Somewhere along the way Caroline had ceased to be his ward and had become his woman.

She meant more to Wolfe than he dared to admit, even to himself.

Now, as she stood in his arms, she looked up at him with a wistfulness in her eyes. "I care about you. I care too much. But you must know that I don't dare love you. And without loving you, I can't—"

He pressed his hand over her mouth, ending her pronouncement. Then, when she quieted, he caressed her face.

"My sweet Caroline, you're very wise not to throw away your love on me. Save it for a man worthy of you."

God help him, how he ached to be that man....

* * *

"Expertly blending romance and suspense, Beverly Barton knocks our socks off with another fabulous adventure of the heart."
—*Romantic Times Magazine*

Also Available from

BEVERLY BARTON

More books in her exciting miniseries

The PROTECTORS

NAVAJO'S WOMAN
(Silhouette Intimate Moments #1063)

WHITELAW'S WEDDING
(Silhouette Intimate Moments #1075)

JACK'S CHRISTMAS MISSION
(Silhouette Intimate Moments #1113)

Look for more books in the coming months from
Silhouette Intimate Moments!

BEVERLY BARTON

The PROTECTORS

SWEET CAROLINE'S KEEPER

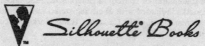

Silhouette Books

Published by Silhouette Books

America's Publisher of Contemporary Romance

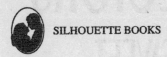

SILHOUETTE BOOKS

THE PROTECTORS: SWEET CAROLINE'S KEEPER

Copyright © 2001 by Beverly Beaver

ISBN 0-373-48430-5

This edition published by arrangement with Harlequin Books S.A.

® and TM are trademarks of Harlequin Books S.A., used under license. Trademarks indicated with ® are registered in the United States Patent and Trademark Office, the Canadian Trade Marks Office and in other countries.

Visit Silhouette at www.eHarlequin.com

Printed in U.S.A.

For the readers who have made
THE PROTECTORS
series a big success!
And special thanks to my editors,
Lynda Curnyn and Leslie Wainger.

Prologue

Caroline asked the Harpers' chauffeur to drop her off at the back of the house. She had her key with her, knew the security code and could easily slip in through the kitchen entrance. If she went in through the front door, Preston would hear her, learn that she was sick and insist on phoning her mother. Lenore wouldn't like being called away from the Mitchells' party. Caroline had learned through experience that it was best to never interfere with her mother's plans, even if that meant trying to handle things that were difficult for a twelve-year-old to handle alone.

Last year, she had overheard her stepfather and mother arguing and had learned something that she had suspected all her life.

"Good God, Lenore, what kind of mother are you?" Preston's voice had trembled with near rage.

"I'm the kind of mother who gave birth to a child she didn't want simply because her husband and her family left her no other choice."

"Even if you didn't want Caroline, you must love her. You

must care about what happens to her. She's a sweet child. Intelligent and—"

"I endure her presence on holidays and breaks from school," Lenore had said. "But next summer, I'm sending her to my sister-in-law Dixie in Mississippi, so don't you dare bring that brat of *yours* here for the summer. Send him off to camp or tell your ex-wife to keep him."

Caroline banished the memory now as she sneaked through the darkened kitchen and up the backstairs of their Baltimore, Maryland, home. Although she spent little time here with her mother and Preston, her mother's third husband, she loved the house and especially her room. Preston had been the one who'd hired an interior designer to prepare the room for her shortly after his marriage to her mother, five years ago. Caroline had no memory of her real father, who had died when she was barely two. And all she remembered about Bruce Verner, Lenore's second husband, was that he'd always smelled of tobacco and had had a boisterous laugh. During that marriage, Caroline had been cared for by a succession of nannies.

As she made her way up the backstairs, Caroline thought she heard voices in the study, but more than likely Preston was just watching something on television. Lately her stepfather had seemed totally uninterested in the glamorous parties her mother so loved. She had noticed, too, that he had been closing himself off in his study a lot, at least for this past week since she'd been home for the Christmas holidays. She suspected that her parents were having marital problems. Her best friend, Brooke Harper, with whom she was supposed to be spending the night, had told her that she'd overheard her mother and father talking about Preston and Lenore Shaw's imminent divorce. Brooke had asked Caroline what *imminent* meant.

"It means something that's going to happen soon," Caroline had explained.

She didn't want her mother to divorce Preston. She loved

her stepfather. He was very good to her. Better than her own mother had ever been. He visited her at school sometimes. And whenever his own son, Fletcher, came to visit for a weekend, he insisted that she come home so that they could share family time together. Her mother had begrudgingly participated in the picnics, horseback riding and theater excursions. What would happen to her, if her mother divorced Preston? She would lose the closest thing she'd ever had to a father.

Caroline couldn't bear the thought of losing Preston.

Another wave of nausea hit her full force. Just as she rushed down the hall and toward her room, the voices downstairs grew louder. Men's voices. Arguing. Preston's voice. Shouting.

Caroline barely made it to her bathroom before the bile spilled from her mouth. Hurriedly, she flipped on the light switch, then leaned over the commode, emptied her stomach and dropped to her knees. Her sleepover with Brooke had come to an abrupt halt the minute she'd started vomiting. With the Harpers attending the same party as Caroline's mother, the task of summoning the Harpers' housekeeper had fallen to Brooke. When Caroline had asked to go home, the housekeeper had quickly awakened the chauffeur to drive *Miss McGuire,* as she referred to Caroline. Caroline supposed she'd caught a virus of some sort. One of those twenty-four-hour bugs. She'd just sleep here on the bathroom floor if necessary and try not to disturb anyone. Maybe if she did her best not to annoy her mother while she was home during the holidays, Lenore might be nicer to Preston and to Fletcher and maybe even to her. And if they could be a family during Christmas, perhaps Lenore would never divorce Preston.

Caroline scooted across the tile floor, lifted a washcloth from the stack on the wicker tier table and reached up to grab the rim of the sink. Hoisting herself up, she stood on shaky legs, her hands gripping the rim of the sink. She turned on the cold water, wet the cloth and washed her soiled mouth.

Her stomach settled somewhat and she breathed a relieved sigh. She had vomited twice at Brooke's house, then once on the way home and again just now. About every thirty minutes her insides churned and she erupted like a volcano.

Maybe she could lie down for a while. Until the next time. Her bed looked inviting. A white French provincial four-poster decked in baby-pink eyelet lace. If she soiled the bed linen and her mother found out…! Caroline didn't even want to consider the possibility. Of course, the housekeeper, Mrs. Claypool, never ratted on her anymore, not after the first time, when Caroline had accidentally spilled cola on the carpet and Lenore had gone ballistic. No, she didn't dare risk sleeping in her bed tonight. She'd have to settle for the ceramic bathroom floor.

But before she settled in for a long night, maybe she should change into her pajamas and then go back downstairs, to the laundry room, and wash the vomit out of her blouse before the stain set in. There would be no way to hide the garment. Maybe if she hurried, she could go down, wash the blouse and return before another bout of nausea hit her.

She stripped out of her clothes. The blouse came first. She draped it across the rim of the bathtub, then removed her shoes, socks and jeans. These items went into the clothes hamper on the floor of the linen closet. She took off her underwear and stuffed them into the small "delicate items" bag that her mother insisted she use. Her mother had taught her that a lady always washes her own intimate apparel.

As she entered the dark bedroom, illuminated only by the light from the bathroom, she caught a glimpse of her naked body in the cheval mirror. She was round and plump, her body just beginning to develop feminine curves. For all intents and purposes, however, she was still a child. If her hair were blond or red, she might resemble a chubby cherub, but she'd never seen a painting of an angel with black hair.

She rummaged in the dresser drawer, found a pair of pink-and-white-striped flannel pajamas, pulled them on and then searched the closet for her fuzzy pink house shoes. She'd have to be very careful not to disturb Preston. He would be sure to notice that she was sick. Her stepfather had a keen sense of observation. He would take one look at her and surmise that she wasn't feeling well, regardless of what excuse she gave him for not spending the night with Brooke.

After returning to the bathroom to retrieve her soiled blouse, she sneaked down the backstairs, trying her best to be as quiet as possible. When she entered the kitchen, she heard a rather odd noise, as if something had fallen over in the den, which was diagonally across the hall. And from the sound of it, whatever had crashed to the floor had been a rather large object. Should she investigate? she wondered.

Suddenly she remembered what Amelia Randall had told the girls at boarding school about her grandfather. He'd had a heart attack, fallen unconscious on the floor, and if it hadn't been for the quick action of her grandmother, the man would have died. Had Preston had a heart attack? He was old—more than forty. It was certainly possible, wasn't it?

Just tiptoe down the hall and peek into the den, she told herself. It's probably nothing. Preston might have accidentally knocked over something. But you should make sure that he's all right before you go back upstairs. Caroline scurried into the washroom, dropped her blouse in the sink, ran enough cold water to cover the garment, then rushed back through the kitchen and out into the hall. The light in the foyer, at the end of the hallway, spread a long, dim glow over the hardwood floor and cast shadows along the corridor walls. The den door stood open. Caroline crept slowly, cautiously down the hall. Preston usually kept the door to his den closed.

When she reached the doorway, she peered into the room; Preston's large oak desk was the one object in her direct line of vision. The banker's lamp on her stepfather's desk emitted the only light in the room. She dared to take one step over the threshold, just to get a better look. But before her eyes could scan the entire room, she noticed that the huge world globe that sat center stage lay on the floor, along with the heavy wooden stand on which it normally rested. And there, beside the globe, lay Preston.

Caroline gasped. Silently. Mercy! Had he had a heart attack, just like Amelia's grandfather? Panic momentarily controlled her. She knew nothing about helping someone who'd had a heart attack. But she had to do something or Preston might die. *Think, Caroline, think. What must you do first?* Call for an ambulance immediately. Without giving her own sickness another thought, she ran into the room, heading for the telephone on Preston's desk. But as she reached for the phone, she noticed blood seeping onto the wooden floor. Blood pooling around her stepfather's head. And then, just as the reality of what had actually happened began to dawn on her, Caroline heard something behind her. Turning abruptly, she saw a man. Tall. Broad-shouldered. Wearing dark clothes. Black slacks. Black pullover sweater. Black gloves. She caught only a glimpse of his face, the light brown beard and mustache, the hawk nose, the shaded eyes as his gaze narrowed and pinned her to the spot. Her gaze collided with his.

Was he a thief? she wondered. Perhaps, but he was also a murderer. For she knew in that one terrifying moment that Preston was dead. Killed by this intruder. The tall stranger still held the weapon in his hand. Caroline stared, hypnotized by the big gun. He would have to kill her, too, wouldn't he? After all, she had seen him, even if not very clearly, hidden as he was in the shadows.

Instinctively, Caroline opened her mouth and screamed. What else could she do? The quivering began inside her body and quickly spread outside, from head to toe. She kept screaming as she trembled. Her eyes squinched with fear. Her heartbeat accelerated wildly, the rhythm drumming in her head. She was going to die. He was going to kill her.

Seconds passed, agonized moments of sheer terror, as she

waited for the sound of the gun firing. Waited for the bullet to hit her. Waited for her life to come to an end.

Minutes flew by. She kept screaming and screaming, unable to control the hysteria that had claimed her. Her vision clouded with unshed tears. Why hadn't he shot her? What was he waiting for? She blinked several times, clearing her vision enough to see that the man had moved out of the shadows. Where was he?

She scanned the room. No sight of him anywhere. She heard the front door open and close. He had left the house. And he hadn't killed her. But why? Why had he let her live?

Caroline glanced down at her stepfather. She shivered. Then as if in a trance, she picked up the telephone receiver, dialed the emergency number, and the moment she heard another human voice, she asked for help. She told the person her name, her address and that someone had just killed her stepfather. Then, while the person asked her several more questions, Caroline stopped speaking. She dropped the phone. The receiver fell to the floor, dragging the base to the very edge of Preston's desk. She turned her head and vomited into the nearby wastebasket. Her mother would scold her for making a mess. But Preston would take her side. He always tried to protect her from her mother's wrath. He was so kind and good and gentle.

Caroline wiped her mouth with the back of her hand, then walked over and sat down on the floor beside Preston's body. She lifted his limp hand in hers and held it tightly.

"I'll stay right here with you," she told him. "I won't leave you alone."

Aidan Colbert parked the nondescript black sedan in the underground parking garage at Peacekeepers International in Washington, D.C. With expert ease, he removed the 9 mm from his shoulder holster, then lifted the case from the floorboard, placed the weapon alongside the silencer and closed the lid. Following instructions, he left the case on the seat,

then got out of the car, locked the doors and walked toward
the elevator. He punched the up button. The elevator doors
swung open. He removed his ID card from his pants pocket,
inserted it into the appropriate slot, and then hit the one-inch-
square, unmarked blue panel.

As the elevator rose higher and higher, taking Aidan toward Ellison Penn's office atop the Peacekeepers building,
he tried not to think about the child. But he knew he probably
would never be able to erase that moment from his mind—
when their gazes had locked and she realized he had killed
her stepfather. For just a split second he had seen Brendan's
little face, Brendan's blue eyes, Brendan's frightened features. Aidan had seen on the girl's face tonight the exact look
that had crossed his little brother's face only moments before
his father had struck the fatal blow that had ended Brendan's
life nine years ago.

The child had thought he was going to kill her.

The elevator stopped. The doors opened to reveal the entrance to the office suite occupied by the current head of
Peacekeepers International. Fellow agent Gavin Robbins, another new recruit, waited for him in the outer office.

"Mr. Penn is waiting for you," Gavin said, his dark eyes
staring accusingly at Aidan. "Word has already reached him
that there was a problem—a witness you didn't eliminate."

Aidan glared at Gavin but didn't respond verbally. There
was something about Gavin that rubbed Aidan the wrong
way. They had disliked each other on sight the moment
they'd met six months ago when they began their training
together. Aidan followed Gavin into the ultramodern office,
dominated by black leather sofas and chairs, contemporary
paintings on the stark white walls and pieces of expensive
avant-garde metal sculpture placed strategically on glass-and-
chrome desks, tables and bookshelves.

Ellison Penn stood a tad over six feet tall, a good two
inches shorter than Aidan, but he possessed a commanding
presence. A professional athlete's build. Large. Muscular.

Without an ounce of fat on his body. His all-seeing eyes were a shade lighter than his steel-gray hair, which gleamed like polished silver against his light olive skin.

"We know that Shaw's stepdaughter was at the house," Ellison stated in a matter-of-fact way. "She wasn't supposed to be there. I'm not sure what happened. Our man followed Preston when he took her to the Harper house several hours earlier."

"She saw me," Aidan said. "I don't think she got a good look, but—"

"You should have eliminated her." Standing as if at attention, Gavin puffed out his chest as he issued his opinion. "By allowing her to live, you compromised the mission."

Aidan glowered at Gavin. "I thought it was our job to protect the innocent, not kill them."

"Aidan is right," Ellison said, a world-weary look on his face. "As a Peacekeeper, he could not have murdered that child without going against the very principles on which our organization was founded."

"But if the child can recognize him—" Gavin said.

"The child is traumatized," Ellison told them. "The initial report I received states that she's in shock and has been unable to help the local police in any way." Ellison surveyed Aidan from head to toe. "Shave the beard and mustache."

"Yes, sir," Aidan replied.

"And to be on the safe side, I'll send you to our London office. You can work from there for the next year or so, until Preston Shaw's death becomes just one more unsolved murder."

Aidan nodded agreement.

"I'll keep abreast of the developments in the case and keep tabs on what happens to the child." Ellison shook his head. "Damn shame she was there. She didn't see you kill him, did she?"

"No, I was just on my way out of the room when she walked in."

"We should have sent backup with you," Ellison said. "Someone to watch the house while you were inside. But we thought our information was reliable and we were sure Shaw would be all alone. One man in and out quickly was less of a risk." Ellison breathed deeply, his washboard-lean belly tightening when he inhaled. "We'll never make that mistake again."

"Sir?" Aidan squared his shoulders and stared point-blank into his superior's cool gray eyes.

"Yes, what is it, Colbert?"

"About the child…I'd like to be kept apprised of everything concerning her."

"That's not a good idea," Ellison said. "Regardless of how you feel, there can be no personal contact between you and Caroline McGuire."

"I was thinking of impersonal contact, sir. I believe I have a right to care what happens to the little girl."

"You're in the wrong business if you allow yourself to get sentimental over Preston Shaw's stepdaughter," Gavin Robbins said. "A professional assassin cannot afford the luxury of caring about his victim's family."

"Robbins, I'd like to speak to Colbert alone," Ellison said.

Aidan didn't glance at Gavin, but could sense the man's displeasure as he strode from the office. "If there is anything I can do to help the child…any way I can… All I ask is that I be informed, that I receive frequent updates on her condition."

Ellison rounded his desk, walked over to Aidan and clamped his large hand down on Aidan's shoulder. "I understand what you're feeling. A man's first assignment is never easy. And unfortunately, with your first assignment things didn't go exactly as planned. In time, you won't be as disturbed by mishaps that occur."

"I'm sure you're right. But that doesn't change the facts in this case. Will you or won't you agree to forward all information on the child to me in London?"

Ellison tightened his grip on Aidan's shoulder. "It's against my better judgment…but, yes, I'll see that you learn everything there is to know about Caroline McGuire. However, I must warn you that you can never contact her personally or reveal in any way who you are or—"

"Do you think I'd ever want her to know me, to find out that I'm the man who killed her stepfather?"

"You were only doing your job. Preston Shaw had to be eliminated. He had become a very dangerous man."

"But that little girl doesn't know the facts. She isn't aware of what kind of man Preston Shaw really was. She'll spend the rest of her life believing he was good. And the man who killed him—" Aidan broke off, shook his head and cast his gaze to the floor. He couldn't bear verbalizing his thoughts, couldn't face the truth of how Caroline must feel about her stepfather's executioner. With Preston Shaw's blood fresh on his hands and the memory of the frightened expression on the child's face vivid in his mind, he was having difficulty convincing himself he was one of the good guys.

Chapter 1

David Wolfe tucked the file folder under his arm and picked up the mug of steaming black coffee from the kitchen counter, then opened the door and walked out onto the wrap-around porch surrounding his log cabin. The drive from Atlanta had been well worth the hours behind the wheel. Even after all these years, nothing felt as right as coming home to the east Tennessee mountains where he'd been born, where generations of his mother's family had lived and died. The Scottish-Irish settlers had claimed these hills as their own, bringing with them their folklore, superstitions and Celtic music. The proud Cherokees to whom this land had belonged long before the first Pilgrim set foot on Plymouth Rock, except for a few who had hidden away, had been transported via the Trail of Tears to Oklahoma in the early part of the nineteenth century. His half-breed mother's ancestors had been among those few who had escaped and found refuge deep within the Smoky Mountains of Tennessee and North Carolina.

David eased into the large wooden rocking chair, which

was constructed of small logs and matched the porch swing and the other chair to his right. Leaning to the side, he placed his mug on the porch floor, then took the thick file folder from under his arm, opened it and spread it across his lap. The face of a child stared up at him. A picture of Caroline McGuire at age twelve, a school photograph taken several months before her stepfather's death. A plump little girl with short, cropped black hair, her bangs hanging in her eyes. A pair of unforgettable blue-violet eyes. Eyes that had haunted him for fifteen years. Hurriedly, he flipped through the folder. Picture after picture came into view, interspersed among data compiled on an unloved and unwanted child whose own mother had tossed her aside, as if she'd been nothing more than an outdated dress.

David knew as much about Caroline McGuire as anyone on earth did. From the size shoe she wore to her favorite brand and shade of lipstick. For the past five years, she had used an expensive label with a seductive name—Passion Pink. And although she enjoyed going barefoot as much as possible, when she purchased shoes, she bought a size 7B. She collected clocks and had an assortment in her St. Michaels, Maryland, home, as well as her Talbot Street photography studio. She had purchased everything from a cheap resin lighthouse clock to an antique mahogany grandfather clock she had acquired at an estate sale.

She didn't smoke. Had never done drugs. And seldom drank. When she did consume liquor, her drink of choice was a strawberry daiquiri, a concoction as sweet as she was. Although she had numerous friends and had dated a variety of men since her first date at seventeen, she had never been married. Lived alone. And at twenty-seven, was possibly still a virgin.

David flipped through the hefty dossier, removed the information and picture Ellison had faxed him at his apartment in Atlanta first thing this morning, just as David had been heading out the door for his long weekend at the cabin. He dropped the thick folder onto the seat of the other rocking chair, then reached down and picked up his coffee. After taking several swigs of the strong brew, he looked at the picture of Caroline at her mother's funeral a week ago. The snapshot, taken at a distance by one of Ellison's flunkies, showed a somber young woman in a dark suit. Surrounding her were her first cousin, Lyle Jennings, her assistant Roz Turner, her stepbrother Fletcher Shaw, and her old friend Brooke Harper, who was Fletcher's girlfriend.

When David swiped his fingers across the picture, down Caroline's cheek, an odd sensation tingled in his fingertips, as if he had actually touched her skin.

He had sent flowers to the funeral, of course, and signed the card simply *David*. He would liked to have been there, to have offered her sympathy and comfort, but of course that hadn't been possible. Any personal contact between them was forbidden.

David couldn't help wondering how Caroline felt about losing her mother, a woman who had shipped her off to her aunt Dixie's in Mississippi less than a month after Preston Shaw's death, and for all intents and purposes had deserted her. From what he knew of Caroline, her kind heart probably wept for the woman who had given birth to her. But how did one ever come to terms with the feelings of anger, hurt and resentment one felt for a parent? God knew he had never been able to accomplish that seemingly impossible feat. But Caroline was a better person than he, so maybe for her it was possible.

He reread the hand-scribbled note from Ellison.

Caroline has inherited the house on Sheffield Street from her mother. I cannot imagine that she'll ever want to go back there. Perhaps she will simply turn the place over to a Realtor. I understand that during the years Lenore leased the house, it fell into disrepair. Gavin assures me that Caroline is holding up well. I did tell you that he is dating her, didn't I? They met at a charity auction in Baltimore a few months ago. He's quite taken with her. But then, who wouldn't be? Your Caroline has grown up to be quite a beauty.

Fifteen years ago Ellison Penn had cautioned Aidan Colbert not to become emotionally involved with Caroline's plight, and yet Ellison had taken a keen interest in the well-being of Preston Shaw's stepdaughter. David had always suspected that Ellison shared some of the guilt that had plagued Aidan for nearly thirteen years—until Aidan's ''death'' in an explosion while on a Peacekeepers assignment in the Middle East more than two years ago.

Aidan Colbert had kept his distance, observing Caroline's life through pictures and reports, helping her financially over the years, yet known to her only as her phantom benefactor, David, a name he had chosen because it had a special meaning to him alone. David Wolfe had been Aidan's maternal great-grandfather, a man who had been much revered by his family.

When Aidan Colbert had died, David Wolfe had risen like a phoenix from the ashes of the bomb explosion that had officially ended Aidan's existence. Then, with Ellison Penn's assistance, he had begun a new life, with a surgically reconstructed face and a fake identity.

I did tell you that he is dating her, didn't I? It was as if David could hear Ellison's voice speaking the taunting words. Ironic that Gavin Robbins, who had once asked Aidan Colbert why he hadn't eliminated Preston Shaw's stepdaughter, was now dating her. David didn't like the idea of Robbins being involved with Caroline. She deserved better. Robbins, still a gung-ho agent, had been promoted only this past year to second in command, directly under Ellison, whom David prayed never retired. He couldn't imagine someone like Gavin taking over the reins of Peacekeepers International, which was a front for an organization of highly trained men and women who worked as contract agents for the U.S. government and its allies. These handpicked agents lived seemingly normal lives. Their families and friends knew them to be employees of Peacekeepers, experts who worked to secure peace throughout the world, as nongovernment negotiators who fostered humanitarian deeds worldwide. But in truth the job that these men and women performed was to protect the cause of freedom and eliminate any problem that might arise that couldn't be handled through ordinary channels. And a small squad of agents were trained as assassins, prepared to kill on command, when no other alternative existed. Aidan Colbert had been a member of that select few. And so had Gavin Robbins.

David tossed aside the faxed note and picture, letting them sail down and settle on top of the file folder. He rocked back and forth, slowing occasionally to sip his coffee. He would call Ellison tonight. Thank him for the update. And suggest that his old mentor find a way to persuade Robbins to end his relationship with Caroline. He had hoped nothing would come of their dating, had thought she would see through that phony gentleman facade Robbins projected and dump the bastard. He couldn't allow Caroline to waste her life on a man unworthy of her. Out there somewhere was a man he could trust with Caroline's heart and her life. Caroline deserved only the best. And that sure as hell wasn't Gavin Robbins.

Caroline held the key in her hand but could not bring herself to unlock the front door. She had purposely never returned to the house on Sheffield Street and had avoided this area of town whenever she'd come to Baltimore. She wouldn't be here now if Fletcher and Lyle hadn't agreed to accompany her. Of course, she could have simply turned the house over to a Realtor without seeing the place herself. But she felt that this was the final step in putting the past behind her—now and forever. Sometimes she would go days without thinking about that night, but then a memory would flash through her mind and it would all come back to her. Thankfully, with each passing year, the memories faded, became less vivid, and she had long since recovered from the emotional breakdown she had suffered after Preston's death.

You can do this, she told herself. Preston is dead. Your mother is dead. And for all you know the intruder who murdered Preston might be dead, too. None of them are inside this house waiting for your return. Only memories await you, and even the most horrific memory cannot harm you.

"Are you sure you want to do this?" Lyle Jennings asked. "I can handle this for you. Or—" he glanced at the other man "—Fletcher can deal with it."

"No." Caroline reached out and squeezed Lyle's hand. Dear, kind Lyle, who was like a brother to her. Lyle's mother had raised the two of them together in her modest Iuka, Mississippi, home. A loving disciplinarian and fine Christian woman, Dixie Jennings had taken in her brother's child and treated her as if she were her own. "I need to do this myself. But I want to thank you and Fletcher—" she smiled up at her stepbrother "—for coming with me. I don't think I could do this without y'all."

"To be honest, this is something I need to do, too," Fletcher said. "I haven't been back inside the old house since the day of the funeral. I remember going into the study that day. The house was filled with people, of course, and Lenore was center stage as the grieving widow." When he stole a quick, apologetic glance at Caroline, she smiled reassuringly, letting him know she, too, had understood her mother's penchant for theatrics. "I slipped away into the study. I wanted to see where it had happened."

"Oh, Fletch, I never knew you'd done that." Caroline patted her stepbrother's arm. "How awful for you."

"Yeah, it was. The servants had tried to clean the floor, but the blood had stained the old wood and I could see the spot where Father had bled after he'd been shot in the head."

Caroline had not talked about that night to anyone in a long time. Not since she had completed years of therapy with the psychiatrist in Memphis. Her aunt Dixie had driven her across the state of Mississippi every other week to visit the doctor, an expensive therapist who specialized in traumatized children. To this day she didn't know how much those sessions had cost. Far more than her aunt could afford. If it had not been for David, she wouldn't have gotten the help she had so desperately needed. David, her mysterious benefactor. David, a man who had known her stepfather, had contacted her aunt through his lawyer to offer financial assistance for Caroline McGuire.

"No use putting this off any longer." Caroline inserted the key in the lock, turned it until she heard a distinct click, then twisted the doorknob and opened the front door. She breathed deeply, inhaling to fill her lungs fully before exhaling slowly.

Taking a small, tentative step, she crossed the threshold into the foyer. A sour, musty smell assailed her senses. The stench of an old house, closed up and unused for many years. The only light came from the sunshine pouring in through the open front door.

"I understand no one has lived here for the past four years," Fletcher said, as he moved inside and came to a halt near Caroline. "So, there's no electricity. I suppose we'll have to open up the blinds if we want to take a good look at the place."

Caroline didn't budge. Lyle entered, put his arm around her shoulders and hugged her to his side. "Would you like for Fletch and me to open the blinds to let in some light and raise a few windows to air out the place a bit?"

"Just open the blinds," Caroline said. "Enough so that we can see our way around in here."

"Will you be all right here by yourself while we do that?" Fletcher asked.

Caroline nodded. Yes, she'd be fine—if she didn't go any farther into the house. If she didn't go into the study.

Fletcher and Lyle disappeared, one taking the rooms to the left of the wide foyer, the other the rooms to the right. Caroline forced herself to move. Although the floor badly needed refinishing, wallpaper was peeling off the walls and the white painted woodwork was stained and yellowed, the empty foyer still retained a hint of its former beauty. She could remember the first time she had walked into the house. She'd been seven years old. Shy. Awkward. And uncertain whether or not her new stepfather would like her.

Preston Shaw, tall, slender and elegant in a Cary Grant sort of way, had come out of his study when Caroline arrived with her nanny. She had looked up at the big man, into his handsome, smiling face and sparkling blue eyes and breathed a sigh of relief.

"Well, hello, Miss Caroline," he'd said. "Aren't you a pretty little thing. You'll probably grow up to be every bit as lovely as your mother."

Before that day, no one had ever told her she was pretty. With those few words, Preston had won her heart—and her loyalty—forever. And during the next five years, she had grown to love her stepfather more dearly than anyone on earth. He had been her champion, her defender and her friend. When her mother had been cruel, he had been doubly kind. When her mother had rejected her, he had lavished her with attention. And when he had died, she had lost the only father she had ever known.

Tears pooled in Caroline's eyes. No, you mustn't cry, she told herself. You have already shed enough tears to last a lifetime. Preston wouldn't want you to cry.

"You have such a lovely smile, my dear little Caroline," Preston had told her. "You should use it more often."

A fragile smile quavered on her lips. She blinked away the unshed tears and wandered out of the foyer and up the hallway. *Face the worst first. Get it over with. Now!* The door to the study stood wide open. Lyle had already opened the blinds and afternoon light poured through the slats, laying stripes of alternating sunshine and shadows across the dirty wooden floor. Since the room was bare of furniture, it appeared even larger than she remembered. A vast empty space.

But suddenly Caroline visualized the way the room had once looked—the way it had looked fifteen years ago. Warm. Inviting. Richly decorated with the best money could buy. In her mind's eye she could see her stepfather. Laughing. Talking. Joking. A personable man, well-liked by everyone.

The images inside her head darkened, fading from joy to sorrow. Preston's body sprawled on the floor. The world globe and its stand toppled. A pool of blood. Fresh. Bright red. And the hooded eyes of a large bearded man standing in the shadows, his hand gripping the weapon that had murdered Preston. Their gazes had locked for a split second. Paralyzing fear. Numbing realization that she was going to die. Shock when he had left the house without harming her. But why had he not killed her, too?

Caroline could hear her own long-ago screams. Incessant. Terrified. Hysterical. Sounds from years gone by.

Someone touched her. She gasped and jerked away.

"Sorry," Fletcher said. "I didn't mean to startle you."

Caroline swallowed. "A part of me would like to burn this place to the ground."

"It's yours. You can do whatever you want with it."

"I could give it to you. After all, this house belonged to your father."

"Yes, but he left it to your mother and she in turn left it to you," Fletcher reminded Caroline. "My dear, I'm afraid this house is your headache, not mine."

A quirky smile lifted the corners of Fletcher's lips. In many ways he reminded her of his father. Tall. Debonair. Good-looking. And quite charming. She laced her arm through his and sighed. "I think Preston would want to see people living here again. A family. Parents. Children. He did so want us to be a family, didn't he?''

"Yes, he did."

"I think I should renovate this place and put it up for sale." Caroline glanced around and this time she saw the room as it was, not as it had once been. Holding the memories at bay, she led Fletcher out into the hall, where Lyle stood, dusting off his hands.

Lyle sneezed. "Sorry. You know I'm allergic to dust."

"Yes, I know that's your story," Caroline said jokingly. "At least you convinced Aunt Dixie of that fact. I always had to dust and vacuum your room for you."

"Yes, you did," Lyle replied. "But in return, I always washed the supper dishes, didn't I?"

"Only because Aunt Dixie made you do it." Caroline glanced at the staircase, which rose from the entrance hall to the second floor. "I want to go up and have a look at my old room before we leave."

"Have you decided what you want to do with this place?" Lyle asked.

"Mmm-hmm. I think I'm going to hire a contractor first thing next week and have the place fixed up enough to sell. The church's charity programs could use a sizable donation, couldn't they?"

Lyle's mouth formed a surprised oval. "Are you really thinking of donating the proceeds from the sale of this house to the church?"

"Mother wouldn't approve, of course, but I think Preston would. Don't you agree, Fletcher?"

"No doubt he would," Fletcher said. "Father was a generous man."

"Then it's settled." Caroline knew in her heart that she had made the right decision. In coming here today—to face a past that still occasionally haunted her. And for choosing to donate the money from the sale of her old home to the church where Lyle had been a minister for the past several years.

So, Caroline was going to renovate and sell the old house, then donate the proceeds, in Preston's name, to the Congregational Church. A fitting tribute to a man she had loved like a father. Preston would have wholeheartedly approved. He'd been a great one for pomp and circumstance. How he had enjoyed his role as an agent for Peacekeepers International, thought to be only a philanthropic organization established for doing good deeds around the world. But Preston had also enjoyed playing secret agent, taking risks. He had loved the cloak-and-dagger games, the adrenaline rush of outsmarting everyone around him.

Despite his job with the Peacekeepers, Preston Shaw had been an asset to his true friends and associates of the Loyalists Coalition, never forgetting to whom he owed his real allegiance. When given an order, he obeyed. Unfortunately, his adherence to the dictates of a cause controlled by a select few had cost Preston his life. Once the Peacekeepers had discovered the man was a traitor, what else could they do but eliminate him?

Unfortunate that the child had been at home the night Aidan Colbert had assassinated the Peacekeepers' rogue agent. Lucky for Colbert that she had been unable to identify him. And even more fortunate that Preston had not lived to follow through on the threats he had made against the organization to which he'd sworn his first allegiance. For several years after Preston's death, *they* had held their breaths, wondering if he might have found a way to reach out from the grave to wreak vengeance. But with each passing year, they had relaxed more and more as they began to believe that Preston had left behind no evidence to link him to their organization or to expose the identities of its other members.

They had kept a close watch on Caroline, just as the Peacekeepers had. But for entirely different reasons. She was no longer of any interest to them and, since Aidan Colbert's death two years ago, apparently of little interest to the Peacekeepers. But since there was and had been for many years a connection between Caroline and him, he still maintained a personal interest in her and even felt affection, to a certain degree.

Perhaps Colbert should have eliminated her that long-ago night. Even some of the other Peacekeeper agents had agreed. But in the end, there had been no need. Preston had told neither her nor her mother anything about his double life. And despite his threats, he had not bequeathed either of them the secret documents he had sworn he possessed.

Caroline was safe. Safer now than she'd ever been in the fifteen years since her stepfather's death.

Chapter 2

When a Talbot County contractor who attended Lyle's church told Caroline that he would contribute his services for free, other church members, including a plumber and an electrician, volunteered their services to renovate the house in Baltimore. Most of the job would have to be done on Saturdays, but the workforce had turned out en masse last week, so things were moving along quicker than anticipated. This was their second Saturday, and the main focus today was stripping wallpaper and tearing out damaged Sheetrock.

While six men worked on the main project, ripping out the mildewed walls in the two basement rooms—one used as a wine cellar years ago and the other a former minigym—Caroline and three other women stripped old wallpaper off the upstairs bedrooms. As she and her friend Roz, who had been her assistant at the studio for the past three years, concentrated their efforts on Caroline's old bedroom, Mrs. Mabry and Allison Sims worked diligently in the master suite.

As she scraped away at the stubborn wallpaper, Caroline

tried to remember only the happy times she'd spent in this house, but try as she might, bad memories kept creeping into her thoughts. Her instincts had warned her to stay away, to put as much distance between herself and the past as she possibly could. But how could she let others work to restore the house while she stayed away? She couldn't, of course.

"Damn!" Roz cried suddenly, and stuck her index finger into her mouth.

"What's wrong?" From where she sat perched atop the ladder, a wet sponge in one hand and a metal scrapper in the other, Caroline glanced down at her friend, who had been attacking the stubborn paper along the baseboard.

Roz sucked on her finger, then removed it from her mouth and held it up for Caroline's inspection. "The stupid scrapper slipped and I nicked my finger on the edge."

Caroline laid aside her equipment and climbed down the ladder. "Here, let me take a look. I've got a first aid kit in my car, if you need a bandage."

"It's just a scratch, but you know how little cuts can hurt like the devil."

Caroline grabbed Roz's finger and inspected it thoroughly. "It's not even bleeding."

"Okay, so I'm a crybaby." As Roz shrugged, she rolled her eyes toward the ceiling.

Caroline adored Rozalin Turner. Few people understood their friendship, not even Lyle, who knew Caroline so well. But she realized that poor Lyle didn't know quite what to think of the flashy, loudmouthed Roz. She wasn't the type of woman he was used to being around—nothing like Aunt Dixie or Caroline or the good ladies of the Congregational Church. Roz wasn't a Southern lady, not by the widest stretch of the imagination. Roz was...well, Roz was Roz. A liberated free spirit.

Roz had come for an interview three years ago, answering an ad in the newspaper Caroline had placed for an "all-around personal assistant to a professional photographer."

Just one look at Roz and Caroline had thought how easily her appearance might offend some of the studio's wealthier clients. Then as now, her curly bleached-blond hair had been piled atop her head, giving her a sexy, tousled look. She wore shorts, a tank top, an ankle bracelet, three toe rings, six pairs of tiny gold hoops in her ears and a belly button ring. But within five minutes of talking to Roz that day, Caroline had realized that to counter the negative effect of her wild-child appearance, Roz possessed a flamboyant, exuberant personality that could charm the birds from the trees.

They had become fast friends and Roz was, without a doubt, the best assistant in the world. She had a way with adults and children alike. And although she tried to hide her softer side, the woman had a heart of pure gold. Almost everyone recognized that fact and appreciated Roz for the wonderful person she was—everyone except Lyle, who was put off by everything Roz said and did. In the beginning, Caroline had tried to bridge the vast gap between her cousin and her assistant, but had finally given up any hope that the two would ever be friends.

Roz's stomach growled. "Isn't it getting to be lunchtime?"

Caroline pulled her wristwatch from the pocket of her faded jeans to check the time. "It's only eleven. Lunch is at noon. Mrs. Mabry brought two big picnic baskets overflowing with food. Just hang on another hour and we'll have a feast."

Caroline surveyed her tall friend's slender curves. How was it possible for someone to eat like a stevedore and keep a model-thin figure? Every extra bite that went into Caroline's mouth wound up on her hips and thighs.

"Caroline!" Allison Sims cried as she rushed into the room. "Steve just called out to me from downstairs and said to come get you. They've found something in the basement they think you should see."

For a brief moment Caroline's heart stopped beating as an

odd thought flashed through her mind. *Had they found a dead body?* Don't be silly, she told herself. You're letting being in this house spook you. Your imagination is working overtime.

"What did they find? A treasure chest filled with diamonds and rubies?" Roz asked, her large, brown, Bette Davis eyes widening with speculation.

"He didn't say," Allison replied. "But he said for us to hurry."

Roz and Caroline joined Allison and the three met Mrs. Mabry on the landing, where she waited for them.

Steve stood at the bottom of the backstairs and motioned for them to come down, which they did. "Caroline, you're not going to believe this, but when we tore out that back wall in the wine cellar we found a…well, we think it's a secret passageway of some sort."

"You're kidding." Caroline's heart fluttered.

"And that's not all," Steve said.

"What do you mean, that's not all?" Roz asked.

"The guys are waiting for you." Steve grabbed Caroline's wrist. "You'll have to see this for yourself."

The image of Preston Shaw's body sprawled out on the study floor appeared in Caroline's mind, but she brushed it aside, telling herself not to be ridiculous. If there was a dead body downstairs, a skeleton hidden away for years, Steve wouldn't be acting so excited, now would he?

Since their plans included working on the house from early morning to late into the night every Saturday, Caroline had arranged to have the electricity turned on, as well as the water. The stairs leading down into the belly of the old house were well lit, plainly revealing several steps with rotting edges and a wall covered in an accumulation of spiderwebs. Steve brought her to a halt at the bottom of the stairs. The other five men, including Lyle, stood circling something as they gazed down toward the floor.

"She's here," Steve informed them.

Five heads popped up and five pair of eyes focused on Caroline, who stood frozen beside Steve.

Roz gave her a shove. "Go on. I'm dying to find out what they've discovered."

As Caroline moved toward the circle, the men separated and one by one moved away from the object resting on the concrete floor. She stared at the metal box, approximately twenty inches square, and immediately recognized it as some sort of small safe.

"Diamonds and rubies," Roz said.

"Or perhaps some stocks and bonds," Steve suggested.

"Could be cash money," Marty Johnson said.

"Might be nothing but an empty safe," Lyle told them.

"It's closed, and unless you can figure out the combination—" Steve looked directly at Caroline "—we may never find out what's inside."

"Why would you think I'd know the combination?" Caroline asked.

"Because of the initials on the safe," Steve said.

"What are you talking about?" Caroline walked closer to the safe and knelt in front of it.

"What were your stepfather's initials?" Lyle asked.

"P. W. S.," Caroline replied. "Preston Wakefield Shaw."

The six men said "Hmm-mmm" in unison.

Caroline dropped to her knees and examined the safe. There, attached to the front, were tarnished silver letters—the initials P. W. S. "This must have belonged to Preston."

"Our guess is that he put this safe in the hidden passageway," Marty said. "Did he ever mention the passageway or the safe to you or your mother?"

Caroline shook her head. "Not to me, but perhaps to Mother. I wouldn't know about that." But as she denied knowledge of the passageway and the safe, a long-forgotten memory tried to resurface. The night he'd been killed, Preston and her mother had gotten into another of their many arguments and her mother had stormed out of the house, on her way to yet another party. Preston had noticed Caroline standing in her bedroom doorway and had come over to her.

"I'm sorry," he'd said. "Don't let the tension between Lenore and me upset you. I love your mother and you very much. Don't forget that."

He had kissed her on the forehead then, as he often did. Preston had given her the only paternal affection she'd ever known.

"I wanted to tell your mother something important, but she didn't have time to listen."

"I have time to listen," Caroline had said. So naive. Such a child.

He had placed his hand on her shoulder and said, "If anything happens—" He had cleared his throat and begun again. "I've put away something downstairs, something important. A sort of life insurance policy to protect your mother and you and Fletcher. But it's not something for you to worry about. I'll tell Lenore about it in the morning."

When Caroline felt someone shaking her shoulder, she glanced up and saw Roz staring at her. "What's the matter with you?" Roz asked. "You're acting like you're in a trance."

"No, I was just remembering a conversation I had with Preston."

"Something about the safe?" Lyle asked.

"I'm not sure. Maybe."

"Do you have any idea what the combination might be?" Steve asked.

"I haven't the foggiest," Caroline replied. "Isn't there another way to get into this thing?"

David dumped his suitcase on the floor beside the simple brass bed, unloosened his tie and removed his sport coat. He reached into the closet and withdrew a wooden hanger, draped the coat around it and returned the hanger to the closet. After whipping off his tie and tossing it in a nearby chair, he flopped down atop the neatly made bed. He had flown in from Miami this evening, after two weeks of playing private nursemaid to a Latin American businessman and his family who were vacationing at Disney World. Jack Parker had been scheduled for the assignment, but at the last minute a client who had used Jack on his previous trip to Egypt had specifically requested him to act as his bodyguard for a return visit. Ellen Denby, CEO of the Dundee Private Security and Investigation Agency, had given David a twelve-hour notice and promised him a bonus, if he'd take the job without giving her a hassle. It seemed a couple of the other agents had worked for this particular businessman in the past and refused to be stuck with his flirting wife and whiny kids, even for a day, let alone two weeks.

David stared up at the white ceiling in his bedroom. He'd done nothing except move in some brand-new furniture when he'd leased this Atlanta apartment six months ago. After taking the job as a Dundee bodyguard fifteen months ago, he'd rented a furnished one-bedroom place, which had suited him just fine. But once he realized he would probably be staying with the Dundee agency for many years to come, he started looking for something larger. With three bedrooms the apartment was spacious, giving him enough room to spread out and move around, which he liked. He hated cramped quarters. A result of having grown up out in the country.

The few people who had seen the inside of this place all said the same thing. That it looked as if he'd just moved in. No pictures on the walls. No personal objects scattered around here and there. A minimal amount of furniture. And not one memento that even hinted he'd had a life before he moved to Atlanta. And in a way, that assumption was correct. David Wolfe had no past beyond sixteen months ago, when he'd been released from a private hospital after enduring nearly a year of surgeries and rehabilitation.

As far as anyone knew—including the other Peacekeepers International agents—Aidan Colbert had died in an explosion in the Middle East. In fact, he *had* almost died. Ellison Penn had had Aidan flown directly to a private hospital where he had been admitted under the name John Doe. Orders were then issued to do everything possible to save the man's life. At this hospital no one asked questions, not even the highly skilled doctors who had performed a miracle and not only saved his life, but had put him back together. Almost as good as new. Except that now he had someone else's face. Not quite as good-looking as he'd once been, but at least his face wouldn't scare small children.

When he'd regained consciousness, after he'd been in the hospital for nearly three weeks, Ellison had paid him a visit and given him a precious gift. His freedom. A new identity. A new life. Few were ever allowed to leave Peacekeepers International. Few actually wanted to leave while they were still in their thirties. But Aidan Colbert had discovered that, after more than twelve years as an agent who was called upon to kill on demand, he had begun to lose his humanity. The killing, which he had once abhorred, had become simply a part of his job. Too easy. Too simple. Not enough regrets or maybe too many.

So, when he'd left the hospital, he had walked away as David Wolfe, with all the credentials to verify his identity to his new employer—the Dundee agency. Ellison had told him that he'd called in a favor from an old friend, Sam Dundee, the agency's retired owner, to get him a good job. As a bodyguard he laid his life on the line every day he was on an assignment, and the job required that he be prepared to kill, if necessary, to protect a client. But he wasn't tied to this job for life. He could leave the Dundee agency anytime he wanted to go. In fact, he already had enough money to last a lifetime—money that Aidan Colbert had earned as a Peacekeepers agent. Money that Ellison Penn had put through a "laundering" process before having it deposited in David Wolfe's account. The problem was, David didn't know *where* he'd go. What he'd do.

David unbuttoned his shirt and scratched his chest, then sat up and removed the wrinkled garment. As he rubbed his neck, he glanced down at his suitcase, then scooted to the edge of the bed, lifted the case and set it against the footboard. He unzipped the black carry-on and lifted the small rectangular velvet box out from under the stretchy security straps that held his clothes in place.

He'd gone straight from the airport to Leander & Smythe Jewelers. He had commissioned the gift two months ago and had inspected it thoroughly when he'd picked it up this evening. He flipped open the box. Beautiful. A pearl-and-diamond bracelet.

Next Thursday was Caroline's twenty-seventh birthday— June 21st. Over the years he had limited his gifts to birthdays and Christmases. The only exceptions had been her high school and college graduations. He would sign the card simply *David,* as he had done for the past fifteen years. And through his lawyer, she would send him a thank-you note. Sweet and sincere, scolding him for being too generous.

He couldn't help wondering if she would celebrate this year's birthday with Gavin Robbins. He sincerely hoped not. Why couldn't that cousin of hers—Reverend Lyle Jennings—introduce her to another nice young minister? Maybe a man of the cloth would prove himself worthy of Caroline.

David closed the lid and laid the jewelry case on the bedside table to his right. Last year he had sent her a pearl necklace and the year before teardrop pearl earrings. After she'd turned twenty-one, he had begun sending her birthstone jewelry.

Just once he would like to see her on her birthday—in the flesh, all dressed up for a night out and wearing the jewelry he'd bought for her. But he would never again see Caroline face-to-face. He, of all people, had no right to be a part of her life.

David removed his shirt, tossed it atop his silk tie on the chair and lay down on the bed. The minute he closed his eyes, an image of Caroline appeared. The picture taken at her mother's funeral. Surrounded by caring friends. Never alone. Never lonely. Thank God she had been able to put the night of Preston Shaw's death behind her and build a good life for herself. He had wanted that for her and had done everything within his power to see that from that horrible night forward everything was made right in her world. As right as he could make it. After all the heartache she had been through, she deserved nothing less.

"Caroline," he whispered softly. "My sweet Caroline."

They sat on the floor in the middle of the kitchen, Caroline and her friends, as she tried for the tenth time to open the safe by using a combination of numbers she thought might have had some meaning for Preston. She had tried his birthday, her mother's birthday and their anniversary. Then she'd tried various other number combinations. Their old phone number, or at least the first six digits. The zip code for that area of Baltimore didn't work, either. Now she was trying Fletcher's birthday.

Marty and Steve had carried the rather heavy metal safe up from the basement and Allison and Roz had wiped the black box with rags. For the past hour no work on the house had been done. Everyone was sure that something valuable would be found inside the safe. Why else would it have been hidden away?

Caroline tried the new numbers. Right. Left. Right. Nothing. The safe remained locked. A collective groan signaled the onlookers' disappointment.

"I give up," Caroline said. "Maybe we should just use a stick of dynamite."

Roz giggled. Mrs. Mabry gasped.

"Have you tried every important date in your stepfather's life?" Lyle asked.

"All that I know, including his birthday, mother's birthday and Fletcher's."

"What about your birthday?" Roz asked.

"Mine?" Why would Preston have chosen her birthday as the combination to this safe? Maybe because no one would have guessed that he would choose those numbers. "All right. What have I got to lose?"

Everyone watched with baited breath as once again Caroline turned the knob on the small personalized safe. She tried her birth date. Nothing happened. Then she tried it backward. Still nothing.

"It's no use," Caroline said, then just as she spoke, an idea hit her. Without saying another word, she spun the dial to eighteen, then to twenty-one and back around to eleven. Fletcher's birth date, February 18th. Her birthday, June 21st. And Preston and Lenore's wedding anniversary, the date that had joined two families. January 11th.

The safe opened, pretty as you please.

Chapter 3

"I can't believe it!" Caroline gasped as she turned the handle and opened the solid steel door.

The others hovered closely, and when they got a good look inside, a chorus of disappointed sighs permeated the kitchen.

"No diamonds and rubies," Roz said.

"It's empty." Steve frowned.

"No, it's not empty." Caroline reached inside and grasped the small manila envelope stuck in the back of the safe.

When she pulled the envelope out and held it up, she saw that her mother's name had been written plainly across the top, in a bold, distinctive hand that Caroline felt certain was Preston's. A tremor shivered along her nerve endings.

"Aren't you going to open it and see what's inside?" Roz asked.

With quivering fingers, Caroline ripped open the envelope, then reached in and pulled out a single sheet of stationery.

"It's only a letter," Allison said.

Yes, it *was* only a letter, but instinct cautioned Caroline as she unfolded the message Preston had written to her mother. What if it were something private, a love letter? They're both dead now, Caroline reminded herself. Reading something personal can't harm either of them.

November 30. The letter was dated only a few weeks before Preston's death.

My dearest Lenore,

If you are reading this, then my worst fears have been confirmed and they have killed me to keep me quiet. When you clear out this safe, you will find this letter and the enclosed key. Safeguard this key and the identical one in your possession. They unlock the means by which to keep our family safe, after I am gone. Look inside your heart for the proof of my love for you and the children. If they try to harm you or either of the children, do not hesitate to use what I have left you. This is my last and most precious gift to you, Fletcher and Caroline.

Your devoted husband,
Preston

"What does the letter say?" Roz asked.

Ignoring her friend's question, Caroline turned the envelope upside down and shook it. A key fell out and into her open palm.

"A key?" Lyle stared at the object Caroline held.

"A key to what?" Roz asked.

Caroline closed her fingers over the mysterious brass key. What *did* it open? It was such an ordinary-looking thing. Not fancy. Denoting nothing specific. "I have no idea what it unlocks."

"Didn't your stepfather say in his letter?" Lyle asked.

Caroline shook her head, then stood and held out the letter to her cousin. "I don't understand why Mother left this envelope in the safe. It's apparent that she knew about the hidden passageway and where Preston kept the safe. She must have cleaned the safe out before she moved from the house.''

"We didn't even see the envelope at first," Roz reminded Caroline. "Wasn't it stuck way in the back? It's possible your mother simply overlooked it."

Lyle scanned the letter hurriedly. "Oh, my, my. If what he says in this letter is true, then whoever killed Preston Shaw wasn't some thief trying to burglarize the house."

"If that letter is true, then my stepfather was assassinated," Caroline said. "And this key—" she opened her hand, lifted the key and held it up between her right thumb and forefinger as she stared at the object "—might unlock the identity of his murderer."

"I think you should call Fletcher right away," Lyle said. "He should know about this letter and the key. Perhaps he'll recognize the key and know what it unlocks."

David woke with a start, sweat drenching his naked chest. He rose from the bed, sat on the edge and placed his bare feet on the floor. He hadn't been plagued by that particular dream in a long time. Not in years. He supposed he had finally reached a point where he'd been able to reconcile his guilt with the knowledge that he had acted under orders and done the right thing. Raking his hand through his hair, he stood and walked across the room and into the bath. He left off the light so that only the dim glow of the moon coming through the window eliminated the complete darkness. He turned on the faucets, cupped his hands to catch the cold water and splashed his face, then lifted a towel from the nearby rack and blotted the cool, reviving moisture.

Preston Shaw had been dead nearly fifteen years. Why did he occasionally still dream about the night the man had died? Preston didn't just die, David reminded himself. *You killed him.* Acting under orders from Ellison Penn. The Peacekeepers' secret agents took care of their own, whether to protect them or to dispose of them. If one went rogue, which rarely happened, then he or she met a swift punishment at the hands of the organization itself. Shaw had been under suspicion for several months, but no one wanted to believe the charming man was capable of subversive activity that might threaten the United States. But despite Shaw's blue-blooded background and the respect he had earned over the years, in the end, he had proved himself dangerous to the very government he had sworn to serve.

Only a handful of people knew the truth—the wealthy, suave, sophisticated, gallant and greatly admired Preston Shaw had assassinated U.S. senator Herbert Harwell, under orders from a secret society of insurgent and highly dangerous powerful men known as the Loyalists Coalition. Preston Shaw had been a double agent.

And two months later, the Peacekeepers' special agent, Aidan Colbert, executed the traitor Shaw had proved himself to be by that one atrocious, deadly act.

David padded through the apartment, out into the large open space that combined a living room and kitchen. He plopped down in the black leather easy chair, hoisted his feet atop the matching, contemporary-style ottoman and picked up the TV remote control. At this time of night, when he suffered with bouts of insomnia, he usually watched reruns of black-and-white comedy shows from the fifties and sixties. He had a weakness for the *Andy Griffith Show* and *Father Knows Best,* both depicting an unobtainable ideal of family life. God knew his own family life had been the furthest thing possible from ideal. The horrors his father had inflicted on them might have come from an Edgar Allan Poe tale of torment and fear.

But that wasn't your past, your childhood, he reminded himself. That life belonged to Aidan Colbert. And Aidan Colbert is dead.

David clicked on the TV but kept the sound muted as he flipped through the various stations. As he zoomed from channel to channel, his gaze traveled back and forth from the television set to various other objects in the room. In his peripheral vision he caught a glimpse of the file folder containing the history of one Caroline Lenore McGuire.

What he needed to do was strike a match to the folder, to destroy it completely. Over the years, he had foolishly allowed Caroline to become an obsession. What had started out as a man wanting to help a child, to watch over her and keep her safe, had turned into more. Exactly what, he wasn't sure. But whatever it was, it wasn't good for him. If he'd been smart, he would have let his observation of Caroline's life end with Aidan Colbert's death.

David turned up the sound on the TV just enough to create a racket, then meandered into the kitchen and prowled around in the refrigerator. After retrieving a bottle of imported beer, he popped the cap and walked back into the living room. The program on TV was an old movie with a scene depicting a light snowfall in a metropolitan area.

His mind drifted swiftly back in time. It had started to snow that night, just as he left the Shaw house. Small flakes at first, but by the time he had returned to the Peacekeepers' headquarters, the ground was covered with a light dusting. The first snow of the season. Had Caroline ever realized it had snowed that night or had most of her memories from that time been banished along with the horror of finding her step-father's body and coming face-to-face with his killer?

Tomorrow morning, he would telephone Ellison and tell him to end the surveillance of Caroline. In all these years no one had tried to harm her, so what was the point of the agency continuing to protect her? *Not the agency,* an inner voice reminded him. The only reason Ellison had continued keeping watch over her was as a personal favor to Aidan Colbert. But Aidan was dead and it was high time to allow his obsession with Caroline to die, too.

It had been three days since she had found her stepfather's cryptic message to her mother, perhaps the last letter he had ever written. And despite everyone's insistence that she not make too much out of what Preston had written, Caroline found that she simply could not let it go. She had discussed the matter with Lyle and Roz, but the minute they saw how upset the revelation made her, they suggested that perhaps Preston had been paranoid for some reason. After all, the police had thoroughly investigated her stepfather's death, hadn't they? And when she had shown the letter to Fletcher, he'd been shocked and at first as convinced as she that someone had murdered his father because he possessed information that could harm someone else. Perhaps someone very powerful. After all, Preston had belonged to a prestigious Washington organization and wielded a great deal of power as second in command at Peacekeepers International. Wasn't it possible that some foreign government had ordered his assassination? Fletcher had immediately contacted Gavin Robbins, who had, as a favor to Fletcher and her, gone straight to Ellison Penn, the head honcho of the Peacekeepers fifteen years ago and now.

"Ellison has assured me that Preston wasn't involved in anything dangerous for the Peacekeepers at the time of his death," Gavin had said. "And the organization conducted their own private investigation and came to the same conclusion as the police—a botched robbery had resulted in the murder of Preston Shaw."

"But what about this letter?" Caroline had waved the handwritten missive under Gavin's nose.

"Caroline, honey, why do you want to dredge up the past this way?" Gavin had asked. "Ellison and I both remember how odd Preston had been acting the last few weeks of his life. Ellison thought he was on the verge of a nervous breakdown because his marriage was in trouble. If Preston's mental state was shaky, then he very well could have become paranoid."

"I do remember the last couple of times I saw Father he

acted rather peculiar,'' Fletcher had said. ''He seemed distracted.''

''I believe that what you both have told me only adds to the evidence in this letter that Preston feared for his life.'' Caroline had paused, looked at the two men, saw skepticism on their faces and then continued, ''And he was afraid for Mother and Fletcher and me.''

''Even if what you suspect is true—and I don't think it is—after all these years, there would be no way to prove it,'' Gavin had said. ''No way to find Preston's murderer. Besides, why put yourself and Fletcher through hell all over again?''

''That's where you're wrong,'' she'd told him. ''I have a key that can unlock the evidence Preston left as an insurance policy to protect his family.''

''Perhaps Caroline is right.'' Fletcher had put his arm around her shoulders. ''If there's any way we can find Father's murderer, then I'm willing to relive that hell, to go back and rehash what happened that night.'' He had looked point-blank at Caroline. ''What about you, kiddo, do you think you can relive what happened? Maybe you'd better think about it before you open that old can of worms.''

Caroline had thought about it. All last night and all day today. And no matter how many times she went over things, she came to the same conclusion. She believed what Preston had written in the letter. Her stepfather had been the victim of cold-blooded, premeditated murder. The bearded man in the shadows had been an assassin. And she had practically witnessed the crime.

Then why didn't he kill you? She had asked herself this question a million times and had yet to come up with a logical answer. If he had been merely a burglar or if he had been a hired killer, why would he have balked at killing a child if it meant protecting himself?

If she could find the lock that the key opened, she might well find the answer to this question as well as all the others

surrounding Preston's death. Unfortunately Fletcher didn't
recognize the key and she had no earthly idea where to start
looking.

Caroline liked parties well enough, although she preferred
quiet evenings at home. She loved sitting on her back porch
in the evenings partly because she had a great view. The
waterfront footage, which was part of the five acres that had
come as a package deal with the house, had been one of the
reasons she had purchased the nineteenth-century ramshackle
wooden structure and remodeled it four years ago. But this
was one party invitation she couldn't decline. When Gavin
had called to ask if he could be her escort to the birthday
party Fletcher was giving for Brooke aboard his yacht, she
was delighted that she wouldn't be attending the event alone.
Even though she had decided not to date Gavin again, she'd
thought one more date wouldn't matter. But after tonight
she'd tell him that she couldn't see him again.

When Gavin and she had boarded the *Lenore,* he had
pulled her aside and said, "You'll be the most beautiful
woman here tonight."

Gavin was always complimenting her, saying all the things
she supposed most women liked to hear, which made her
wonder if Gavin's womanizer reputation wasn't well
founded. They had been dating on and off for the past few
months. More off than on, but that was her doing, not his.
When she'd made it perfectly clear after their third date that
she had no intention of hopping into bed with him, she had
assumed he wouldn't be back. She'd been wrong. After that,
his pursuit of her had intensified, as if he liked the challenge.
Perhaps he believed he could wear her down with his gentlemanly charm. It was past time for her to be totally honest
with him. She liked Gavin well enough, enjoyed his company
occasionally and was inordinately flattered by his attention,
but she wasn't in love with him and never would be. Call

her old-fashioned, but she wanted to wait for love, wanted her first time to be with a very special man.

Caroline strolled along the deck of the *Lenore,* the motor yacht Fletcher had inherited from his father. Preston had purchased the yacht new when he'd married Lenore and took her on a honeymoon cruise in the Caribbean. As a child Caroline had loved the three summer vacation trips aboard the wide-beam cruiser. Fletcher had kept the yacht in perfect condition, and the vessel maintained the original cockpit and gorgeous oak interior throughout. Below were three staterooms with their own baths and the galley up layout offered a deck-level powder room, too.

Fletcher kept the yacht anchored at the marina and often loaned the boat to friends for excursions in the bay. Much like his father before him, Fletcher was known to be generous to those nearest and dearest to him.

A balmy spring breeze swept across the deck, caressing Caroline's hair. As the evening had worn on, she'd grown tired of dancing, first with Gavin, then later with Fletcher and several of his friends, each progressive dance partner just a little drunker than the one before him. She had lost track of Gavin in the throng of well-wishers, about thirty minutes ago, shortly after Brooke had blown out the candles on her enormous birthday cake and ripped into the stack of elaborately decorated gifts. Caroline was more than ready to head back to St. Michaels right now and wished she could locate her date. As she had made her way along the congested deck, she had asked people she knew if they'd seen Gavin, but no one seemed to have any idea where he was. She couldn't help wondering if he'd found some willing female and was making use of one of the staterooms.

Why on earth would you continue dating a man you thought capable of having sex with another woman while on a date with you? she asked herself. *Because you didn't want to come to this party alone, that's why.*

As Caroline tried to find a less-congested area on the yacht

so she could at least breathe without smelling liquor or cig-
arettes, her mind filled with thoughts of her own upcoming
birthday. She had never had a gala celebration like the one
Fletcher was hosting for Brooke, but since she'd turned thirteen, her birthdays had been special events. Made special by
one person. One man. *David.*

Each year a gift. A signed card. A birthday cake delivered
by a local bakery. And balloons equal in number to her age.
Since that first year when she had felt so alone, after her
mother had sent her to live with Aunt Dixie and Lyle, she
had never again dreaded a birthday. Because of David's generosity.

She longed to meet her benefactor, but after years of having her request to meet with him and thank him personally
denied by his attorney, Caroline had finally accepted the fact
that for some reason known only to him, David did not want
the two of them to ever meet. Over time she had played out
more than one scenario in her mind. Perhaps he was very
ugly and even deformed—a true beast of a man. Or maybe
he was married and thought his wife might be jealous of all
he had done for an old friend's daughter. Whatever the reason, David had become a mystery she dreamed of one day
solving. She could not deny that she had built his image into
one of a knight in shining armor, someone who would willingly slay dragons for her.

She couldn't explain to anyone why she loved a man she'd
never met, why she believed that for the past fifteen years
David had been the one constant in her life, the only adult
who had never betrayed her, never left her, never stopped
loving her. As a child she had clung to his phantom image,
thinking of him as a substitute father, a protector and a benefactor. Because she had lost her own father and two step-
fathers, and then her mother had abandoned her, she had
transferred her desperate need for these lost parental figures
and loved David as if he had truly been in her life.

David's presence in her life, albeit from afar, had been like a light at the end of a lonely tunnel and she had developed an attachment to his kindness when she had felt herself to be nothing more than an unloved and unwanted child. Even Aunt Dixie's love and concern had not been enough to fill the void she had felt. But somehow knowing that David cared, that David would always be there for her, he had in an almost miraculous way made her feel less alone, less abandoned, less unloved.

She wasn't quite sure when her affections for David had begun to change, to alter from a child's adoration to a woman's admiration and respect. For many years now, her dearest wish had been to meet this special man who had cared so greatly for her all her life. And she couldn't deny that in her heart of hearts, she fantasized that David would become a real part of her life.

Suddenly someone near her gasped. "We're moving."

Another said, "I didn't know Fletcher was going to give us a trip out into the bay as a finale for Brooke's party."

Caroline sighed and shook her head. Now she was stuck aboard, probably until the wee hours of the morning. She continued making her way around the deck, finding it less crowded toward the aft side. She walked past a handful of couples wrapped in each other's arms as the *Lenore* left the dock. At last she was alone, with only the sea breeze around her and the starry sky overhead. She had never been a party girl, not even as a teenager, and now less than ever. She much preferred small, simple dinners at home with a few well-chosen friends. At this precise moment, she would much rather be sitting on her back porch, barefoot and in a pair of tattered old shorts, than dressed to the nines and bored out of her mind.

Suddenly, without any warning, someone came up behind Caroline. She sensed the hovering body before she actually felt it as it pressed against her back. Was it Gavin? Had he finally come looking for her? As she started to turn around, she found herself trapped, held in place by the man's big arm, which quickly draped around her. She opened her mouth to protest, but before she could make a sound, a foul-smelling rag covered her nose and mouth. She whimpered as her head began to spin. Overwhelmed by complete helplessness, she quickly drifted off into a semiconscious state. The very last thing her fuzzy brain registered was the feeling of being lifted. Raised up into the air and over the railing. Then released.

Floating. Down. Down. Down. And into the water.

Chapter 4

David had no idea why Sam Dundee had summoned him to his island home, but David's gut instincts warned him of trouble. He had met the owner of Dundee Private Security and Investigation Agency the first day he'd come to work there. The big boss had flown into Atlanta to personally introduce his newest agent to Dundee's CEO, Ellen Denby, who normally did the hiring and firing. David had gotten this job because Ellison Penn knew Dundee personally and had called in a favor. So maybe Ellison's involvement with Dundee was the reason David felt so uneasy as he followed along behind Manton, the seven-foot mahogany-skinned guardian of Dundee's private island retreat. David had realized almost instantly that the giant of a man was mute, but his keen black eyes seemed to look into David's very soul. The last thing David wanted was someone seeing past the David Wolfe facade and finding Aidan Colbert.

When they reached the porch of the huge raised cottage that sat perched atop a small hill, which gave the house a magnificent view of the gulf, Manton opened the door and held it for David. Once inside, David was greeted by Sam Dundee himself, who apparently had been waiting for him in the foyer.

Sam offered his hand. "I hope the boat ride from Biloxi wasn't too bad. The waters are a bit choppy this morning."

David exchanged a handshake with the big man. Although they were close in height, Sam had the build of a football linebacker, with massive shoulders and arms.

"The boat ride was fine," David replied.

"Join me in the den," Sam said. "I have another guest who came in late last night and he's anxious to speak to you."

David's stomach tightened. Another guest? He vanquished several thoughts and settled on one. Ellison Penn. There was no one else it could be. But why would Ellison risk contacting him personally? They had both broken several cardinal Peacekeepers' rules in order to bury Aidan Colbert and resurrect him as David Wolfe two and a half years ago.

Sam led David to the den, which was Caribbean light and airy. Cream walls. Massive windows, open to catch the spring breeze and illuminate with morning sunlight. Overstuffed chairs and sofa. An ornately carved blond oak desk, placed in front of floor-to-ceiling bookshelves, dominated the room. Behind the desk, in the large cream leather swivel chair sat Ellison Penn. Ellison's attire of tan slacks and navy-blue short-sleeved shirt took David aback; he didn't think he'd ever seen the white-haired gentleman in casual clothes before. The man's friendly gray eyes were as deceptive as his healthy tanned face and gregarious smile. Ellison Penn looked like any affluent American businessman. One would assume this seventy-year-old gentleman incapable of harming a fly. But David knew better. This grandfatherly-looking man, as the commander of the secret squad of Peacekeepers agents, had over a period of twenty years ordered the assassination of several dozen people.

Ellison rose to his full six-foot height. "Good to see you,

Mr. Wolfe. I appreciate your meeting me on such short notice.''

David stared at his former boss, a man who had served as his mentor for many years. Ellison held a thin file folder in his hand. ''Mr. Penn.'' David nodded.

''I'll leave y'all alone.'' Standing in the doorway, Sam glanced at Ellison and then at David. ''Lunch will be in an hour. Jeannie and I would be pleased if both of you would join us before Mr. Wolfe returns to Biloxi this afternoon.''

''We'd be honored to join you and your lovely wife,'' Ellison said.

Sam closed the den door, sealing the two men together within the privacy of the room.

Inclining his head toward the door, David said, ''He doesn't know who I am...or rather who I was, does he?''

''No one knows, except the two of us. Safer that way.'' Ellison rounded the side of the desk and came toward David. ''I trust Sam implicitly, but he's safer not knowing your true identity.''

''Why are you here?'' David asked. ''Or better yet, why did you have me summoned here?''

''Let's sit.'' Ellison indicated the sofa.

Ellison took a seat, laid the file folder on his lap and relaxed against the enormous cushions. Sitting on the opposite end of the sofa, David stared inquisitively at the file folder.

''As you know, Caroline McGuire inherited the house on Sheffield Street in Baltimore when her mother died,'' Ellison said.

David nodded but remained silent. What was he supposed to say? *Yes, I well remember that house, that December night and what transpired between Caroline's stepfather and me.*

''Unknown to us, the house had a hidden corridor in the basement.'' Ellison ran his fingertips around the edge of the folder. ''It was probably constructed by the original builder, but there are no blueprints on record for the old house, so there's no way of knowing for sure.'' Ellison kept his gaze fixed on the folder. "When Caroline and members of her cousin Lyle's church were working in the basement, they found the hidden passageway and a small, portable safe that Preston had put there."

Now Ellison had gained his attention. David's heartbeat accelerated. A secret passageway? A hidden safe? "Were they able to open the safe?"

Ellison nodded. "Yes, Caroline finally figured out the combination and was able to open the safe."

"I assume there was something inside—something important. Otherwise you wouldn't be here."

"The safe was empty—" Ellison paused for effect "—except for an envelope. And inside that envelope was a letter Preston had written to his wife, Lenore." Ellison lifted the folder and handed it to David. "We didn't get our hands on the original, so this is only Gavin Robbins's account of the letter that Caroline showed him."

David flipped open the folder, scanned the typed page and cursed under his breath. "Goddammit!"

"Somewhere out there Preston Shaw left some damning evidence against some very important people," Ellison said. "People who have, for the past fifteen years, thought they were safe. Leaders of the Loyalists Coalition who ordered Preston to kill Senator Harwell."

"How did Caroline react to the letter? And Fletcher Shaw? What did he have to say?"

"Gavin tried to convince them to let the matter drop. He told them that after all these years—"

"Let me guess…" David bounded off the sofa, slammed the folder against the palm of his hand and glared point-blank at Ellison. "Caroline is determined to find out what the key unlocks. She wants to find out who killed her stepfather and why."

"Since she discovered the letter and the key, she's been relentless in pursuing the search." Ellison rose to his feet. "She's tried the locks on every door in the house on Sheffield

Street, but to no avail. And she is in the process of contacting everyone who ever knew Preston. She even telephoned me, but I was able to avoid taking her call."

"Sooner or later, you'll have to talk to her." Years ago David had feared something like this would happen. During the weeks and months directly following Preston Shaw's death, the Peacekeepers had kept a vigilant watch over Shaw's wife, son and stepdaughter. Then when nothing had materialized, no evidence to point the finger at Shaw's accomplices in the Senator Herbert Harwell assassination scheme, David had hoped that Caroline was safe. That she would always be safe. "If these people find out she has a key that will unlock the evidence against them, then Caroline is in danger. You'll have to keep her under surveillance…make sure she's—" The look in Ellison's eyes, a mixture of regret and sadness, warned David of bad news. "What's happened? Is Caroline all right?" David's heartbeat roared in his ears.

Ellison grasped David's arm, manacling his biceps through the material of his shirt. "While Caroline was attending a party aboard Fletcher Shaw's yacht, someone chloroformed her and dumped her into the bay."

Every muscle in David's body tensed. Every nerve screamed. He jerked free of Ellison's grip, narrowed his gaze and glared at the bearer of evil tidings. "Is she…?" He couldn't bring himself to say the word. The file folder slipped from his hand and sailed smoothly down to the floor.

"She's alive," Ellison said. "No thanks to our would-be assassin, however. If his plan had worked, Caroline's body might not ever have been found. It would have probably been hours before anyone aboard the yacht discovered her missing."

"She's alive?" David released the breath he'd been holding. "Does that mean she's all right?"

"That means she's fine and recuperating at home after a brief stay in the hospital. And she's understandably unnerved." Ellison shook his head. "I'm afraid the police got involved, but they aren't overly concerned. Considering the fact that the yacht was filled with drunken partygoers, they assume Caroline had been drinking and might have accidentally fallen overboard."

"If you had somcone watching her, why didn't—"

"It seems that Gavin got sidetracked by a rather luscious blonde," Ellison admitted sheepishly. "Not conduct I approve of in any of my agents, but as you know, Gavin has a weakness for the ladies."

"And this is the man who was only recently promoted to the number two position at Peacekeepers?" David wanted to smash something—anything—but preferably Gavin Robbins's face! "Caroline needs a twenty-four-hours-a-day bodyguard. They've already tried to kill her once to stop her from using the key. They'll try again and again, if necessary, until they put a stop to her investigating."

"You're right, on both counts," Ellison agreed. "These people—whoever they are—will continue their efforts to stop her permanently. Therefore, she needs constant protection."

"We can dispatch someone from Dundee's... Ah... Has Sam already chosen someone to...?"

"Fletcher Shaw got in touch with his lawyer and told him to find the premier agency in the country and request their best bodyguard for his stepsister, so naturally the lawyer recommended Dundee's. I made a recommendation to Sam last night. That's why he telephoned you and requested your presence here today."

"I'm afraid I don't understand."

"I don't know of a man on earth who has a bigger stake in protecting Caroline McGuire than you do." Ellison clamped his hand down on David's shoulder.

David swallowed hard. "No. Not me." Surely Ellison wasn't suggesting that he act as Caroline's bodyguard. The idea was out of the question. There could be no face-to-face contact with Caroline. Not ever. *You were ordered not to go near her. You were allowed to be her caretaker only from a distance.*

"Aidan Colbert is dead," Ellison said. "There is no connection between David Wolfe and him."

"It would be wrong for me to take this assignment."

"I thought you'd jump at the chance. You've acted as her secret guardian, her protector, her keeper for nearly fifteen years." Ellison squeezed David's shoulder. "Tell me that you believe there's another man who is capable of keeping watch over Caroline the way you can. Tell me that everything within you isn't chomping at the bit to go to her side as quickly as possible." Ellison released his hold on David and met his gaze. "This is your chance for redemption."

"Do you think I need redemption?"

Ellison held up his hand in a stop gesture. "Don't try to convince me that you haven't been eaten alive with guilt ever since that night. Do you think I don't know what it did to you having to confront Caroline only moments after you had killed her stepfather?"

Ellison was right and he damn well knew it. Of all the assignments Aidan Colbert had completed as a Peacekeeper none had tormented him the way that first assassination had. There had been no doubt in his mind that he had done the right thing, that Preston Shaw had to be eliminated. In that instance as in many that had followed, he had done his duty, had lived by the Peacekeepers' code, and his actions were those of an honorable man doing a dirty job for his country. Innocent people sometimes got in the way and were hurt or killed. But not by him. Never by him. Only that one time when the innocent victim had been Caroline McGuire. Memories of her still haunted him. It was her little cherubic face he saw in his nightmares, that terrified look in her eyes. The look of a child who knew death awaited her. He had seen that fear in another child's eyes once, long before the night of Preston Shaw's execution. When he had recognized the terror in Caroline's eyes, her face had been overlaid with the features of another. His little brother Brendan.

"Are you all right?" Ellison asked.

"What?" David blinked several times, bringing himself out of a bad place, an evil moment from his childhood that plagued him to this day. "Yes, I'm all right. And yes, I'll take the job as Caroline's bodyguard. You're right about me. You know that I would die before I'd let anyone harm her."

"Yes, I'm sure you would." Ellison reached down and picked up the file folder from the floor. "I'll have Sam contact Fletcher Shaw and let him know that a Dundee agent named David Wolfe will arrive in St. Michaels tonight. Sam has arranged for Matt O'Brien to fly you straight from Biloxi to Maryland. And Jack Parker is on standby to join you, if you need backup later on."

"You were awfully sure I'd accept this job."

"My boy, you must remember that I'm the man who has worked as your accomplice in taking care of Caroline all these years. I, better than anyone, know what she represents to you and exactly to what extent you would go to keep her safe."

"If it means breaking every rule in the book, I'll do it," David said in a calm, controlled manner. "Know this from the start—Caroline's well-being comes first, before anyone or anything else. And that includes the Peacekeepers."

Ellison nodded. "While you're guarding Caroline, you'll also be investigating Preston Shaw's death along with her. The key she has holds the one and only possible means of finding any evidence as to who Preston's cohorts were. Those men still exist and have continued their work, even if somewhat less obviously. With enough proof, we could put those men in jail where they belong and eliminate an ongoing threat to this country."

"You make sure I get what I want and I'll do my best to help the Peacekeepers get what they want." David offered Ellison his hand.

"You have a deal." The two men sealed their pact with a powerful handshake.

Caroline felt trapped inside her own home and it was a feeling she detested. Since her release from the hospital yesterday, she had been surrounded by well-meaning friends. Roz, Brooke, Lyle and Fletcher had all four spent the night, and at least two of them had been with her throughout the day. Brooke's parents, Oliver and Eileen Harper, had stopped by while she'd been in the hospital and had driven down from Baltimore earlier today. Eileen had even sent a beautiful bouquet of get-well flowers. Then Gavin had shown up about an hour ago and joined the fearless foursome. Now the five of them sat around in her living room, each one hovering like a mother bird waiting for her chick to hatch. As much as she enjoyed their company and appreciated their concern, she was accustomed to the peace and quiet of living alone. But for some undetermined amount of time, she would have to forego her privacy and greatly treasured solitude. Once the bodyguard Fletcher had hired for her arrived, she wouldn't be alone again. Someone would be at her side, day and night. Watching her. Protecting her from harm.

"What time is this bodyguard supposed to arrive?" Brooke asked.

"He should be here within the next half hour," Fletcher said. "I spoke to the CEO of Dundee's and was assured that they're sending one of their top agents."

"What's his name?" Gavin asked.

"Wolfe," Fletcher replied. "I don't know if that's a first or last name."

"If he turns out to be a big, gorgeous hunk, I may move in with you," Roz said.

Lyle gave Roz a condemning stare. "Is that all you think about, Ms. Turner, men and sex?"

Roz's cheeks flamed red, but she kept her temper in check

as she skewered Lyle with her gaze. "Unlike you, *Reverend*, some of us actually enjoy the sins of the flesh."

"You make that more than obvious," Lyle countered. "Most people have the decency not to flaunt their sins in front of the world. But you seem to have no qualms—"

Roz got right up in Lyle's face, which immediately stopped his condemnation. "Now, you listen here you Bible-thumping, pulpit-spouting—"

"That's enough!" Caroline put one arm around Roz's shoulders and the other around Lyle's, then adeptly separated the two warring parties. "I wish that just once the two of you could be in the same room together without going for the jugular."

"If you ask me, they've got the hots for each other," Brooke said. "If they'd just hop in the sack and get it over with—"

"You're crazy if you think I'd be interested in a holier-than-thou *virgin*," Roz said, putting special emphasis on the last word. "I like my men rough, tough and experienced."

"I can assure you, Ms. Turner, that you're safe from me." Lyle turned and stormed out of the room.

"Now, look what you two have done." Caroline glowered at Roz and then at Brooke. "You know how sensitive Lyle is."

"I'm sorry," Brooke said. "Lyle is such an easy target, but I forget how serious-minded he is."

"The man can't take a joke," Roz complained, then forced a smile as she wrapped her arm around Caroline's waist. "I shouldn't have gotten into an argument with him. Not tonight of all nights. Lyle and I were able to act civilly toward each other when you were in the hospital, so there's no reason we can't continue to be civil toward each other. The last thing you need is having your cousin and your best friend at each other's throats."

"And I thought I was Caroline's best friend," Brooke said, with a half-joking pout on her lips.

"All of you are my friends," Caroline said. "My dear friends. And although having y'all here is driving me nuts, it's also distracting me from thinking about what happened the night before last on Fletcher's yacht."

"I can't believe someone actually chloroformed you and threw you overboard," Fletcher said. "If I'd thought that damn key would put your life in danger, I'd have insisted you toss it into the bay. I'd rather never know what the key opens if searching for it puts your life at risk."

"Don't you see? Someone doesn't want us to find out what this key opens." Caroline lifted the key, which she had slipped onto a gold chain and placed around her neck. "I truly believe that when we find what the key opens, we'll find proof of who killed Preston and why."

"Perhaps you should give Fletcher the key," Gavin said. "After all, Preston was his father, and if anyone has the right to unearth any secret truth about his murderer, then Fletcher does."

"I don't need the damn key," Fletcher said. "However, my dear sister, I think you should hand the thing over to this fellow Wolfe. His agency, Dundee's, is going to be working with him to investigate Father's death."

"Do you think that's wise?" Gavin asked. "The bigger the stink you stir, the more danger there is bound to be for Caroline."

"I'm not going to back down," Caroline said. "Being almost drowned had the adverse effect on me from what my would-be killer intended. Not only am I still alive, but I'm more determined than ever to find what the key unlocks and retrieve whatever evidence there is against Preston's killer."

The soft tinkle of the doorbell chimed throughout the house. Caroline froze for an instant. All eyes turned toward the foyer.

"Shall I go to the door?" Fletcher asked. "It's probably your bodyguard, Mr. Wolfe."

"Why don't we go together?" Caroline suggested.

Fletcher nodded and with a magnanimous sweep of his hand indicated for her to precede him. By the time Fletcher and she reached the foyer, Roz, Brooke and Gavin were only a few steps behind; then Lyle came out of the room across the hall and halted several feet away from the others. Caroline grasped the brass handle and opened the door.

She wasn't quite sure what she'd been expecting, but the man standing on her front porch wasn't it. He was tall, broad-shouldered and lean, with a bronze tan, thick dark blond hair and tinted aviator glasses that hid his eyes. He wore a cream-colored sport coat and a teal-blue shirt, casually elegant attire that a man with money might wear to project both a fashionable and yet masculine image. He wasn't handsome, but he was devastatingly attractive, in a self-assured way that professed to the world he was a man to be reckoned with. A shiver of apprehension fluttered in Caroline's stomach. She heard an indrawn breath and assumed it came from Brooke. Then a low, soft whistle told her that Roz had just made a comment.

"I'm Wolfe," the man said, his voice dark and rich and distinctively Southern, as he removed his sunglasses and slid them into his pocket.

"Won't you come in, Mr. Wolfe. We've been expecting you. I'm Caroline McGuire."

When she held out her hand, he simply stared at it for endless seconds, then encompassed it within his own huge hand. The moment they touched, a current passed between them. A shocking sensation of awareness. And when their gazes met, Caroline gasped. She had never seen such cold eyes, moss green and void of any emotion.

"Hello, Caroline," he said.

Startled by her reaction to the stranger, Caroline snatched her hand away but couldn't stop looking directly at him in the same way he continued staring at her. Did he feel it, too? she wondered. That odd sense of recognition, as if she had known this stranger all her life, perhaps even in a dozen other lifetimes?

Chapter 5

He couldn't take his eyes off her. She was more lovely than any picture he'd ever seen of her. This was Caroline—his Caroline. He wasn't sure exactly when he'd begun to think of her that way. It had been a gradual thing, taking place so imperceptibly that he had no way of pinpointing the precise moment that his thoughts of her had become possessive. Perhaps if he'd had a family of his own, his feelings for Caroline wouldn't have taken on such monumental proportions. Aidan Colbert had had a few distant relatives, but no real family to speak of, and David Wolfe had no one. There were no parents, no siblings, no wife and no children. Only Caroline.

When he noticed the flush on her cheeks and the way she suddenly broke eye contact, Wolfe realized he had been staring at her for longer than was socially acceptable. In the future, he would have to be careful and take advantage of unguarded moments, when no one else was around, to drink his fill of her. He wondered if a thousand lifetimes would be enough.

Someone cleared his throat. Wolfe glanced behind Caroline to where four people stood guard over her, each inspecting him thoroughly. The two men glowered at him as if they didn't quite trust him. The two women surveyed him from head to toe as if he were an item up for auction. He recognized all four people from photos that had been included in the packet Sam Dundee had given him this afternoon before he'd left Le Bijou Bleu, Dundee's private island. The dossier contained brief bios and photographs of the people most important in Caroline's life.

Fletcher Shaw came forward and extended his hand to Wolfe. He sized up the handsome young man quickly as he reached out to accept his gesture of greeting. They were about the same height, but Shaw was more slender, his handshake weaker. Caroline's stepbrother possessed an air of superiority, one that declared without words that he was the master and considered David the servant.

"Fletcher Shaw."

"Wolfe." He looked directly into Fletcher's blue eyes and noted just a hint of uncertainty there. Most of his adult life he'd had that effect on other men. A wariness they tried to disguise, but couldn't. A primitive fear that admitted a more dominant male had just arrived on the scene.

"I'm the one who hired you," Fletcher said. "Ms. McGuire is my stepsister and I'm quite concerned about her welfare. I've been assured that you're one of the best at what you do. I want only the best for Caroline."

So do I, Wolfe thought. *That's all I've ever wanted.* "I can assure you, Mr. Shaw, that Ms. McGuire's safety is my top priority. No one is going to get to her, except through me."

"Caroline, you lucky girl, you." Tall, fashion-model elegant, Brooke Harper sauntered across the foyer, all the while sizing up Wolfe, flirting subtly as she held out her hand. "I'm Brooke Harper, Caroline's oldest and dearest friend." She sighed dramatically when Wolfe shook her hand. She held on just a fraction too long, then when Fletcher moved to her side, she laughed and said, "Fletch, darling, if I'm ever in danger, will you hire me a Dundee bodyguard like Mr. Wolfe?"

Before Fletcher could respond, Roz rushed forward. "Hi. I'm Rozalin Turner. Since I'm Caroline's assistant, I'm sure we'll be seeing a great deal of each other."

"Ms. Turner." Wolfe acknowledged her presence by looking directly at her.

Caroline motioned for the other man, who hadn't moved since Wolfe entered the foyer, to come to her. "This is my cousin, Reverend Lyle Jennings."

Surprisingly the short, stocky reverend's handshake had more power than Shaw's, and the wariness Wolfe saw in the man's eyes had more to do with concern over Caroline than with masculine dominance. He liked Lyle on sight, which made him second-guess his own judgment. He seldom liked anyone immediately. But reason told him that his knowledge of Lyle Jennings's place in Caroline's heart preconditioned him to like the man who truly was a brother to her.

"Mr. Wolfe, I'm very glad you're here," Lyle said.

Wolfe nodded, then looked past the others to where a third man stood, arms crossed over his chest and his dark, hooded eyes focused on Wolfe. The last time he'd seen Gavin Robbins was a few days before Aidan Colbert had left the country on his final Peacekeepers assignment. Although the two had worked together for nearly thirteen years, neither had ever moved beyond their initial hostility toward each other. David wondered what Gavin would do if he realized Aidan Colbert had become David Wolfe. Not that there was any reason Gavin would recognize him. All resemblance to Aidan Colbert was practically gone.

Caroline turned around and smiled at Gavin. "Come meet Mr. Wolfe," she said.

Gavin made no move to approach. Instead he remained aloof, deliberately setting himself apart from everyone else. "Fletch tells us that you come highly recommended. I think you should know that I have every intention of checking out your credentials.''

Caroline gave Gavin a disapproving look, apparently appalled by his bold rudeness. "I'm certain that's not necessary."

"On the contrary," Wolfe said. "If I were your boyfriend, I'd want to make sure the man who was to be at your side day and night was someone trustworthy."

Brooke and Roz giggled. Fletch coughed and cleared his throat. Lyle glanced at Caroline as if wanting to gauge her reaction.

Caroline walked over and closed the still-open front door. "I was just about to prepare some coffee, Mr. Wolfe. Won't you join us in the living room?"

"Thank you," Wolfe replied. "But if you don't mind ending this evening with your friends a bit early, I'd like to familiarize myself with your house and the grounds tonight and go over a few rules with you that can't wait until morning."

"Oh, I see." Caroline stared at him strangely, as if she didn't quite comprehend the necessity of such discourteous haste. He feared that Caroline would find his abrupt and oftentimes tactless actions disturbing. One of the many things he knew about her was her penchant for good manners. Something Dixie Jennings had drilled into her as a girl.

"Well, I guess we've been asked to leave," Fletcher said, obviously not pleased by Wolfe's take-charge attitude.

"You've hired me to do a job," Wolfe reminded him. "From this moment on, everything I do will have one objective—to protect Ms. McGuire."

"Yes, of course." Fletcher hugged Caroline, then glanced at Brooke. "Get your things, darling, and we'll leave Caroline in Mr. Wolfe's capable hands."

"I'm sorry we have to end our lovely evening so early," Caroline said as she scurried around after her guests while they prepared to depart.

Wolfe stood in the foyer, waiting and watching, while she shared hugs and kisses and goodbye waves with her friends. Gavin was the last to leave, but when he did go, he made a production of planting a rather intense kiss on Caroline's lips. Every ounce of Wolfe's willpower came into play at that precise moment, stopping him from jerking the cocky Robbins away from Caroline and forcefully tossing him out into the yard. The very second that the last car left the driveway, she turned to Wolfe, a look of annoyance on her face.

"Was that necessary?" she asked.

"I apologize if I was rude," he said. "But good manners aren't a priority in my business." He glanced around the foyer, taking note of the rooms to the right and left and the staircase that led up to the second level of the roomy clapboard house. "Familiarizing myself with your surroundings as quickly as possible will enable me to do my job more efficiently. I'll need to inspect the house from top to bottom, cover the grounds, check out your security system and do the same thing at your studio downtown."

"I don't have a security system here at the house," she said.

"Yes, I know. One is being installed first thing tomorrow. I'll check out the one at your studio in the morning and then the newly installed one here tomorrow evening."

"I see."

He turned to her and forced himself to avoid direct eye contact. "You won't leave this house, not even to go outside for a walk, without me. Before you get in your car, I'll inspect it. At work and at home, I'll be at your side. I'll require a bedroom directly across from yours and ask that you sleep with your door open...or we can arrange for a cot to be put in your room."

"I prepared the bedroom across the hall from mine."

Wolfe nodded. "I realize this isn't easy for you, Ms. McGuire. But a few minor changes in your lifestyle can help me keep you safe. I've already arranged not only for a security system to be installed at your home tomorrow, but as a precaution, the locks on your doors will also be changed.''

"That seems rather drastic, doesn't it?"

"Someone tried to kill you and will, more than likely, try again. I will do whatever is necessary to make sure any future attempts fail. From this moment until the day you are no longer in danger, my only purpose will be to protect you.''

Caroline's mouth opened on a silent gasp, as if she were startled by his vehement declaration. Did she think he had overstepped his bounds? he wondered. Had what he'd said or the way he'd said it made her suspicious of his motives?

Wolfe cleared his throat. "As a professional bodyguard, it's my duty to put your welfare above everything else."

"I understand." She glanced toward the closed front door. "Do you have a suitcase in your car?"

"I came from the airport in a taxi," he told her. "My bag is on your porch."

"If you'll get it, I'll show you upstairs to your room, then I'll give you a tour of the house. It will be easier to show you around outside in the morning when it's daylight.''

"That will be fine."

"Mr. Wolfe...I'm going to be honest with you. I feel awkward having you living here in my house. I realize that you're a professional, but you're...you're—"

"A man?"

"Well, yes."

"I will do my utmost not to invade your privacy. I won't come into the bathroom with you or enter your bedroom without knocking, unless there's potential danger involved. However, I'm afraid that my being with you might cramp your love life a bit. I'll have to tag along on all your dates.''

"Believe me, you won't be cramping my love life." Caroline sighed. "I'm not seeing anyone in particular right now."

"Is that right? Hmm-mmm...what about Gavin Robbins?"

Caroline laughed. Wolfe loved the sound. He'd never

heard her laugh before, never heard the sound of her voice. Never been close enough to reach out and touch her. And he realized that he was finding the sight and sound and scent of her intoxicating.

"I won't be dating Mr. Robbins again."

"Good."

She lifted her eyebrows and stared at Wolfe.

"Your not dating anyone simplifies my job as your bodyguard."

"Oh. Yes, of course." She glanced toward the front door. "Please, get your bag and I'll show you upstairs."

Wolfe followed her instructions, retrieved his black vinyl bag, closed and locked the front door and followed his client up the stairs. He tried not to focus on her body as she moved with such easy grace, taking the steps slowly, her round hips swaying to her body's own particular rhythm. She wore gray cotton slacks and an oversize white blouse that hung to mid-thigh. Her only jewelry, other than a simple wristwatch, was a gold chain that disappeared inside her shirt and a pair of small pearl-and-diamond ear studs. He recognized the earrings immediately and his chest tightened. A gift for her twenty-first birthday from her illusive benefactor, David.

When they reached the landing, Caroline turned abruptly and almost collided with Wolfe. Gasping, she took a couple of hasty steps backward in an effort to keep their bodies from touching. Noting the pink flush that stained her cheeks, he came to the conclusion that Caroline blushed easily. Always? With everyone? Or just with him? he wondered. Did she sense the tension between them as acutely as he did? As much as he wanted to deny the attraction as anything physical, as remotely sexual, he knew better than to lie to himself. She was reacting to him as a woman does to a man, and her shy sweetness reinforced his suspicions that she was sexually inexperienced.

She stared at him, seemingly unable to speak. Her chest rose and fell steadily as her breathing accelerated just a fraction. She was a vision. Lovely beyond belief. Flawless, creamy skin. Shoulder-length black hair that glistened with healthy vibrance. Full pink lips, which she licked nervously. Wolfe's body tightened. He gazed into the depths of her blue-violet eyes and lost himself in their mesmerizing power. He broke eye contact suddenly and darted his gaze from one of her earlobes to the other.

"Nice earrings," he said, using any excuse to end the accelerating tension between them.

She took a deep breath. "Thank you. They were a twenty-first birthday gift and are favorites of mine. I wear them quite a lot."

I gave them to you, he wanted to say but knew he couldn't. He had no rights where she was concerned. None whatsoever. He could never be more to her than a bodyguard, an intruder into her private world.

"My room?" He looked right and then left.

"Oh, yes." She moved hurriedly, leading the way into the bedroom on the right side of the narrow corridor. "There are only two bedrooms finished up here. There are two more that I intend to eventually redo, but since I live here alone, I really don't need the extra... Forgive me. I'm rattling. A sign of nervousness."

"I'm sorry if I make you nervous, Ms. McGuire. Perhaps once you become accustomed to my being here, you'll feel more comfortable." He followed her into the spacious guest bedroom.

"You have your own bathroom and I cleared out closet space—" she indicated the closet by pointing "—and the top two drawers of that dresser—" she inclined her head toward the box-shaped, cherry dresser "—are empty."

"Nice room." He scanned the area hurriedly, taking note of very little except the color scheme of neutral shades and the uncluttered simplicity. He hoisted his bag up and onto the foot of the cherry sleigh bed.

"If you'd like to settle in first, we—"

"I'd prefer to check things out now."

"Yes, of course. Where would you like to start?"

"With your bedroom," he said.

She blushed again, and it was all he could do not to slide the back of his hand over her cheek and caress it the way he had her photograph on more than one occasion.

Roz had noticed the car following her about five minutes ago. At first she'd felt uneasy, since there weren't many cars on this lonely stretch of road at this time of night, but when she recognized the vehicle as a Ferrari, she relaxed. Caroline must have given Gavin Robbins his walking papers tonight. And who could blame her? Why would anyone want Gavin, hunk that he was, when a hottie like Mr. Wolfe was sleeping just across the hall? Of course, Caroline wasn't the type to make the most of propinquity. If the luscious Mr. Wolfe was guarding her body, Roz knew exactly what she would do. She'd invite him into her bed ASAP. Roz chuckled softly as she reached out to turn up the volume on the cassette player. She sang along with Faith Hill's latest hit and pressed her foot down on the accelerator.

She liked her music loud, her cars fast and her men hard. She'd bet her life that Gavin was pretty hard right about now. He might want Caroline, but he'd be willing to settle for what he could get. Roz figured that was the reason the VP of Peacekeepers International was chasing her along the back roads, like a hound after a fox. There had been a time when she wouldn't have cared, that it wouldn't have mattered to her that she was second choice. Hell, there had been a time when she'd screwed around indiscriminately and hadn't given a damn whether mutual respect or affection was involved. Odd how she'd changed gradually over the past few years, but especially during the last eight months since her breakup with Jason Stanley. She supposed she could blame Caroline's goody-two-shoes influence, but she'd be lying to herself if she attributed her changed-woman ways to her employer and dear friend.

"Lay the guilt where it belongs," she mumbled under her breath. "You've done something really stupid, Rozalin Marguerite Turner. You've let some man get under your skin. And not just any man."

She whipped her older-model Corvette into the drive at the side of her little house in a quiet neighborhood of other older homes, some well-kept and others a bit shabby. Her own place fell somewhere in between. It wasn't as if she owned the place and could fix it up herself. She'd signed a one-year lease eight months ago when she'd moved out of Jason's place in Easton.

By the time she got out of her car and made it to her front door, the sleek black Ferrari turned into her drive. She hesitated for a moment, then unlocked her door, reached inside and flipped the switch that turned on lights inside her living room. But she didn't go into the house. Instead she waited for Gavin.

He called out to her the minute he emerged from his car. "Roz, wait up."

She turned around leisurely, letting him know that she wasn't surprised to see him. When he approached her, she smiled. "Not driving back to D.C. tonight?"

"That depends." The dimples in his cheeks appeared when he grinned. "If a friend offered me a place to sleep..."

"I have only one bed."

"I don't mind sharing." Gavin moved closer, stopping when only inches separated their bodies.

And I wouldn't mind sharing more than a bed, Roz thought. Being celibate wasn't her thing and she'd gone without for eight months now. Besides, she could sure do a lot worse than Gavin Robbins. She'd bet the guy was a tiger in the sack.

"Come on in," Roz said, giving him a come-hither gesture with the crook of her index finger.

Gavin followed her inside and didn't waste any time putting the moves on her. She had no sooner locked the door when he wrapped his arms around her and pulled her backside up against his arousal. He was hard, all right. Hard as a rock. And ready to rumble.

"You know that whatever was between Caroline and me is over," he whispered against her ear. "You can sleep with me and still have a clear conscience."

"If I hadn't already known that Caroline didn't want you, I wouldn't have invited you in," Roz told him as she turned around to face him. "There's one thing I don't do and that's betray a friend."

Gavin nuzzled her neck as he delved his hands low and cupped her buttocks, lifting her up and into his erection. "I don't want you to think you're my second choice or anything."

Roz kissed him with a passion she forced, with a hunger she felt not for him, but for another man. But her wicked body didn't know the difference, didn't care who was kissing and fondling her. Their tongues dueled as Gavin removed her blouse. She broke free from the demanding kiss to help him take off her bra. When his mouth touched her nipple, she shivered.

"I don't mind being your second choice," she told him. "As long as you don't mind being mine."

He halted momentarily and glanced up at her. "Pretend I'm the freaking Prince of Wales if it'll help you get in the mood."

Just what she wanted to hear—that he was in this for an easy lay. No emotions involved. No commitment beyond tonight. As she led Gavin to her bedroom, an unwanted and totally unbidden thought passed through her mind. If she were with *him* right now, how would she feel? What would *he* say and do at a moment like this?

Roz finished undressing hurriedly and hopped into bed, then opened her arms and invited Gavin to come to her, to take her so completely that all thoughts of any other man would vanish from her mind. When he shucked off his clothes and came down over her, she lifted her hips. He delved deeply with one powerful thrust. As physical pleasure spiraled through her body, tears gathered in the corners of her eyes.

There would never be a moment like this with him, the one she really wanted. He would never want her. She knew she wasn't good enough for him, that he thought she was a tramp and probably always would.

Holding her shoes in one hand, Brooke tiptoed down the hall, hoping not to disturb her parents. Of course, this wasn't the first time she'd come home in the wee hours of the morning, and being well over twenty-one she hardly owed either her mother or her father an explanation of her whereabouts. The antique grandfather clock in the foyer downstairs chimed the hour. Three o'clock. She supposed she should have stayed the rest of the night with Fletch, but her mother enjoyed seeing her each morning at breakfast. And it had been for her mother's sake that she had sublet her apartment and moved back home. Like most children she supposed she had thought of her mother as invincible, but Eileen Harper's recent bout with breast cancer had proved that theory wrong. Although the doctors assured them that they'd gotten it all and her mother's chemotherapy and radiation treatments officially ended a few weeks ago, Brooke intended to live with her parents until she and Fletch married.

She hummed softly to herself as she reached out to open her bedroom door. Fletch hadn't proposed, at least not officially, but she knew it was only a matter of time until he did. After all, they'd been sweethearts since childhood, and even though each had experimented with other romances, they always came back together. They were two of a kind, whether Fletch realized it or not. Both born into old moneyed families, blue bloods by heritage. Former debutante mothers and wealthy, powerful fathers. And since Fletch intended to run for Congress next year, he would need the right wife at his side, someone who was part of the Washington crowd. What more could he ask for? After all, her father was his staunchest supporter, and with her dad's connections, Fletch would be a shoo-in for the party's nomination.

"Brooke?"

She stopped when she heard her father's voice and turned to face him. With a smile curving her lips she greeted him. "What are you doing up at such an ungodly hour?" she asked. "I hope I didn't waken you."

"You didn't." He slipped his arm around her shoulders. "Sometimes old men don't sleep well."

"Dad, you aren't old. You're the youngest sixty-nine-year-old man I've ever known."

"Did you have a nice time tonight?" Oliver Harper asked.

"Yes." She nodded as she slid her arm around her father's waist. "We all stayed with Caroline until her bodyguard showed up. Roz and Lyle stayed and Gavin Robbins dropped by, too."

"What's this bodyguard Fletcher hired like? Did he seem capable?"

Brooke chuckled. No way could she tell her father just how very capable Mr. Wolfe actually looked. She suspected the man was lethal, even in small doses. Pity that all that machismo was wasted on Saint Caroline. Oh, she loved Caroline dearly, but after a while it became rather tedious having a friend who was so incredibly good. Just once she'd like to see Caroline screw up. Maybe then all the men in her life would finally take her down off that damn pedestal they had her on. Fletch included!

"Mr. Wolfe came from the Dundee agency, headquartered in Atlanta," Brooke said. "I'm sure you can ask around and find out all you need to know about this man."

"I may do that," Oliver said. "After all, we don't want just anyone looking out for Caroline. She's practically family...or will be once you and Fletcher are married. And I owe it to Preston to be concerned about the girl. He was quite fond of her, you know.''

"Odd, isn't it, about that letter Caroline found in the safe hidden in the basement of that old house where they lived when Mr. Shaw was killed.''

"I had hoped Caroline would disregard the message," Oliver said. "It's apparent Preston was delusional when he wrote it. The poor man actually thought that someone intended to murder him because he had important secret information. I can't believe an intelligent girl like Caroline has bought into such a ludicrous fabrication."

"Then you don't think there's any chance that Mr. Shaw was involved in some sort of espionage?''

"Preston Shaw was no more a spy than I am." Oliver hugged Brooke to his side. "How about a brandy with your old man before you head off to bed."

"I can't think of anything I'd like better. But only one. I want to get some sleep before I have breakfast with Mama."

"You can't imagine how much it's meant to Eileen having you back home these past few months. You're a good daughter, my love."

"And you're the best father in the world."

Brooke considered herself fortunate, far more so than most of the women her age. Few of her friends and acquaintances had not only both parents living, but parents who were still married to each other. And being an only child, she had been the center of her parents' universe. When she and Fletcher had children, she hoped that they could be the kind of parents her own had been. But why shouldn't they be? They were the same type of people, weren't they? And as her mother had told her countless times—blood will tell.

Chapter 6

An overcast sky veiled the morning sun, diffusing the light and cloaking the springtime warmth. Caroline loved it when the weather cooperated enough for her to have breakfast on the back porch as they were doing today. When she had followed Lyle to Maryland's eastern shore after the local Congregational Church hired him as their minister, she'd felt a sense of coming home. She found a serenity and beauty by the bay unlike any she'd ever known. And an unparalleled freedom. After college graduation, she had worked for another photographer in Richmond and then a couple of years later opened her own small studio. She always tried to stay within driving distance of wherever Lyle settled. He was the only family she had left and both he and she were determined to stay together and not allow too many miles to separate them. It was what Aunt Dixie would have wanted. She could almost hear her aunt's voice. *Blood is thicker than water.*

"It's inadvisable for you to be out here," Wolfe said. "You're too accessible. Someone could come out of the woods or in from the bay and get to you. After this morning, all meals will be eaten inside.''

"I realize that you know better than I what's safe and what isn't," Caroline said. "But I'm not sure I can live like a prisoner in my own house."

"I'm sorry." He stared at her over the rim of his tinted glasses, which had slipped down his nose. The moment he caught her looking directly at him, he shoved up the glasses and averted his gaze. "Let's hope we find what your key opens soon and put an end to the danger in your life. That way you'll be rid of me and can resume your normal activities."

"Mr. Wolfe, I have a career...a job, with clients depending on me. And I have responsibilities that can't be put on hold."

"Just Wolfe," he said.

"What?"

"Call me Wolfe, not Mr. Wolfe."

"Oh. All right...Wolfe." What was it about this man that repeatedly frustrated her? Was it the way he looked at her through those damn tinted glasses, as if while he remained hidden from her, he could see straight through into her mind and her heart? Or was it the way she felt in his presence— small and vulnerable and totally feminine? Or was it having a stranger know so much about her personal life? She realized that in order to protect her, his agency had to know a great deal about her, but she got the feeling that Wolfe knew a little too much.

Perhaps the problem was that she wasn't accustomed to his type of man. One who sits at the breakfast table wearing a hip holster. An aura of strength and danger surrounded her bodyguard, a man trained to protect others, with both defensive and offensive tactics. Has he ever killed in the line of duty? she wondered, and a shiver of apprehension shimmied along her nerve endings.

"You can go to work," Wolfe told her. "You can go

anywhere that I feel isn't dangerous, anyplace where I can protect you. And if you're insistent on not changing your lifestyle, I can call in another Dundee agent as backup.''

"I'm sure you're costing Fletch a small fortune. I can hardly expect him to pick up the tab for a second bodyguard.'' Caroline shook her head. ''Let's give it a try, doing things your way, and if I find that to be too confining, I'll pay for the second bodyguard myself.''

Wolfe nodded. ''Before I drive you to your studio, do we have time this morning to discuss the reason you believe someone tried to kill you?''

"I thought you already knew.'' She spread strawberry jam on her toast, then offered the jar and knife to him. He declined the offer. ''From some of the things you said last night, I assumed you knew everything there was to know about me.''

''No one knows everything there is to know about another human being.''

''You're right.'' Caroline sighed, realizing that no one would win an argument against this man, especially not her. He was far too logical in his thinking, whereas she usually acted on pure emotion. ''What do you want to discuss?''

''I want to see the letter you found in your stepfather's safe and I'd like a better look at that key.'' He eyed the chain hanging around her neck. ''Fletcher Shaw has given us permission to go through any personal files that he has in his possession that once belonged to his father. I'd like your permission to have a copy of the key made and sent to our lab in Atlanta.''

Caroline lifted the chain and grasped the key in her hand. ''No.'' She shook her head. ''I don't mean to be uncooperative, but I'm not willing to allow copies of this key to be made. The copies could fall into the wrong hands.''

''And just who do you suspect would wind up with the copies, Ms. McGuire?''

''I don't know.'' Caroline scooted back her rustic wooden

chair and stood. She tossed her napkin on top of the table and walked away, down the steps leading out into the back-yard, which faced the shoreline.

He immediately followed her, catching up with her quickly, before she had a chance to go more than a few feet. He grabbed her arm to halt her. She turned on him, a protest on her lips. A tingling sensation radiated up the entire length of her arm from where his big hand held her.

"Do you have any idea how much I hate all of this?" she asked him. "For nearly fifteen years I've believed that an intruder, a burglar, killed my stepfather. Now I know better. Now I have the proof, in his own handwriting, that someone assassinated him because he was in possession of some damaging information. Someone ordered Preston Shaw's execution and someone carried out that command." She fingered the chain around her neck. "This key is the only weapon I have against those people. I won't let it out of my possession."

"Then we have no choice but to use trial and error to try to find out just what your key opens." Wolfe tugged on her arm. "Don't run away from me again, Ms. McGuire. Your life could well depend upon my being at your side."

And my sanity might well depend upon putting some distance between us, she wanted to say, but didn't. "Are all the Dundee agents like you?" she asked as he led her back to the porch.

"All the Dundee agents are highly trained professionals," he said. "Their former professions vary somewhat—military, law enforcement and government agents, mostly. Ages vary, too, as do personal histories."

"What description would fit you?" What did it matter? she thought, the moment she asked the question. This man is a temporary fixture in your life. Here today, gone tomorrow. You shouldn't get personal with him. He isn't here to be your friend.

"If you've finished breakfast, let's clear away the dishes and get you back inside," he said.

"Oh, I see. You get to know all about me and my life, but I'm not supposed to ask you any personal questions. Is that how this works?"

"Something like that." He stacked their dishes, laid the silverware crossways atop the plates, then handed them to Caroline. He removed the butter and jam from the table with one hand, then picked up the blue linen napkins and stuffed them into his pants pocket.

"You really think someone is going to appear out of nowhere and try to kill me on my own back porch?"

"It's been known to happen." He nudged her into action, keeping step with her as she walked into the kitchen.

She set their dirty plates and silverware in the sink, then turned to face him and held out her hands to accept the butter and jam. Their hands touched in the transfer, a momentary brush of flesh against flesh. An electrical current sizzled through her. Frozen to the spot by her reaction, she glared at him and found him looking right at her, as if he had been shocked by the same surge of energy.

"Is it against the rules for me to see your eyes?" she asked, her voice uncharacteristically breathy.

He hesitated, then with a slow, precise movement reached up and removed his glasses. But he didn't allow their eyes to meet. Not immediately. She waited, heart thumping in an erratic rat-a-tat beat, as he lifted his gaze from where he had focused on the floor and stared straight at her. The cold, hard glimmer in his daring green eyes paralyzed her momentarily. There was no warmth, no sympathy, no understanding in his gaze. Not one shred of human emotion, almost as if he were a robot. She could not control the involuntary quivering that shook her body from head to toe.

Without saying a word, Wolfe put his glasses back on, then stepped away from Caroline. This time he was extra careful not to touch her. That was when she knew he wasn't as immune to her as he wanted her to believe.

Gavin Robbins was not one of his favorite people, so listening to him brag about his recent sexual conquest didn't go well with Ellison's morning tea. The man was every bit the cocky bastard he'd been fifteen years ago as a young recruit, but he possessed something the Peacekeepers prided themselves on—loyalty to the organization. Robbins had proved himself to be a top-notch agent time and again, and despite Ellison's personal dislike of him, the man didn't have one black mark against his record. When the second-in-command position came open at the unexpected death of the former VP from a heart attack, the other agents had immediately recommended Robbins. When the vote was counted, Robbins had been elected to the position by a landslide. If there was one thing Robbins did almost as well as he did his job, it was kiss ass.

"So, even if things are over with Caroline, I can still keep close enough to her to be apprised of everything going on in her life. Now that I'm bonking Roz Turner, she'll keep me updated on what's happening."

"And using Ms. Turner as an unknowing informant was your sole reason for instigating an affair with her?" Ellison lifted the china cup to his lips and sipped the imported tea that was blended in a small London shop specifically for him.

Gavin chuckled. "Hey, a man does what a man has to do. Right? Besides, it's not exactly a hardship. Roz is one talented lady, if you know what I mean."

Ellison heaved a deep sigh, signifying his displeasure, but the subtle gesture escaped Gavin's attention. Robbins was like many men of Ellison's acquaintance. Self-absorbed. Overly confident. And a bit of a braggart. He dreaded the day when he would be forced by old age to relinquish the reins of Peacekeepers International to a man more suited to the military than diplomacy. His personal choice would have been Aidan Colbert. But the man known as Aidan Colbert was dead.

"So, have you found out everything we need to know about Caroline's bodyguard?" Gavin asked as he plopped down in the chair directly across from Ellison's desk. "Is he somebody we can trust?"

"My sources tell me that Mr. Wolfe is as trustworthy as they come." Ellison took another sip of the delicious tea, then placed his cup on the saucer atop his desk. "Caroline McGuire is in good hands."

"Yeah, well, I'll bet Aidan Colbert is turning over in his grave at the thought of some young stud sharing a house with Caroline. If you ask me, Colbert had a sick obsession with our Ms. McGuire."

"There was nothing sick about Aidan's concern for Caroline. He was a man of principle, a man with a conscience. He deeply regretted that she'd practically been a witness to her stepfather's execution."

"Colbert let his conscience get in the way sometimes," Gavin said. "In my opinion, he'd be alive now if he hadn't tried to get that group of grade-school kids out of the way before that bomb went off. The guy's own actions screwed him."

"I didn't ask you."

"Yeah, yeah. Okay. I know the guy was a favorite of yours and you were priming him to take over your job one day, but face it, Ellison, Colbert never really had what it took for our line of work."

"Until I tell you otherwise, you will now and in the future refer to me as Mr. Penn." Ellison eased back his chair and stood. "Only my family and friends call me Ellison and you, Gavin, are neither."

"You've made your point, *Mr. Penn.* So, how about a look at whatever information you have on Mr. Wolfe?"

"The information I have on him is right up here." Ellison tapped his right temple. "All you need to know is that if

Caroline finds this so-called evidence Preston Shaw supposedly hid away somewhere, we can count on Mr. Wolfe to see that only the proper authorities will have access to the information.''

"I'd like to know how you can be so sure of Mr. Wolfe."

"Suffice it to say that I am sure." Ellison skewered Gavin with a deadly glare that issued a silent warning for his subordinate to back off immediately. He realized that he risked piquing Robbins's curiosity with his evasiveness, but he wanted to postpone sharing any vital information about Wolfe with a man he didn't completely trust.

Photography by Caroline was located in a renovated building in downtown St. Michaels. The waiting area resembled an old-fashioned parlor, with turn-of-the-century reproduction furniture. Two college-aged gofers acted as receptionists and hostesses, booking appointments, welcoming clients and serving coffee and tea as well as pacifying crying babies and entertaining restless children. The pale cream walls in the parlor boasted a lineup of brilliantly photographed babies, children, brides and families. Wolfe knew that Caroline had become a renowned portrait photographer, but until seeing her work today he hadn't fully comprehended how truly talented she was. In each picture she had captured the very essence of her subject.

"She's very good," Wolfe said without realizing he had spoken aloud.

"The best," Roz agreed. "She has clients who come here from all over the country. Every young girl dreams of having her bridal portrait taken by Caroline, and we have expectant mothers making appointments with us for their unborn child's first-year pictures the minute they discover they're pregnant."

Wolfe glanced over his shoulder, checking on Caroline's whereabouts as she padded barefoot across the wooden floor and introduced herself to her first two clients of the day—a mother with a toddler in tow and an elderly gentleman barely restraining the friendliness of his springer spaniel. Caroline bent on one knee in front of the little boy who, judging by his size, was probably no more than three.

"Hello, Justin, I'm Caroline. My, you're a big boy. Your mother told me that you like bugs...spiders and flies and scorpions. Did you know that I have a whole box filled with bugs in my studio?"

The curly-headed child grinned and said, "You've got bugs?"

"Dozens of them."

"You got a scorpion?"

"At least three of them." Caroline held out her hand to the toddler. "Would you like to go with my friend Roz...you and your mommy...and see my scorpions?"

The child jumped up and down, then tugged on his mother's hand. "Let's go now, Mommy. Go see the bugs."

While Roz led mother and child into the studio area used primarily for shots of babies and children, Caroline made her way to her next customer. She sat down on the sofa beside the old man, then leaned over and let his dog sniff the back of her hand. Immediately the spaniel wagged his tail and lifted his front paws onto Caroline's knees.

"Hello, old boy," Caroline said as she rubbed the dog's ears. "What's his name?" she asked the owner.

"Freddy."

"Well, Freddy, you're a sweetie, aren't you?" She glanced at the pet's master. "Mr. Dalton, do you mind if I give Freddy a doggie treat?"

"I don't mind at all. Freddy's like me, he's getting up there in years and one of the few pleasures left to him is eating." Mr. Dalton laughed good-naturedly and patted his potbelly.

"Sandy—" Caroline motioned for the plump redheaded gofer "—will take you and Freddy outside in the garden, and when I finish with little Justin Payne, I'll join y'all. If you'd like coffee or tea or if Freddy needs a bowl of water, then you just tell Sandy.'' Caroline dipped into the deep pocket of her baggy blue slacks and pulled out a bone-shaped dog treat. She waved it under the dog's nose. He caught a sniff and snapped it up immediately.

As soon as Mr. Dalton and Freddy disappeared down the corridor that led to the garden at the back of the studio, Caroline motioned to Wolfe. ''There's only one door in and out of the children's studio, so if you guard that door, no one can get to me.''

''Is that your subtle way of telling me to stay out of your way while you're working?'' Wolfe asked.

''You catch on fast,'' she replied.

He walked behind her down the hallway, past the curtained alcoves young clients used to change clothes and into the large, colorfully decorated room she used as the children's studio. After scanning the area and noting only one window, which overlooked the enclosed garden courtyard where Sandy entertained Mr. Dalton and Freddy, Wolfe closed the single entry door and leaned back against it.

He watched as she maneuvered the lighting, first setting up what he later learned from Roz was a 350-watt diffuser fill light to the front right of the squirming Justin Payne.

''Roz, place that quartz key light behind him while I get the metal deflector in place.'' Caroline made a funny face at Justin, who had his hands filled with an assortment of plastic bugs.

Caroline and Roz worked tirelessly as a team, each in perfect timing with the other. Roz maneuvered the child with expert ease, returning him to a posed position time and again while Caroline checked lighting and angles as she snapped picture after picture of her energetic subject.

Wolfe couldn't take his eyes off Caroline as she worked. Her face glowed with enthusiastic zeal, and any fool could see how much she loved what she was doing. She and the camera became one, joined into a single entity capable of producing photographic masterpieces. If Aidan Colbert had done nothing else of any consequence in his life, he could take some credit for having helped this incredible young woman achieve her goals.

Bubbly, blond Kirsten, the other studio gofer, brought in lunch for two on a tray and placed the tray on Caroline's cluttered desk. "Crab cakes," she said. "Enjoy." Her smile flirted with Wolfe, but he purposefully ignored the girl.

When he pulled a chair up to the other side of the desk, Wolfe glanced at Caroline, who gave him a condemning glare.

"What?" he asked.

"Did you have to be so rude to Kirsten?"

"I wasn't rude," he said. "If I'd been rude, I would have told her that she was wasting her time with me. I have no interest in eighteen-year-old girls."

"Oh, I see. No point in encouraging her." Caroline opened the lid on the food container. "Tell me, just what age bracket does interest you?"

Wolfe lifted the coffee mug off the tray. "Definitely over twenty-five."

"How old are you?" she asked.

"Thirty-six."

"Hmm-mmm."

"Too old?" he inquired.

"For what?"

"For someone twenty-seven?"

Caroline blushed. "I'm twenty-seven, or at least I will be on Thursday."

"Yes, I know."

"You're not too old." She immediately averted her gaze, concentrating on the food before her.

He'd never been particularly adept at playing games with women, certainly not a lighthearted flirting match like the one he'd just exchanged with Caroline. But with her, he felt different. With her, he *was* different.

While sipping his coffee, he glanced around her office, taking note of the photos on the walls, personally significant portraits confined to her private space. There were three shots of Brooke Harper and the same number of Fletcher Shaw. Two pictures of Roz, each capturing a vulnerability that surprised Wolfe. And dispersed among the other framed photographs were half a dozen shots of Lyle Jennings at various ages, from a chunky teenager in a baseball uniform to a majestic shot of him in his minister's garb. Glass-enclosed shelving lined the wall space on either side of the unused fireplace. Wolfe surveyed the contents. Clocks of various kinds and sizes. A couple of sculptures. And on a shelf by itself, a small 35 mm camera.

Wolfe set the mug on the tray, shoved back his chair and stood. As if drawn to the object by some magnetic force, he walked across the room for a better look at the little black camera. He peered through the glass, then lifted his hand as if to touch the object. Was this what he thought it was? Could it actually be the camera Aidan Colbert had bought Caroline for her thirteenth birthday?

He sensed rather than heard her when she came up behind him. She was so close he could smell the sweet scent of her delicate perfume.

"That was my first camera," she said, a trace of nostalgia in her voice. "It's my most prized possession."

"An inexpensive 35 mm camera is your most prized possession?" Inclining his head slightly, he glanced back at her.

"Yes. You see, it was a gift."

He nodded, afraid to speak, uncertain he wouldn't blurt out some sentimental hogwash that she couldn't possibly understand.

"Someone very special gave it to me for my thirteenth birthday." She opened the glass door, reached inside and removed the small camera. "My love for photography began with this camera. Taking pictures with it opened up a whole new world for me.''

Wolfe swallowed hard. Had his insignificant little gift, purchased in London on a whim, actually done so much for the young Caroline?

''Who gave you the camera?'' he asked.

''Someone very important to me.'' Caroline sighed. ''A man I know only as David. He's been my benefactor since my stepfather died. He knew Preston and has sort of looked out for me for that reason. I have no idea who he is or what he looks like or how old he is. But in my heart, I see him as my knight in shining armor.''

Wolfe watched silently as Caroline placed the camera back in its honored spot. When he glanced at her again, he noticed the tears glistening in her eyes and the slight tremble in her hand. Realization hit him like the blow of a sledgehammer.

''You're infatuated with this man,'' he said.

''Yes, I know. But it's a harmless infatuation. My David has made it abundantly clear that we can never meet.''

My David. She referred to him in the same possessive way he thought of her. *My Caroline.*

''What if you could meet him? What would you say? What would you do?'' Wolfe asked.

Would you run into his arms? Would you tell him that you love him?

''That will never happen,'' she said. ''The only place I'll ever meet my David is in my dreams.''

Chapter 7

"So, you think searching through this old place might turn up a clue?" Roz asked

"It's worth a try," Caroline said. "Wolfe and I agree it's possible the key fits something other than the doors."

Wolfe stayed at Caroline's side, constantly alert to the surrounding stimuli. Every sound. Every sight, especially things he caught in his peripheral vision. He even took note of the odors, having learned long ago to use all his senses when safeguarding his life and the lives of others. There was no way to know for certain when another strike would be made against Caroline or from what direction a second attempt on her life would come. Everyone was suspect. The postman whistling as he delivered mail across the street. The taxi driver picking up a fare half a block away. The woman planting flowers along her sidewalk two houses up.

Lyle Jennings came around the side of the house on Sheffield Street, paused and took a deep breath. His freckled face was slightly flushed from having run around the entire yard, back and front.

"The back door's locked," Lyle said, huffing a bit from exertion. "No windows open or broken and no one in sight out back."

"Thanks," Wolfe said, then held out his hand for the door key. "Roz, you take Caroline to the end of the porch and stay there until I have the door completely open."

"Aren't you being overly cautious?" Caroline asked. "What are you expecting—someone to jump out and grab me?"

"That's a possibility." Wolfe removed his tinted glasses. "But I was thinking more along the lines of an explosive device being triggered when the front door opens."

Caroline gasped. Roz grabbed her hand and tugged. Lyle ran toward the porch, then bounded up the steps.

"Come on. Let's do what he says." Lyle came up behind the two women, placing one hand on Caroline's back and the other on Roz's shoulder.

"Please be careful," Caroline called to Wolfe as Lyle led her and Roz to the far end of the wide front porch.

Wolfe felt fairly confident that the door was clean, but he wasn't willing to take any chances with Caroline's life. He slipped his glasses, which corrected his slight nearsightedness, into the inside pocket of his sport coat, then checked the door thoroughly, inserted the key and unlocked the door. He waited for a couple of minutes, then turned the doorknob. Once the door stood wide open, he motioned to the others. Caroline came to him immediately and they entered the house together.

"What's the matter, Rev, the tension too much for you?" Roz asked Lyle. "You're as white as a sheet."

"I suppose I am, but then I have enough sense to realize the danger in this situation," Lyle said. "Of course, you're not the least bit afraid, are you? A wild woman like you, with a tattoo on her leg and holes pierced in various body parts, lives for excitement. Tell me, Ms. Thrill Seeker, if a bomb had exploded just then, would that have given you your kicks for the day?''

"Oh, bite me, Lyle. You're such an uptight, goodie—''

Caroline stopped in the foyer, turned around, put her hands on her hips and yelled, "For heaven's sake, will you two give it a rest. If y'all can't get along while we're here, then one of you can go sit in the car.''

"Sorry." Roz breezed past Lyle, her nose upturned as she entered the foyer. "Are you sure that guy—'' she hitched her thumb backward in Lyle's direction ''—is a blood relative of yours?''

"If we can proceed—'' Wolfe looked from Roz to Lyle, who stood in the open doorway ''—then I suggest Caroline and I search down here and in the basement and you two try upstairs and then the attic.''

"Remind me again what we're looking for," Roz said.

"Anything that requires a key to open," Wolfe told her. "Before we leave, we'll try it on all the doors again, just to be sure, but my guess is that Caroline's key doesn't open a door. I think it's a key to a drawer, a trunk, a box... something like that. I had Caroline take several snapshots of the key and we've sent them to Dundee headquarters. If it fits any type of standard lock, our lab should be able to identify some definite possibilities.''

"Let's get with it," Roz said. "I have a hot date tonight, so I need to go home in time to get ready.''

"Who's the unfortunate man?" Lyle asked.

"Lyle, that wasn't very nice." Caroline frowned, but Wolfe noticed her lips twitching and knew she was on the verge of smiling.

Roz narrowed her gaze, glanced pensively at Caroline and grimaced. "Well, actually, my date is with Gavin Robbins. Gee, Caroline, I hope you don't mind. I mean, you did say that you weren't going to see him anymore and—''

Caroline laughed. "You're more than welcome to Gavin. But Roz, honey, I think you could do better. Gavin's a good-looking charmer, but if you get serious about him, he'll break your heart.''

"Amen," Wolfe said under his breath. Caroline certainly had figured out Gavin's true nature without any warnings from a friend. He couldn't help wondering if Roz were half as astute.

Caroline glared at Wolfe. Had she heard his quiet comment?

"Get serious about him? Not me." Roz stared pointedly at Lyle. "I'm the quintessential good-time girl, just in it for fun.''

"One of these days, you'll have to pay a price for having all that fun," Lyle said.

Roz made a face at Lyle, then stuck out her tongue. He just rolled his eyes toward the ceiling and headed up the stairs. Before he made it to the landing, Roz caught up with him. Wolfe could hear them mouthing off at each other as they tramped along the upstairs hallway.

"What is it with those two?" Wolfe asked.

"They're opposites who don't attract," Caroline said.

"Or maybe opposites who do attract and are fighting the attraction?"

"Hmm-mmm. Maybe." She reached out and laid her hand on Wolfe's arm. "You don't like Gavin Robbins, do you? Why? You don't even know him."

"Sorry about my comment," Wolfe said. "You're right, I don't know him, but I have pretty good instincts when it comes to people, and my gut reaction to Robbins was negative." Wolfe glanced at Caroline's hand resting on his arm. "I'm glad you saw through his gentleman facade."

Caroline's fingers tightened around Wolfe's arm. Their gazes met and locked. He jerked away from her abruptly, unnerved by the powerful sexual urges she ignited within him. *Dammit, man, this isn't just any woman. This is your sweet little Caroline!* Ah, but that was the problem—she *was* his sweet Caroline. But she was no longer a little girl.

"Where do we start?" she asked, obviously willing to overlook his blatant rudeness.

"The kitchen, then the laundry room and the pantry," he said. "After that we'll walk from room to room and look for anything that locks with a key."

Wolfe tried not to think about the past, tried not to remember the only other time he'd been inside this house. One cold December night nearly fifteen years ago. Fresh snow falling. Christmas lights blinking all over town. On his way down the hall that night, he had passed the living room, noticed the decorated tree and the presents stacked high underneath. Preston Shaw had been sitting behind his desk in the study when he looked up and saw Aidan Colbert standing in the doorway. He'd jumped out of the chair and come forward, his expression one of outrage at first, and then when he'd realized the intruder in his home was an executioner sent by the Peacekeepers, fear etched his classic features.

David wondered how he could now enter that same room…with Caroline? He wasn't the man he had been then, not by appearance nor identity. And there was no way Caroline could know he was the man who had executed Preston Shaw. But God help him, he knew who he really was and what he'd done that night.

There would be no way to avoid going into Shaw's study. Wolfe knew he had no choice but to walk through the door, Caroline at his side, and confront the demons from his past without letting on to her that anything was wrong. But Caroline would be forced to relive that night again, too. Perhaps he could persuade her to stay just outside the door while he searched the room. But if she insisted on coming into the room with him, then he would be her protector, her strong shoulder to lean on if she needed one. However, not by word or deed could he dare let on that he was familiar with any of the intimate details concerning what had occurred in that room when a twelve-year-old child had come face-to-face with her stepfather's killer.

* * *

"We have one last room on the first floor to check before we head down into the basement," Caroline said. She had deliberately left the study for last, dreading to go in there again. It had been difficult enough when she'd opened up the old house a few weeks ago and forced herself to enter Preston's study for the first time since the night he was murdered. How could she possibly go in there again?

"If you'd rather not go into the study, you can wait out in the hall where I can see you, while I check for a lock of some kind," Wolfe told her.

"You know about what happened that night, don't you? Fletcher must have explained to you how his father died."

"When a Dundee agent takes on a case, the persons involved are thoroughly investigated and a dossier put together on them as quickly as possible," Wolfe explained. "I have copies of the police report concerning Mr. Shaw's death, as well as old newspaper clippings. So, yes, I'm aware of the fact that Preston Shaw died in that room." Wolfe glanced up the hall at the open door.

"Do you have a report on me?" Caroline asked. "If you do, then you know that I had a nervous breakdown that night, after I called the emergency number. I saw the killer…was in the room with him…but later I couldn't identify him. I was helpless because I was upset and confused. And my memories were fuzzy. A murderer is probably out there now, walking the streets a free man, because I couldn't give the police a good description of him."

"You can't blame yourself for something you weren't a part of."

"If what Preston wrote in the letter he hid away in the safe is true, then he wasn't killed by some burglar. He was assassinated because he had information that was dangerous to someone very powerful. Don't you understand—the man who shot Preston was a professional killer. So tell me this, why didn't he kill me, too?"

Tears pooled in her eyes. That same old unanswerable question still haunted her. More so now than ever—now that this new evidence had been discovered. She turned away from Wolfe and hurried down the hall toward the study, feeling as if somehow she could solve the mystery only in the room where it had begun.

"Caroline!"

Wolfe was running after her. She could hear his heavy footsteps, could sense him drawing nearer and nearer. But she couldn't stop, couldn't wait. She raced into the study, halting in the middle of the room, at approximately the same spot where Preston had lain sprawled on the floor. She gazed down at the scuffed, dusty wood and could almost see the bloodstains that had, in reality, been removed years ago. Suddenly she looked up and saw a large, dark figure near the door. Her heartbeat thundered in her ears. Moisture coated the palms of her hands. Tremors racked her body.

He was going to kill her. Shoot her the way he had shot Preston. She couldn't escape. And there was no one else in the house she could call for help.

A child's chilling screams echoed inside Caroline's head. The room began to spin around and around. She desperately wanted to find that poor, pitiful screaming child, but how could she? Her feet seemed glued to the spot and her vision was beginning to blur.

Wolfe had seen that look on Caroline's face before. The sheer terror. The fear that she was going to die. Salty bile rose in his throat. His stomach knotted painfully. He couldn't bear seeing her this way. Remembering. Reliving that moment when the two of them had gazed into each other's eyes on a snowy winter night so long ago. Over the years, his nightmares had been filled with that ungodly moment when a little girl had thought he was going to kill her. He had gone over that moment in his mind again and again, and each time he had thought about how ironic it was that he, of all people, had put that kind of fear into a child. Aidan Colbert, who had killed his own father to stop him from murdering a child.

"Caroline." He spoke her name softly. "Don't be afraid. You're not in any danger. No one is going to hurt you."

He recognized the glazed look in her eyes. How many times had he seen traumatized men and women relive a terrifying moment? In her mind, Caroline was twelve again, Preston lay dead on the floor—and Aidan Colbert hovered in the shadows, the deadly weapon still in his hand.

All color drained from her face. She began swaying, just a fraction, the movement almost indiscernible at first. But he knew the signs. She was on the verge of fainting.

"Caroline…Caroline…"

He rushed forward despite the horror he saw on her face as he approached. She opened her mouth on a silent scream. He suspected that in her mind she was screaming at the top of her lungs. Just as she started to topple over, Wolfe reached out and grabbed her, swooping her into his arms. She lay limp as a dishrag. He carried her out of the study, down the hall and into an area that had once been the living room. There nestled beneath the arched bay windows was a window seat. He walked across the room, sat down with Caroline in his lap and very gently patted her cheek. Her eyelids fluttered. He patted her face again. Her eyelids opened and closed. She moaned.

"Caroline?"

This time when she opened her eyes, she looked straight at Wolfe. "What happened?" she asked.

"You fainted."

She lay there in his arms, a delicious weight. Warm and soft. The delicate scent of her flowery perfume permeating the air he breathed. Her silky black hair draped over his arm.

"Oh, Wolfe, I'm so sorry…I was remembering that night and…" She bit down on her bottom lip. "It was you."

"What?" Fear grabbed him by the throat in a stranglehold. No, it wasn't possible. She couldn't have recognized him as the man who'd shot Preston Shaw because he no longer resembled that man.

"I saw you there in the doorway, didn't I? And I thought…oh, God—" She sat straight up and looked at him so sadly. "I thought you were Preston's killer. For just a few seconds I thought I was twelve again and it was that night. I looked up and saw you and thought—" She gasped, then flung her arms around Wolfe and buried her face against his chest.

He held her securely but without force. Everything within him longed to comfort her, to find a way to put an end to her torment. But could he trust himself to act purely as her bodyguard, as an objective employee whose sole duty was to protect her? *There is no rule that says you can't comfort her, is there?* he asked himself. It seemed to him that he had spent a lifetime longing to comfort Caroline, wanting to erase the past and give her a happy future. He had sought any and all means to aid her, hoping that in some small way he could atone for what had happened to her—for what his actions had done to her. In photographs and written reports from Ellison, he had watched her grow up, change from a shy, chubby little girl into a beautiful, successful woman. How many times had he watched the videos Ellison had sent him of Caroline's high school and college graduations? He had freeze-framed her face on both videos so many times he had lost count. Exactly when his concern for a child had turned into an obsession with a woman, he wasn't quite sure.

She mumbled softly, her lips moving against his shirtfront. "Why didn't he kill me?"

Wolfe slipped his hand between her neck and his chest and cupped her jaw. She allowed him to tilt her chin just enough so that he could see her face. He looked into her eyes, the color of the blue-tinted violets that his mother had grown in pots on her kitchen windowsill. Of its own volition, his thumb tenderly raked across her parted lips.

She sighed and said his name. "Wolfe?"

"You won't ever have to come back here again," he said. "I promise."

"Can you answer my question?" She stared at him pleadingly. "In your line of work, you must have been confronted by hired killers more than once. Why would a professional hit man let me live? Why didn't he kill me?"

Because my job was to eliminate a rogue agent who posed a threat to our government, not to harm an innocent child. The explanation swirled around inside his head. The desire to tell her what he was thinking became an overpowering need. Now is not the time for true confessions, he reminded himself. He had joined Peacekeepers, hoping to help others, to save the innocent whenever possible—because he had failed in his efforts to save his own younger brother and his mother from the wrath of a mean drunk. And every day of his life, since he was a boy of thirteen, Aidan Colbert had lived with the knowledge that even though he had taken his father's life, he had acted too late to save the two people dearest to him. If he could have helped his brother, his mother might still be alive, too.

"I'm not sure why he didn't kill you," Wolfe said, his voice deceptively calm. "If he was a professional, then he'd been sent to do a job. You weren't part of that job. And if you couldn't identify him, he had no reason to kill you, did he?"

"But he couldn't possibly have known that I couldn't identify him, that he had been partially hidden in the shadows and—"

Wolfe cradled her face with his hands. "Stop torturing yourself. I thought you'd gotten over this, that you had put it in the past."

"What?" She stared at him, puzzlement written plainly on her face.

Damn! He should have kept his mouth shut. He'd gotten sentimental and said too much. "I assumed that since you live a very normal life and aren't under any type of psychiatric care that you had dealt with Preston Shaw's death years ago."

"I thought I had."

Wolfe scooted Caroline off his lap and helped her to her feet as he stood. "Are you all right now? You don't still feel faint, do you?" Get back in bodyguard persona, he thought. And keep it that way. He couldn't afford to let his personal feelings for Caroline show.

She stared at him, a fragile frown drooping her mouth and a wounded expression in her eyes. "I'm fine, Wolfe, thank you."

The moment she moved away from him, he wanted to grab her and pull her back into his arms. He wanted to tell her that he was David. Her David. The man she thought she could meet only in her dreams. How he wished he could admit to being her caretaker, her guardian angel, without having to confess that he was a fallen angel, a man with blood on his hands—the executioner who had killed her stepfather.

"I suppose we should check the basement next," Caroline said, her back to Wolfe.

"Certainly." He had to keep his distance from her, no matter how tempted he was to be more to her than a temporary employee.

After suggesting that she take the rooms on the left while he took the rooms on the right, Lyle had tried to avoid Roz as much as possible. Just being around the woman unnerved him. The first day Caroline introduced them, they had taken an instant dislike to each other. And that bothered him. Then and now. As a general rule, he liked everyone he met. But there was something about Roz, something in her manner, in her speech, in the way she dressed that simply drove him crazy. And it didn't help that she seemed to thrive on annoying him, on poking fun at his appearance, his demeanor and his profession.

But the most disturbing aspect of their unfriendly relationship began a few months ago. The first time he'd had one of those dreams about Roz. It wasn't the sexual content of the dream that had bothered him so much—after all, he was a man as well as a minister—but the fact that the woman in the dream had been Roz. Wasn't she the last woman on earth he would find appealing? Apparently not. If it had been only one dream, he would have dismissed it, but the first one had been followed by more—many more. Now it had reached the point that whenever he was around Roz, his body responded to her. If she ever found out that he was getting sexually aroused whenever he just looked at her, she would take great pleasure in tormenting him.

"Hey, Rev, are you about finished in there?" Roz called from the hallway. "If you are, then let's head to the attic."

"Be with you in a minute," he replied. The attic would be dark, warm and confining. Not someplace he'd want to be with Roz. He could tell her that he'd check the attic without her, but knowing her, she would veto any suggestion he made.

Taking several deep breaths and willing his traitorous body to cooperate, Lyle met Roz in the hall. When she looked at him and smiled, his stomach turned over.

"Ready?" she asked.

Why her, dear God, why her? Lyle prayed. We are totally incompatible. She's the exact opposite of everything I want in a woman. Is this some sort of test? Are you throwing temptation in my path to see if I can resist? Or is this some sort of joke you're playing on me?

"Hey, are you okay?" Roz asked. "You've got this goofy look on your face. What were you doing, praying?"

"Yeah, something like that."

"Odd time to pray, don't you think? You're the only guy I know who's ever taken one look at me and started praying." Roz sashayed closer and closer, her smile slightly sinister. "Were you praying for my soul, Rev? Or for your own?"

When she reached out and ruffled his hair in a playful manner, he jumped away from her. She burst into laughter.

"What's the matter, are you afraid I'll contaminate you, that my evil ways will rub off on you?"

"Yes, as a matter of fact, I am afraid of exactly that."

Her warm, exuberant smile faded quickly, replaced by a killer glare so sharp it could have cut through steel. The minute Lyle saw the hurt look in her eyes, he wished the words back. But it was too late.

"Let's go in the attic and check things out." Roz headed toward the door that enclosed the hidden staircase leading to the third level of the house. "I need plenty of time to get gorgeous for my late date with Gavin. He's the kind of guy who loves being around a woman like me."

Lyle wanted to explain and to apologize, but he did neither; instead he remained silent—hadn't he already said more than enough?—and followed her up the narrow winding stairs and into the attic.

"It's awfully dark up here," Roz said. "If it weren't for that one little window, we wouldn't be able to see a thing."

"Stand aside and let me see if I can find a light switch."

He fumbled around in the semidarkness and accidentally ran smack dab into a lightbulb hanging at the end of an electrical cord that was attached to the ceiling. Amazingly the bulb still burned and gave off enough dim light to partially illuminate the space. Only a fraction of the area had flooring, the rest was a beehive of wooden boards and high arched beams.

"Looks pretty empty to me," Roz said. "I doubt we'll find anything up here."

As Lyle glanced around, he spotted something in a far corner, a large, bulky object. He walked toward what he soon realized was some sort of old trunk. He ran his hand over the battered lid and dust flew everywhere. The particles danced in the air and tickled his nose. Suddenly he went into a sneezing frenzy.

"Bless you," Roz said as she approached him. "Are you okay?"

"I'm fine. Just allergic to dust."

"What have you found?" She eyed the dusty, battered old trunk. "Does it have a lock?"

Lyle knelt down and inspected the trunk. "Yes, it does."

"Well, hallelujah. This is the first thing, other than the doors, that we've found in the house that actually has a lock."

While he was still bent over and without warning of any kind, Roz let out an ear-splitting scream and all but jumped on top of him.

"What on earth?" he mumbled as he toppled to the floor and landed flat on his back.

Roz, who was hanging on to him for dear life, fell on top of him. He looked up to find her face only inches from his. Her slender form draped his body like a blanket.

"There are mice up here." Roz's voice quivered. "I hate mice!"

"You knocked me down and jumped on top of me because you saw a mouse?" *Get off me this minute. Please. If you don't, I'm not going to be responsible for what my body does in the next sixty seconds.*

"Not just a mouse. Two mice. They went scurrying across the floor—over there." She pointed the direction.

God help me, Lyle prayed. His lips twitched. Roz glared at him. His mouth turned up in a smile he could not control.

"Don't you dare laugh at me," she said.

"Sorry."

Their gazes connected and for one timeless moment they stared at each other. Breaths stilled. Heartbeats stopped. The world beyond their two entwined bodies ceased to exist. He couldn't prevent what was happening. Heaven help him! She had to be able to feel his arousal.

Almost immediately she shoved herself up and off of him. "We wouldn't want anybody to catch you rolling around in the dirt with the likes of me, would we?" Forcing a laugh, she shrugged. "What would they think?"

Lyle rose to a sitting position, then looked up at her. "They'd probably wonder why a pretty, sexy girl like you would have jumped my bones."

Roz stared at him, apparently as surprised by his statement as he was. A soft little giggle erupted from her throat, followed by genuine laughter. "Hey, Rev, you actually have a sense of humor, don't you?"

Her good humor ignited his own and he started laughing, too. She had thought he was joking, when he'd actually been dead serious. Why would a girl like Roz be interested in a quiet, self-contained minister, who wasn't anything special? After all, he was a slightly overweight carrottop who most definitely resembled Howdy Doody much more than Tom Cruise. Thank God Roz had diffused the tension between them by injecting the situation with a healthy dose of humor. Lord only knew what he would have done if she'd taken his comment seriously.

When they heard Roz scream, Wolfe grabbed Caroline's wrist and pulled her along with him as he rushed out into the hall and toward the backstairs. "Stay behind me." He undid his holster and removed his Sig Sauer P228.

Together they crept up the stairs, Wolfe cautious and prepared for whatever he might find. He could sense the tension in Caroline, could smell the fear and understood her concern for her friend. He felt an odd sensation of being connected not only to Caroline's thought processes, but to her emotions as well.

Following his instructions, she stayed at his back, close enough to him so that whenever he paused he could feel the warmth of her breath. Suddenly, as they neared the open door that revealed the bottom of the narrow steps that led to the attic, they heard laughter.

"Hey, up there," Wolfe called. "What's going on?"

"Roz, we heard you scream," Caroline said. "Are you all right?"

"I'm fine," Roz yelled. "Come on up. We think we might have found something."

Wolfe stepped back and motioned for Caroline to go first. She nodded and began to climb the tight passageway. Before her feet reached the top step, her head and shoulders cleared the opening. When she hesitated, Wolfe gave her a gentle shove to set her in motion again. A single lightbulb, hanging from the ceiling by a frayed electrical cord, dispersed a dim light. Sitting atop the only visible object in the attic—an old trunk of some sort—Roz waved them forward. Lyle stood at her side, a wide grin on his face. Then suddenly he sneezed.

"Excuse me. Dust is everywhere."

"One of you want to tell me what's going on?" Wolfe asked.

"Look what we found." Roz stood, moved to the side and waved her hand in a gesture of introduction. "Ta-da. It's an old trunk. And it's locked." Her big brown eyes rounded wide with delight, like those of a child who had discovered a treasure trove of toys.

"I think what Wolfe meant was why did you scream?" Caroline looked point-blank at Roz. "I suppose you know you scared me half to death."

"It wasn't anything," Lyle said. "Our wild, fearless Roz saw a mouse run across the floor and screamed like crazy."

"It wasn't just one mouse," Roz told them. "It was two mice."

"Whatever." Lyle shrugged. "She was so scared she tried to climb me like a tree and we wound up falling on the floor and—"

"I suppose that's when y'all started laughing?" Caroline asked.

Roz nodded. "Who would have thought the rev would actually have a sense of humor about the whole thing. Go figure." Roz grinned at Lyle, who smiled sheepishly, as if he were slightly embarrassed.

"Glad you two are getting along better," Wolfe said.

"Now, how about we give the lock on that trunk a try. If the key doesn't fit it, then we might as well leave because we've searched this place thoroughly."

They gathered around the old trunk. Caroline dropped to her knees in front of it and eased the chain over her head, then she tried to insert the key into the lock. It didn't fit. She removed the key, turned it upside down and tried again. Still no fit.

"It won't even go in." Caroline draped the chain back around her neck. "So much for solving the riddle today."

"I thought you were going to Fletch's house after we left here to go through the things of his father's that he's kept stored all these years," Lyle said, then sneezed again. "You might find something there."

"Fletch is in D.C. today, so we're going over tomorrow at lunch," Caroline said. "Fletch wants to be there with us when we check through Preston's things. Besides, tonight is my volunteer evening at the church. Remember?"

Lyle nodded. "People at the church are going to wonder who Mr. Wolfe is and why he's sticking to you like glue. You probably don't want to tell them that he's your bodyguard."

"We'll just tell them that he's a friend," Caroline said.

"If it were me, I'd tell them that he's my new boyfriend." Roz sighed dreamily as she batted her eyelashes at Wolfe.

Caroline's and Wolfe's gazes collided. Tension wound inside Wolfe's gut. Caroline's cheeks flushed a soft pink.

Don't let your mind wander into forbidden territory, he cautioned himself. You are Caroline McGuire's bodyguard, hired by and paid for by her stepbrother. David Wolfe has no past with her and most certainly no future. You are a temporary necessity in her life and that's all. You are here to protect her, to keep her safe. And once she is no longer in danger, you will disappear from her life—forever.

Chapter 8

Wolfe stood in the doorway and watched her while she slept. Moonlight covered her bed like a creamy, transparent blanket. He knew he had no right to invade her privacy this way, no legitimate reason to hover outside her bedroom. But God help him, he could not resist the temptation to observe her without her being aware of his presence. Whenever he stared at her for a moment too long, she gazed at him questioningly and he could give her no explanation for being so fascinated with her. He could hardly say, "I'm David. Your David. The man who has kept watch over you all these years. I gave you the camera that is your most prized possession and the pearl-and-diamond earrings that are your favorites. You have been the most important person in my life for the past fifteen years. Through all the dark and lonely nights, the unemotional and controlled days, you have been my heart…my soul…my secret treasure."

Since coming into her life two nights ago, he had already discovered that Caroline was all that he had believed her to be. He had observed her with her friends, employees and clients and marveled at the way people were drawn to her. At Lyle's church, where they had gone after leaving the Sheffield Street house earlier in the evening, Caroline had spent an hour tutoring an underprivileged child in reading and then worked in the church's cafeteria for two hours serving meals to the homeless. Lyle had told him that she devoted at least one evening a week, occasionally two or three evenings, to her volunteer activities, but her generosity didn't end there. Caroline paid for clothes for needy children and provided financial assistance to deserving students who desperately needed help with college tuition.

"She knows from firsthand experience what having a caring benefactor can mean in a young person's life," Lyle had said. "No doubt she has told you about David. Everyone who knows Caroline knows the story of her David."

Wolfe closed his eyes to shut out the sight of her lying peacefully, innocently in her bed. The sheet and blanket draped her hips, leaving her upper body unveiled. She rested on her side, the curve of one bare arm fitted beneath the swell of her breasts. He felt ashamed that his body betrayed him, reacting to her beauty in a purely physical way. He was here to protect her, not to ravage her. But every instinct he had was urging him to take possession of this woman. The primitive male within him told him that she was his. His alone. In a way she had not—nor ever could—belong to another man.

He envisioned her awakening, looking at him and smiling. She rose from the bed, her gown diaphanous and flowing, her hair hanging in disarray around her shoulders. With her arms outstretched, she came to him and enveloped him in her sweetness. He swept her up into his arms and carried her back to the bed. She whispered his name. "David. My David." And then with her lips a hairbreadth from his, she gazed adoringly into his eyes and said, "I want you. Please, make love to me."

Wolfe's sex hardened painfully, need riding him hard. He

opened his eyes, took one final look at the woman he longed
for, then turned and walked across the hall to his room. To
his lonely bed. Back to the reality that Caroline was as out
of his reach as the stars in the night sky.

Caroline woke with a start, the feeling of having been
touched, of a large, strong hand caressing her body overpow-
eringly real. After tossing back the covers, she sat up and
scooted to the edge of her bed. A shiver of longing shuddered
through her, a sexual tingling she had never experienced before that moment. She had dated her share of men, had always immensely enjoyed kissing and had even experimented
with some heavy petting a few times, but in the end she had
always drawn back, always put a stop to things before they
got out of control. Whenever that had happened, she had
convinced herself she simply didn't want sex without a lifetime commitment, but in retrospect she admitted to herself
the real reason. Caroline felt, in her heart, that she could not
give herself to a man without loving him.

She flipped on the bedside lamp, slid her feet into her plush
cloth slippers and stood. A tender quiet permeated the house,
disturbed only by the soft, comforting sounds of night whis-
pers. The distant lull of water lapping against the shore. The
hum of springtime insects. The sigh of a nighttime breeze.
The gentle creaking of old timbers. She picked up her cotton
robe from the nearby chair, put it on, walked across the room
and out into the hall. Was Wolfe asleep? she wondered.

Caroline tiptoed across the hall, halting in the open doorway of his bedroom. Moonlight illuminated the area enough
for her to make out his shape where he rested flat on his back
atop the covers. With his arms lifted to his head and his
entwined fingers resting at the nape of his neck, his position
accentuated the breadth of his wide shoulders and the muscles in his big arms. Her heartbeat accelerated instantly when
she realized he wore nothing but a pair of dark pajama bottoms. An aura of breathtaking power and masculine strength

surrounded him and a subtle sensuality exuded from every pore in his magnificently proportioned body.

As if drawn to him by some magnetic force she was powerless to resist, Caroline stepped over the threshold and into his room. Wolfe shot straight up in bed and reached for his weapon hidden under his pillow. Before Caroline realized what was happening, he was beside her, every muscle in his body tense, a look of predatory energy on his face.

"Caroline?"

She released her indrawn breath on a long, relieved sigh. "I'm sorry. I didn't mean to wake you. I shouldn't have come in here. I'll go—"

When she turned to leave, he moved quickly to snap on the bedside lamp and lay his gun on the nightstand. Then he caught up with her and clamped his hand down on her shoulder with gentle strength. "Are you all right?"

Without glancing back at him, she nodded. His hand on her shoulder was hard and hot. His rough fingertips absently massaged her muscles. A man's touch had never taken her breath away. Not like this. Powerless to stop herself, she pivoted slowly until she faced him. He maintained his hold on her shoulder and increased the pressure just a little as he moved his hand down to cuff her bare upper arm. Unable to bring herself to look him in the eye, she cast her gaze toward his chest and what she saw startled her. She gasped, then lifted her hand and laid it on his brutally scarred upper torso. He grabbed her hand and she thought he was going to snatch it away. But instead he held it there where she'd placed it over his heart.

"What happened to you?" she asked, hypnotized by the viciousness of his scars.

"An accident," he told her, his voice low and husky.

"Oh, Wolfe. How awful for you. You must have suffered terribly. You poor darling."

He lifted her hand away from his chest, turned it palm up and brought it to his lips. When his warm, moist mouth grazed her sensitive flesh, she trembled. There was such gentleness in the way he stroked her, the way he eased his hand up and down her arm, caressing her with a lover's touch. Her gaze lifted to his and a tremor of pure undiluted sexual longing spiraled up from the core of her femininity when he looked at her as if he intended to take her, here and now.

She swayed toward him, unable to resist, swept away by the moment and the heady sensual experience. His gaze narrowed, shrinking his eyes to mere slits. His nostrils flared. His breath became labored. She sensed that he was an aroused beast and she was his appeasement. Excitement dulled her fear as pure animal instinct took control of her mind and body, telling her that he was her mate, the man she had been waiting for all these years.

Abruptly Wolfe shoved her away. Startled by the unexpected action, she caught her breath and glared at him, not understanding his sudden rejection of her.

"You should go back to bed," he said, a hint of regret in his commanding voice.

She nodded, then swallowed hard and said, "Yes. Yes, I should." Embarrassment claimed her with a vengeance and she all but ran from his bedroom, across the hall and into her own room. She started to slam the door shut, but remembered his orders to always leave the door open. With her pulse pounding at breakneck speed, her face hot with shame, Caroline hurried into her bathroom, closed the door and dropped to her knees. Tears streamed down her face.

What had she almost done? Wolfe must think her a hussy to have come into his room and all but attack him. He would have no way of knowing that she had never reacted that way to another man. Only to him.

Ellison stood and rounded his desk when Oliver Harper entered his office. He hadn't seen Oliver in nearly a year and then it had been a brief hello at some political function they'd both been obligated to attend. Although they'd known each other since their days at Harvard, they had never actually been friends. More friendly acquaintances than anything else. Ellison had always liked Oliver, despite the differences in their political leanings and the fact that Oliver had all but stolen Eileen from him when they'd been a couple of young bucks vying for her affections.

"What brings you to Peacekeepers International?" Ellison asked as he extended his hand.

Oliver exchanged a cordial handshake with Ellison, all the while bestowing his most charming smile on his old rival. "Nothing to do with international affairs. I can assure you that I leave all that diplomatic stuff to you do-gooders. You know me, Ellison, I'm of the persuasion to bomb 'em and ask questions later."

Ellison chuckled. Oliver never changed and never apologized for his beliefs. He was the same old right-wing, militant conservative he'd always been. "Then to what do I owe the honor of your visit this morning? I'm afraid if there's trouble on Wall Street, you've come to the wrong organization for help." Ellison indicated a chair to Oliver, then stepped back and leaned his hip against the front edge of his desk.

"No financial complaints." Oliver nodded and sat in the proffered leather chair. "What I've come to you about is something of a personal nature."

Ellison's brows lifted as his eyes rounded with curiosity. "Would you care for some coffee? Or perhaps a cup of tea?"

"No, thank you." Oliver relaxed his tall, lean frame in the chair and crossed his legs. "I suppose you know all about the attempt on Caroline McGuire's life recently."

Ellison nodded. "Hmm-mmm."

"I figured Gavin Robbins was keeping you informed. Brooke told me that Caroline dated Gavin for a while and he was actually her date that terrible night aboard Fletch's yacht. He was rather lax in his duty, wasn't he? If he'd been with her—"

"Get to the point," Ellison said, his voice a bit more testy than he'd intended. "What personal interest do you have in Caroline McGuire, other than the fact she and your daughter are friends?"

"Isn't that enough? If not, then surely you recall that Preston Shaw was a friend of mine. Our families have been socially connected for generations. And Preston adored Caroline. You know the poor child had a nervous breakdown after Preston's murder, so naturally Brooke and I are concerned about her mental health now. Caroline seems convinced that there's some credence to that ridiculous letter Preston left."

"What makes you think the letter is ridiculous?"

Oliver laughed. "I knew Preston. He was a bon vivant, a man who loved the good things in life and got a great deal of pleasure out of his role as a diplomat. He wasn't the type to be involved in espionage."

"Perhaps you didn't know Preston as well as you thought you did. Perhaps none of us really knew him."

"Of course it's possible you're right." Oliver sighed. "At this late date, that's neither here nor there, is it? There isn't anything we can do to help poor old Preston, but Caroline is a different matter. Considering the fact that Preston was one of your own, I'm sure you're as interested as my family is in safeguarding his stepdaughter."

"I understand from Gavin Robbins that Fletcher Shaw hired a professional bodyguard for Caroline. I don't see that there's anything else to be done."

"Now you've hit upon my concern." Oliver leaned forward, his gaze connecting boldly with Ellison's. "I'd like for you to use your connections and have an in-depth security check done on this Mr. Wolfe. I've already made some phone calls and found out that the Dundee agency has an exemplary reputation. It's one of the best, if not *the* best security and investigation agency in the country. But I wasn't able to get any real information on Mr. Wolfe. His background seems to be a mystery and that fact bothers me. If there's the re-mo st possibility that there is any truth to what Preston wrote in that letter, then we can't afford to trust anyone.''

''Not even each other,'' Ellison said in a deadpan manner.

Oliver guffawed loudly. ''I trust you, Ellison. You're probably the most trustworthy man I know. That's why I've come to you with my concerns. Find out what you can about this man Fletcher hired to protect Caroline. Let's make sure that she's safe in his hands.''

''All right,'' Ellison replied. ''As a favor to you and because Caroline is Preston Shaw's stepdaughter, I'll run a check on Mr. Wolfe.'' Ellison realized that he would have to pacify Oliver with a fake report on David Wolfe; otherwise his old friend was bound to become suspicious. And that was something he couldn't allow to happen.

Oliver rose to his feet. ''You'll let me know the minute you get the information on him?''

''It could take a few days.''

Oliver stepped forward and clasped Ellison's hand. ''A few days would be perfect. We can discuss your findings at the dinner we're having this weekend to raise funds for Fletcher's political campaign. You are planning to attend, aren't you?''

''Didn't receive an invitation.'' Ellison pulled his hand from Oliver's grip.

''Consider yourself invited.'' Oliver grinned. ''I'll see that Eileen adds your name to the guest list. She'll be delighted to see you again. It's been what—five years or more since you two saw each other?''

''Give or take a year,'' Ellison said.

''Caroline will be at the dinner, escorted by her bodyguard. If there's any reason Fletcher needs to dismiss Mr. Wolfe, then we can present a united front and I can immediately call in a man from the agency I use. Eastbrook, Inc., out of Richmond. We've used their bodyguards for years, whenever there was any need.''

Ellison followed Oliver into the outer office, past his sec-

retary and all the way down the corridor to the private
vator. The door to Gavin Robbins's office, directly across
hall from the elevators, stood wide open and Gavin's assistant, Mike Latham, glanced up from his desk to make eye
contact with Ellison. Gavin had hand-picked his assistant,
just as Ellison had, and with his legal background, Latham
had proved himself an invaluable asset to the Peacekeepers.
The minute the elevator doors closed, Ellison reversed directions and headed straight back to his office. He paused momentarily at his secretary's desk. Barry Vanderpool, whose
father had been a Peacekeepers agent until his untimely
death, was the most efficient secretary Ellison had ever had.
The young man had a knack for anticipating Ellison's every
need. He was quite proud of the fact that he had handpicked
Barry from a long list of applicants and his instincts had
proved him right.

"I don't want to be disturbed for the next half hour."

"Yes, sir," Barry replied.

Ellison closed and locked his office door, then removed
his cellular phone, which worked off a scrambled security
frequency, thus preventing interception. He dialed the number that he had memorized and waited, tapping his foot on
the floor, while the phone rang.

When the familiar voice answered, Ellison said, "We've
got a big problem."

"I can't believe we didn't find anything, not even a hint
of a clue in all these things." Caroline dropped the handful
of old, yellowed letters back into the ornately carved wooden
box lying in the middle of Fletcher Shaw's attic.

"I felt certain when we finally unearthed this box that the
key would fit it," Fletcher said. "But the thing wasn't even
locked."

Brooke leaned over the back of the dilapidated chair in
which Fletcher sat, among the array of stored antique furniture and boxed family items. She wrapped her arms around

neck and kissed his right temple. "I'm so sorry, dear. I know how disappointed you and Caroline must be."

"Is there anything else that you can think of?" Wolfe asked. "Something that your father could have left somewhere else?"

"Lenore cleared out his safety deposit box," Fletcher said. "So that's ruled out. And the key doesn't fit any locks in the Sheffield Street house that he shared with Lenore, nor does it fit any locks in this house, where he once lived with Mother."

"What about his office at Peacekeepers International?" Brooke asked.

"I'd already thought of that," Fletcher said. "I phoned Ellison Penn and he assured me that every key issued to Father by the Peacekeepers was accounted for shortly after Father's death. Besides, none of the old keys fit any of the new locks in the Peacekeepers building."

"There has to be something we're overlooking." Caroline paced the unfinished wood floor, trying her best to avoid eye contact with Wolfe. Ever since what had occurred between them in the wee hours of the night, she'd felt a keen sense of embarrassment. When he didn't mention the incident this morning, she felt relieved and thankful that his demeanor toward her had returned to robotic efficiency. Their breakfast conversation had consisted of nothing more than the plans for the day. Then at the studio, while she'd photographed four different clients before noon, Wolfe had stood guard quietly, his gaze only occasionally meeting hers and then moving on quickly.

"Everything that belonged to Father is stored right here," Fletcher said. "And as far as I know, when Lenore left for Europe, she didn't take any of Father's personal items, just his money and her jewels."

"By any chance, did your father have an apartment in D.C.?" Wolfe asked.

"No." Fletcher shook his head.

"What about cars? Did Lenore sell his cars or did you get them?" Wolfe glanced first at Fletcher and then at Caroline.

"I have no idea," Caroline admitted. "Mother left for Europe only a few weeks after Preston's funeral and she'd already shipped me off to Aunt Dixie's by then."

"She sold her Mercedes and Father's BMW," Fletcher said. "But I still have the '39 Alfa Romeo coupe. He willed the thing to me."

A flash of color swept through Caroline's mind. Wind blowing her hair. She and Fletcher giggling. Preston smiling happily. Caroline remembered how she'd loved taking rides out to the Maryland countryside with Fletch and Preston in that fabulous old car. Preston had adored antique cars and had bought and sold several over the years, but he'd always kept the Alfa Romeo—the 8C 2900 Sport Spider. Odd that she would remember that tidbit of information. But then whenever Preston had taken them out in the old car, which he'd had repainted a brilliant red, he had raved on and on about it to them. "Where is the Alfa Romeo now?" she asked.

"I stored it in the garage at my grandparents' cottage in Windhaven." Fletch sighed. "I'm afraid I haven't even seen the old car in years. I didn't inherit Father's love for antique vehicles." Fletch's eyes widened as a suspicion came to mind. "I say, you don't think the key fits the Alfa Romeo, do you?"

"I doubt it," Wolfe said. "But there's a possibility that your father could have stored something in the trunk or the glove compartment that requires a key to unlock."

Caroline focused her gaze on Fletcher. "Would it be all right with you if Wolfe and I drive down to Windhaven and have a look at the car?" She glanced at Wolfe, anticipation glowing in her eyes. "I can call Roz and have her reschedule my afternoon appointments and we could leave right away."

Wolfe looked to Fletcher for approval. "Do we have your

permission to check the car over and remove anything we find?''

Fletch disengaged himself from Brooke's clinging embrace and stood. He shoved his hands into the pockets of his tailored slacks and paced across the attic. ''I'd drive down with you, but I have a meeting with Senator Marshall and Congressman Williams at three today.'' He paused, looked directly at Caroline and then reached out to grasp her by the shoulders. ''I want to find out the truth about Father's murder as much as you do, but not at the cost of your life. I'd rather never know than to risk your getting hurt. But if you're determined to continue with the search, then—''

''I am determined.'' She laid her hands over his where he held her shoulders securely. ''I have no intention of letting someone get away with murder, not if there's the remotest possibility that I can bring Preston's killer to justice.''

''Very well.'' Fletcher kissed Caroline's cheek, then released his hold on her. ''I'll call up Teddy Richards, the caretaker there at the cottage, so he'll be expecting you. I'll explain to him why you're driving down. '' Fletch turned to Wolfe. ''You have my permission to tear the damn car apart if you think you can find anything. And whatever you find, by all means bring it back with you.''

''Then we can leave from here?'' Caroline asked Wolfe. He nodded.

''I'll call Roz right away.'' When Caroline headed toward the attic stairs, Brooke followed her.

When the women were out of earshot, Fletch said, ''I'm holding you personally responsible if anything happens to her.''

''I can promise you that nothing is going to happen to her as long as there's breath in my body.'' Wolfe glared at Fletcher, his gaze and stance vowing as surely as his words that he was completely and wholeheartedly dedicated to protecting Caroline.

Fletcher narrowed his gaze and stared at Wolfe oddly, as

if he couldn't quite figure out what motivated his stepsister's bodyguard. Wolfe didn't give a damn. Let Fletcher Shaw think what he would. David Wolfe was in Caroline's life now, her constant companion, and until she was safe from all danger, only an act of God could sever him from her side.

Chapter 9

Interstate 97 took them to Annapolis. Then Caroline stayed on Highway 2, heading south, until they reached their turnoff onto a county road that would take them to the coast and the tiny village of Windhaven, which wasn't even a speck on the map. Wolfe sat on the passenger side, riding shotgun, while Caroline drove. He read aloud Fletch's directions that would lead them to his maternal grandparents' waterfront cottage— and hopefully to a discovery inside Preston Shaw's antique car stored there in the garage. Nothing would suit Wolfe better than to learn what the mysterious key opened. Not only would that disclosure put an end to the threat on Caroline's life, but it would enable Wolfe to hand over, to Ellison Penn, the unquestionable proof of Preston Shaw's guilt as well as the evidence against Shaw's cohorts. The Peacekeepers had had enough proof of Shaw's guilt to order his death and Wolfe had simply been following orders when he executed Caroline's stepfather. But having recently seen a new per-spective of Preston Shaw through Caroline's and Fletch's eyes made him wonder if there was even the slightest possibility that the Peacekeepers had made a mistake. Wolfe's conscience would rest easier when even the tiniest glimmer of doubt was removed from his mind.

The truth would no doubt break Caroline's heart. She still thought of Preston Shaw as not only an honorable person, but as a good and kind man. Wolfe regretted that it would be necessary to ruin her cherished memories of the man she'd thought of as a father. But now that she had found the mysterious key and had become obsessed with locating the hidden evidence, there was no other way to protect her. As much as he would like to see the other members of the highly secret, traitorous group of which Shaw had been a leader revealed and punished, Wolfe would prefer Caroline never know the complete truth about her stepfather. If they found the evidence Shaw had professed to have in his possession, then Wolfe decided that he would do his best to keep her from being exposed to all the ugly details.

But what if they didn't find what the key unlocked? What if weeks went by, even months, without unearthing the damaging evidence? Would Caroline give up the quest? Dear God, he hoped she would. If not, she would live in constant danger from an unknown enemy.

Wolfe would have felt more at ease right now if fewer people knew their whereabouts. Fletcher and Brooke had taken part in making the plans to go to Windhaven, so it was only reasonable to assume that Brooke might tell her parents, despite his warnings to tell no one. Roz knew, too, and it was possible that she had disregarded instructions and had by now told Gavin and/or Lyle. If Gavin knew, then he might have informed Ellison, or if the boss had been unavailable, then Ellison's trusted secretary. It wasn't that Wolfe suspected anyone in particular, but he had learned the hard way that a cautious man trusted no one. Sometimes even the closest friend might prove to be a person's most deadly enemy.

Wolfe spread his right hand and, using his thumb and middle finger, clasped the side of the frames and repositioned his tinted glasses to rest more securely on the bridge of his nose. Without moving an inch and alerting Caroline, Wolfe scanned their surroundings. She slowed her Lincoln LS when a forty-five mile-per-hour speed limit sign appeared along the side of the road. The area in which they had been traveling was definitely rural and was now becoming more coastal with each passing mile.

They had spoken very little on the long ride from Fletcher's home in Baltimore. No idle chitchat. No heart-to-heart conversation. He read the directions whenever necessary. She commented occasionally on this or that roadway scene. He suspected she felt every bit as awkward as he did after their middle-of-the-night sensual exchange in his bedroom. Try as he might, he couldn't get the sight of her, the scent of her, the feel of her out of his mind. It had taken a great deal of willpower to release her, to reject the offer he'd seen in her lavender-blue eyes. She had wanted him as surely as he had wanted her. How was he going to continue guarding her night and day and resist the sweetest temptation on earth?

"Directions, please." She glanced his way hurriedly, then refocused on the road. "Is our turnoff close?"

Wolfe looked over the directions again, then gazed out the window. "Harcourt Road should be about two miles from here. Fletch says we can smell the sea from that point on."

Caroline grinned, then sighed. "I'm desperately trying not to get my hopes up about finding anything in the Alfa Romeo. But it would be just like Preston to have hidden something important in the car he dearly loved. I keep wondering that if he wanted Mother to find the evidence, why would he leave the car to Fletch?"

"Good question."

They remained silent until Wolfe spotted the turn. "There's Harcourt Road."

She whipped the Lincoln off onto the rough, uneven course, slowing almost to a standstill after hitting a rather

large pothole. She grumbled under her breath. The narrow
two-lane local roadway was in bad need of repair. If they
hadn't been traveling at such a slow speed, they would have
probably missed the town of Windhaven, which consisted of
a gas station-minimart and little else. A row of empty build-
ings and a few boats docked in the small harbor comprised
what had no doubt been a small, active seacoast village years
ago. As they wound their way through the remnants of the
old town, Wolfe noted a few signs of new life on the outskirts
and wondered what group of wealthy investors had gobbled
up the place, probably intending to turn it into a tourist
mecca.

"We go half a mile and then turn off onto a gravel road
that leads to a dirt road that will take us straight to the cottage," Wolfe said.

She nodded. "Looks like Windhaven will be another tourist destination in a year or two. Pity."

In less than five minutes, they found the cottage, located
on a dirt road close to the bay and within walking distance
of five other old waterfront houses, built decades ago as summer homes. Standing outside the cottage, his hand raised in
greeting, stood a man Wolfe guessed to be at least seventy-
five, his bald head gleaming in the late afternoon sunlight.

"That must be Teddy Richards." Caroline pulled the Lincoln to a stop in the overgrown driveway.

"And there's the Alfa Romeo." Wolfe pointed toward the
garage, which was the exact shade of yellow as the house.
On both the paint was faded and peeling. The rather rickety-
looking open garage door hung precariously on rusted hinges.

Caroline removed her seat belt, flung open the door and
jumped out and onto the ground. Wolfe hurried so that she
got only a few steps ahead of him on her way toward the
garage.

"Hey there, you Caroline McGuire?" the elderly man
asked.

Caroline held out her hand as she approached him. Wolfe

barely restrained himself from halting her friendly greeting. What were the odds that this old codger was a hit man? Slim to none. But pure instinct guided Wolfe as he slipped his hand beneath the edge of his lightweight sports coat to undo the snap on his hip holster. His hand hovered close to the weapon as Caroline shook hands with the man who identified himself as Teddy.

"Mr. Fletcher said to let y'all do whatever you wanted with the car," Teddy said. "So there she is. Like to take a closer look?"

Wolfe grabbed Caroline's arm as she headed straight for the garage. "Wait a minute."

She glanced over her shoulder, giving him a puzzled stare. "We can hardly check the trunk and the glove compartment or whatever else from this distance."

Wolfe looked at the garage. Nestled inside the small structure's belly was a magnificent antique car, its sides and fenders a single molded unit that tapered to a teardrop rear end. The long curved roofline swooped forward to a split and curved windshield. Like an ageless lady of great style and beauty, Pinin Farina's classic automobile outshone any present-day models. Wolfe owned several vintage vehicles himself, having begun his collection shortly after his resurrection from the dead and his move to Atlanta. He kept his '59 Corvette and his Ferrari 250 swb garaged at his home in Tennessee.

"I'll bring her out so you can get a good look at her," Teddy said. "Not much room to maneuver in the garage and no electricity out there, so no lights."

While Teddy made his way, rather briskly for an old man, toward the garage, Caroline turned to Wolfe. "Are you suspicious of Mr. Richards?" A closemouthed smile spread across her face. "My heavens, he's probably eighty years old."

"A professional weakness," Wolfe admitted. "Not trusting anyone. Suspecting even the most innocent-looking person."

He placed his hand in the small of her back. She stiffened instantly. He assumed that Caroline had been as curious as he to know how they both would react when they touched again. For him it was a blend of pleasure and agony. His instincts told him that for her it was the same.

"Move over to the side of the house," Wolfe suggested. "I'm not sure I trust Teddy's driving skills."

Caroline laughed softly as she allowed Wolfe to guide her to what he considered a safer location. They both watched as Teddy opened the driver's side door of the antique car and slipped behind the wheel. Suddenly a pure gut reaction prompted Wolfe to call out to the old man. He had allowed the physical contact with Caroline to momentarily distract him and that distraction had sidetracked his normally astute instincts.

"Wait! Don't start the engine," Wolfe cried.

Caroline looked at Wolfe, her eyes widening in surprise, as if questioning his sanity. But within seconds, her look changed to one of shock and then of horror. A loud, ear-splitting blast rocked the ground on which they stood as the Alfa Romeo, the garage and Teddy Richards were blown to kingdom come.

"Son of a bitch!" As the sound of the explosion reverberated in their ears, Wolfe shoved Caroline to the ground and covered her with his body.

Debris sailed high into the sky—pieces of yellow wood, fragments of red metal, gravel, grass, dirt and the minuscule particles that had once comprised a human body. Bits and pieces of the remains rained down on them, peppering Wolfe's body and showering across the yard and the cottage. Fire singed the earth where the garage had once stood and little outbreaks flamed up all around them. Wolfe prayed that Caroline's Lincoln was far enough way from the blast to have survived intact. It was their only means of escape. His guess was that the explosives had been wired to the ignition, set to activate the moment the car was started. Maybe the person who had placed the bomb in the Alfa Romeo was long gone. But what if he or she had waited around to make sure the blast had done its job? Caroline had been the target, not Teddy Richards.

As soon as the dust settled, Wolfe rose to his knees and closely surveyed the destruction all around them. His tinted glasses, which had fallen off when he'd hit the ground, lay broken only a couple of inches from his right foot. His gaze moved to settle on the Lincoln, which was covered with dust and particles from the blast. Flying debris had smashed in the back window and pockmarked the side of the vehicle. Wolfe rose to his feet, then jerked Caroline to a standing position. She shivered uncontrollably. He ran his hands up and down her arms, then shook her gently.

"We've got to get out of here. Do you understand?"

She nodded and obediently let him lead her hurriedly toward the car. He opened the passenger door and shoved her inside, then closed and locked the door and rounded the hood. The minute he slid behind the wheel, she held out the car keys, which she had earlier slipped into the pocket of her slacks. Her hand shook uncontrollably.

"Poor old Teddy Richards," Caroline said, tears in her voice.

Wolfe reached over, caressed her dirty cheek, then inserted the key in the ignition and started the Lincoln. With only one thought in mind—to protect Caroline—he reversed the car, whipped it out onto the road and slammed his foot down on the gas pedal.

When Wolfe pulled the battered Lincoln into the driveway at Caroline's home at fifteen past eleven that night, four people came rushing off the well-lit front porch where they had been waiting. Roz was the first to reach Caroline, with Brooke a close second. Wolfe allowed the two women to push him aside as they rushed to smother their friend with hugs and dampen her with their tears of relief and joy.

"Oh, God, Caroline, when you phoned Lyle from the Calvert County sheriff's office and told him what happened, he called me immediately." Roz brushed strands of Caroline's disheveled hair out of her eyes. "We've been worried sick."

"Lyle called Fletch, too, and the four of us have been out of our minds with worry," Brooke said. "My poor Fletch has been blaming himself for Teddy Richards's death. And he's been frantic about you."

Wolfe glanced over his shoulder at the two men who stood nearby, as if waiting their turn, then focused his attention on the two women flanking Caroline. Someone had passed along information, whether maliciously or innocently, that had enabled a professional to prepare a booby trap for Caroline. Was one of these four dear friends capable of such treachery? He wanted desperately to rule out Lyle, and if not for his cynical nature, he would have. For the life of him, he couldn't see Reverend Jennings harming a hair on anyone's head, let alone willingly helping someone murder Caroline. The other three, each in his or her own way, were a possibility, even though his instincts told him their affection for Caroline was genuine.

"Caroline." Lyle held out his hands as Roz and Brooke led her up the walkway.

Caroline paused, pulled away from her girlfriends and grabbed Lyle's hands, then put her arms around him and hugged him fiercely. Tears streamed down Lyle's cheeks as he clung to her.

"I'm so thankful you're all right," Lyle said. "I've prayed almost nonstop since you called me, letting the Lord know how grateful I am that he spared your life."

"Did you thank the Lord for sending Mr. Wolfe to me?" Caroline asked, as she pulled back from her cousin and searched for Wolfe.

Fletcher came forward but didn't block the path or prevent

Wolfe from being able to see Caroline. With a fragile, tentative tilt of her lips, she smiled at her stepbrother.

"If only I hadn't sent you down to Windhaven..." Fletcher's voice cracked with emotion.

Caroline caressed Fletcher's cheek, then kissed him with sisterly affection. "Stop blaming yourself for what happened. You had no way of knowing that someone would get there ahead of us and plant a bomb in Preston's Alfa Romeo."

Wolfe followed closely, just behind the foursome as they escorted Caroline to her front porch, then he moved around them to unlock the door. He went in first, turned on the lights, punched in the security code and scanned the foyer before motioning for the others to come inside. Once they were congregated in the foyer, Wolfe disengaged Caroline from her quartet of concerned friends. She gasped when he grabbed her arm. The others stood rigidly still, their gazes riveted to Caroline.

"I have a few questions for y'all," Wolfe said. "And after I get the answers, I want all of you to leave."

"What?"

"Now, see here..."

"I had planned to stay...."

"What sort of questions?"

Wolfe jerked Caroline to his side. She went without protest, although the look on her face warned him that she would confront him later.

"Come with me." Wolfe led the way, hauling Caroline with him. He gently shoved her down into an overstuffed easy chair and took his guard post behind her. The others made their way into the living room. The women sat side by side on the sofa. Lyle took the rocking chair to Caroline's left. Remaining on his feet, Fletcher crossed his arms over his chest and glared at Wolfe.

"Only six people knew that Caroline and I were going to Windhaven to search through Preston Shaw's antique Alfa Romeo," Wolfe said. "Caroline and I. Fletcher, Brooke and

Roz. And Teddy Richards. But I think we can rule out Mr. Richards as a suspect.''

''A suspect?'' Brooke gasped and looked point-blank at Caroline. ''What is he talking about?''

Before Caroline could speak, Wolfe cut off her reply and asked, ''Did any of you tell someone else where Caroline and I were going and why?''

''I didn't,'' Fletcher replied immediately, a smug look of satisfaction on his face.

''I did,'' Roz confessed. ''I told Lyle, but that hardly counts. He phoned the studio and asked to speak to Caroline, so naturally I explained where she'd gone and why.''

''Naturally.'' Wolfe focused on the reverend. ''Did you tell anyone what Roz told you?''

Lyle's face paled. He shook his head. ''No. Not a soul.''

''Anyone else?'' Wolfe asked.

Roz's forehead wrinkled when she puckered her lips in an oh-dear-me pout. She bobbed her head up and down slowly, regretfully admitting that she had gone against Wolfe's instructions and told someone other than Lyle. ''I told Gavin. He called to invite me out and just happened to ask if I'd mentioned to Caroline that he and I were seeing each other. I know I wasn't supposed to tell anybody where you two went and why, but it's not as if Gavin is the guy out to kill Caroline.''

Wolfe growled, deep and low, the sound emitting roughly from his throat. Caroline tilted back her head and glanced up at him. He reached down and clamped his hand on her shoulder. She broke eye contact and looked away from Wolfe and at her friends, but she lifted her hand and laid it over Wolfe's for a brief moment.

Wolfe's gaze moved on to Brooke. ''What about you, Ms. Harper?''

''I think I might have mentioned it to Mother and Dad,'' she said.

"Either you did or you didn't." Wolfe's voice held a deadly, accusatory tone.

"See here, Wolfe, I don't like your attitude," Fletcher said.

"I don't really care what you like or don't like," Wolfe replied. "Pleasing you is not part of my job description. Protecting Caroline is the only thing that matters. Someone in this room is responsible for giving information about Caroline's activities to the wrong person. That act, innocent though it might have been, could have cost Caroline her life. I cannot allow something like that to happen again."

"Yes, I mentioned to Mother and Dad that Caroline was going to Windhaven," Brooke said. "And it's possible that one or more of the servants overheard me. I didn't think you meant my family when you warned us not to tell anyone. My parents love Caroline."

"Thank you for your honesty, Ms. Harper," Wolfe said.

"You know, come to think of it, Kirsten and Sandy knew why Caroline had canceled her afternoon appointments." Roz shot up off the sofa. "I didn't think twice about telling them. Gosh, Caroline, I'm sorry."

"It's all right," Caroline assured her.

"I have to disagree," Wolfe said. "It's not all right. However, what's done is done. In future, something like this will not happen again. I don't want any of you pressing Caroline for specifics about the plans she has beyond her normal work schedule. Starting in the morning, she will be curtailing her activities until further notice."

"Is that what you want, Caroline?" Fletcher asked. "If not, say the word and I'll fire this overzealous commando."

"No," Caroline said. "If you fire Wolfe, I'll simply rehire him. He and I will work things out between us."

Roz exchanged a quick what's-up-with-those-two look with Lyle, then said, "Since you came by and picked me up tonight, you'll have to drive me home, Rev."

Caroline slipped her shoulder out from under Wolfe's possessive clasp and stood. Lyle nodded agreement to Roz's request, then got up out of the chair. After he and Roz kissed Caroline good-night, they showed themselves out the front door. Brooke stood, walked over to a scowling Fletcher and slipped her arm through his.

"We should be going, too," Brooke said, then dragged her reluctant and angry boyfriend toward Caroline. "If you need us for anything, don't hesitate to call." She glanced at Wolfe. "But I believe we're leaving you in good hands."

Caroline hugged her childhood friend and her stepbrother, then Wolfe shoved them out the door, locked it and punched in the code to secure the house for the night. The minute he turned to face Caroline, he realized she was fighting mad. Angry with him. For being rude to her friends?

"How dare you accuse one of them of being at fault for what happened at Windhaven!"

"I accused no one."

"No, you didn't out-and-out accuse one of them specifically, but you might as well have." She marched right up to him and pointed her finger in his face. "Those four people are the dearest friends I have on earth. Lyle and Fletch are like brothers to me. Not a one of them would ever do anything to harm me."

"Are you willing to bet your life on that?"

"What?"

He manacled her wrist. She glared at him. "From this moment on, until you are no longer in any danger, the only person you can trust one hundred percent is me."

"You? You're a stranger to me. A hired bodyguard. Why should I trust you more than four people I've known and trusted for years?"

With one quick jerk, he hauled her up against him and lowered his head enough so that their breaths mingled. "I think you already know the answer to that question."

Chapter 10

"Thanks for the ride home." Holding the passenger side door open on the minivan, Roz peered inside at Lyle. "You wouldn't want to come inside for a cup of coffee, would you?"

Lyle didn't respond immediately so she figured he was trying to find a tactful way to decline her offer. It had been stupid of her to suggest that he come into her house, even for something as innocent as coffee. Wasn't he the man who had told her that he was afraid she'd contaminate him, that her wickedness would rub off on him?

"Sure. I'd love a cup of coffee. Have you got decaf?" He opened the driver's side door and hopped out.

Too stunned to speak, Roz stood there for a couple of seconds, her mouth hanging open and her eyes slightly glazed from shock. "Oh...yeah...I've got decaf. Got it in three flavors." She slammed the minivan door. "Hazelnut. Macadamia chocolate and French vanilla."

Lyle rounded the van, then stopped hesitantly. "French vanilla sounds nice."

Reverend Lyle Jennings was actually going to come inside her house, at night—heck, at past midnight—for a cup of coffee. Was she dreaming or had some alien being possessed the rev's body?

Oh, God, her house was a mess. She couldn't remember the last time she'd dusted. There were dirty dishes in the sink. Unfolded clothes in the laundry basket on the kitchen table. And her bed was unmade. Forget about unmade beds, Roz, she told herself. Lyle certainly isn't going to be in your bedroom tonight.

As they walked toward the front door, side by side but not touching, Roz began feeling uncertain about having issued the invitation. "Look, I'm not much of a housekeeper. The place is untidy. Actually, it's an unholy mess. Oh, bad choice of words. Sorry."

"Roz?" Lyle halted at the door.

She turned to face him. "Huh?" she replied nervously. She loved that adorable freckled face of his, those sleepy hazel eyes and that shock of wavy red hair. Put him in a cowboy outfit and he'd look like Howdy Doody all grown up. Yet she could picture a couple of adorable kids who looked just like him. One of these days some really lucky woman would give him those kids. Why the heck did she have to wish she could be the mother of Lyle's babies, the woman he loved and wanted to spend the rest of his life with? Of all the women on earth, she'd be his last choice.

"My place isn't very neat, either," he admitted. "When some of the ladies at the church dropped by, they suggested that I needed a wife. I suspect they took one look at my lack of housekeeping skills and figured—"

"I'll bet they've been bombarding you with likely candidates, haven't they?" Roz could just picture the uptight plain Janes the church ladies had paraded before him. Prim. Proper. Pious. Boring. And completely suited to life as a minister's wife.

As Roz unlocked the door, Lyle sighed. "I've tried every

courteous way I know how to tell the ladies that I'm perfectly capable of finding a wife without any assistance. But they do seem determined for me to choose one of the young women they deem suitable.''

She glanced over her shoulder and saw that he was blushing. ''Come on in.'' After turning on the light in the living room, she spread out her arm in a gesture of welcome. ''Be it ever so humble.'' Immediately she flitted about, picking up magazines strewn on the floor, stuffing scattered clothing beneath sofa and chair cushions and jerking up a couple of beer bottles from an end table. Holding the bottles behind her hips, she backed toward the door to the kitchen. ''Make yourself at home. I'll put on that coffee—French vanilla—and be right back.''

''Thanks.'' Lyle chose the sofa, sat and glanced around the room.

She plastered a fake smile on her face and shoved the door open with her butt, then escaped into the small, cluttered kitchen. Breathing a quick sigh of relief, she tried to remember where she'd stored that unopened bag of French vanilla decaf coffee Caroline had given her, along with the other flavors, in a Valentine's Day gift basket. It's got to be here somewhere, she thought. Ah-ha! In the freezer! Caroline had told her to store the small bags of gourmet coffee in the freezer so they'd stay fresh.

Hurrying, she retrieved the coffee, opened the sack and prepared her four-cup coffeemaker. With that done, she rummaged around in the refrigerator and in the cabinets for something to serve with the coffee. Cake? Pie? Danish? She didn't have any of that stuff. Cookies. She had cookies. Oversize peanut butter cookies she'd picked up at the bakery a few days ago.

While the coffee brewed, she cracked open the door and called out to Lyle, ''Cream and sugar or just black?''

''Sugar, please. One teaspoon.''

''Coming right up.''

Damn, she didn't have a silver coffeepot or any good china. She didn't even own a set of matching thrift-store dishes. The best she could offer Lyle was a pink Bitch's Brew mug. When she had seen the mugs in a speciality shop several years ago, she'd thought they were cute, so she'd bought half a dozen. Most of the guys she dated either didn't even notice the feminist logo or got a good laugh when they read it. Lyle was likely to take offense. What the hell! She couldn't serve hot coffee in her Wal-Mart Looney Tunes glasses, could she? Another purchase that she had, at the time, thought was cute.

Five minutes later, she shoved open the door with her hip and emerged from the kitchen carrying a floral metal tray. The moment she entered the room, Lyle stood. What a gentleman, she thought. She wasn't used to guys with good manners. Lyle's Southern charm had a way of disarming her and making her feel inferior. She knew he didn't come from money or anything like that, but he'd had a mama who was a real lady. Caroline's aunt Dixie had instilled old-fashioned rules of decorum in her son and niece.

Roz placed the cheap metal tray on the cocktail table, wishing with all her heart that it was the finest silver. She sat on the sofa, then Lyle joined her, sitting on the opposite end.

"I thought you might like some cookies." She indicated the plate of cookies by pointing at them, then remembered that pointing wasn't polite. "Peanut butter. I hope you like them."

"Did you bake them?" he asked as he lifted the bright pink coffee mug and reached for a cookie.

Roz chuckled. "Me?" She shook her head. "Honey, I've never baked anything in my life." She gasped. "Sorry, Rev, I didn't mean to call you honey. Just a slip of the tongue."

Lyle blushed again, then picked up a cookie and took a bite. After chewing, sipping the coffee and swallowing, he smiled. "The cookie's quite tasty and the coffee's really good. Thank you."

Roz tried to think of something to do or say to make this less awkward for him. She tried to think of a subject to discuss. Surely they had at least one thing in common. "What do you think of Mr. Wolfe?" she finally asked, then picked up her coffee mug.

Lyle stared at the mug she held, seemingly mesmerized by it. Suddenly Roz realized he hadn't paid any attention to his own matching mug and was reading the logo on hers. His mouth curved into a smile. She giggled.

"Sorry. They're all I've got. I bought them a few years back because I simply couldn't resist them."

"Stop apologizing to me for every little thing." Lyle scooted a little closer to her, his gaze never leaving her face. "I may be a minister, but I'm not a saint, not some perfect human being whose job it is to judge you. I think the mugs are cute. They're—" he paused, as if trying to come up with the right thing to say "—they're so you, Roz."

"Oh?" Was that an insult? A compliment? Neither? "Is that good or bad?"

"Definitely good," he said.

"You mean there's something about me that you think is good?"

His smile widened into a sheepish grin. "I suppose I deserve that." He shook his head and laughed. "There's a lot about you that's good. Buying these mugs is an example of your great sense of humor, and a sense of humor is a good thing."

"Does that mean you don't think the mugs' logo suits my personality? Do you think I'm a bitch, Lyle?" Oh, that's it, Roz, ask a leading question. Brace yourself for the answer, she cautioned herself. The rev doesn't lie, you know.

"No more or no less than any other female of my acquaintance," he replied—and with a straight face.

She stared at him for a moment, then realized he was joking. She punched his arm playfully, laughing as she leaned toward him. Their gazes connected. Warmth suffused her body. Sexual heat. *Don't go there, Roz,* an inner voice warned. Just because he's being nice to you for a change doesn't mean he's interested in you in *that way*.

"I...er...I think Mr. Wolfe takes his job very seriously." Lyle cleared his throat. "And that's good for Caroline. I believe Fletch was wrong to take offense at the things Mr. Wolfe said."

"I agree. I think Wolfe would die to protect Caroline."

"That's his job, isn't it? To be prepared to kill or to die to protect her." Lyle finished off the cookie and washed it down with his coffee.

"Yeah, I suppose it is, but I think there's more to it. Didn't you pick up any vibes between them? If I didn't know better, I'd swear he and Caroline have something going on."

"Caroline just met the man," Lyle said. "She is not the type of woman who would—"

"Honey, any woman is the type who *would* with—"

"With a man like Mr. Wolfe, you mean."

Roz shook her head. "No, I wasn't going to say with a man like Mr. Wolfe. I was going to say, with the right man. A woman would do just about anything for a guy who is her soul mate."

"I hardly think Caroline and Mr. Wolfe are soul mates. They have nothing in common."

Roz gazed into Lyle's eyes. "You might be surprised. Besides, I don't think you have to come from similar backgrounds or be just alike to be soul mates. Do you?"

"I don't know," Lyle admitted. "I've never given the subject much thought." He added in a whisper, "Until recently."

"Yeah, I know what you mean. The idea of having a soul mate is sort of sappy and sentimental, isn't it?"

"And romantic," Lyle said.

"Yeah. Very romantic."

Moment by moment, inch by inch, Lyle and Roz drew closer and closer until they were sitting right beside each other on the sofa. Their arms and legs touching, their gazes locked, their breathing labored.

"You're very pretty," Lyle said.

"Thank you. You're pretty cute yourself."

Lyle blushed, yet again. "I've never thought of myself as cute."

"You are." She reached out and ruffled his thick red hair. "You're awfully cute. And as you know, I just love cute things."

They came together, their lips almost touching. Roz's stomach fluttered. Was he really going to kiss her? Please, let it happen, she prayed. *I promise I'll be good for him. So good. Just let him want me the way I want him.*

The telephone rang. Lyle jumped away from Roz as if an invisible hand had shoved him. Roz groaned. Who the hell would be calling at this time of night? She grumbled to herself, cursing the Fates for interrupting at such an auspicious moment. Another ten seconds and all her dreams might have come true. She stomped across the room, lifted the receiver and growled.

"Whoever this is, it had better be a damn emergency!"

"Roz, sweet thing, did I wake you?"

"Gavin?"

She sensed Lyle's movement and when she glanced his way, she almost cried. The look on his face said it all. Disappointment. Anger. Hurt. He rose to his feet quickly and accidentally hit his knee on the edge of the coffee table. Grimacing, he groaned and rubbed his knee. She looked at him pleadingly. *Don't go! I'll get rid of Gavin. The man means absolutely nothing to me. You're the man I want...the man I love.*

"Gavin, this isn't a good time for me," she said.

"Should I be jealous? Are you in the sack with another guy?"

"Don't be ridiculous."

Lyle was heading for the front door. Damn!

"Call me back when it's daylight outside, okay?"

Lyle opened the front door.

"Better yet, Gavin, don't bother calling me again. Ever!"
Roz slammed down the telephone and ran toward the door,
catching up with Lyle just as he stepped over the threshold.
"Wait!"

Lyle turned and glared at her, his face flushed with anger.
"You shouldn't have been rude to your boyfriend on my
account. Heck, Roz, it's not as if you and I are friends. We
don't even like each other, do we? The only reason we're
ever civil to each other is for Caroline's sake."

She bit down on her bottom lip to keep from bursting into
tears, then bobbed her head up and down to agree with him.
"Drive carefully. Okay?"

He nodded. "Good night, Roz. Thanks for the coffee and
the cookies."

"Sure. Anytime."

He hesitated, as if he wanted to say more, but instead he
turned and walked away. Roz stood in the doorway for several minutes after the red taillights on Lyle's minivan disappeared down the road. Then she slammed the door, leaned
against it and sank to the floor. She keened softly as tears
trickled down her cheeks, over her nose and across her lips.

Caroline had all but run from Wolfe, and he had allowed
her to escape—from him and his brutally honest statement.
Of course she knew why she should trust him and him alone.
But she couldn't admit that to him. She barely had the cour-
age to admit the reason to herself. She had locked herself in
the bathroom, turned on the shower and stripped naked.
While standing under the warm, pelting water, she relived
every moment of her life since Wolfe had showed up at her
front door. She had wondered how it was possible that on

such short acquaintance a perfect stranger had come to mean so much to her.

Now, sitting at her dressing table, combing the tangles from her damp hair, she confronted herself about her true feelings for Wolfe. If she trusted him with her life, as she trusted no one else, wasn't it time to be totally honest with herself? A powerful sexual attraction existed between them. She felt it and so did he. It was unlike anything she'd ever known. But that wasn't the reason why she trusted him. There was more to her feelings than sexual attraction. From the first moment she saw him, she sensed a bond, as if she already knew him. Was reincarnation possible? she speculated. Lyle would say it wasn't. Roz would say it definitely was. Brooke and Fletch would say whatever was currently in vogue with their set of society friends.

No matter what she believed or didn't believe, one fact was clear. Wolfe was a man capable of protecting her, a man who had proved that he was dedicated to keeping her safe. In some odd sort of way, his interest in her seemed personal. Was it the sexual thing? she asked herself. Did he, like some primitive male, think of her as his possession, his woman? As a modern-thinking female, with politically correct views on many subjects, she supposed she should resent that type of macho thinking. After all, maybe Wolfe was the kind of man who thought it was his right to sleep with his female clients. Was his desire to have sex with her at the root of his willingness to go to any lengths to protect her?

Caroline laid the silver comb on the dressing table, eased back the satin-covered bench on which she sat and rose to her feet. It was time for her to have a talk with her bodyguard. She had to find out if she was simply one more woman in a long line of conquests.

What if you are? What will you do then?

She donned the matching satin robe that covered her bare arms and swept to the floor. The lace hem glided along behind her as she marched out of her bedroom. Naturally he had left his door wide open. She paused momentarily outside his bedroom, took a deep, fortifying breath and knocked softly on the door frame. She glanced into the room but didn't see him anywhere.

"Wolfe, I'd like to speak to you, please."

His bathroom door opened. She gasped. He emerged with a large towel draped around his hips, the rest of him completely nude. Taken aback by his lack of clothing, she froze to the spot and swallowed hard.

"I'll come back after you've put on something."

She turned and headed toward her room, but he caught up with her before she'd taken more than a few steps. His big hand clutched her upper arm. She whirled around to face him, her breathing harsh, her cheeks flushed with emotion.

"What are you so afraid of, Caroline?" he asked, his cold, jade-green eyes focused on her face. "You must know...you must feel it here—" he laid his open palm over her heart "—that I would never hurt you, that I will protect you, with my life if necessary."

"Because it's your job?" She held her breath, waiting for his reply. His big hand on her chest felt hot and heavy.

"Yes, partly because it's my job." His palm glided upward, over her collarbone, until he spread apart his fingers and gripped her throat with the utmost tenderness.

"And..." she prompted.

"And because I couldn't bear for anything to happen to you."

He lifted the hand at her throat and circled around to grasp the nape of her neck, while he released his hold on her arm to cup her hip. She gazed into his eyes, hypnotized by the intensity of emotion she saw revealed in their depths. He was going to kiss her, with or without her permission. Had he guessed that this was what she wanted? He covered her lips with his, a gentle possession but forceful enough to brook no denial on her part. When she succumbed to the kiss, he pulled her closer and deepened the contact.

This was unlike any kiss she'd ever known. Powerful enough to propel her from pleasurable experience to raging sexual hunger in one minute flat. Every fiber of her being acknowledged this man as her mate. Primeval forces surged through her body, demanding satisfaction of the most primitive nature. Caroline pressed herself intimately against his erection and a sense of feminine power overwhelmed her. She lifted her arms to drape his shoulders and became an equal participant in the carnality of their kiss.

As quickly as he had instigated the kiss, Wolfe ended it. Caroline felt bereft and breathless, as if her oxygen supply had suddenly been cut off and she was smothering. When he stepped away from her, she reached out for him pleadingly.

"Unless you have no doubts about what you want, then I suggest you turn around and go back to your room," Wolfe said.

He wanted her as desperately as she wanted him, didn't he? So why was he rejecting her? *No, he's not rejecting you,* an inner voice told her. *He is giving you a chance to think twice about what you're doing.*

"If you are sure that you will have no regrets in the morning, then come to me." He held out his hand. "I'll make love to you."

Passion tried to overrule common sense. The temptation to succumb to the most basic human desires fought a battle with her self-preservation instincts. Would she regret it in the morning if she gave herself to Wolfe? She honestly didn't know.

Undoubtedly she hesitated a moment too long to suit him. He dropped his proffered hand. "When it's right...if it's ever right between us, you won't have to think about it. You'll know."

"Wolfe, please..."

"You've had a rough day," he said. "You've been through a traumatic experience. You aren't in any sort of emotional shape to make a decision as important to you as this one. You haven't saved yourself all these years to give yourself to the wrong man now.''

''How did you know—''

''That you're a virgin?''

Her face burned with embarrassment. ''Was it that obvious to you? Am I that inept? Is that why you stopped things when you did—because you prefer your women more experienced?''

''You could never be just another woman to me. If I were to ever take you to my bed, you would become my woman forever. I put a stop to things not because of your innocence, but because I'm the wrong man. I'm not worthy of you, my sweet Caroline.''

He left her standing in the hallway, feeling totally dazed by his statement. Heaven help her, she was more aroused and more confused than she'd ever been in her entire life. And in the morning, she would have to confront him again, this powerful, commanding man. How would she be able to control her attraction to him now that he knew she found him irresistible? But hadn't Wolfe proved himself to be an honorable man? He could have taken advantage of her, but he hadn't. It wasn't Wolfe she had to fear, but her own desire.

Chapter 11

Having dealt with stubborn clients before, Wolfe had learned the art of compromise. But being forced to accommodate Caroline's determination not to drastically change her lifestyle had proved difficult for him. He understood that she didn't want someone else dictating what she could do, where she could go and with whom she could associate. But dammit all, couldn't she understand that he had her best interests at heart? If she would let him have his way, yes, he would lock her away from the world until she was no longer in danger. And yes, he would keep her apart from everyone, even those she loved. Caroline trusted too easily, believed the best of everyone, and thus opened herself up to people who might not deserve either her love or her trust.

And God help him, he was one of those people. But the difference between him and all the others in her life was that he knew what motivated him. He might prove a threat to Caroline's heart, but never to her life. There was absolutely nothing he would not do for her. And on some instinctive level, he believed she knew that.

Since the morning after their kiss in the hallway, Caroline had been more reserved with him, as if she thought putting up a barrier between them would prevent any repeat performances. And that same morning, she had made it perfectly clear to him that although she knew her life was in danger, she could not live in a glass bubble and would not alter the basic pattern of her life. He had presented every feasible explanation of why she would be wise to follow his suggestions, and in the end, they had compromised. She would temporarily give up her volunteer work and all social activities—after the dinner party hosted by the Harpers—but she would continue her normal work schedule. And they would continue their search, wherever it might lead them, to find the lock Preston Shaw's key opened.

Wolfe had been totally opposed to this evening's outing, but Caroline had insisted on attending the dinner for Fletcher Shaw. Her unwavering loyalty to her stepbrother was commendable, but exposing herself this way was foolhardy and he'd told her as much.

"It is important to me to be there for Fletch, to lend my support," Caroline had said. "Humor me about this one night and I promise that I'll spend every night from now on under lock and key."

Reluctantly, he had agreed. "I'll need backup for this evening. There's no way I can guarantee your protection without extra agents to help."

He had hoped to talk her out of going but soon realized she would not change her mind. That's why, at this precise moment, they were pulling up outside Oliver and Eileen Harper's mansion in Alexandria, Virginia. He and Caroline sat in the back seat of the Mercedes he had rented for the night and had personally gone over it with a fine-tooth comb. Caroline's damaged Lincoln would be in the repair shop for another few days. Two Dundee agents, who had flown in from Atlanta that morning and would return on a flight the next day, were in the front seat. Matt O'Brien, acting as their chauffeur, would be on hand outside the Harper mansion and alert him to anything that was even vaguely suspicious. Jack Parker, wearing a black tux, black snakeskin boots and a black Stetson, would play the good-old-boy Texas millionaire friend, someone Caroline had supposedly met when she'd taken a family photo for him. Jack would be Wolfe's backup during the buffet dinner, a second set of eyes and ears inside the house. The main players at tonight's little social event would know that Wolfe's relationship to Caroline was professional; however, they would present themselves to the other guests as a couple.

"Mighty fancy digs," Jack said when Matt stopped the Mercedes in the drive directly in front of the white-columned portico. "Almost as nice as my place back home."

"Don't overdo it," Wolfe said. "Play the part whenever necessary, but don't enjoy yourself too much."

"Ah, shucks. And here I was all ready to lasso me a filly or two and tell 'em about my oil wells."

A white-jacketed servant opened the car's back door. Wolfe emerged first, scanning the area as subtly as possible, then he offered his hand to Caroline and assisted her out of the vehicle. He could barely take his eyes off her. She was so beautiful in her simple black silk dress that clung to her curves and accentuated her hour-glass figure. Shirred around a band collar, the bodice covered her completely in front, but her back was bare almost to her waist. She had swept her hair atop her head in a fluffy, loose topknot. Fine tendrils curled between her ears and face. Her only jewelry was her favorite diamond-and-pearl earrings…and, although it was well hidden beneath her dress, the gold chain on which the key was kept.

"How about moseying along," Jack said, "and let a fellow get out of the car."

Realizing that he had stared at her just a little too long, Wolfe took Caroline's arm, draped it over his and moved forward, enough to allow Jack room to step out of the Mercedes. Once the threesome headed up the steps to the veranda, Matt drove off to park the car and join the other chauffeurs.

Inside the house, Jack and Wolfe remained on either side of Caroline. The place was an example of wealth and good taste, and the party itself, which was already in full swing, seemed to be a great success. No doubt Mrs. Oliver Harper had planned and executed countless of these little private dinners—for a hundred guests—on more than one occasion. As Aidan Colbert, a member of Peacekeepers International, Wolfe had attended his share of social functions and had then, as now, felt a bit out of place in a tuxedo. At heart he had always been and always would be just a country boy.

Wolfe surveyed the crowd, then removed his tinted glasses, replacements for the broken ones he had left in the debris at Windhaven. These people were the rich and powerful. The famous and the infamous. Each invitee handpicked because he or she had either enough money or enough influence to help Fletcher Shaw get elected to Congress. Wolfe slipped his glasses into the inside pocket of his tuxedo jacket.

"Caroline, sweetheart." Fletcher zeroed in on them, all smiles and warm greetings. Brooke Harper, in a strapless royal-blue number, a diamond-and-sapphire choker around her slender neck, looked every inch the debutante heiress. She clung to Fletcher's arm as if she'd been born attached to him.

Try as he might to like Fletch, Wolfe found the man a little too smooth, a little too charming. But then country boys were usually suspicious of their refined city-boy counterparts. And Wolfe knew Brooke's type. He'd dated a few just like her and had found rich girls could be amusing, but incapable of surviving in the real world without Daddy's money.

"Fletch thinks you're very brave to come out tonight, considering how dangerous it could be for you," Brooke said to Caroline, but her gaze was fixed on Wolfe. "But I told Fletch that your Mr. Wolfe wouldn't let anything happen to you."

Brooke glanced at Jack Parker and smiled. "Caroline, it's terribly unfair that a good little girl like you winds up with two dates...and both absolute hunks."

"Howdy, ma'am. I'm Jack Parker, from Texas. And you'd be?"

"She would be—" Fletch cleared his throat. "She *is* Brooke Harper, your hosts' daughter and my future wife."

"Fletch, dear..." Brooke all but cooed. "If this is a proposal, I must say it's a strange one."

Fletcher Shaw turned beet red. Wolfe would bet his last dime that the man hadn't been embarrassed since he was in short pants.

"Stop teasing him, Brooke," Caroline said.

Ignoring Fletcher completely, Brooke slid between Caroline and Jack and slipped her arm through his. "Why don't I show you to the buffet and we can get better acquainted, Mr. Parker? That is, if you're allowed to leave Caroline's side."

Jack grinned, exchanged a casual glance with Wolfe and accepted the lady's offer. "It would be my pleasure, ma'am."

As they strolled into the adjoining room, Brooke glanced over her shoulder and called out, "Caroline, do find Mother and Dad. They're eager to see you and to meet Mr. Wolfe."

"And by all means mix and mingle and enjoy yourselves," Fletcher said. "I must meet and greet. This isn't an official fund-raiser, you know, but Oliver has assured me that we'll get at least five million in pledges tonight, maybe more. That's a good start, don't you think?"

"Wonderful start," Caroline said. "Good luck. We'll find you later to say goodbye."

As soon as Fletcher saw new arrivals, he gave Caroline a hurried peck on the cheek and moved on. Wolfe cupped Caroline's elbow. He intended to remain stuck to her like glue throughout the evening. Jack could scope out the partygoers while Ms. Harper entertained him. The man had a knack for keeping a lady's attention while surveying a crowd and picking out suspicious characters. In the year he'd known Jack Parker, Wolfe had learned the man's easygoing cowboy charm was deceptive. In any battle, Wolfe could think of no one he'd rather have at his side.

"What next, Ms. McGuire?" Wolfe asked. "Since you were damned and determined to attend this affair to show your support of Fletcher and he's already acknowledged your presence, who else do you need to impress with your sisterly loyalty?"

Glowering at Wolfe, Caroline jerked away from him, but didn't protest when he grabbed her arm and draped it through his.

"I realize you're upset with me because I insisted on attending this dinner party," she said.

"I'm not upset," he replied. "Furious, maybe, but not upset."

"Do you honestly think that someone will be bold enough to try to kill me at a party with so much press in attendance?"

"It's been known to happen," he told her. "I just don't want it to happen to you."

"Let's say hello to Oliver and Eileen, get a bite to eat and then we can leave early. Will that make you happy?"

"Not coming here would have made me happy."

"You're impossible to please, aren't you?"

You could please me, my sweet Caroline, he thought. You could heal my wounded soul and teach me how to be happy for the first time in my life. But my dream is as impossible as your fantasy. Neither is destined to be fulfilled.

"Caroline!" Roz Turner called from halfway across the crowded room.

"Roz?" Caroline searched the direction from which the voice had come and said to Wolfe, "I had no idea Roz had been invited."

The exuberant blonde came barreling toward them, Gavin Robbins in tow. Roz's attire seemed out of place in this crowd of designer dresses. She wore a silver lamé miniskirt and matching bustier covered by a sheer gray overblouse. A pair of half-dollar-size silver hoops dangled from her earlobes.

"Isn't this party fab or what? I've already met an oil sheikh, an English earl, two senators, three congressmen and a TV soap opera star."

"I didn't know you were coming here tonight," Caroline said.

"Neither did I, but then Gavin called me at the last minute and said his date had canceled on him. So I'm doing him a big favor, aren't I, Gavin?"

"Yes, a big favor," he agreed. "I had already accepted for myself and a date. Then the lady had a family emergency. A man hardly likes to admit that he's been stood up."

"Hey, when this shindig's over, what do you say the four of us go dancing or out somewhere for a sunrise breakfast or something," Roz suggested.

"I'm afraid that won't be possible," Wolfe said.

"Sorry, Roz." Caroline patted her friend's arm. "I had to twist Wolfe's arm to get him to bring me here tonight. We're not staying long. But I had to put in an appearance, for Fletch's sake."

"Oh, sure thing. I understand." Roz shook her head sadly. "I wasn't thinking or I'd have known it was a bad idea. I'll sure be glad when all this cloak-and-dagger stuff is over and you can get back to leading a normal life."

"Me, too," Caroline said.

Wolfe cupped her elbow again. The sooner she made the rounds and he got her out of this place the better. He couldn't pinpoint exactly what was wrong—maybe nothing except in his overactive imagination—but his gut instincts told him that something wasn't right. He couldn't leave Caroline's side to do any investigating on his own, so he had to count on Jack and Matt to do what they could to spot any potential trouble before it got too close to Caroline. Anything that came at her, point-blank, he'd deal with himself.

Caroline had decided it was about time to leave the party. With each passing minute Wolfe was becoming more and more agitated. There was no point in prolonging his agony. Just as she started to tell him they could go, she noticed a short, stocky middle-aged man staggering toward her. When he approached, she tried to recall if he was someone she might know. But by the time he came up to her, his face only inches away, she realized two things—he was horribly drunk and he was a stranger.

"Hi, there, boo-te-ful," the guy said, slurring his words as he spoke. "How's about a little kiss."

With a sharply indrawn breath, Wolfe tensed at her side.

The moment the man's damp lips puckered, Wolfe twisted the man's arm behind his back, then shoved him against the nearest wall.

Jack Parker appeared out of nowhere, taking a guard post at Caroline's side. People stopped their conversations to gasp and stare and mumble. Caroline's palms dampened with perspiration. Her pulse raced maddeningly. Everything had happened so fast, she'd barely had time to realize what was going on before Wolfe sprang into action.

"What the hell's wrong with you?" the man Wolfe had just subdued grumbled, his speech slurred.

Wolfe frisked the drunken man, then shoved him toward Jack. "He's just drunk. How about escorting this gentleman to the door? I think our host and hostess would appreciate it."

"Be glad to accommodate you." Jack grabbed the guy by the shoulder. "You're going to cooperate, aren't you?"

The man nodded and made no protest when Jack led him away. Wolfe clasped Caroline by the forearms and inspected her from head to toe.

"Are you all right?" he asked, concern evident in his voice.

"Yes, I'm fine. Really. Don't you think you overreacted just a bit? He tried to kiss me, not kill me, and you practically broke his arm."

"I've told you before, everyone is suspect. Even an inebriated Lothario."

Caroline didn't know how much longer she could bear living this way. Guarded night and day. Increasingly afraid of every noise in the dark. Wary of strangers. Her normal activities drastically curtailed. And Wolfe watching her closely when he thought she wasn't looking. He was like a predatory animal, waiting to strike, constantly in search of danger. And anyone who dared come too close to her might find his life in jeopardy.

How many times had she gone over in her mind what had happened between them the night Wolfe had kissed her in the hallway? Those incredible moments when passion ruled her completely had changed her relationship with Wolfe, making them each careful of what they said and did with regard to each other. Wolfe seemed less patient, more critical and demanding with his orders, while she couldn't help being less cooperative and more argumentative. They were both using discord to keep their sexual urges in check. If they could remain on edge, just a little angry and slightly hostile, then perhaps they wouldn't make another mistake. And kissing each other had been a monumental mistake. At least it had been for her.

Thank goodness Wolfe had called a halt when he did; otherwise she would have given herself to him, willingly, gladly allowing him to take her virginity. And she would have regretted it later. In the cold, hard light of day, when the heat of the moment had passed. As much as she was attracted to Wolfe—and merciful heavens, she was—he'd been right when he had told her that he was wrong for her.

She abhorred violence in all its forms. Since the night of

Preston's murder, she had kept herself as far removed from anything and anyone even remotely connected to violence as humanly possible. She supposed other than the fact he was like a brother to her, one of the reasons she involved herself in Lyle's life and church work was because he and the life he lived represented gentleness and kindness and brotherly love. And she had dated Gavin because he was associated with Peacekeepers International, the nongovernment organization devoted to world peace through diplomacy. Perhaps she had hoped Gavin would be the kind of man Preston had been. Unfortunately, he hadn't lived up to her expectations.

So why had she ever entertained the notion that she could love a man like Wolfe, a man who made his living protecting people from violence and thereby living violently himself? He carried a weapon and knew how to use it. She suspected that in his line of work he had shot someone, perhaps even killed someone. Wolfe had chosen his profession as she had chosen hers—and he was as good a bodyguard as she was a photographer. Despite his often gentle manner and the tenderness with which he touched her, he was a man capable of physical violence.

"Caroline?" Wolfe said her name softly, against her ear.

She shuddered. In her peripheral vision she caught a glimpse of him, alarmingly attractive in his black tuxedo. Standing at her side, his hand cupping her elbow, Wolfe suddenly seemed as threatening as an unknown assailant lying in wait.

"Caroline, are you all right?"

"Yes, I'm fine." She breathed deeply, willing herself not to respond to him in a physical way. *Don't look at him*, she told herself. *If I allowed herself to care about this man, then he* would *be as dangerous to her as a killer. Loving a man like Wolfe would destroy her.* "Let's find Oliver and Eileen. I want to thank them for hosting this party to help Fletch raise money for his campaign next year. After doing that, we can leave."

"You don't want to go through the buffet line?" Wolfe asked.

"No. I'm afraid I don't have much appetite." When she moved, he moved with her, staying in step as she led him through a throng of chatting people.

"You're upset about what happened with that idiot drunk, aren't you? He didn't hurt you. I prevented him from—"

"Yes, I know what you did."

He slid his hand from her elbow to her waist before she realized what he was doing, his action immediately halting her search for their hosts. "I did my job, dammit." He kept his voice low so that only she could hear him, but he might as well have shouted at her, so powerful was his statement.

"Let's not argue," she said. "Not here. Not now."

She could sense the frustration, the barely controlled anger within him. The evidence showed on his face, in the tightening of his muscles and in the agitation in his cold green eyes. She held her breath and waited, then began to breathe again when he released his tenacious hold on her.

Across the room, standing by an older, rather attractive man she thought she recognized but couldn't quite place, was Eileen Harper. Eileen Wendell Harper, the wealthy heiress whose family had been New England bankers for the past two centuries. Eileen was tall, elegantly slender and youthfully vibrant for a woman of sixty who had survived breast cancer this past year. Caroline had always envied Brooke because she and her mother shared such a loving relationship.

As Caroline led Wolfe closer to her objective, she felt an odd reluctance in him, a strange tension that made her wonder what was going on inside that mysterious mind of his. Eileen saw Caroline and smiled. The white-haired man standing next to her paused in their conversation to seek out the person who had captured his hostess's attention. When she approached, Eileen reached out, grasped Caroline's hand and pulled her closer.

After planting a light kiss on Caroline's cheek, Eileen said,

"Dear girl, how simply delightful to see you." Eileen then glanced at Wolfe. "This must be your...er...Mr. Wolfe of whom Brooke has spoken."

Wolfe nodded but didn't reply verbally. Caroline noticed that Wolfe glanced from Eileen to the man at her side.

"Yes, this is Wolfe," Caroline finally said when it became apparent that Wolfe had no intention of saying anything.

Eileen slipped her arm through the arm of the tall, well-built man beside her. "Caroline, do you remember Ellison Penn? He's the president of Peacekeepers International, and knew your stepfather quite well. El was at Harvard when Oliver was there and we've known him for years."

The man whom Eileen referred to quite intimately as El greeted Caroline with a placid smile and a firm handshake. "Hello, Caroline. I don't think you and I have seen each other since Preston's funeral. You've grown up to be a lovely young lady, and from what I understand quite a successful photographer."

When she shook Ellison Penn's hand, she smiled warmly and wondered why her stepfather's former superior at Peacekeepers would even remember her, let alone know any details about her life. She certainly didn't remember him from the funeral. Of course, she had been sedated that day.

"Hello, Mr. Penn," Caroline said. "It's nice to see you again after all these years." She turned to Wolfe. "May I introduce my friend, Mr. Wolfe."

The two men stared at each other for only a couple of seconds, but in that brief glance, Caroline noticed an odd expression on Wolfe's face. The two men shook hands and mumbled hellos.

"Here comes Oliver," Eileen said. "He will be so pleased that you've come to our little party. He was afraid you'd hide away there in St. Michaels, after those two perfectly horrible incidents." Eileen clasped Caroline's hand again. "My dear, I do wish you'd give up this quest to find whatever it is that key of Preston's unlocks. It seems to me that all that nasty business should be left in the past. Dead and buried with poor Preston. If I were you, I'd throw that key in the trash.''

Oliver Harper slid his arm around his wife's waist and bestowed a wide, gregarious smile on Caroline and her companion. She had always liked Oliver, even as a child. He had, in many ways, reminded her of Preston. Soft-spoken, gentlemanly and devoted to his family. She recalled several times when Brooke's father had treated them with an afternoon trip to the zoo or to a museum or even to a matinee at the theater. Besides being quite wealthy and extremely powerful, he was a handsome man, with graying brown hair and warm chestnut eyes.

''What's this about Preston's key?'' Oliver asked. ''Any new developments?''

Caroline glanced meaningfully at Ellison Penn, wondering just how much the Harpers had told him about the key she had found in Preston's hidden safe. Was it possible that Preston had discovered damaging information about his former boss or about the Peacekeepers organization and Mr. Penn was the person behind the attempts on her life? He certainly didn't look like a criminal. But maybe Wolfe was right. Maybe she did trust too easily.

''Oh, Caroline, you look simply mortified, my dear,'' Eileen said. ''You mustn't be concerned because El knows about the key. He's totally trustworthy. And because of his former association with Preston, he's quite concerned about your welfare.''

''Ms. McGuire, I want to assure you that Peacekeepers International is as interested as you are in finding out just what sort of information Preston might have kept hidden,'' Ellison said. ''And if there is anything that our organization can do to help you—''

''As a matter of fact, there is,'' Wolfe said. A collective silence followed his unexpected statement. ''I'd like to take a look at Preston Shaw's files. Would that be possible?'' Wolfe didn't give a damn about Preston Shaw's files. He and

Ellison had gone over those files with a fine-tooth comb fifteen years ago. What he wanted—what he badly needed—was some sort of cover so that he could meet with Ellison now and perhaps again in the future without anyone being overly suspicious. The unimportant files were the best excuse he could think of.

"Well...er... Yes, I'm sure that could be arranged." Ellison looked straight at Caroline when he replied. "I can assure you, however, that there isn't anything in those files that might prove useful to you."

"What about tomorrow morning?" Wolfe asked. He needed this meeting with Ellison as soon as possible. His gut instinct was telling him that there was something Ellison hadn't told him about Preston Shaw, something that he needed to know. "I can be at your office by nine."

"The young man seems quite anxious." Oliver Harper's gaze rested directly on Wolfe.

"The sooner we discover what Ms. McGuire's key unlocks and reveal that information, the sooner she will be out of danger," Wolfe said.

"I agree." Ellison Penn nodded. "Although I doubt Preston's files will help you, I will make them available to you tomorrow." He lifted Eileen's hand and kissed it, then nodded to Oliver before turning his attention briefly back to Wolfe. "My personal assistant is here tonight. I'll find him now and arrange for him to bring Preston's files out of storage first thing in the morning and have anything that's been transferred to our computer system put on a disk for you."

"My goodness, Ellison, you're being very trusting, aren't you?" Eileen asked. "After all, what do you know about Mr. Wolfe, other than he's a reliable bodyguard?"

"I know a great deal about Mr. Wolfe," Ellison said, making quick yet consequential eye contact with Wolfe. "After all, I did have a thorough check done on him as a favor to your husband."

"You did?" Eileen tilted her regal head and stared at Oliver.

Oliver cleared his throat, then smiled at his wife. "I thought it best to find out all we could about the man guarding Caroline. And I must say I was quite impressed with his résumé. Let me see if I can summarize in just a few succinct sentences. David Wolfe, thirty-six years old. No living relatives. Never married. No children. Dundee agent for less than two years. Before that a CIA agent who lived and worked in Europe, Asia and the Middle East for most of his career." Oliver looked boldly at Wolfe. "You have an exemplary record, Mr. Wolfe. You're almost too good to be true. But Ellison assured me that he dug quite deep and came up with nothing but the most impressive facts about you."

Caroline withdrew from Wolfe, just enough to put a foot of space between her body and his. She looked at him, but he avoided making eye contact with her. She had found his profession as a bodyguard upsetting, knowing it was fraught with violence. But now she had just learned that his former profession had involved violence on a grand scale and at an international level. There was no telling what he had been required to do as an agent for the CIA.

"Well, it's good to know that our dear Caroline is in such capable hands," Eileen said. "Now, let's put all this aside for the time being and see if we can't have an enjoyable evening."

Caroline stood rigidly, her spine stiff, her chin lifted. Her heartbeat drummed in her ears. She forced a smile and waited until Eileen and Oliver moved on to other guests and Mr. Penn had gone in search of his assistant. She had one question to ask Wolfe about a matter far more personal than anything to do with his former profession.

Caroline confronted him. "Why didn't you tell me that your name is David?"

Chapter 12

Wolfe's gut tightened painfully. Hell, why hadn't he told her his name was David? By not telling her, he'd made concealing it a big deal and given her reason to be suspicious. What if she asked him if he were *her David,* her mysterious benefactor? Don't be ridiculous, he told himself. Why should she think he was that David? She had no reason to connect him with the man who had watched over her and provided for her after Preston Shaw's death. His guilty conscience had made that giant leap, but Caroline's mind wouldn't.

"No one calls me David," he replied. "My clients, my associates and my acquaintances call me Wolfe."

"I understand," she said. "But that still doesn't explain why you purposefully neglected to mention that your given name is David."

"It wasn't purposeful," he told her, then when he saw the skepticism in her eyes, he amended his statement. "At least not at first. Then when you told me about your benefactor and what he meant to you and…things happened between us…" He lowered his voice to a mere whisper. "I didn't want you getting me and this other David mixed up in your mind and reacting to me because of the way you felt about him.''

Caroline didn't say anything, she simply stared at him for several minutes, as if judging the sincerity of his words. Finally she slipped her arm through his and said, ''I've changed my mind. I think I'd like to stay a while longer and maybe eat a bite. Why don't we take a look at the buffet? I'm sure we'll both find something we like. Eileen uses only the best caterers and always has a marvelous variety.''

Was that it? he wondered. Had Caroline finished interrogating him? Had his explanation actually satisfied her? If so, he was thankful. But a niggling little doubt chipped away inside his head and that bothered him. She had definitely let the matter drop too easily. So that meant something else was going on in Caroline's mind. But what?

Two hours later, without any more incidents with drunken Lotharios and no other personal revelations, Wolfe escorted Caroline back to the waiting Mercedes. He'd never been so glad to leave a party in his life. Jack Parker, who had been, as he always was, a big hit with everyone—especially the ladies—said his good-nights and followed them outside, without anyone being aware of the fact that he was the rear guard. Jack was smooth. The best of the best. After the three of them were safely ensconced in the car, Matt exited the circular drive. Within no time they were traveling on the Interstate 495 loop that circled D.C. and the outlying cities, heading toward the Annapolis exit.

After what seemed like an endless silence, Jack, who sat in the front seat with Matt, turned around and smiled. ''That turned out to be fairly harmless, didn't it? Other than Wolfe capturing the kissing bandit, everything went off without a hitch.''

''The kissing bandit?'' Matt asked.

''Some drunk took an instant liking to Miss Caroline and thought he'd steal a kiss,'' Jack explained.

"So that was the guy I saw you escorting outside." Matt chuckled. "I'm surprised Wolfe didn't shoot him. You did know that our Wolfe is an expert marksman, didn't you, Ms. McGuire?"

"Yes," Caroline said quietly. "I believe Fletch mentioned that being an expert with guns was one of Mr. Wolfe's credentials."

"We were lucky," Wolfe said, deliberately changing the subject. "Things could just as easily have gone the other way."

"I'm glad Matt and I were both free to come in and help you tonight," Jack said. "It just so happened that we'd both come off our last assignments when you called Ellen and asked for a couple of agents. Sure am happy I got to meet you, Miss Caroline. As a matter of fact, if you get tired of having a bodyguard as solemn and serious as Wolfe, then I'd be more than happy to—"

"Cut the crap, Parker," Wolfe said brusquely.

Jack rolled his eyes and clicked his tongue, his expression saying, *Uh-oh, what's up with him?*

Matt cleared his throat and glanced in the interior rearview mirror to steal a quick glimpse of the back seat's occupants.

Caroline giggled. "You'll have to excuse him. I've found that your David Wolfe is rather proprietary about me. Is he that way about all his clients?"

"David?" Matt glanced in the rearview mirror again, and when he made eye contact with Wolfe, he returned his focus to the road, pronto.

"Yeah, Matt, didn't you know that Wolfe actually has a given name?" Jack chuckled. "And Miss Caroline, I think Wolfe…can be forgiven for being proprietary where you're concerned. It'd be hard for a man not to be."

"Dammit, Parker, I thought I told you to—"

"So, Jack, what time is our flight out in the morning?" Matt asked.

"Nine-thirty," Jack said.

"I'll need y'all to cancel and take a later flight, possibly even stay over another day," Wolfe said. "I have a nine o'clock appointment in the morning with the president of Peacekeepers International. He's given me permission to go through all of Preston Shaw's old files to see if I can come up with any information that might help us."

"How did you manage that?" Matt asked. "I'd have thought those files were confidential."

"Boy, don't you know by now that the Dundee agency has a way of getting a look at whatever files they need to see?" Jack said. "It seems Sam Dundee's got connections with every government agency in the U.S., as well as organizations like the Peacekeepers."

"Wolfe didn't go through the Dundee agency," Caroline said. "He met Mr. Penn tonight and simply asked to see the files."

Jack and Matt said "hmm-mmm" simultaneously.

"While I'm in D.C. tomorrow morning, I want you two to stay at Caroline's studio with her," Wolfe said. "And you might as well wait until day after tomorrow to leave."

"Sure thing," Jack replied. "When you drop us off at the motel tonight, I'll cancel our morning flight to Atlanta and book us for something day after tomorrow. That is if you're sure you won't need us to hang around longer than that, just in case Miss Caroline wants to attend another fancy shindig."

"Your services won't be needed after tomorrow." Wolfe's voice lowered to a feral growl.

Gavin Robbins left Roz with the pudgy, bug-eyed federal judge who seemed smitten with her, despite the fact that Roz was young enough to be his granddaughter. But Roz didn't seem to mind. The silly woman was dazzled by all the important people she'd met here tonight. She'd probably be so grateful later that she would invite him to spend the night with her. Why else would he bother with a no-class, airheaded bimbo like Roz Turner, except for the sex? What he needed for a lifetime mate was a class act like Brooke Harper, a woman with brains and looks who was the heiress to a fortune. Unfortunately Fletcher Shaw had beat him to the punch there, but since his promotion at Peacekeepers, he'd been receiving more and more invitations to all the right parties. It was only a matter of time until he snagged himself a rich wife. He'd thought Caroline McGuire might be his ticket to respectability and the power he longed for, but they had been all wrong for each other. That ice queen needed to find herself a man like her cousin Lyle, somebody as harmless as a fly. Caroline wouldn't know what to do with a real man if she fell over one in the dark.

While the judge kept Roz entertained, Gavin decided to take the opportunity to say hello to his host and hostess, something he didn't want to do with Roz on his arm. He spotted Oliver Harper in the adjoining room, talking and laughing with General Bishop and Senator Howard.

"Gavin," a male voice behind him called.

He glanced over his shoulder and saw Ellison Penn's flunky, Barry Vanderpool, motioning to him. Ellison thought Barry was something special just because he'd graduated from one of those Ivy League schools and could speak half a dozen foreign languages. Well, Barry could enjoy being the big man's favorite while Penn held the top position at Peacekeepers. But sooner or later the old man would either die or retire, and when that day came, Gavin intended to take over. Then he'd ship Barry off somewhere overseas, never to return to D.C., and promote Mike Latham, his own handpicked man.

"What's up, Barry, my man?"

"I wanted to speak to you about something that concerns me, however…" Barry glanced nervously around, as if checking for eavesdroppers. "You know how highly I think of Mr. Penn."

"Yeah, sure, he's like a father to you."

"I wouldn't go that far, but yes, I do admire and respect

him greatly, as you know my father did when he worked with Mr. Penn.''

"Does this story have a point, Vanderpool? If it does, how about getting to it."

"My first allegiance is to Peacekeepers International. That's the only reason I'm mentioning this to you." Barry took a deep breath. "Mr. Penn told me that first thing in the morning I'm to put together all of Preston Shaw's files and search the computer system for anything that might be stored there."

Gavin knew that he was one of a handful of Peacekeepers agents who knew the truth about Preston Shaw's betrayal and about why he was killed and by whom. Was Ellison afraid that something in Preston's files might have been overlooked when they'd gone through them nearly fifteen years ago? Did he just want to make sure that nothing showed up now—that nothing came back to bite them in the butt?

"This thing with Caroline McGuire has gotten old Ellison curious, is that it?" Gavin asked. "Or did he seem unduly concerned about something in particular?"

"You don't understand," Barry said. "Mr. Penn asked for those files because he intends to allow Mr. Wolfe, Caroline McGuire's bodyguard, to go through them to see if he can find anything that will help him in his investigation. I must tell you, Gavin, that I find Mr. Penn's willingness to allow a *civilian* to view classified documents highly irregular."

Gavin nodded. "Yeah. Highly irregular." What was that wily old fox up to? Gavin wondered. Who had persuaded Ellison to give Wolfe a look at the files? Oliver Harper, maybe? Who else with that much power would be interested in Caroline? Surely Ellison planned to check the files himself before he allowed Wolfe to see them. Or was there something else going on? Just exactly who was this Mr. Wolfe? Was it possible that Ellison knew the man? Whatever was going on, he intended to find out. After all, his own future could very well depend on it.

Gavin grabbed Barry's hand and shook it soundly. "Thanks. You did the right thing coming to me. I'll talk to Ellison and find out what's going on. No need for you to worry."

No need for anybody to worry about anything. Gavin smiled. If Ellison Penn was keeping secrets—or giving away secrets—then he intended to catch the man in the act. Best way to find out what you need to know is try the direct approach first. Go straight to the horse's mouth.

When Gavin found Ellison Penn, he was deep in conversation with their hostess, a strikingly attractive woman, for someone of her age. But then Brooke's mama had probably gone under the plastic surgeon's knife more than once. Half the old biddies here tonight had gotten everything on their faces and bodies lifted, tucked or suctioned.

Ellison saw him approaching and gave him a don't-bother-me glare, but Gavin ignored the warning. As Gavin neared him, Ellison disengaged himself from the charming Mrs. Harper and headed Gavin off before he reached their hostess.

"What do you want, Robbins?" Ellison asked.

"I hear you're making Peacekeepers International files open to the public."

"You heard wrong," Ellison said.

"So Caroline McGuire's bodyguard won't be given access to all of Preston Shaw's old files?"

"Allowing Mr. Wolfe access to those files does not constitute opening them to the public."

"Does Mr. Wolfe have a top-priority clearance?" Gavin demanded.

Ellison hesitated. His square jaw tightened. Gavin would give a million bucks for a two-minute glimpse into the old man's steel-trap mind right now.

"As a matter of fact he does," Ellison said, with a hint of a smile playing at the corners of his mouth. "Just between us, Robbins, I've checked out Mr. Wolfe thoroughly. And

I've seen a rather interesting personal file on him. He's former CIA.''

Heat crept up the back of Gavin's neck and suffused his face. Damn! He should have known it would be something like this. Wolfe was former CIA, was he? Gavin found that fact very interesting. Interesting enough to do a little checking of his own. And soon.

Caroline placed her shoes on the rack, then unzipped her dress and removed it. Just as she hung the black silk creation on a pink satin padded hanger, she heard a soft rap on the outer door to her bedroom. Without looking, she knew it was Wolfe. Who else would it be but David Wolfe?

She had known several men named David over the years, and other than the fact that the name itself held a special meaning for her, none of those other Davids had meant any more to her than guys named John or Jim or Tom. But David Wolfe was different. From the moment she saw him standing at her front door, she had felt an odd sense of recognition, as if she already knew him. Of course that wasn't possible. She'd never met the man before in her life. But that feeling wouldn't leave her, no matter how hard she tried to reason it away. On a purely emotional level, her body and her heart had immediately responded to him.

There was no way on earth he could be her David. The very idea was ludicrous. So, why did it matter so much to her that his name was David? Why was she so upset that he had deliberately not told her his given name? Dope, she chided herself. He didn't tell you because of this very reason—because he knew you would put too much emphasis on the name. Even before you knew his name, you were practically trying to seduce him. And failing miserably, she reminded herself. Being a femme fatale was not her forte. She had never seduced a man…had never wanted to seduce a man.

Another knock, louder and a bit more forceful, brought

Caroline's wayward thoughts into focus. She grabbed a lavender silk robe off a hanger and put it on over her black bra and half-slip, then walked out of the huge closet. Wolfe stood on the threshold, leaning against the door frame. He had removed his tuxedo jacket and bow tie, undone the top three buttons on his white shirt and taken off his glasses. How was it possible for one man to look so good? she wondered. Large and lean and devastatingly male. With just enough muscles, just enough body hair, just the right amount of self-assurance without coming across as cocky.

"Is there something you want?" she asked, trying her level best to sound cool, in control and totally unemotional.

He looked her over, from head to toe, his gaze pausing a couple of times. Once on her face and then at her breasts, which swelled over the top of her low-cut, black lace bra. Feeling as if he had stripped her naked, Caroline pulled the lapels of her thin robe together and ran her hand around to the back of her waist, searching for the tie belt. When she realized it wasn't there, she simply held the lapels together with one hand.

He lifted his gaze to her face again. "Unless I find something in your stepfather's Peacekeepers files to give us a clue or we can figure out where else to look, I'd say the odds of our finding the object your key opens aren't very good. The Dundee lab hasn't been able to definitely identify the key from the photos we sent."

"And your point is?" She stayed where she was, keeping the width of her bedroom between them. Having learned the hard way how dangerous it was to get too close to an open flame, she had no intention of being burned by the same fire a second time. And for her, David Wolfe was definitely a blazing inferno.

"I suggest that you give it one more week and if nothing shows up, you—"

"I'm not giving up!"

"As long as you have that damn key in your possession,

your life will remain in danger." Wolfe stepped over the threshold. "All I'm suggesting is that you take yourself out of the equation. Give me the key and let me continue the search on my own, until I've exhausted every possibility."

"I thought you just implied that after looking through Preston's Peacekeepers files tomorrow we will have exhausted all known possibilities." She couldn't—wouldn't—let anyone have the key. And she had no intention of stopping the search. Not until she was convinced that it was a hopeless cause.

"Caroline, please be reasonable." He took several steps toward her, then stopped in the middle of her bedroom. "It's only a matter of time before another attempt is made on your life. Is finding the object that your key unlocks worth risking your life?"

She lifted the chain around her neck enough so that she could grasp the key. "This key will unlock the identity of the person who killed Preston and the reason he murdered him. I owe it to my stepfather to see that his killer is brought to justice."

"Damn!" Wolfe stormed across the room, grabbed her shoulders and shook her soundly. "It's clear from the way he was killed that Preston Shaw was executed. That probably means the man who killed him was simply following orders. He was simply a tool, just as the gun was, in Shaw's killing. The man who pulled the trigger on that gun is unimportant. There is no point in your tormenting yourself this way when you will never know the identity of that man."

Caroline's pulse raced, her heart beat wildly. She looked into David Wolfe's eyes—no longer cold, but deadly hot—and shivered with a combination of fear and longing. "How...do...you know? How can you be so sure? And you're wrong about his identity not being important. Even if he was only a trained assassin—"

Wolfe tightened his hold on her shoulders. "You have to

let this go. If we don't unearth something in another week, I want you to give me the key.''

When she opened her mouth to protest, he lifted his hand from her right shoulder and placed his index finger over her lips. ''What if I promise to find your David, a man who knew your stepfather, and give him the key? Would you trust him to do everything in his power to solve the mystery?''

She stared at him, dazed by his question. ''Do you think you could do that, find David—*my David?*''

''If it's the only way to get you out of danger, then yes, I'll find your David for you. He will probably refuse to meet with you, to allow you to know who he is, but my guess is that he will want to do whatever is necessary to help you.''

''All right,'' she said. ''We will give it another week, from tomorrow. And if by that time we still haven't found whatever the key unlocks, then you find my David.''

''And you'll let me give him the key.''

''Find him first and then I'll decide.''

His hands skimmed down, over her arms, across her elbows and to her wrists, which he manacled in his tight grasp. ''You shouldn't waste your life waiting for a man who's never going to be able to give you what you want and need. You have to stop fantasizing about this mysterious David of yours.''

''You couldn't possibly understand what it's been like for me.'' Try as she might, she could not break eye contact with David Wolfe. She felt as if he held her spellbound. ''To have someone in your life who has somehow become a part of you and yet you can never see him, never touch him, never talk to him. This man whom you say can never give me what I want and need has spent the past fourteen years doing just that. Don't you understand at all? David has been giving me what I needed, everything I needed, since I was twelve years old.

''The money for the best psychiatrist in the South. Money for nice clothes and piano lessons and swimming lessons and school trips. He paid for my senior trip. He put me through college. He arranged for my first job with the photographer in Richmond and he saw to it that I got a bank loan when I opened my own studio. He doesn't know that I'm aware of everything he's done for me, but I am. When Aunt Dixie died, she left me a letter explaining everything that David had done for me.''

Dixie Jennings had broken the promise she had made to him. No, actually, she hadn't. She had said in their one telephone conversation, ''I vow that as long as I live, I'll never tell Caroline how generous you've been to her.'' Apparently, she had not kept that truth hidden after her death.

''All right, so he was a man who took care of an old acquaintance's child. Good for him. But you're a woman now. A successful woman who doesn't need a keeper. You need a man who can love you and marry you and give you children. Your David can never be that man!''

''How can you be so sure?'' Tears collected in her eyes, swimming over the surface.

''Because I'm a man.'' His fingertip brushed across her upper lip as his thumb cradled her chin. ''Believe me, if your David could come to you and claim you for his own, he would have done it already. He can't come to you. Not now or ever.''

Wolfe released her abruptly. ''But just because he can't be a part of your life doesn't mean he won't help you in any way he can.''

Odd, Caroline thought, the way Wolfe spoke of a man he didn't know. But his words hadn't been a revelation to her. In her heart of hearts she already knew the truth—her David could never be a part of her life.

''Even though I understand that what you say is true, I'm not quite prepared to give up my fantasy,'' she said.

He nodded, a sad look in his eyes as he gazed at her. ''Just don't hang on to that fantasy too long, sweet Caroline, and let life pass you by.'' He turned and walked out of her room.

She waited, her breath caught in her throat, until he disappeared across the hall, then she rushed toward her bed, threw herself across it and let the tears fall. The cards that her David attached to her birthday and Christmas presents always read *My sweet Caroline.* Why of all the endearments in the world had David Wolfe chosen to use that one? Her heart was breaking into a million pieces and no one could help her, no one could heal her. Neither of her Davids. Neither of her guardian angels.

Chapter 13

Wolfe arrived at the Peacekeepers International building in Washington, D.C., at precisely ten minutes till nine and was passed through the security check on the ground level. He had left his Sig Sauer in the car. As the lone occupant of the private elevator to the top floor, which housed the president and vice president's suite of offices, he had a few minutes to prepare himself. It had been nearly three years since he'd been in this building, since Aidan Colbert had reported to Ellison Penn. He reminded himself that he must act as if, before today, he'd never been in this building or the suite of offices with which he was so familiar.

When the elevator doors opened, Barry Vanderpool, the boy wonder at Peacekeepers, was standing there like a sentinel. The twenty-four-year-old had piercing black eyes, shortly cropped auburn hair and a lean, hard body that was obvious despite the cover of a business suit.

"Good morning, Mr. Wolfe."

Barry possessed a military stance and carried himself like

a trained soldier. Wolfe halfway expected the man to salute him.

Wolfe nodded. "Good morning, Mr. Vanderpool."

"Mr. Penn is expecting you. If you will follow me, please."

As the highly efficient Barry escorted Wolfe down the hall, Gavin Robbins emerged from his office, coffee cup in hand. Barry paused and nodded to Gavin.

"I hope Ellison's secretary is giving you the red-carpet treatment," Gavin said as he followed them down the hall. "We here at Peacekeepers like to maintain a good working relationship with all the federal agencies, especially you CIA boys."

"Former CIA," Wolfe said. "I'm retired."

"Retired kind of young, didn't you?" Gavin asked.

Wolfe paused and glared at Gavin, but didn't respond to his question. Instead he continued walking, which prompted Barry to do the same. Wolfe sensed rather than saw Gavin stop and stare at his back. Barry knocked on the closed door to his superior's inner sanctum.

"Come in." Ellison's voice rang out clearly.

Barry opened the door, stepped back and indicated with a wave of his hand that Wolfe was to enter. Wolfe glanced across the room to where Ellison rose from his desk. When they met in the middle of the office, they shook hands, then Ellison closed the door.

"I have all of Preston Shaw's files on the table over there." He indicated with a nod. "I had Barry set things up for you this morning." He pointed to the portable table, stacked with file folders, computer disks and an assortment of boxes. "As you know, Preston was with Peacekeepers for a good many years."

"Is there anything on that table that we didn't go over with a fine-tooth comb nearly fifteen years ago?" Wolfe asked.

"You know there isn't," Ellison replied. "So, want to tell

me what this is all about, why you made such a production of requesting to see Preston's files?''

''Two reasons. First, it gave me a front for meeting with you without anyone asking questions. And second, I want to know exactly what you've been concealing about Preston Shaw. And don't try to tell me that you have no idea what I'm talking about.''

''You already know that we suspected Shaw of being involved with a secret organization of men who had a long-range plan to gain control of the government, partially by gradually putting their people in place in Congress and top-ranking government positions. Hell, they even infiltrated Peacekeepers International by recruiting Preston.''

''As you say, I already know all of this. What don't I know?''

''The proof we were given that Preston was the man who assassinated Senator Harwell might have been falsified.''

Wolfe suddenly felt cold, then went momentarily numb. As if something was draining the blood from his body. He stared at Ellison, his mind screaming accusations, but all he said was ''Are you telling me that I was given orders to execute an innocent man?''

''What I'm telling you is that there is a possibility the Loyalists Coalition wanted to get rid of Preston and planned to use us as the means by which to achieve that end, then changed their minds when they realized he had damning evidence against them. But somehow...by mistake, the information was sent to us, anyway. It doesn't mean that Preston didn't kill Senator Harwell.''

Wolfe closed his eyes momentarily, the impact of this new information dropping like a lead weight into his stomach. God in heaven, was it possible that Preston Shaw had been innocent? If that were true, how could he ever justify what he'd done? ''If there's any possibility that Preston Shaw was an innocent man—''

''You're thinking about Caroline, aren't you?''

"Yes."

"Dammit, man, if the truth comes out, you can't protect that girl." Ellison clamped his hand down on Wolfe's shoulder. "Believe me, Preston Shaw was guilty. Even if he didn't actually pull the trigger, he was part of the assassination plot. Once you find the evidence Preston hid away, there's a good chance we can blow the Loyalists Coalition sky-high and arrest their top men. When that happens, Caroline will learn the truth about her stepfather. There's no way to avoid it."

"She will be devastated," Wolfe said. "But it may never come to that. I'm beginning to have my doubts that if there is any such evidence, we'll ever find it. But regardless, I want Caroline taken out of the line of fire."

"And how do you intend to do that?" Ellison released his hold on Wolfe's shoulder and stared at him quizzically.

"She has agreed that if within a week's time we haven't found the object the key opens, she'll consider turning the key over to someone else and allow him to continue the search."

"Who?"

"The man she knows only as David. I've promised her that I'd find this man for her."

"Have you lost your mind? How the hell do you intend to find yourself? You can hardly present yourself to Caroline and tell her that you're the man who has acted as her benefactor all these years."

"I have no intention of introducing Caroline to *her* David. But if I can persuade her that he has been found and is willing to continue this search, in order to free her from danger, then we'll all get what we want. Caroline will be safe. And I can continue the search for the evidence against the Loyalists Coalition."

"You realize this plan of yours will work only if Caroline is convinced that her David is involved in this scheme. And you must know that if you tell her you've found him, she will insist on meeting him."

"And he will insist that their relationship remains the same, that he not reveal himself to her."

"Let's say your plan works and she gives you the key for you to give to her David and then you unearth what the key opens and find the evidence against the Loyalists Coalition. What will you tell Caroline?"

Wolfe looked squarely at Ellison. "I'll tell her everything, except about Preston Shaw's involvement with the Loyalists Coalition. I intend to let her continue believing her stepfather was a hero, that he died because he had gotten hold of evidence against some evil characters."

"In other words, you're going to lie to her."

"Yeah. I'm going to let her hold on to at least one fantasy while she's forced to let go of another."

"And what fantasy would that be—the one she'll be forced to let go of?" Ellison asked.

"The one about her benefactor David. It will be necessary to eliminate him. Once everything else is settled, she will receive a letter from his lawyer telling her of his death."

"You already had this planned, didn't you, before Caroline found the key? You were going to cut your ties to her."

Wolfe nodded. "I should have gotten her benefactor out of her life years ago, once she outgrew the need for him. But selfishly, I allowed things to continue as they were."

"Satisfy an old man's curiosity…" Ellison smiled, but there was a rather sad, lonely look in his eyes. "Is she all that you thought she was, all you had hoped she would be?"

Quiet fell on the office. A hushed stillness. Wolfe breathed softly. In and out, in and out. "Yes," he replied. "All that and more."

"She need never know who you really are," Ellison said. "You could be with her, if that's what you want."

If that's what he wanted! As emotional pain radiated through him, Wolfe shut his eyes, refusing to acknowledge that there was even a glimmer of hope. "I would know the truth—that I killed Preston Shaw—and eventually the lie standing between Caroline and me would destroy me. No, it's better this way.''

''Very well.'' Preston pointed to the table piled high with Preston Shaw's files. ''You'd better spend the morning looking through that mess, just to continue the farce. And in a week's time, if you can persuade Caroline to go along with your plan, we can use some excuse concerning your rechecking those files to arrange another meeting.''

Wolfe nodded agreement, then pulled out a chair and sat at the desk. During the next couple of hours, he would work his way through these files, then he would call Jack Parker and let him know it would be this evening before he could make it back to Caroline's St. Michaels studio. He had several errands to run, certain arrangements to be made and a few decisions to make. Glancing down at the date displayed on his wristwatch, he was reminded of what day it was today. This would be his one and only chance to spend Caroline's birthday with her. Was he wrong to want to make it a memorable event?

Despite her concern about what information Wolfe might have uncovered when he went through Preston's files today, Caroline finished the last photo shoot of the day feeling pleased with the photographs she'd taken. Lindsey Chapman, a June bride-to-be, had driven in from Wilmington with her groom. Seeing the young couple so much in love and so totally devoted to each other had evoked mixed emotions within Caroline. Joy for the couple and a reaffirmation that true love existed. But also a sense of sadness and perhaps a little jealousy because she doubted she would ever share that kind of happiness with someone.

''Weren't they absolutely disgusting,'' Roz said. ''And God, don't you envy them.''

Caroline laughed, thankful for Roz's sense of humor. Somehow her dear friend always knew the right thing to say to lighten a dark mood.

"Do you think either of us will ever be that lucky?" Caroline flopped down in the padded swivel chair, lifted her feet and propped them on her desk.

"You, maybe," Roz said. "If you'll ever quit mooning over that phantom benefactor of yours and start taking notice of what's right under your nose."

"Meaning?"

"Meaning that six-foot-two hottie who's living in your house." Roz opened the compact minifridge sitting on a corner table, retrieved a couple of bottles of lemon-flavored iced tea and tossed one to Caroline.

"I don't think Wolfe is the type for long-term commitments." Caroline twisted off the bottle cap, shot it into the wastebasket by her desk and lifted the refreshing drink to her lips.

"My theory is that no man is prepared for marriage, not until the right woman comes along and he realizes that he can't live without her." Roz uncapped her drink, tossed the lid at the wastebasket, missed by a couple of inches, then shrugged and took a big swig of tea.

Jack Parker suddenly appeared in the open doorway, a friendly good-old-boy smile on his face and a small package in his hand. "Pardon me, ladies, but this little item just arrived special delivery for Miss Caroline."

Caroline eyed the small parcel that Jack laid on her desk, which she could tell had been opened and hastily rewrapped. From the untidy appearance of the shiny paper and the lopsided bow, she suspected that neither Jack nor Matt was adept at giftwrapping. When she glanced up at Jack, he grinned.

"Sorry about not getting it put back together all pretty like, but I did the best I could," he said.

"You opened Caroline's package?" Roz asked.

"Had to, ma'am," Jack explained. "Never know what might have been in there. Could have been something dangerous."

"Oh, stupid me." Roz grimaced. "I keep forgetting. So, I take it the package is safe."

"Yes, ma'am."

"Go on. Open it," Roz said. "I'm curious to see who's sending you presents and it's not even Christmas."

"No, it's not Christmas," Caroline said. "But it is my birthday. And I'm pretty sure I know who sent this gift."

"Damn, why didn't you remind me it was your birthday?" Roz whined, and gave Caroline an apologetic look. "What kind of friend am I to forget your birthday."

"It's okay, really." As Caroline reached for the gift, she caught a conspiratorial glance exchanged between Roz and Jack and wondered what it was all about. Knowing Roz, she was simply flirting with the Dundee agent. "When this whole mess about Preston's hidden key is resolved and I can resume my normal life, we'll celebrate. You and Lyle, Brooke and Fletch and I. We'll go out somewhere really nice and make a night of it."

"Excuse me, Miss Caroline," Jack said.

"Yes?"

"Wolfe just called about five minutes ago and said he's only a few miles from here. So I just wanted to say goodbye and good luck, since Matt and I'll be heading to the motel as soon as Wolfe gets here."

"Thank you, Jack." She had been waiting all day for word from Wolfe, but he hadn't bothered speaking to her personally either time he'd called his co-agent. He'd simply informed Jack Parker that business was keeping him in D.C. longer than expected.

"I'll be right outside, if you need me," Jack said. "Matt's locking up out there now that Kirsten and Sandy have left for the day." Jack closed the door behind him.

"Texas Jack there is going to make some woman mighty happy one of these days." Roz sighed dramatically. "Actually, he's probably already made quite a few women mighty happy." She giggled. "I was just thinking about the lucky girl who gets him for keeps." Roz plopped down on the edge of the desk and eyed the poorly rewrapped gift. "So, are you going to open it or not?"

Caroline knew before opening the gift or reading the card, which would be lying inside, that the birthday present was from David. Her David. Not once since her thirteenth birthday had he forgotten. With nervous fingers she removed the bow, untied the ribbon and pulled apart the white wrapping paper to reveal a black velvet jeweler's box. Since her twenty-first birthday, he had sent jewelry as a gift. She eased back the lid to reveal a stunning pearl-and-diamond bracelet. Roz let out a long, low whistle. There sitting atop the present was the familiar white card. She lifted it and read the brief message. *Happy birthday, my sweet Caroline.* And below in the bold, flowing script was his signature. *David.*

"I'll say one thing for this guy, he's no cheapskate."

Caroline lifted the bracelet from its velvet bed, draped it around her wrist and fastened the catch. "It matches the other diamond and pearl jewelry he's already given me."

"You've never worn all of them, have you? I'm sure I would have remembered seeing them if you had."

"I've considered selling them and giving the money to charity," Caroline said. "You know, except for an occasional event that Fletch or Brooke invite me to attend, I'm not much of a social butterfly. And I have so many lovely pieces of jewelry, most of them gifts from David, that I hardly need them all."

Roz hopped up, came around the side of the desk and gave Caroline a hug. "Happy birthday, hon. I'll remind Lyle when I get over to the church that today's your birthday. I'm sure he's just so busy with getting things together for this weekend's church yard sale that he let it slip his mind."

"I'm sure that's it. And Roz, thanks again for taking my place and meeting my obligations at the church until—"

"Don't think another thing about it," Roz assured her. "You may find this hard to believe, but I'm actually enjoying myself. And the rev and I haven't had one single knock-down-drag-out. At least not yet.''

"I'm glad to hear it. Lyle is a great guy. But I have a feeling you already know that."

Roz grinned. "Hmm-mmm. Maybe."

Caroline waved goodbye. Heading out, Roz almost collided with Wolfe when she opened the office door.

"Sorry," Wolfe said. "Are you leaving for the day?"

"I'm on my way over to the church to do Caroline's good deeds for her." Roz winked at Wolfe.

"That's an interesting idea," he said. "Good deeds by proxy."

He entered the office as soon as Roz left. Caroline immediately noticed that he had changed clothes, that he wasn't wearing the charcoal pin-striped suit he'd left her house in this morning. Instead he was now dressed more casually in navy-blue slacks and a white cotton shirt, the top two buttons undone. But the ever present hip holster remained. Caroline rose to her feet slowly and confronted him.

"Did you find anything in Preston's Peacekeepers files?" she asked.

"Yes and no."

"Can't you be more specific?"

"No information that will help us find the object the key opens," he said. "But some information about why your stepfather was executed."

She tensed. Nausea stirred in her stomach. "He *was* executed, wasn't he?"

"Yes. It seems that he definitely had come into possession of some critical information about a group known as the Loyalists Coalition, comprised of unidentified powerful men who posed a threat to our government. These men were probably responsible for Preston Shaw's murder."

"And these men who had Preston executed don't want me to find the evidence against them and that's why they've been trying to kill me."

"Ellison Penn is as interested as we are in finding that evidence," Wolfe said. "He's pledged to do whatever he can to assist me, including contacting your benefactor's lawyer and asking for his help."

"Mr. Penn knows my David, doesn't he?" She had suspected for years that her David was somehow connected to Peacekeepers International, and that her stepfather's boss had always known the identity of her benefactor. And she was just as certain that had she ever asked him about David, Mr. Penn would have denied knowing him.

"We could end this nightmare for you right now, Caroline. Give me the key and then we'll let it be known that you no longer have the key and have given up the search, but that the Peacekeepers are continuing the investigation."

Caroline stroked the chain at her neck and considered her options. "You said you'd give us another week working on this together. I want that week."

"What difference do you think another week will make?"

"If that's true, then you shouldn't have a problem keeping your promise to me, should you?"

Shaking his head, he huffed loudly. "All right. One week."

There, that was settled. One week wasn't long, but if her prayers were answered, a week would be long enough. Enough time to find what the key unlocked. Enough time to come to terms with her feelings about David Wolfe. "Okay, I'm ready to go home and be locked in for the night." What a way for a woman to spend her twenty-seventh birthday, Caroline thought. No dinner with friends. No birthday cake. No presents. No cards. Nothing special. Just another day.

She lifted her wrist and stroked the pearl-and-diamond bracelet. David hadn't forgotten. He never forgot. But what good was an expensive gift when all she truly wanted was to be with her David, to share just one of her birthdays with him?

"New bracelet?" Wolfe asked.

"Yes. A present from my benefactor."

"A birthday gift."

"Yes, but how did you—"

"Your birth date is listed in the file I have on you."

"Of course."

"If you're ready…" He motioned to the door.

She rose from behind the desk, followed him and turned the light off in the office before closing the door. When he led her toward studio one, which she used for all her adult photography, she tugged on his arm.

"I thought we were going home," she said.

"Later."

"What do you mean, 'later'?"

"I have something I want to show you in the studio," he said. "It's something I think you'll like. So just humor me, okay?"

"Would you mind telling me what's going on?"

He took her hand, led her down the hall and straight to studio one. He placed her in front of him, reached around her to open the door, then gave her a gentle shove over the threshold. The moment she entered the studio, she gasped.

Chapter 14

Caroline could not believe her eyes. The studio had been transformed into a magical, romantic scene, complete with soft lighting, mellow jazz and a table set for two. The tune—"Sorry Seems to Be the Hardest Word"—coming from some unknown source was from a CD of hers. The mournful wail of the saxophone wrapped around her, a musical lover's caress. Hundreds of white balloons filled the room. Some floated across the ceiling like bubbly clouds. Others danced around over the floor, covering every inch of space like an airy, undulating carpet. Huge white candles had been strategically placed on two food-laden tables behind the small center table that had been set with china and crystal for two. Cream-white roses in spiraling vases graced all three tables.

"What is all of this?" Caroline asked.

"Do you like your surprise?"

She whipped around and stared at him. The look on his face sent shivers along her nerves. This was a man intent upon pleasing her. She saw it in his eyes, sensed it as surely as if he had spoken the words aloud...*I want everything to be perfect for you.* But why? Why this man and why this moment? He had to know that he was the wrong David to fulfill her fantasies.

"It's incredible," she replied. "How…when…? Is this the reason you've been gone all afternoon?"

He nodded. "I had some help," he confessed. "From Roz and Kirsten and Sandy, as well as Matt and Jack. The girls helped me set things up in here while Roz kept you in your office. And Matt and Jack haven't actually left. They're outside, keeping an eye on the place. This is why I asked them to stay over until morning."

"Was this your idea or—"

"Totally my idea," he said. "I knew it was your birthday, and since you're confined to quarters, so to speak, I decided you deserved something more than a birthday cake."

"I can't believe this." She glided through the balloons, which separated and floated around in every direction. "I would never have dreamed that you could come up with something this sentimental and romantic." She whirled around and around, letting the balloons dance at her feet as she moved to the sensuous rhythm of the music.

"Then you like it?" he asked.

"Like it?" She stopped twirling and smiled at him. "I love it."

Wolfe closed the door behind him, then stood in place, his arms crossed over his chest, and watched Caroline McGuire savor the fantasy world he had created for her. How many times had he longed to do something special for her? How often had he envisioned a moment like this? If it was wrong of him to want this particular birthday to be memorable, then God forgive him. But this would be the one and only birthday he would ever spend with her. He intended to do everything in his power to make the night unforgettable for both of them. Soon the Fates would condemn him to hell, into a world without Caroline. Damned for past sins. Unforgiven.

She reached up and pulled the scarf holding her ponytail

in place and let the small square of lavender silk sail down to disappear in the ocean of balloons at her bare feet. Her hair fell around her shoulders, strands of shimmery onyx that beckoned him to run his fingers through them, to grasp her head and hold her face to his. He had long ago memorized the features of her beautiful face from having spent hours gazing at photographs of her. But no picture could capture the vibrant loveliness of this woman. She swayed to the music, her green-and-lavender floral skirt whirling around her calves.

Caroline held out her hand. He walked across the room, removed his hip holster and laid it on a side table, then went to her. Without a word being exchanged, he took her into his arms. Their bodies came together, touching tenderly, undemanding and totally at ease, as if they had danced together countless times. In tune. Perfectly matched. A man and a woman. A night filled with promise. Unhurried. As if each moment had no beginning and no end.

Wolfe knew he had no right to expect anything beyond giving Caroline pleasure. And that would be enough. It had to be enough! A part of him longed to tell her that he was her David, the man she had turned into a larger-than-life hero that no mortal man could possibly live up to. But with that sort of revelation would come questions that he could never answer, inquiries into a past he must keep secret from her. He had one more week with her and then he would disappear from her life and her David would also cease to exist. It was the only way—for him and for her. She could never have a normal life as long as she clung to the impossible hope that someday her David would become a part of her world.

Caroline's body heat invaded his skin, seeped beneath the surface to warm his muscles and bones and set afire the desire he had been keeping under control. She tilted her head and gazed up at him. A dreamy smile opened her mouth and curved her soft lips. How could he resist the temptation to sample such sweetness? He brushed his lips over hers. She shivered ever so slightly, an almost indiscernible quiver that shook him as much as if a volcano had exploded inside her. He was so in tune to her body, so in sync with every little nuance, every varying shade of Caroline McGuire. Wolfe cursed himself for the doomed fool that he was. She had not been the only one with a fantasy—an unrealistic dream—as equally impossible and with as little hope of existing in reality as his was.

Like her, he had been alone for most of his life, having lost his entire family by the age of thirteen. Although he had pretended to be strong and fearless, to be self-contained, needing no one, there had been a hunger inside him, a deep, human longing to have something—someone—of his own. For the past fourteen and a half years, he had allowed Caroline to become that someone—the center of his universe. From a safe distance he had watched her grow from a child into a woman and his feelings for her had changed just as gradually. In the beginning he had cared for her as a big brother, a generous friend and a man eaten alive by guilt. And then one day he realized that his thoughts about Caroline were the thoughts a man entertained about a desirable woman. Somewhere along the way she had, in his mind and heart, ceased to be his ward and had become his woman.

Always separated. A safe distance between them. It was easy being infatuated with a phantom lover, one who could never reject you, never disappoint you, never leave you. His sexual appetite had been appeased by numerous women, but not a one of them had taken anything from him because he'd given them nothing beyond the moment, nothing except sex. He had risked nothing. Expected nothing. But Caroline was different. She meant more to him than he dared to admit, even to himself.

"This evening isn't real, is it?" she asked as she lifted her hand to the nape of his neck.

Her question brought him to the present, to this moment in time, with Caroline secure and happy in the safety of his arms. "No, this evening isn't real. It's a birthday present that ends at midnight."

She slowed her movements but stayed in his arms. Looking straight at him, a melancholy wistfulness in her eyes, she whispered, "I care about you. I care too much. But you must know that I don't dare love you. And without loving you, I can't—"

He pressed his hand over her mouth, ending her pronouncement, then when she quieted and simply stared at him, he caressed her face. "My sweet Caroline, you're very wise not to throw away your love on me. Save it for a man worthy of you. But don't wait for your David."

She sighed and her fragile smile vanished. "Did you know that's what he calls me, what he's always called me? My sweet Caroline."

Wolfe hadn't realized how easily those words rolled off his tongue. How many times had he referred to her as sweet Caroline? "Then he and I are in agreement. I think that any man who truly knew you couldn't think of you in any other way. You are so very sweet."

"And just what does that mean?" she asked.

He released her, then cradled her face with his hands. "You possess a loveliness that goes beyond the physical. You have a kind heart and a generous spirit. And although you've experienced tragedies and traumas that would have destroyed a lesser person, you came through it all still possessing a goodness I can't even begin to understand."

"Wolfe…David…why can't you be—"

Her words were like a knife stabbed into his heart. How odd that he should be competing against himself, that he was his only rival for Caroline's affection.

"I'm so sorry," she said. "You've gone to so much trouble to make everything wonderful for me, and instead of being grateful, I tell you that I wish you were another man."

She tried to turn from him, but he grabbed her wrist and

jerked her up against him. Their gazes locked. Their heated breaths mingled.

"It's all right," he told her, his voice thick with passion and deceptively soft. He wanted to tell her that all Davids were the same in the dark, but wisely didn't make a joke of the matter. In his case, it was true. He *was* her David. "You may think you love him, but you want me, don't you, Caroline? Even if you feel that you're being unfaithful, you can't help wanting me. Loving a phantom is so much safer than caring about a flesh-and-blood man, isn't it?" He could tell her that he knew only too well the truth of his words. Hadn't he spent years, just as she had, investing all his deepest emotions into a relationship that was nothing more than smoke and mirrors? An illusion of love.

"You're the one who told me that you and I are all wrong for each other," she said.

"We are." *For many reasons, most of which you can never know.*

"Sometimes we want what is bad for us, don't we?" She shut her eyes, breaking the visual link that bound them. "I've never understood that before, not until I met you. I thought desire was a part of love and that love was a simple thing. I believed that you love and are loved in return and the two of you make a lifelong commitment and then..."

"In the best of all possible worlds, that's true."

"But not in our world. Not for you and me. We're both afraid of love, aren't we?"

He didn't respond verbally. There was no need. He saw the acceptance and the disillusionment in her eyes. God help him, he was destroying her dreams. When she eased out of his arms and walked away from him, he did not try to stop her. Had he made a mistake in trying to give them both a moment out of time, one evening that could belong to them alone, that nothing and no one could ever take from them? Had he prepared this surprise more for himself than for her, knowing that he was the one who would need the memory to cling to, not Caroline? She would have a future, free from him and from her David. Eventually she would fall in love and marry and have children. But what would he have? A lifetime alone.

Caroline had to put some distance between them, had to escape from the seduction of his strong arms and hypnotic gaze. It would be so easy to love this man and so very difficult to get over him once he left her. And he would leave her, return to the life he'd had before he had taken the job as her bodyguard. She knew that he wanted her... sexually...just as she wanted him. She couldn't even begin to explain the strange fascination he held for her. Why, after all these years and all the men who had come in and out of her life, was she drawn to this one man? David. But not *her* David. If she hadn't been attracted to him when she'd known him only as Wolfe, she would have suspected that his name alone had seduced her, that she had allowed herself to confuse the two men in her mind. But she had experienced that inexplicable pull, that irrefutable chemistry the moment she met him.

If Wolfe was right—that she would never meet her David, would never be allowed to see him, touch him, love him— then would it be so wrong to experience passion with another? With this David, whom she could see and touch and...love.

How could she show him the way she felt? How did she tell him that she wanted him, but was afraid that if she gave herself to him physically, she would fall in love with him? *You're already halfway in love with him as it is,* an inner voice whispered. But once they became lovers, there would be no going back, no return to the safety of loving her David. Was she prepared to relinquish her dream for reality? Would a few days in David Wolfe's arms, becoming his woman on a temporary basis be worth what she would have to give up?

Yes. Yes. Yes!

Having made her decision, Caroline searched the shelves

that held some of her photography equipment. She knew of one way—a way very personal to her—that she could seduce David Wolfe. Glancing over the variety of cameras at her disposal, she quickly chose her Rollei, one of her favorites, which was easy to operate, thus giving her flexibility and creative control. Even in candlelight, she could count on this camera to capture more than the eye could behold. Before Wolfe became aware of the fact that he was her subject, she aimed and shot, then aimed again, repeating the process several times.

He faced her. Boldly. Surprised by her actions. For several minutes, he stood before her. Unmoving. He was a magnificent man and the camera loved him. The high cheekbones. The slanted shape of his eyes. The hard, chiseled imperfection of his features. The wide shoulders encased in a loose white shirt. The sleek, fluid lines of a superbly honed physique.

Long after he was gone, she would have these photographs to remind her of this special man.

Suddenly she realized that he was coming toward her, an agitated expression on his face. Without hesitation she continued taking pictures. Hurriedly. Furiously. Moving around the studio, keeping just out of his reach. She knew he intended to stop her. When he finally captured her, he manacled her wrist and jerked the camera out of her hand. She gasped aloud the moment he grabbed her by the waist.

"Why did you do that?" she asked. "I took those shots for me. I promise that no one else will ever see them. Please..." She reached down to where he held the Rollei at his side.

He held the camera just out of her reach. "You were trying to make love to me with the camera, weren't you?" He circled her waist and pulled her close, then lowered his head. "As sensual as we both found the experience, it's a poor substitute for the real thing."

She looked up, thinking he was going to kiss her. Hoping

he would. Afraid he would. But instead his tongue touched
her throat. Light. Moist. A faint, tingling caress that moved
down her throat and onto the flesh exposed by the V-neck of
her billowing lavender blouse. When he released his hold
around her waist, she didn't move, didn't pull away. He
tugged on her blouse until he loosened it from beneath the
waistband of her skirt, then he reached underneath, his big
hand flattening across her midriff. She sucked in her breath.
She quivered as her nipples tightened. He undid the front
snap of her bra, pulled back the cups and freed her breasts,
still covered by her blouse.

His mouth opened over one breast and his lips encompassed her nipple through the thin barrier of cloth. When he
sucked, she leaned her head back as if it were too heavy for
her neck to hold upright. He moved to the other breast, giving
it equal attention. Caroline began unraveling, coils of pleasure spiraling, swirling inside her like wind-tossed streamers.
While she was in the throes of passion, consumed by pure
sexual hunger, Wolfe released her. She lifted her head, her
gaze searching for him. He stood several feet away, the
Rollei in his hand, the lens pointed at her.

"It's my turn," he said. "To make love to you."

She understood his meaning. She would be his subject.
The object of his desire. She looked at him, knowing that all
she was feeling in that moment showed plainly in her eyes.
He snapped the first shot. She began moving, swaying this
way and that, to the soft, jazzy beat of the music. He took
picture after picture, his actions frenzied. She had never felt
so alive. And for the first time in her life she knew she was
sexy and seductive.

She lifted her hair in her hands and then let it cascade
through her fingers. She turned her back to him and removed
her blouse and bra, then glanced over her shoulder. He captured that seductive pose on film, exploring the fantasy and
the pure sexuality of the moment. A clutching pressure built
between her thighs, a prelude of longing so intense that it

overwhelmed her. She licked her lips, moistening them, and looked at David, knowing he would recognize the invitation.

He came toward her, then stopped to lay the camera on the table where their uneaten food awaited them. She held her breath, anticipating what was to come. He eased up behind her and wrapped his arms around her. She leaned her head back to rest on his chest. He lowered his head and placed his cheek against hers. She curved her arms backward so that her hands rested on his hips.

All rational thought ceased to exist for Caroline. She gave herself over completely to the moment and to the man who held her captive. When his hands lifted to cup and then cover her breasts, she rubbed her hips seductively against his erection. Wanton, alive with a desire unequaled by any previous experience, she surrendered and yet simultaneously conquered.

Wolfe turned her to him and took her mouth in a kiss of unleashed passion, as if a dam of control had burst free inside him. She flung her arms around his neck and participated in the kiss with equal abandon. He unzipped her skirt and pulled it down her hips. It fell to her feet, draping over the nearby balloons like a voluminous tent atop quivering white sand dunes. She clung to him, totally nude except for her lavender satin panties.

He touched her. Everywhere. Her face. Her hair. Her throat. His hands skimmed her arms, her waist, her hips and down her legs. He knelt before her and buried his face against her belly. She threaded her fingers through his thick golden hair and held him to her, glorying in his adoration. He made her feel as if she were the most precious thing on earth to him.

When he hooked his forefingers under the elastic of her panties, she waited, breathlessly, for him to remove the last barrier, the last fragment of cloth that covered her. The panties slid over her hips and down her legs. She lifted one foot and then the other. He grabbed the panties and tossed them aside. His mouth touched her intimately, kissing her, arousing her unbearably. As he spread her legs farther apart, she gripped his shoulders to balance herself and within moments succumbed to the passion of his marauding lips and tongue. He held her in place, his palms on her buttocks, as he brought her to the edge of release.

Caroline wanted the fulfillment desperately. Her body yearned for him to take her that final step into completion. "Please, David, please," she whispered, calling him by his given name in her passion.

And he did please her. The intensity of her climax bolted her knees and shook her from head to toe. While the rippling aftershocks trembled through her, Wolfe swept her up into his arms and carried her across the room, sending balloons flying in every direction as he strode through their midst. He shoved open the door to the nearest dressing room and eased her down on a white damask sofa, then stripped off his shirt and tossed it to the floor.

Caroline reached up, her hands trembling as she unbuckled his belt and unzipped his slacks. He removed his clothes and stood there, hovering over her, gloriously, magnificently naked. Only the candlelight from the studio illuminated the dark dressing room, so her view of him was shadowed, but she could see the scars that marred his big body. A crisscross of scar tissue bisected his brown chest hair in several places and zigzagged atop his thighs.

"Be very sure this is what you want," he said, his voice a hoarse, heavy growl. "We have no future together. This will change nothing between us."

Caroline lifted her right arm and reached up with her left hand to undo the closure on her new diamond-and-pearl bracelet. When she removed the valuable piece of jewelry, she dropped it to the floor atop the small lambswool rug beside the sofa. Not without some regrets, she set aside the past, disengaging herself from a dream that she had outgrown.

She held open her arms to Wolfe, beckoning him to come to her. She would accept him on his terms, take whatever he offered. But he was wrong if he thought this would change nothing between them.

Wolfe knelt, dove his hand into the pocket of his discarded slacks and removed his billfold. She watched, sighing when she saw him remove the wrapped condom. Even in this, in a moment of supreme passion, he was protecting her. She gazed at him. He was big and savage-looking and overwhelmingly male. She knew a moment of panic, of uncertainty that she could accommodate him fully, but when his body covered hers, she surrendered to her own needs.

"I don't want to hurt you," he whispered against her ear, his breathing ragged, perspiration dotting his brow.

"I want you so. Make love to me..." *David. My David.*

She felt his fingers touching her between her legs, dipping inside and spreading the moisture he found. Then he slid his hands beneath her and lifted her to meet him. His first thrust was shallow, entering her with only the tip of his sex. Clinging to his shoulders, she lifted her legs, urging him to delve deeper. He took her by slow degrees, careful to allow her time to accommodate the length and width of him. When he encountered her virginal barrier, he paused, but she would have none of it. She lifted her hips higher, taking him deeper into her body as she wrapped her legs around his hips. The moment he broke through, she gasped, then held on to him, whimpering his name. As if he could hold back no longer, he took her completely, plunging himself fully into her.

Tears trickled from the corners of her eyes. He kissed them away. "I've wanted you so much...for so long...."

Their bodies moved together in perfect unison. Unparalleled passion. Indescribable pleasure. An earth-shattering loving. Caroline could not believe that her body was capable of a second climax so quickly following the first or that the second would surpass the first. She fell apart, crying, moaning, her body trembling only moments before his body tensed and his face contorted into an expression of pain. And then an animalistic moan erupted from deep in his chest when he came. Spasms rocketed through him as her body drained the last ounce of strength from his. He kissed her, devouring her with a passion that a thousand climaxes could never appease.

"Mine," he murmured. "My sweet Caroline."

Chapter 15

Lying beside Caroline, Wolfe watched her while she slept. He intended to savor every minute with her and store up enough memories to last a lifetime. He had disregarded doing the decent, honorable thing and done the unforgivable. But what man, under the same circumstances, could have denied himself the thing he wanted most in this world? She would never know his deep, dark secret. He promised her that—a solemn, heartfelt vow. Even Caroline, as loving and understanding as she was, would not be able to forgive Aidan Colbert's sins. And if it turned out that Preston Shaw had been executed because of falsified evidence…! But now was not the time for soul-searching, for dredging up guilt and adding more to his already overburdened conscience. He would not waste these precious days he'd been given with Caroline. They were a gift from the gods, one he didn't deserve, but clung to tenaciously and with gratitude.

Just being near her aroused him. Her sweet, feminine smell. Her soft, vulnerable beauty. The steady rise and fall of her full, round breasts only half-covered by the sheet. He leaned over and kissed her forehead. Her eyelids fluttered. He kissed each cheek and brushed his lips over hers. She wriggled against him and sighed.

He couldn't justify what he'd done with her, what he intended doing again, as often as possible. But at this point, he was beyond caring. It wasn't as if he planned to stay in her life, become a permanent fixture. One week. One damn week—that's all he was asking for. After that, he would free her and free himself. He had no choice. To ask for more would mean taking a huge risk—a risk that she would discover the truth about him. Not only that he was her benefactor, but that he was Aidan Colbert, the Peacekeepers agent who had killed her stepfather.

Wolfe lifted the sheet, then slipped his hand between her thighs, palming her mound as his fingers curled over her tender flesh. Gasping, Caroline opened her eyes and looked up at him.

"How sore are you?" he asked, his voice heavy with desire.

Smiling, she lifted her hand to clamp the back of his neck, then dragged his mouth down to hers. "Not terribly sore," she said against his lips. "I think my body can survive making love one more time. But after this, you might have to let me recuperate for the rest of the day." She kissed him, not like a lady, but like a woman. Wet and hot. Tongue thrusting, body arching.

"Don't you know that for more of your sweet loving, I'd promise you anything…give you anything?" His heartbeat picked up speed as he fondled her, dipping a couple of fingers into the moisture that told him how ready she was for what he wanted.

"I understand." She closed her thighs, trapping his hand between them, and rubbed her body sensuously against his. "Nothing should be this good…this wonderful…."

Wolfe leaned over and lifted a condom off the nightstand. This was his last one. He always kept one in his wallet, which he had used when they'd made love at the studio. When he was on an assignment there was no need for a supply of condoms, so he hadn't packed any. By the time he and Caroline had left the studio, he realized there wouldn't be a store open where he could purchase more, so he'd been forced to do something he hadn't done since he was a green kid. He'd borrowed condoms from another guy. He'd figured that a ladies' man like Jack Parker would be prepared at all times, on an assignment or not. And he had to give Jack credit, the man hadn't made one rude comment. He had simply handed over three condoms without saying a word.

After preparing himself, David swooped Caroline up and over him, knocking the sheet to their feet as he positioned her on top of him. She straddled his hips. He bucked upward, seeking entrance. Because of her lack of experience, the three previous times he had been the aggressor, but this time he wanted her to set the pace, to take charge.

"Think you can handle me?" he asked.

"Ooh...ooh." The taunting sound came through her puckered lips as she lifted herself up on her knees, ran her hand between their bodies and circled his erection. "I'm willing to try really hard. Later, you can let me know how I did." A tantalizing, bewitching smile curved her lips.

She brought him to her, then positioned herself and took him into her body. Gradually. Inch by excruciating inch. Why the hell didn't she end this torment and take all of him? Now! Before he died from the tension building inside him? But he had taught her well, the art of slow torture. It took every ounce of his willpower not to thrust up and into her.

As her sheath enveloped him, she slid her legs along the side of his body until they were joined completely from their hips down, then she pressed her breasts against his chest and lay there. Still. Perfectly still. Their heartbeats synchronized. Their breathing set to the same rhythm. His sex instinctively quivered inside her, begging for relief.

"I'm warning you, sweetheart," he said. "Don't make me wait too long."

"Is teasing the beast dangerous?" She lifted herself up, gliding over him, withdrawing until her body clutched only the head of his sex. "Will he devour me?"

David grabbed her by the hips and plunged her down so that she was forced to accept all of him. She cried out when he filled her completely, stretching her to the limit. Her body could not resist the urgent pressure, the throbbing need that prompted her to move. Up and down. Appeasing the beast within him...and discovering her own untamed animal nature. Once unleashed, the primitive woman within her took control. While she rode him, hard and fast, he mouthed her breasts. Sucking, nipping, licking. Her sheath tightened around him and she keened, softly at first, then louder and louder until she was all but screaming when she came. The force of her release triggered his and within seconds of her climax, he shuddered with completion. Needing nothing more. Totally fulfilled.

"Yeah, thanks, Art," Gavin Robbins said. "Let me know if you find out anything else."

He hung up the telephone, then slammed his fist down on his desk and cursed. Art Singleton was a friend who worked at CIA headquarters in Langley, Virginia. He and Art had done favors for each other more than once over the years, and neither hesitated when it came to bending the rules when necessary. Gavin had given Art a name—David Wolfe—and asked his old buddy to run a check on the man. That task hadn't taken long, but had yielded nothing of any significance. Wolfe had been recruited straight out of the army and had been assigned overseas for most of his thirteen-year career. Art assured Gavin that the records didn't show anything out of the ordinary, nothing that red-flagged Wolfe as anything other than what Ellison Penn had said he was—a former agent who had retired and gone into the personal security business.

"The guy's record is as clean as a whistle," Art had said.

"What about his personal life?"

"Hell, man, as far as I can find out, he didn't have one."

"No friends? No women?"

"I'm telling you that the guy might as well have not existed. Nobody seems to remember him. And I checked with people who've been around for years."

"What about men who worked overseas the years Wolfe was there? Surely somebody remembers him."

"Some of those guys are dead and others are still out of the country, but I can keep checking, if that's what you want. But so far, nothing."

"That's what I want. Keep digging," Gavin had said.

There was something all wrong about David Wolfe. Gavin would bet his last dime on it. And he intended to find out just what it was. His instincts warned him that Ellison Penn was trying to pull a fast one. But why? For what purpose? He figured that the whole thing had something to do with Preston Shaw. What, dammit, what? Gavin had racked his brain until he couldn't think straight. But he wouldn't let anything get by him. He was too close to achieving his goals to allow anyone or anything to interfere at this late date.

Wolfe remained by the door of studio two, quiet and out of the way, keeping watch while Caroline worked. He found her totally fascinating. Every inclination of her head. Every twist of an arm or leg. Each smile. Each frown. The way her ponytail bobbed up and down as she bent and swerved, leaned and switched directions, all the while snapping away. Pose after pose. Picture after picture. And during the entire process, Caroline captured the playful mischievousness of a five-year-old little hellion named Abigail Faith Lasley. He had to give Roz a great deal of credit for managing not to beat the precocious child within an inch of her spoiled-rotten life as she worked with Abigail to return her to the poses needed for the photographs. Perhaps no one else noticed the maternal potential in Rozalin Turner. But Wolfe saw it. Roz was a natural, the type of woman who would be able to handle half a dozen screaming kids and make the job look easy.

He glanced toward Lyle Jennings, who had arrived ten minutes ago, early for the lunch date he'd made with Caroline. A sort of day-late birthday celebration. Wolfe had asked Kirsten to order something for their lunch and then run out and pick it up from a local restaurant. It was simply easier to guard Caroline within the confines of her studio than it was to keep her safe in public areas. Wolfe noticed that Lyle seemed as captivated as he was—but by another woman. Roz. Wolfe barely suppressed a chuckle. If any man could recognize *that look* in another man's eyes, Wolfe could...today...considering the fact that Caroline had him mesmerized. So, the good reverend had a thing for the wild and free Roz. And from the occasional sidelong glances that she was giving Lyle, Wolfe suspected the feeling was mutual. The bad girl and the preacher. A classic case of opposites.

The photo shoot ran over fifteen minutes, due mainly not to the subject of the session, but because of her demanding mother. Mrs. Bradford Lasley simply couldn't be satisfied, requesting "just one more shot" half a dozen times. Finally Caroline politely called a halt and with her Southern charm assured Mrs. Lasley that the pictures of Abigail would be sheer perfection.

The minute mother and daughter had been escorted out to their waiting limo, Kirsten told Wolfe that lunch was set up in the enclosed courtyard, per his instructions. Caroline led Lyle and Roz outside, while Wolfe followed behind. He remained constantly on alert, always mindful of even a hint of danger. The June sunshine was half-hidden behind gray rain clouds and a whisper of wind breezed through the boxed shrubbery and springtime flower beds. The fancy wrought-iron table was spread with sandwiches, chips and colas.

"We'll have to rush," Roz said. "Forty-five minutes won't give us time to do more than gulp down lunch and then get things set up for the afternoon session with Mrs. Welch and her two daughters."

Wolfe pulled out a chair for Caroline. She graced him with a warm smile, then sat and kept her gaze connected to his while he took the chair beside her. Roz tapped her foot, apparently waiting for Lyle to prove he, too, knew how to be a gentleman. Much to Lyle's credit, he picked up on Roz's cue. When he held out a chair for her, she all but cooed.

The foursome sat quietly, unwrapping their sandwiches, spreading apart napkins and inserting straws through the plastic lids on their drinks. Wolfe would have preferred lunch alone with Caroline. Actually, he would have preferred skipping lunch and having Caroline. Ever since his first sexual encounter when he'd been a teenager, he had been a man with a healthy sexual appetite, but as he'd grown older he had learned to control his baser instincts and curtail his encounters. But he was finding out that his hunger for Caroline wasn't easily sated. After having become her lover, he discovered that he wanted her more than ever.

"So, was the birthday surprise Mr. Wolfe planned for you yesterday evening a success?" Lyle asked.

Caroline almost choked on the bite of Reuben sandwich in her mouth. Roz lifted Caroline's arm and slapped her on the back. Caroline coughed until she dislodged the morsel from her throat, then grabbed her cola and slurped down several huge swallows.

"Are you all right?" Lyle inspected his cousin's flushed face.

"I'm fine," Caroline assured him. "And the surprise Wolfe planned for me was wonderful." She glanced at Wolfe, everything that had transpired between them evident in that heated look.

Wolfe had to break eye contact with her. If she kept looking at him that way, he wouldn't be able to stop himself from reaching out and grabbing her. Damn!

Roz giggled nervously. Caroline took a deep breath.

"Is there something going on that I don't know about?" Lyle glanced from Wolfe to Caroline and then to Roz.

"Let's give Caroline her presents now," Roz said, reaching in her pocket and pulling out a small, gift-wrapped box. "No sense in waiting until after we've eaten."

Wolfe realized that Roz was using the birthday present as a means to draw Lyle's attention away from what he had undoubtedly sensed as sexual tension radiating from Wolfe and Caroline. Perhaps it was best that Caroline's minister cousin not become aware of the fact that she had lost her innocence to a man totally unworthy of her.

Caroline grabbed the gift and unwrapped it hurriedly. Just as she opened the lid, Sandy appeared in the studio doorway, the portable telephone in her hand. She looked directly at Wolfe, then motioned to him.

"Finish opening your gifts," Wolfe said. "I'll take the call."

When he approached Sandy, she held out the phone and said, "It's Fletcher Shaw. He asked to speak to you."

Wolfe took the telephone from her and said, "Wolfe here."

"Yes, Mr. Wolfe, this is Fletcher Shaw. I wanted to run this by you before mentioning it to Caroline." He paused, as if waiting for Wolfe to respond, and when he didn't, Fletcher continued. "I was talking to Mother this morning. She's been away on a cruise, she and her husband, Neall, and they just returned to Baltimore yesterday. Anyway, I was filling her in on everything that has happened to Caroline. Her finding the key and the attempts on her life and my hiring you to protect her."

"Is there a point to this story?" Wolfe asked impatiently.

"Of course there is," Fletcher replied. "As I was saying,

Mother and I were discussing the situation. Naturally, she was upset to learn that poor old Teddy Richards had been killed. She'd known him since she was a young girl. But the crux of the matter is this—Mother remembered something, a place where Father could have hidden the evidence he mentioned in his letter to Lenore.''

"What place?" Wolfe smiled at Caroline when she held up a pair of theater tickets, Roz's gift, then laid them aside and began ripping the paper from Lyle's gift.

"It's a hunting lodge, or at least it used to be a hunting lodge years ago," Fletcher said. "I vaguely remember Father taking me there when I was a boy. I'd forgotten all about the place, until Mother mentioned it. She said it's a rather large old cabin. Several of father's friends, including Oliver Harper, co-owned the place at one time. They mostly used it to get away from D.C., just the guys, to do a little fishing."

"Where is this cabin?"

"Over in the western end of the state, in Garrett County."

"Do you have any idea when your father went there last?" David asked.

"I can't be sure, but I do remember him getting away by himself for a long weekend, sometime during the month before he died. I can call Oliver and ask him if he still owns the place. He might recall the last time my father went there."

"After you speak to Oliver Harper, call me back," Wolfe said. "If your father spent any time there the last few months of his life, then it might be worth checking out. But I don't intend to mention this to Caroline, unless there's a good reason."

"I agree. That's why I asked to speak to you. Caroline has been through more than enough."

"Thanks, Fletcher."

"No need to thank me. I care very much for Caroline. Her happiness and welfare are of great importance to me. The sooner we solve this damned mystery about the key, the better for her. The better for all of us.''

Wolfe grunted. ''Get back in touch with me after you've spoken to Oliver Harper.''

Caroline waved at Wolfe, motioning him to her. He tossed the portable phone on a nearby chaise longue and walked across the courtyard.

Caroline held up the theater tickets and pointed to the multicolored scarf she'd wrapped around her neck. ''The tickets are for next month's performance at the little theater, if things are safe by then. And look at this beautiful scarf from Lyle.''

Wolfe nodded. ''Nice.''

''Who was that on the phone?'' she asked.

''Fletcher.''

''And he wanted to speak to *you?*'' Lyle inquired.

''Yes.'' Wolfe sat down beside Caroline and could not resist touching her hand where it rested on the table. ''He was just checking on you. I assured him that you're all right.''

''Better than all right,'' Caroline said, her gaze locking with Wolfe's.

Lyle cleared his throat and glanced away.

''You two could be a little more subtle, you know,'' Roz said. ''Lyle might still be a virgin, but he's not blind. Even the uninitiated could pick up on the vibes between you two.''

''I do wish you would quit making pronouncements about my assumed lack of sexual experience.'' Lyle lifted the paper napkin from his lap, tossed it on the table and stood, glowering angrily at Roz during the entire melodramatic process. Then, as if a lightbulb came on in his mind, he gasped and turned his attention to Caroline. ''Is she saying what I think she's saying?''

''Oh, get real.'' Roz threw up her hands in a sign of exasperation. ''Lyle Jennings, don't you dare act shocked.''

''Please, Lyle, sit back down,'' Caroline said. ''All Roz meant was that Wolfe and I...we're attracted to each other.''

Lyle glared at Wolfe. "Is that ethical in your line of work, to become romantically involved with a client."

"Technically, no," Wolfe admitted. "But Caroline is different."

"I agree. She's not the type of woman...well...she isn't...she wouldn't..." Lyle stammered, seemingly unable to find the right words to express his high opinion of his cousin's morals.

"For heaven's sake, Rev, every woman's the type," Roz said. "It's just that for some women it takes the right man. If you had a little more experience, you'd understand—"

"What would a woman like you—who apparently finds every man she meets the right man—know about someone with Caroline's moral standards?" Lyle's cheeks flushed scarlet. He balled his meaty hands into tight fists. "I may be a thirty-year-old virgin, but you're nothing but a slut!"

Roz jumped up from her chair, then slapped Lyle. Caroline gasped. The moment Roz's hand fell away from Lyle's cheek, he turned and all but ran from the courtyard. Caroline rose to her feet, but before she took one step, Wolfe clasped her wrist.

"I think Roz is the one who should go after him," Wolfe said.

Roz snapped her head around and stared at Wolfe, a blank look on her face. "What?"

"Lyle's got to be feeling pretty bad right about now," Wolfe told her. "He's probably really sorry for what he said to you. Maybe you should go after him and give him a chance to apologize."

"Oh" was Roz's only response, but she whirled around and raced after Lyle.

"Do you think that was wise?" Caroline asked. "They might wind up killing each other."

"Yeah," Wolfe said. "Either that or kiss and make up."

Caroline's eyes widened in surprise, then a slow, soft smile spread across her face.

* * *

Roz caught up with Lyle in the hallway that bisected studios one and two. "Lyle, please, wait a minute."

Ignoring her, he kept walking. She reached out and grabbed the back of his shirt. He jerked free, then spun around to face her.

"Go away and leave me alone," Lyle said. "Can't you see that you bring out the absolute worst in me? Every time I'm around you, I want to…to…"

"To what?" she asked. "Strangle me? Tar and feather me? Have me run out of town on a rail?"

"No, dammit!" Lyle glared straight at her. "I keep telling myself that you're bad, a bad woman, with the morals of an alley cat, and that I'm an idiot for thinking you would change, that all you need is a man who truly loves you." He took a tentative step toward her.

She stared at him, her eyes round, her mouth agape, totally stunned by what he'd said. "You're right, you know. For a man who truly loved me the way I loved him, I could be good. Oh, so good. And faithful to my dying day."

"Roz, I'm sorry," Lyle said. "I had no right to say such awful things to you. It was just my way of protecting myself."

"Protecting yourself from what?"

"From you," he admitted, his voice a mere whisper.

Before she had a chance to do more than suck in her breath, Lyle grabbed her by the back of the neck, hauled her up against him and kissed her passionately. Roz's knees buckled. Her head started spinning. Butterflies danced in her stomach. She melted against him and returned the kiss, slipped her tongue inside his mouth and placed her hands on his chest. The kiss went on and on until they finally had to come up for air.

Lyle released her. "Stay away from me, Roz. Please, stay away from me."

He turned and ran down the hall, leaving Roz breathless, aroused and deliriously happy. A silly, wicked little smile curved the corners of her lips. The rev had the hots for her. Hot damn!

Chapter 16

As she sat beside Wolfe in the leased Mercedes, Caroline felt giddy with excitement. And if she were totally honest with herself she would have to admit that there was a certain amount of apprehension and nervousness intermingled with the anticipation bubbling inside her. They were on their way to a cabin co-owned by Oliver Harper, located in Garrett County, outside of McHenry. Since the 1920s and the formation of Deep Creek Lake, the isolated county had been gradually turning into the year-round resort area it was today. When she and David had gotten the key and directions from Oliver, who had driven to Fletch's home in Baltimore to save them from making the trip to Alexandria, he had invited them to stay a few nights at the cabin on the lake. And he'd even suggested that they take advantage of the great fishing.

"It would do Caroline a world of good," Oliver had said. "The fishing is at its best this time of year. You can pick up a couple of fishing licenses at any tackle shop. And even if you don't find what Preston's key unlocks hidden away up at the cabin, you wouldn't have completely wasted your time.''

She and Wolfe had left straight from Fletch's home this morning and taken I-70 out of Baltimore, then hit I-68 to Keyser's Ridge and were now heading south on Route 219. Located in the heart of the Allegheny Mountains, Garrett County was a paradise for adventurous sportsmen. Hiking, biking, rafting, skiing, backpacking and camping vied with boating and fishing to lure outdoorsmen from across the country.

Caroline glanced down at the map and written directions that lay in her lap. They should be at the cabin within the next few minutes. Just two more turns and they should be on the road that would take them directly to the cabin. She had used the past three hours on the hundred-and-ninety-mile drive from Baltimore to try to calm down, to prepare herself for the possibility that this trip might very well turn out to be a burnt-run, a totally wasted trip. After all, what were the odds that Preston had hidden away some sort of trunk or box or case at a cabin that had belonged to friends and was used by a variety of people? But Oliver had recalled that Preston made a weekend trip to the cabin less than a month before his death, making it possible that he had stored something there.

"You're awfully quiet," Wolfe said.

"Just thinking," she replied.

When he stole a quick glance at her, Caroline's stomach did silly flip-flops. Would she ever get used to the way he made her feel? All hot and bothered. Arousing her sexually with something as innocent as a glance, a touch or a smile. Then she remembered that she wouldn't have the chance to become accustomed to this all-consuming passion. Wolfe wasn't going to be a part of her life for very long. She couldn't bear the thought of their affair ending so quickly, when it had just begun. But he had made it perfectly clear that he was a temporary man, unwilling to make a commitment. Wasn't his way for the best? she asked herself. Although her body yearned for his and she was more than halfway in love with him, she really didn't know David Wolfe. He was little more than a stranger to her. Common sense told her that there were hidden depths to him, things she might never know.

"This turnoff?" he asked.

"Huh?" She checked the map quickly. "Yes, this is the one."

"Try not to be disappointed if we don't find anything," he said. "You know the odds aren't in our favor."

"That's just what I was thinking. And I want to thank you for understanding why I had to make this trip, to try this one more possibility. If we don't find anything then—"

"Then we'll spend the night and head back to St. Michaels tomorrow."

"You believe we're wasting our time, don't you?"

"Hmm-mmm. Probably. But I promised you another week to search, didn't I?"

She reached over and laid her hand on his shoulder. He tensed, then relaxed, never taking his eyes off the road. "I can sense that you're concerned. You are anticipating some sort of trouble, aren't you?"

"Always," he said. "Trouble comes with the territory. And it's my job to stay one step ahead of the game."

"In what way specifically?"

"Several ways," he told her. "This Mercedes is equipped with bulletproof glass for one thing."

Why wasn't she surprised? "Then you didn't lease it from just an ordinary car rental place, did you?"

"No."

"What else?"

"Someone has already been to the cabin and checked it out for me."

"What?"

"A necessary precaution."

"How did they get in without a key?" she asked. "And how did they know where the cabin was located?"

"Let's just say I have friends and the Dundee agency has friends with all sorts of talents."

"You realize that it frightens me when you talk this way," she told him. "It reminds me of what you do for a living, of the government agency you worked for in the past and how violent your life has probably always been."

"Don't think about it," he said. "Who I am or who I was won't affect your life in the future."

Did he really believe what he'd said? she wondered. Did he truly think that once they went their separate ways, she would be able to forget him, stop wanting him, no longer love him? And would she be that easy for him to erase from his life, as if she had been nothing more than just another brief affair. He might think so, but he was kidding himself. There was no doubt in her mind that she would leave an indelible mark on his heart, as he would on hers. Perhaps they were unsuited for each other and fate had simply brought them together by accident, but one irrefutable fact remained—they were soul mates. Mismatched soul mates. A contradiction in terms, but nevertheless true. On some basic, instinctive level, she had recognized him the moment they met and he had recognized her, too.

"Check the map," he said. "I think the next turnoff should be coming up soon."

She glanced at the map. "The second road on the left. Probably a quarter of a mile."

That one-quarter of a mile zipped by hurriedly. Wolfe pulled the Mercedes up alongside a two-story log-and-rock structure with a big front porch. Through a thin crop of pines, they had a perfect view of the lake. When Wolfe killed the engine, he threw his arm out to prevent Caroline from releasing her seat belt.

"What's wrong?" she asked.

"Nothing. Just stay here in the car for a couple of minutes, until I make a phone call." He removed his cellular phone from the inside pocket of his sport coat, flipped it open and hit a preprogramed number. "We're here," he said, then listened intently. "Good. Thanks."

"All clear?" She placed her hand over his and pressed it to her stomach. A shiver of longing raced up her spine.

He undid her seat belt, then curled his hand over her hip. "All clear for the moment, but that doesn't mean you can have free rein around this place. You'll stay with me at all times. No strolling on the porch. No gazing out the windows."

"Just like at home."

He grinned. "Yeah, sweetheart, just like at home."

"They took the bait. Hook, line and sinker," he said. "Of course, I'm sure Wolfe is being very cautious."

"He'll be one against three," the man said. "Even a hotshot like David Wolfe can't overcome three-to-one odds."

"Only a fool would underestimate him. Mark my word, there's more to him than meets the eye. He's not just an ordinary bodyguard."

"You know he's former CIA, so that makes him very dangerous."

"There's something else," he said. "We'll just have to dig deeper until we find out what."

"If this plan comes off without a hitch, it won't matter, will it?"

He shook his head. "Make sure there are no foul-ups this time."

"There won't be. Just tell me when you want our men to move in," the man said.

"Early in the morning. Say around three-thirty. Even if Wolfe is awake, he should be less alert at that time. He is only human."

"Your plan is a good one. It'll be a lot easier for our men to make a clean getaway from that isolated cabin than it would if we made the hit at Caroline's home or studio. We can go in, strike and get out quickly, with practically no chance of any witnesses. And this way you were able to maneuver things so that you won't be suspected of any wrongdoing.''

"When Caroline and Mr. Wolfe are killed, I shall be shocked and appalled and even blame myself a little that I couldn't have done something to have prevented their deaths.''

"There isn't anything at the cabin they might find while they're searching the place, is there?'' the man asked.

He chuckled. "Don't be stupid. Our people went over the cabin with a fine-tooth comb the day after Preston was killed. The only thing Caroline and Wolfe will find up there are fishing tackle, old clothes and some books and magazines.''

"When do you want me to contact you again?''

"Not for a few days,'' he said. "I'm sure I'll get a call as soon as the county sheriff discovers the identity of the two victims.''

"Nothing,'' Caroline said as she tossed the stack of old magazines back into the closet. "We've gone through every closet, every dresser and chest, every cabinet and cupboard. There isn't anything in this entire cabin that opens with a key, other than the front and back doors.''

David pushed up his glasses, which had made their way down his nose about an inch, then fastened his hand atop Caroline's shoulder. "I'm sorry we didn't find anything.''

She sighed, then inclined her head to the side, bringing her cheek down on his hand. "But it's what you expected, isn't it? You didn't think we'd find anything.''

Yeah, sure, it was what he'd expected. His instincts had warned him from the minute Fletcher Shaw telephoned him and told him about the old hunting lodge over in Garrett County that the whole thing was a setup. Not that he suspected Fletcher, no more so than anyone else. It would have been easy enough for someone to have used Caroline's step-brother to put a devious plan into action. All it would have taken was a phone call to Fletcher's mother, Pamela. But trying to retrace things by that route might prove impossible since the first Mrs. Shaw's circle of friends included most of the suspects on Wolfe's list and a few that hadn't been there before, but were now. Fletcher, of course. All three Harpers—Oliver, Eileen and Brooke. Gavin Robbins, whom Fletch's mother actually dated a few years back, despite the difference in their ages. Barry Vanderpool, whose mother had been the bridesmaid at Pamela's wedding to Preston. And Ellison Penn, who had been her lover for a few months, shortly after her divorce from Preston nearly twenty years ago. The only two people who weren't connected to Pamela Shaw Larson were Lyle and Roz, and he'd pretty much eliminated those two from his suspects list.

Wolfe had never intended for Caroline to find out anything about this place, had in fact planned to send a couple of Dundee agents—hopefully Jack and Matt would have still been free—to check the place out and report back to him. But Brooke Harper had opened her big mouth and mentioned it to Caroline, who had immediately gotten excited. Brooke's slip of the tongue might have been no more than that, but then again, she could have had an ulterior motive for passing along the information.

"You're awfully somber," Caroline said as she lifted her head from his hand, turned and wrapped her arms around his waist. "Something you want to tell me?"

He forced a smile. "Nothing for you to worry about right now."

Maybe he should tell her now instead of later, but if he did, she would only worry until it happened and possibly work herself up into being a nervous wreck. If it came from out of the blue, she would more than likely act out of survival instinct instead of fear, at least at first. If he explained that someone—someone she trusted—had sent them up here to be killed, she wouldn't want to believe him. But she would. And then she'd fret over who and drive herself crazy about when. No, he would wait as long as possible before telling her just what he thought was going to come down here at this cabin. Either tonight or in the morning. He would lay odds that it would be tonight. These people had been playing the waiting game for a while now. They had to be anxious to get Caroline out of the way, and him along with her.

He could have told her everything before they left Baltimore and allowed her to decide whether or not she wanted to put herself in the line of fire. Reason told him that she was in no more danger here at the cabin than she would have been at home, so he had made the decision for her. Sooner or later, her stepfather's former comrades would have to come after her again. He suspected that if and when she turned the key over to him, they would still want her eliminated, thinking that without her to urge him on, he would eventually give up the search. He hated admitting that she wouldn't be safe—not ever again—until these people were identified, arrested and stopped once and for all.

"I think we should make use of the hot tub before we go to bed," Caroline said, lifting her arms to twine around his neck. "A good long soak would relax us and make us sleep like babies."

He didn't dare sleep like a baby. A few catnaps, maybe. Just enough rest to be able to function at top capacity when the time came. David planted his hands on her buttocks and lifted her up and into his arousal. "I know a better way to relax."

A throaty giggle bubbled from her throat. "Why not both? Sex in a hot tub is deliciously sensuous."

He rubbed himself against her. "And just how would you know? You've never had sex in a hot tub."

She kissed him playfully. "I want to find out if what I've heard is true."

"Can't do it. Not here. Not now."

"Why not? We're here. The hot tub is inside the house, all safe and cosy. And you've already got a...er...you're..."

"I've got a hard-on," he said. "Don't you know that I walk around with one just about all the time when you are around? All I have to do is look at you and I want you."

"The feeling is mutual."

He gripped the back of her head, his fingers forking through her hair. She stared at him, her eyes wide. Their gazes locked and held.

"What's wrong?" she asked. "Why can't we make love?"

Although he calculated the hit wouldn't come until the middle of the night, he had to stay alert. There was always the off chance that he had misjudged his unknown opponent and something would go wrong.

Instead of replying to her question, he removed his glasses, tossed them on the nearby bed and then urged her closer, until her body aligned with his. He lowered his head and kissed her. She responded immediately, kissing him back with equal fervor. Her hands lifted, gripped his biceps and held on tightly. His lips moved to her throat. She tossed back her head and flung her arms around his wide shoulders. He grabbed the fabric of her green cotton skirt and, inch by inch, bunched the fabric in his hand as he lifted the shirt higher and higher.

He was going to have her here and now. Not in the hot tub. Not in one of the beds in the many bedrooms. He didn't dare risk the time it would take or the vulnerable position they would both be in for the sweet, unhurried loving they both wanted.

"How badly do you want it?" He mouthed the words against her throat as his hand snaked beneath her skirt and cupped her hip. "Badly enough to take it raw?"

"Yes." Her hands went to his zipper and her fingers quickly undid his pants.

He slid her panties down her hips and when they fell to

her ankles, she stepped out of them. He walked her backward, straight to the wall, then lifted her enough so that when he reached inside his briefs, she was positioned to take him into her body. She wrapped her arms around his neck and her legs around his hips as he began thrusting and retreating, bumping her hips against the wall, the frenzy inside them building fast.

They mated hurriedly, stealing kisses between each undulating movement of their bodies. He kept up a steady rhythm, making sure pressure was applied to the right spot. She tightened around him, her body milking his, bringing them both closer to fulfillment. His release came first, then hers. Shuddering, gasping, they clung to each other and Wolfe covered her mouth with a kiss that claimed her body and soul.

While the aftershocks of pleasure subsided, he held her for just one more minute, then slid her down over his body until her feet touched the floor. Reluctantly he released her and stepped away, never taking his eyes off her as he readjusted his underwear and zipped his pants.

"Go wash up." He nodded toward the bathroom. "Then put your panties on and—"

"What's wrong?" She looked at him questioningly. "Why the rush?"

"Nothing's wrong, but I'd feel a hell of a lot better knowing that if for any reason we have to run out of here during the night, we'd both be fully dressed."

"And do you think we might have to run out of here during the night?"

He hated that worried look in her eyes, the tension on her face. He grabbed her by the shoulders, then kissed her forehead. "I'm a cautious man. Humor me. We're out in the middle of nowhere in an area I'm not familiar with, so on the off chance something were to happen, I don't want to be caught with my pants down."

She didn't question him further, but immediately did as he

had asked. When she returned from the bathroom she found him placing his glasses and his 9 mm on the bedside table.

"We might as well see if we can get some sleep." He lay down on top of the bedspread, lifted his arms and crossed them behind his head.

"You're expecting an attack, aren't you?" She stood over him, her gaze riveted to his face. "You think they're going to come after me tonight."

"We told Oliver and Fletcher we'd stay overnight," David said. "That means they'll strike either tonight or in the morning."

"You brought me up here knowing… Are you telling me that you think Oliver or Fletcher—"

"Don't jump to conclusions. I'm not accusing either of them. They could easily have been used by someone else and be totally unaware of the fact."

She slumped down onto the edge of the bed. "So, what do we do, wait?"

"Yeah, we wait until I get a signal. My cell phone will ring as a warning that someone is approaching the cabin."

"Then you have Dundee agents posted as watchdogs, don't you?"

"Jack and Matt and a third agent they brought with them. A guy named Domingo Shea."

Caroline lay down beside David, at his side, but not close enough to touch. "Why didn't you explain all of this to me before we left Baltimore?"

"I put it off to save you the worry."

"Gee, thanks."

"Try to get some rest, even if you don't think you can sleep."

Minutes ticked by, endless, silent minutes. He turned off the lamp, pitching the room into darkness. Light from the three-quarter moon filtered through the closed wooden blinds, shooting thin ribbons of illumination across the wooden floor. He lay there and listened to her breathing. Slow and steady.

Finally, after what seemed like hours, he turned to her and drew her into his arms. She resisted at first, as he had known she would, but when he whispered her name, she cuddled close and buried her face against his shoulder.

This woman was meant to be his, ordained by the forces that be, long before their paths had crossed. But an evil trick of fate had placed him in the role of her enemy. And then he had anointed himself her keeper, her phantom benefactor, her secretive and elusive David. But suddenly fate had stepped in again and given him a once-in-a-lifetime opportunity—to meet her, to get to know her, to become her protector when she needed him most. And he had been unable to resist claiming her, making her his.

She lifted her hand and caressed his cheek. "You had to do this, didn't you? By bringing me here, by walking into their trap, you have the advantage because you knew in advance it was a trap."

"You got it." He grabbed her hand, brought her open palm to his lips and kissed it. "I'm not going to let anything happen to you. I promise."

Time passed slowly, each minute seeming like an hour. Every sound tensed his nerves. He had been in situations like this before. Waiting. Adrenaline pumping. Mind whirling. Dozens of other jobs, with countless lives at stake. But never someone he personally cared for the way he cared for Caroline. He was prepared to do anything, risk anything to keep her safe.

"You haven't been able to sleep, have you?" she asked.

"I don't sleep a lot," he said.

"Goes with the territory?"

"Yeah, a bodyguard learns to get by on less sleep."

"That's one more thing I've learned about you. It isn't fair that you know everything about me," she said, her voice warm and soft. "You have a file that tells you my entire history." She paused. "I don't know anything about you. Only the most superficial things."

"What do you want to know?" he asked.

"Have you ever been married?"

"No."

"Ever been in love?"

"No."

She laid her hand on his chest, then fingered his scars. "How did this happen?"

"A bomb exploded. I didn't get out of the way fast enough."

"Oh, Wolfe."

"A hazard of my old job."

"With the CIA?"

"Hmm-mmm."

She threaded his chest hair around her fingers. "Where were you born? Where did you grow up? What were your parents like? Do you have any brothers and sisters?"

He sucked in a deep breath, then released it slowly. "I was born in the hills of Tennessee. My mother's family had lived there forever. She was part Cherokee. My father was a drunk. He liked using my mother as a punching bag, and after we were born, he started beating the hell out of me and my little brother on a regular basis. But he seemed to get a special pleasure out of tormenting my brother."

Caroline wrapped her arms around David and held him. "Oh, Wolfe, I'm so sorry. So very sorry. Your childhood must have been a nightmare."

"Yeah," he said. "But then so was yours, wasn't it, sweetheart?"

"You know it was."

Why he was baring his soul this way, he wasn't quite sure. He'd never talked about his childhood to anyone. But this wasn't just anyone. This was Caroline. His sweet Caroline, with the loving heart and generous soul, who had survived her own tormented childhood. Once he'd begun, he couldn't seem to stop pouring out the truth about Aidan Colbert's tragic young life.

He pulled away from Caroline and sat upright in bed. "There's something you should know...something I should have told you before...."

"What is it?" she asked, lifting herself into a sitting position beside him. "You can tell me anything and I'll understand."

Oh, God, if only that were true. If only he could truly bare his soul to this special woman. His woman. "When I was thirteen, I killed my father."

Caroline gasped. Wolfe got out of bed. He stood in the center of the room, rigid as a statue, his breathing stilled for a minute. Even though she moved quietly, he knew when she climbed out of bed and walked toward him. He waited. Not breathing. Not thinking. Not daring to hope. Just waiting and praying.

She came up behind him and wrapped her arms around him. "Do you want to tell me about it?"

Not moving a muscle, not glancing back at her, he stood there and let her hold him, feeling inexplicably secure and unafraid. Could he explain to this gentle woman about a violent act for which he had never been able to forgive himself?

"I was just a scared kid." When he spoke, the words came slowly, painfully and quietly. "I knew what he was capable of doing. What he'd done to all of us countless times. But things had been getting worse. I knew that sooner or later he'd kill one of us, probably Brendan because he was so little and weak.

"I warned him that if he ever hit Brendan or Mama again, I'd kill him." He shuddered as the memory of that day came back to him, as vivid and real as if it had happened yesterday. "I was coming in from school that day. Brendan had been sick with a cold and Mama had kept him home. I heard them before I even reached the porch. Him hollering and Mama begging. And then Brendan screaming."

"You don't have to tell me the rest of it." She hugged him fiercely.

He felt the moisture of her tears as they seeped through his shirt and onto his back. "I ran around the side of the house and came in through the kitchen door. Then I went straight to my bedroom, got my hunting rifle and went out to the living room. Brendan was lying on the floor, staring up at my old man, who was slapping my mama around. I warned him. I told him if he didn't stop, I'd kill him.

"He dared me to do it. Told me I didn't have the guts to kill him. Then he kicked Brendan. And when he raised his foot to kick him again, I shot him. Twice." Wolfe knotted his hands into tight fists. "Once in the heart. And once in the head. I was a crack shot, even then."

Holding on to him, she eased around his hard, tense body until she could gaze up into his face. He couldn't bear to look into her eyes. She released him, then reached up and framed his face with her hands.

"Forgive yourself," she said. "You were forced to make a terrible decision and you did the only thing you could have done. You protected the innocent, the helpless. You saved your mother and your brother."

He looked at her then, but could barely see her through the fine mist coating his eyes. "That's just it. I didn't save them. Brendan died from his injuries that night. And Mama never recovered from the trauma of her baby boy dying and her older son killing his own daddy."

Standing on tiptoe Caroline kissed him. With care and sympathy. With understanding and compassion. And with love. Her love encompassed him, wrapping around his wounded soul like a soothing balm. Taking him by the hand, she led him to an overstuffed armchair in the corner of the room. She urged him down, then sat on his lap, laid her head on his shoulder and put her arms around him once again.

She fell asleep that way, nestled in his lap, with him soaking up her sweet, precious understanding and forgiveness. He drifted off into a light sleep. Visions of his mother and Brendan wafted through his mind, followed by images of Caroline. The only three people who had ever been important to him, the only ones he would have willingly died to protect. But he had not been able to save Mama or Brendan....

Wolfe woke with a start. The telephone had awakened him, but the sound of a loud crash had roused him. What the hell? He realized Caroline was in his lap and he was still sitting in the chair. Their gazes collided.

"What was that?" she asked.

"My cell phone," he said. "A signal to alert me of danger."

He shoved her up and onto her feet, then jumped up and hurried to the bedside table to remove his Sig Sauer from the holster. Suddenly another crash and then a third followed in quick succession. He grabbed Caroline's hand and flung open the door into the living room. Flames shot up to the ceiling and spread in every direction. Firebombs! Firebombs tossed through the windows. Dammit to hell and back.

"We've got to get out of here," he told her. "Looks like their plan is to smoke us out and be waiting for us when we come outside. They intend to shoot us like sitting ducks."

Chapter 17

Smoke quickly filled the house, folding in on them from every direction. Black, hot and heavy. Like a thick, smothering fog. Wolfe figured he didn't have much choice. The back door was not accessible because of the fire blazing in the kitchen area. Their only escape route was through the front door. Not that it mattered much one way or the other. There was bound to be a man posted at the rear as well as the front. He had no way of knowing how many there were, but his guess would be no more than three or four. And with three Dundee agents in place, the odds were better than even—in his favor. Tugging on Caroline's arm, he led her toward the front door. As they made their way through the smoke-clogged foyer, Caroline began coughing.

"When I open the door, we're going to drop and roll off the porch," he said. "They'll be wearing night-vision goggles and be able to see us, so they're going to start shooting the minute we come out. Don't panic. Don't think. Just move." He grabbed her shoulders and gave her a forceful shake. "I'm going to be right there with you every minute and my guys will be responsible for half the gunfire you hear.''

He felt her trembling and wished he could take longer to reassure her, but time was of the essence. This old cabin was quickly burning down around them. If the smoke didn't get them soon, the ceiling would cave in on them.

"Ready?'' He squeezed her shoulders, then released her and retrieved his Sig Sauer from his hip holster.

"Ready,'' she said, her voice shaky.

He flung open the door. Gunfire erupted all around them. They dropped to the porch floor. Bullets flew over their heads, splintering wood and sending chips flying, some peppering their skin as they rolled. A barrage of gunfire followed, tearing up the floor behind them. Son of a bitch! The Dundee agents would be moving in to strike their attackers at any moment. All he had to do was get Caroline out of the way, keep her safe and wait.

He shoved Caroline off the end of the porch and came down over her on the rock-strewn ground behind the Mercedes. The earth exploded nearby, too close for comfort. Grass and dirt and gravel danced into the air. Without giving her a chance to catch her breath, David tumbled Caroline past the car, over the driveway and into the ditch. Not a deep ditch, but hollowed out enough to give them some protection. He lifted himself off her just enough to allow her to breathe, but placed his hand down on her head as a warning for her to stay put. With the pistol in his hand, he scanned the area behind them, black as pitch, except for the moonlight that barely made its way through the trees. Toward the lake, the view was brighter because the trees were sparse. And in front of them the blaze from the burning cabin lit up the night sky.

An unnatural silence fell. He could hear Caroline breathing as well as the thumping of his own heartbeat. The usual nocturnal noises had ceased, as if every living thing around them had fallen prey to their assailants' attack. Wolfe sensed Caroline's fear, could smell her terror. His own fear ate away at his gut like deadly acid. He was afraid—not for himself, but for Caroline.

The sounds were faint, almost inaudible. But he heard them. Since boyhood, when he'd been raised to hunt wild game in the hills, he had relied on his acute sense of hearing. Without seeing them, he knew there were two shooters closing in on them, from opposite directions. He sensed no more than two men, so where were the others?

Suddenly a single shot rang out, coming from behind the cabin. About damn time, Wolfe thought. He'd begun to wonder if the Dundee agents were ever going to make their move. As he had suspected, a third man had been posted at the back door, just in case he and Caroline had made their escape by that route. But the guy out back wouldn't be helping his buddies. Not now. One of Dundee's best had eliminated him. The approaching footsteps stopped. Their attackers now had to realize Wolfe wasn't alone, which meant they were aware that they, not Wolfe and Caroline, had walked into a trap.

He wanted just one of them to live. Just one. Whichever man survived was going to do some talking. Whoever ordered the hit on Caroline wouldn't have done his own dirty work, but for a mission this important, he would have sent the best snipers. Please, God, let one of them still be alive. And give me five minutes alone with him. That's all I need. Five minutes.

Caroline tugged on Wolfe's shirttail, which partially hung out of his pants. "What's happening?" she whispered. "Why is it so quiet? And who—"

He clamped his hand over her mouth. Be quiet, sweet Caroline. For just a little longer. He could hear movement again. Heavier. Deliberate. The men moving around now weren't trying to disguise their footsteps. They had the advantage. The Dundee agents were coming in for the kill. That probably meant there had been only three attackers and one had already been eliminated.

Gunfire erupted again. Close enough for Wolfe to see

shadows and hear grunts. A battle that ended almost before it began. Wolfe waited. He eased his hand from Caroline's mouth and down her throat. She trembled.

"All clear," Jack Parker shouted. "There were only three of them and they've been contained."

Caroline wanted to breathe a sigh of relief, but her chest hurt too much to do more than whimper. And a burning ache ripped through her side when she moved. Wolfe grabbed her hands and lifted her up and out of the ditch. Moaning, she fell against him, her legs too weak to hold her. Dammit, don't pass out now, she told herself. You're alive. Wolfe's alive. The bad guys are...*contained*. As if from out of nowhere three large dark figures appeared and surrounded them. For a split second her heart stopped, but when one of the men removed his night-vision goggles and grinned, she recognized his grimy face. Jack Parker, looking for all intents and purposes like a commando. Oh, God, that's what he was, she realized. That's what they all were, including David Wolfe. Men trained for deadly missions, capable of subduing an enemy with superior efficiency.

"You took your own sweet time," Wolfe said, glowering at Jack. "Where the hell were y'all?"

"We had everything under control," Jack said, a wide grin revealing a set of white teeth, bright against the dark war paint he wore. "Your orders were to wound, not kill at least one of them, so that took a little more effort."

Wolfe wrapped his arm securely around Caroline, giving her even more support as she began to tremble. "Well, did you accomplish that goal?" he asked.

Matt O'Brien and another Dundee agent flanked a wounded attacker as they dragged him forward. Jack reached out and ripped the man's dark mask from his face. Caroline gasped. She felt Wolfe tense.

"They get younger all the time," Jack said.

"He's just a kid," Caroline cried.

"We're going to have to get him to a hospital for a little

repair work," Matt said. "That is if you want him to live long enough to tell us who sent him on this little hit-and-run mission."

"Take him to the hospital," Wolfe said, his voice deadly. "I want him to live. Just make sure that one of you guards his sorry ass every minute until he's well enough for my interrogation."

Lifting his head, the young man glared angrily at Wolfe. He cleared his throat and spit on the ground. Bloody drool trickled from the side of his mouth. "Interrogate me all you want, Mr. Wolfe. I'll never tell you anything I don't want you to know." He fixed his gaze on Caroline. "Don't think he can keep you safe forever. He can't."

"Get him out of here," Wolfe said.

"The fire department and the sheriff's department will be showing up soon," Jack said. "I can handle this kid by myself, so if you'd like I'll leave Matt and Dom here to explain to the local authorities what happened. I called Sawyer McNamara in on this, so he can help us out with the sheriff."

"Who's Sawyer..." Caroline's vision blurred. The world began to spin around and around.

"FBI," Jack replied. "Hey there, Miss Caroline, are you all right?"

Wolfe pivoted her in his arms. She cried out as pain sliced through her side. Wolfe lifted his hand from her rib cage and cursed a blue streak. "She's bleeding," he yelled. "Goddammit, Caroline, why didn't you tell me you were hit!"

"Hit?" What did he mean? Why was he screaming at her?

Wolfe swung her up into his arms and ran toward the Mercedes. Matt opened the car door. Wolfe deposited her on the seat, then knelt and lifted her arm so he could inspect her side. She glanced down and saw that a huge red circle stained her tattered blouse. Wolfe grabbed the soiled material and ripped it apart, exposing the bruised and bloody flesh. He probed gently. She cried out in pain.

"Where's the nearest hospital?" Wolfe demanded.

"Follow me," Jack said.

The last thing Caroline remembered was Wolfe slamming his door as he got behind the wheel.

Caroline had been trying to awaken for the past half hour. He'd been at her side constantly since she'd come out of surgery early this morning. The bullet had gone through her side, doing no major damage, but she had lost a lot of blood and she would carry a couple of nasty scars the rest of her life. He'd been wild with worry when he carried her into the local hospital's emergency room. In retrospect, he realized that he'd scared the ER staff half to death with his rage when he had demanded immediate care for Caroline. He had blamed himself for not realizing sooner that she was wounded. But she hadn't said a word, hadn't let on that she was in pain. His brave little trouper. She hadn't even realized she'd been shot.

While he had walked the floor in the waiting room, Jack Parker at his side, he had mouthed and grumbled, blaming himself, blaming the Dundee agents and cursing God for allowing something like this to happen to someone as dear and good as Caroline. At one point, Jack had all but dragged him outside to the parking lot.

"Take a deep breath of fresh air and chill out," Jack had said. "You're not doing Miss Caroline any good by the way you're acting. She's not going to blame you or us or anybody except those damn snipers who attacked y'all. That's who you should be wanting to rip apart, so stop screaming at everybody and stop beating up on yourself."

"That kid is going to talk. He's going to tell me what I want to know or—"

"It may be a few days before we can get our hands on him, if then," Jack said. "We may have to get in line behind the FBI, the local sheriff and maybe even Peacekeepers International."

"What do the Peacekeepers have to do with this?"

"Seems our kid sniper, Seth Horton, is a new Peacekeepers recruit," Jack said. "What do you make of that?"

"If Ellison Penn pulls any strings to get his hands on that kid, he'd better be doing it so he can hand him over to me. Otherwise, he'll be as good as admitting he was involved with the attack. Ellison's too smart for that."

"You talk like you know the guy personally and that you suspect him of being part of the plot to kill Miss Caroline."

"I know Penn by reputation," Wolfe said, realizing how close he'd come to revealing himself.

Ellison wasn't on his suspects list. He had always trusted him implicitly. After all, the man had been his mentor and had done a great deal for him over the years, including giving him a new life. He couldn't see Ellison as a rebel, as a crazed right-wing insurrectionist, but at this point, he didn't dare rule out even the most unlikely suspect. Perhaps he had eliminated Lyle and Roz from his list too quickly. He honestly didn't think Roz was the type. And Lyle's love for Caroline seemed too genuine for him to take part in anything that would harm her.

"Find out who recommended Seth Horton for his job at Peacekeepers International," David had told Jack.

"You don't suspect a network of Loyalists Coalition members within the Peacekeepers organization, do you?"

"Not a network, but possibly a few moles working their way into key positions, the way Preston Shaw did."

Wolfe decided that until he had proof of any kind against Ellison, he would go with his gut instincts and trust his old friend. But Gavin Robbins was another matter altogether. He didn't trust that bastard any farther than he could throw him. Especially not where Caroline was concerned, he thought now, gazing down at her as she slept.

"Wolfe?" Caroline opened her eyes.

He took her hand in his as he leaned over and smiled. He'd never seen a more beautiful sight than Caroline awake and recovering. "How do you feel, sweetheart?"

"Groggy." She wriggled, then groaned. "And sore."

"You'll be sore for a few days and then the stitches will itch awhile, but the bruises will fade and so will the scars, eventually."

She lifted her hand to his cheek. "You look terrible." She ran her fingers over the day's growth of beard stubble covering his face. "How long have I been asleep?"

"They knocked you out before surgery around five this morning," he said. "It's six in the evening now. After surgery, you woke for a few minutes and then went right back to sleep. I was beginning to worry about you, but the nurses assured me that some patients don't come out of it as quickly as others. Your body needed the rest, so you just didn't wake up again until now."

"I'm hungry." She giggled, then moaned. "Even laughing is painful. Isn't it silly that after what I've been through, I'd wake up hungry."

"What do you want to eat?" he asked. "Name it and it's yours."

She caressed his face. "I'm going to be all right, aren't I?"

The fear and pain of losing her lodged in his throat, an emotion that prevented him from speaking. If anything had happened to her... Finally, he nodded.

"Then don't you think you should stop feeling so guilty," she said. "You saved my life."

"I risked your life," he managed to say, his jaw tense. "I knew that damn cabin was a trap and I deliberately took you there thinking I could protect you and look what happened."

"You did protect me," she told him as she framed his face with both hands. "And y'all caught one of the snipers. He must be a member of the Loyalists Coalition, the people who ordered Preston's execution. That means if he doesn't know who killed Preston, he can give you the name of someone who does know."

David clasped her hands, pulled them away from his face,

turned her palms over and kissed each one. "Whoever gave the snipers their order to kill you is the person I want."

"Do you think you can persuade him to talk?"

"You can count on it."

The look of deadly intent she saw in Wolfe's eyes frightened her. What would he do to the sniper, who wasn't much more than a boy, in order to make him talk? She couldn't bear even thinking about the methods she'd heard that certain people used to obtain information from an unwilling captive. Wolfe couldn't…wouldn't… Caroline shuddered.

"What's wrong?" Wolfe asked, gently grasping her shoulders. "Do you need a nurse?"

She shook her head. "Can't the police question him? You don't have to do it yourself, do you?"

"Yes, I have to question him myself," Wolfe said. "But you shouldn't be worrying about that kid. All you need to do is concentrate on recovering and going home."

"Wolfe…?"

"By the way, there are some people outside waiting to see you," he said, obviously determined to change the subject. "Lyle and Roz have already been in, about two hours ago, but of course you were still sleeping. And Fletcher and Brooke got here about forty-five minutes ago."

"How did they know—"

"I had Jack phone Lyle and he took it from there." Wolfe nodded to the door. "I'll go out and let them come in to see you. But I won't be more than a few feet outside the door."

"All right."

The moment he exited her room, Caroline's friends swarmed around him, bombarding him with questions. He held up his hands in a cease-fire gesture.

"She's awake and wants to see y'all," Wolfe said. "But no questions about what happened up at the lodge. And in ten minutes, I'm running y'all out of there until later."

The foursome piled into the room. When Fletcher reached out to close the door, Wolfe grabbed the handle and held the door open. He and Fletcher exchanged a question-and-answer glance, then Fletcher released his hold, nodded his understanding and left the door open.

Jack Parker laid his hand on Wolfe's shoulder and said, "I've got something for you."

Wolfe followed Jack farther out into the hall, but still close enough so that he could see into Caroline's room. "What is it?"

Jack held out a pair of tinted glasses, identical to the pair Wolfe had left behind at the lodge, which had been just like the ones destroyed at the lakeside cottage in Windhaven. "Thought you might need these, so I ordered you several extra pairs after the bomb explosion."

Wolfe grinned, took the glasses from Jack and put them on. "Thanks."

"While I talk, just keep smiling," Jack said. "Sawyer tells me that you and Miss Caroline will have to give statements to the local sheriff. Just the basic facts. He says there won't be a problem."

"I can handle that."

"And it seems there's already quite a bit of interest in Seth Horton. A request for custody."

"The County Sheriff has a deputy guarding Horton and will take him into custody when he leaves the hospital." Wolfe grimaced. "So what agency thinks it can usurp the Sheriff's authority?"

"Peacekeepers International, Gavin Robbins in particular. And it seems that Robbins was the one who recommended Horton for the job at Peacekeepers." Jack tightened his hold on Wolfe's shoulder. "Sawyer says that Horton belongs to the FBI, that the feds want to get their hands on him and the Peacekeepers don't have the authority to save the guy's sorry ass. But he also said that past history shows that the Peacekeepers take care of their own."

Yes, they do, Wolfe thought. The Peacekeepers took care

of its own, but not only in the way Jack meant. They did protect one another, but they also executed their rogue agents. Which motivated Robbins—the need to protect Horton or the decision to execute the man?

Chapter 18

Wolfe lifted Caroline out of the car and into his arms, then carried her up the walkway to her house. Roz and Lyle stood in the open door. Matt O'Brien, Domingo Shea and Jack Parker followed. Matt and Dom brought in the flower arrangements Caroline had received during her hospital stay, while Jack remained on guard duty.

"I'm perfectly capable of walking," Caroline said.

"Humor me." Wolfe stepped up on the porch. "It gives me pleasure taking care of you."

A peculiar sensation fluttered inside Caroline. Whenever David Wolfe mentioned looking after her, protecting her, caring for her—as he had done so often in the past few days—unbidden thoughts of another David came to mind. Memories of the David who had watched over her for so many years couldn't be erased from her mind and heart, not even by the passion she felt for David Wolfe. And not for the first time, a ridiculous thought occurred to her—how perfect it would be if her two Davids were one, if she could somehow combine them and never lose either of them.

"Lyle and I cleaned the house and cooked dinner together," Roz said, as Wolfe brought Caroline into the living room and deposited her on the sofa. "Lyle's quite a cook. He's going to make some girl a really good husband."

"Hey, don't let Roz sell herself short." Lyle grinned at Roz. "She actually baked the apple pie."

"It was a frozen pie, straight out of the box." Roz grinned. "All I did was put it in the oven."

Matt and Dom lingered in the foyer. "Hey, what do you want us to do with these flowers?" Matt asked.

"Oh, let me have one of the arrangements and I'll put it on the table for a centerpiece." Roz rushed over and took the smaller of the two vases that Matt held.

"Please put the others in my bedroom," Caroline said.

Matt nodded, then he and Dom headed upstairs.

After sighing dramatically, Roz whistled softly under her breath. "Those two guys are dreamboats, aren't they?"

Lyle cleared his throat and glowered at Roz disapprovingly. Jack Parker chuckled.

Laughing, Roz shrugged. "Okay, so the habit is hard to break. I've spent years collecting men. You can't expect a girl to stop looking and appreciating, just because she's given up the habit."

"I didn't know you'd sworn off men," Caroline said. "When did this happen?"

"Recently." Roz stared meaningfully at Lyle. "I'm testing my willpower to see if it'll earn me any brownie points with a guy I'm trying to impress."

"Lucky guy, if you ask me," Jack Parker said. "Miss Roz, a man would have to be a first-class fool not to be downright flattered that you'd want to impress him."

"Well, Texas Jack, I appreciate your saying that. Let's just hope the guy I want feels that way." Roz continued staring at Lyle until his face turned red.

"Oh, by the way, Caroline, a delivery came for you this afternoon," Lyle said. "Roz and I had them put the things in the storage area off the laundry room. I hope that was all right.''

"What sort of delivery?" Wolfe asked, tension wrinkling his brow.

"Several suitcases and a couple of boxes," Roz said. "Your mother's husband sent them from Europe." Roz crammed her hand into the pocket of her cutoff jeans and pulled out an envelope. "This came with the stuff."

Wolfe took the letter, inspected it and handed it to Caroline, then glanced at Jack. "You and Matt and Dom take a look at that special delivery." He glanced at Roz. "Would you show them where y'all put the items?"

"Sure." Roz's mouth fell open. "You don't think there's a bomb or—"

"Probably not, but it's best to make sure," Jack said.

Caroline ripped open the envelope and withdrew a one-page letter. While she read the message, Matt and Dom came back downstairs and Jack motioned for him to follow as Roz led the way out into the kitchen.

"It's from Armand Mahieu, my mother's sixth husband." Caroline's gaze remained glued to the letter. "He says that although it wasn't my mother's request that I be sent her personal things, he thought it only right that he send certain items to me since I was Lenore's daughter."

"If it's going to be too painful for you to go through those things, I can do it for you," Lyle said.

"No, thank you, Lyle." Caroline folded the letter neatly and returned it to the envelope, then reached over and laid it on the end table. "I'll go through them myself. Just not this evening. Maybe tomorrow."

"Well, Roz and I have plans, so we won't be staying much longer," Lyle announced. "As soon as we serve your dinner, we're going to a church softball game. Roz has joined the team, and after only a couple of games she's already our star pitcher."

"You're kidding me?" Caroline laughed, then glanced up

at Wolfe, who stood behind the sofa. She raised her arm and gently grasped his hand.

Wolfe looked down at her and smiled, but she could tell that his mind was elsewhere. Was he concerned about the special delivery that the Dundee agents were at this very moment checking over to make sure it wasn't booby-trapped? Of course he was. He was a professional, trained to protect. His first thought would always be regarding her safety. He was a man whom life had taught from the cradle that you could trust no one, that you could count on no one but yourself and that you were smart to suspect everybody. In his eyes, no one was innocent until proved so. Nothing was harmless unless thoroughly inspected.

Roz reentered the living room first, carrying a tray of tall iced tea glasses. ''Refreshments, anyone?''

By the time Roz had distributed the tea, Jack, Matt and Dom reappeared. Jack grinned. ''The delivery is harmless,'' he said. ''Looks like a bunch of old clothes, books, pictures and a jewelry box. Nothing lethal. The jewelry box came with a key, so we unlocked it and checked it out. Hope that was all right with you, Miss Caroline. Seems your mother had some pretty nice jewels. Expensive stuff.''

''Yes, my mother had very expensive taste. Monsieur Mahieu, her sixth husband, is a multimillionaire. My guess is that he kept the jewelry he'd given her and gave me the things she'd brought with her when they married.'' Caroline gazed up at David and squeezed his hand again. ''See, now you can stop worrying. At least until after dinner. The delivery really is nothing more than some of my mother's belongings.''

''Speaking of dinner,'' Roz said. ''We fixed plenty, so if you three guys—'' she looked at Jack and Matt and Dom ''—are staying, I'll set a couple of extra plates.''

''Nothing for us now, Miss Roz,'' Jack said. ''We've got a couple of errands to run and then Matt and I will be taking turns keeping watch outside tonight, while Dom heads back to the hospital to make sure the sheriff's deputy is keeping Seth Horton off limits to any unauthorized visitors.'' When he glanced at Wolfe, Jack inclined his head to one side in a come-with-me gesture.

Wolfe released Caroline's hand. ''I'll walk the guys outside and be back in just a minute.''

She hated the secrecy, the cloak-and-dagger tension surrounding Wolfe and the Dundee agents as well as the ever-present danger that was so much a part of her life now. She had no doubt that Wolfe was, at this very minute, discussing with the Dundee agents not only a plan to get their hands on Seth Horton when he left the hospital and was turned over to the FBI, but also the escalation of protection for her. Wolfe insisted on keeping the extra agents on hand, and when she'd asked just how expensive that would be, he had told her that the extra cost had been taken care of. By whom? she had asked. Fletcher? No, not Fletcher. And when she had looked squarely into David Wolfe's eyes, she had seen the answer. Her benefactor had somehow learned about what was happening to her and had once again come to her aid.

Seth Horton wasn't sure exactly what his fate would be, but he felt certain he would fare better being turned over to the FBI than winding up in David Wolfe's hands. The two G-men who had escorted him from the hospital this afternoon told him very little, except that they were taking him to meet with their superior. He realized his only hope of avoiding prison was if the Loyalists Coalition rescued him and got him safely out of the country. He had always been told that the organization took care of its own. He believed wholeheartedly in the cause to which his father had dedicated his life and he would die before he would betray his brethren. The feds might be harsh in their treatment of him, but their methods would remain civilized. If he had been subjected to questioning by Mr. Wolfe, Seth doubted that he would have survived.

The big black car in which he was a passenger pulled into a building that resembled an abandoned warehouse somewhere in the D.C. area, but Seth wasn't sure exactly where. During the trip, he had been confined to the back seat and his view obscured by the dark windows and the screen that closed him and the agents off from the driver. The car doors swung open on either side and he was dragged to the right and escorted inside the warehouse, straight into an empty, unused office.

"What the hell is this place?" Seth asked. "Why did you bring me here?"

"Because I asked them to bring you here," a familiar voice said.

Seth whipped around to face the man who had authorized the sniper mission to Garrett County to kill Caroline and her bodyguard.

"You?" Seth glanced from one FBI agent to another, and the realization of just who these men were hit him. He chuckled. "They aren't FBI, are they? They're a couple of our guys. How the hell did you manage that?"

"You must know by now, Seth, that we can accomplish practically anything we set out to do," he said. "FBI agents were on their way to take you, but our guys, as you called them, intercepted the federal officers."

"So what's the plan now?" Seth asked. "How soon can you get me out of the country?"

"There won't be any need for that," he said.

"Do you think the organization can successfully hide me out here in the U.S.?"

"Actually, no, I don't."

"Then—"

The two phony FBI agents grabbed Seth, one on either side. Adrenaline pumped through his body at an alarming rate. He looked point-blank at the Peacekeepers agent and saw his own fate reflected in the double agent's eyes. These phony FBI agents were members of the Loyalists Coalition.

Seth had failed in his mission. Failure was not acceptable to the Loyalists Coalition. They weren't going to give him a second chance.

"But it wasn't my fault," Seth said. "I had no way of knowing that the trap we set for Caroline and Mr. Wolfe would actually be a trap for us."

"These things happen," he said. "No one's fault. But you have become a liability to us, Seth. Your identity is known and there is no way we can guarantee that you won't reveal privileged information."

"You know that I would die before I'd betray the organization."

He nodded. "I'm glad you understand."

Yes, Seth understood. He understood only too well.

As she headed into her kitchen, Roz lifted the edge of her T-shirt and wiped the sweat from her face. "We whipped their butts good, didn't we?" She jerked open the refrigerator door and searched inside for the beer she hoped would be ice cold.

"You really need to work on cleaning up your language now that you're playing on the church softball team," Lyle said.

"Oops, sorry." She retrieved two frosty bottles of beer, closed the refrigerator and tossed one of the bottles to Lyle. "Is it a sin for you to have a beer to cool off after the game?"

"One beer isn't a sin," Lyle said. "Getting drunk is the sin."

"Then we won't get drunk." She popped the lid on her bottle and lifted it to her lips. She caught a glimpse of Lyle in her peripheral vision and noticed that he was staring at her breasts. She took a hefty swig of beer, then glanced down at her chest. Perspiration and dirt stained her T-shirt and her puckered nipples pushed against the tight cotton cloth.

"Are you hungry?" she asked.

"What?" Lyle's face flushed with embarrassment, like a

kid who'd been caught looking through his father's stash of *Playboy* magazines.

Roz laughed. "Are you hungry...for food? I can fix us some sandwiches."

"Thanks, but a beer will be fine for now," he said. "Would you mind if I cleaned up a bit? Washed my face and hands. I feel pretty grimy."

"Sure thing. The powder room is down the hall and to the right. While you're doing that, I think I'll catch a quick shower."

"Well, it is late...." Lyle backed toward the door. "I should probably head on home and let you get to bed."

"No, don't leave. The night's still young. Stick around and we'll fix some popcorn and watch TV. Do you like old horror movies?"

"Yeah, I love them. To be honest, I'm addicted to them."

Yes, she knew he was. One of the many things Caroline had told her about Lyle that she had stored away for future reference. "There's a movie marathon of classic horror flicks on right now."

"Okay," Lyle said. "I'll wash up while you're showering...." He cleared his throat. "I can fix the popcorn if you'll just tell me where you keep it."

"Top left cupboard over the sink," she replied, then headed toward him. As she passed him, she deliberately brushed up against him, then slowly moved around him to shove open the door.

She hurried into her bedroom, took several deep swigs from her beer, then stripped off her shirt on the way into the bathroom. She set the beer bottle on the vanity, then tossed her shirt in the open hamper before reaching inside the tub to turn on the shower. When she opened the linen closet to get some towels, she suddenly remembered that she hadn't put out fresh towels in the powder room after she had thrown the soiled ones in the washer this morning. She grabbed a pink towel and matching washcloth, rushed through her bedroom and down the hall. She didn't hesitate when she reached the powder room and found the door closed. She knocked twice, then flung open the door, squinted her eyes shut and held out the towel and cloth.

"You'll need these," she said.

"You can open your eyes, Roz. I'm decent."

She lifted one eyelid and then the other. Lyle was decent, despite the fact that he had removed his T-shirt and stood there with his bare chest exposed. Her gaze settled on that broad chest, taking in every inch. Thick swirls of reddish brown hair formed a T that spanned the area between his tiny male nipples and bisected his freckled belly. Her hand itched to reach out and touch him.

God, if I shouldn't do this, then give me the strength to resist, she prayed silently.

Of its own accord her hand snaked out and she laid her open palm over his chest, between those tight little nipples that peeked out from beneath all that glorious manly chest hair. Lyle sucked in a harsh, startled breath. Roz dropped the towel and cloth that she held in her other hand onto the edge of the sink, then zeroed in on Lyle. She brushed against him. Her breasts, covered by only a thin layer of lace, pressed against his naked chest. She sighed, loving the feel of his body so close to hers.

"Roz, we really shouldn't—"

She placed her index finger over his lips. "You know I'm crazy about you, don't you? I mean crazy in love. I've never felt about anybody else the way I feel about you. You've got to believe me."

He kissed her finger and smiled, then lifted her hand and held it securely in his. "I believe you."

"I won't lie to you. There have been a lot of guys. I've made some bad mistakes."

"I don't care about the other guys or the mistakes you've made," Lyle told her. He reached out and ran the back of his hand across her cheek. "I preach about forgiveness and

God's love that washes us clean from past sins. I believe what I preach. I live my religion.''

''I've never known anybody like you. You're the most wonderful, kind, honorable, decent—''

''Enough. You make me sound like some sort of saint, and believe me, Roz, I'm just a man…a very ordinary man who lives one day at a time doing the very best he can.''

''Oh, honey, you're not ordinary. Not by a long shot. You're the most extraordinary man in the world.'' She draped her arms around his neck. ''I'd give anything if you'd kiss me again the way you did that day at Caroline's studio.''

''Considering the fact that we're alone in your powder room and we're both half undressed, I'm not sure—''

She kissed him. After huffing loudly, grimacing and shaking his head as if he'd just admitted to himself that he'd lost an inner battle, he pulled her into his arms and deepened the kiss. Their hands went wild, touching, exploring, fondling. And their lips mated passionately, imitating the basic sexual act. When they came up for air, Lyle pushed Roz away and then clasped her shoulders.

''We've got to stop,'' Lyle said.

''Oh, Lyle, honey, I want you so much.'' Roz knew she was begging him, but she didn't care.

''And I want you.'' He gazed at her with hungry eyes.

''Then what's the problem? Sex between two people who care about each other can't possibly be a sin. Didn't God invent sex? With Adam and Eve.''

Lyle chuckled, then clasped her face between his hands. ''I'm a minister who preaches abstinence for unmarried people. That's the reason I'm still a…a virgin. I do practice what I preach. Sex isn't a sin, but for me to give in to temptation would be wrong. Can you understand?''

''Yeah, I understand.'' Roz frowned. ''I'm not going to get laid tonight, am I?''

''No.''

''But you'd like to have sex with me, wouldn't you?'' she

asked, hopeful that she could bring him around to her way of thinking.

"No, I wouldn't like to have sex with you. Not tonight or any other night."

She glared at him, unable to believe what he'd said. He was lying. He had to be lying. "I thought you—"

"I do want you," he said. "I want to make love to you, not just have sex with you. But for me sex and love must be one. And that act must take place within the sanctity of marriage. That's the only way it can be right for me."

Roz reached out, flopped the lid down on the commode and sat. "Well, I guess that leaves me out." She looked up at him and smiled weakly. "Don't suppose you can fool around just a little. I know all kinds of things to do without going all the way."

"If I started fooling around with you, I wouldn't be able to stop," Lyle confessed. "So while we're dating, we'd better keep our relationship under control and stop at kissing. But once we're married, I'm going to keep you in bed for at least two weeks without letting you ever leave the bedroom."

"Just kissing while we're—what did you say?" Roz shot up off the commode lid fast as a rocket blast, almost toppling over Lyle's empty beer bottle. "Did you say when we're *married?*"

"Yeah." Lyle blushed a shade almost as dark as his hair. "I'd kind of planned on proposing in a more romantic place, after I'd bought you a ring and—"

"You—" she pointed to him "—want to marry me?" She pointed to herself.

"More than anything."

"Have you lost your mind? What will people say? Those little old blue-haired ladies at your church will never accept someone like me. They'll excommunicate you!"

"The worst the church will do to me is ask me to resign and I don't think they will do that. Not once they see what a wonderful woman you are and how happy you make me.

Besides, with your enthusiasm and energy, you'll be an asset to my ministry.''

"One of us has lost his mind."

Lyle pulled Roz into his arms and kissed her forehead. "We've both lost our minds because we're crazy in love."

Chapter 19

Caroline's whimpering cries instantly jolted David from his uneasy sleep. She tossed and turned beside him in bed, obviously having a bad dream. And why shouldn't she? Within a few weeks time, someone had tried to drown her, blow her sky high and gun her down. What he found amazing was that she was able to sleep at all. But he credited himself with her feeling safe and secure enough to rest, even if that rest was plagued by nightmares. She knew he would protect her with his life, and not only he, but the Dundee agents he had charged with guarding the house. He reached out and took her by the shoulders as he whispered to her.

"Caroline, sweetheart, it's all right. You're safe. You're here with me and I won't let anyone hurt you."

She stopped wriggling, but she tossed her head back and forth on her pillow as she continued whimpering. "Please, don't leave me. Don't ever leave me."

He flipped on the bedside lamp. "Caroline, wake up." He shook her gently.

She gasped, then opened her eyes and stared at him. Terror turned to surprise and surprise to relief. "Wolfe?"

"Mmm-mmm." He swept the flyaway tendrils of her lustrous black hair away from her face. "You were having a nightmare."

She nodded, then snuggled against him as he enveloped her in his embrace, being careful not to press too tightly and irritate her healing gunshot wound. "You were leaving me," she murmured against his bare chest. "I needed you, but you wouldn't stay."

"You know that I'll stay with you as long as you need me, as long as your life is in danger."

"But then you'll leave. Once I'm safe." She tilted back her head and gazed at him. "What if I'm pregnant, will you still leave me?"

He closed his eyes and called himself all kinds of a fool, as he'd done again and again over the past few days. He hadn't meant to take her without protection; he had made sure he was always prepared. But the night at the cabin, when he had made love to her quickly, standing up, both of them still dressed, reason had taken a back seat to passion. He had tried not to think about what he'd done or the possible consequences. Surely God wouldn't punish Caroline for his mistake.

"I'm sorry that I didn't take the proper precautions that night." Wolfe kissed her temple. "But I think it's highly unlikely that you're pregnant, don't you?"

"The timing was all wrong," she admitted. "I'm sure I'm not pregnant. I had my period while I was in the hospital. I just wanted to know that if you had gotten me pregnant, would you stay when this is all over?"

He lifted himself up and braced his head with his elbow as he looked down at her. She lay halfway beneath him, gazing up at him as if he were the beginning and end of her world. The last thing he wanted was to leave her. But he would have no choice. Because of who he was, because of the part he had played in her tragic past, they couldn't have a future together. No matter how much he wished for a miracle, there would be no happily ever after for Caroline and him.

If only he could tell her the truth—that he was her benefactor, the man who had safeguarded her from afar, the David who had loved her and provided for her and longed to be near her. But that would be only half the truth. He could not confess to one without confessing to the other. She would want to know why he had taken on the role of her keeper all those years ago. He could never tell her that he was Aidan Colbert, the Peacekeeper executioner assigned the task of eliminating a rogue agent who had just happened to be her stepfather. He could never look her in the eye and say, "I'm the man you came face-to-face with in Preston Shaw's study. I'm the man you thought was going to kill you."

"Wolfe, what's wrong?" Caroline asked. "You have the most peculiar look on your face. Was my question that difficult for you to answer?"

He covered her with soft, light kisses. Adoring her. Worshiping her. Wanting her more than he had ever wanted anything. "If you were pregnant, I'd take care of you and the baby, but—"

She kissed him to silence him, then pulled back, her face only inches from his, and whispered against his lips, "I love you."

Her confession took him aback. Heat swelled up inside him, pervading every inch of his body as the meaning of her words became a part of him. He knew that she cared deeply for him, that she was infatuated with him due to their sexual compatibility. But he figured that was only because sex was new and exciting for her. He had not expected her to fall in love with him. Wasn't she in love with *her David?* Wasn't her phantom benefactor the man she truly wanted? Wasn't he just a substitute for the man she couldn't have?

But you are that David, he reminded himself. And even if

Caroline doesn't realize that fact on a conscious level, isn't it possible that subconsciously she knows that you and he are one and the same?

"You're in love with the way I make you feel when we have sex," he told her. "You've never been with a man before and you're mistaking great sex for love."

"Maybe you can separate the two in your mind and heart," she said. "But for me the two things go together. Don't you realize that without my being at least halfway in love with you, I wouldn't have had sex with you?"

What would happen if he told her that half truth right this minute? What would she do if he told her he was her benefactor? If he did that, then he could tell her how much she meant to him, how deeply he cared. He could find a way to kept the other half of the truth from her, couldn't he? Would it be so wrong to take what she was offering? They could go away together. Far away, where no one knew her and no one had ever heard of Aidan Colbert.

But his conscience got in the way, as it always did. Hadn't he caused Caroline enough harm already? "I can't offer you anything beyond what we have now," he said. "I'm sorry. I wish…" *You don't know how much I wish that I could give you the moon and stars, that I could lay the world at your feet. This is one time, my sweet Caroline, that I cannot give you what you want.*

"Then I have no choice…I'll take what you can give me." She reached for him, all the love and longing she felt alive in the depths of her blue-violet eyes. Eyes that had haunted him for years and would continue to haunt him until his dying day.

"You're recuperating from surgery," he reminded her. "I don't want to do anything that—"

"You won't hurt me," she said. "You know how to make gentle love. I need you so. Once I give you the key and you feel that I'm no longer in danger, you will leave me and we'll both be alone. Let's not waste what precious time we have left together."

No man alive could refuse such a request. Not from a woman like Caroline. She had no idea how alone he would be once he left her. Although he had been alone most of his life, the loneliness in his past couldn't begin to compare to what lay ahead for him.

Tears gathered in her eyes and spilled down her cheeks. He kissed them away, tasting their sweet saltiness with his tongue. "Don't cry. Please, don't cry."

He undid the buttons on her silk pajama top, slowly, prolonging the pleasure for both of them. She lay still, her chest rising and falling with each expectant breath she took. When he released the last button, he spread apart the shimmery, soft garment and bared her breasts.

He touched her. Featherlight. Hesitant. Her nipples puckered. His mouth could not resist. His lips closed over one nipple while his fingers played with the other. She moaned and squirmed. His hands traveled beneath her breasts to the flesh below. Licking. Nipping. Kissing. Careful to avoid the small bandage that covered the stitches in her side, both front and back, and sealed her recent wounds. He hooked his fingers beneath the elastic of her pajama bottoms and eased them down and off, leaving her totally nude.

"You are the most beautiful thing on earth," Wolfe said.

"Please…I want to see all of you, too."

He could refuse her nothing. He lifted his hips and removed his boxer shorts, leaving himself totally exposed. His erection thrust forward as if searching for Caroline's body. She was everything to him. Without her— No! He wouldn't think beyond the moment. She was his tonight.

He touched her everywhere, his hands examining and petting. Her face. Her breasts. Her belly. The inside of her thighs. He eased her to her uninjured side and became intimately acquainted with every inch of her back, her hips and buttocks. He lavished attention on her body, arousing her and at the same time arousing himself. Almost beyond endurance. But this loving was for her. His lips joined his fingertips, kissing her mouth and then moving to explore her neck, her ears, her throat. She shivered and his tongue came out to play, traveling over her arms and legs, painting trails between her fingers; then under, over and around her breasts until she lifted her hips and arched her back as her heels dug into the rumpled covers at their feet. Placing his hand in the middle of her belly, he soothed her while he spread her legs apart with his other hand and lowered his mouth to kiss her intimately.

Only a few strokes of his tongue and she was crying out for him. Close, so very close to fulfillment. He ached to be inside her, free from all barriers, but he had risked too much that one time at the cabin. In the last moment of sanity before he could no longer control his actions, he reached out for protection and found the box of condoms he'd picked up at the drug store the other day when he'd picked up Caroline's pain medication, the day she came home from the hospital. The box was still inside the nightstand. He hurried, his hands unsteady, his fingers fumbling. Need rode him hard. The moment the sheath was in place, he braced himself over her, his knees on either side of her legs, and looked down into her eyes as she gazed up at him and held open her welcoming arms.

"I'll be...very...careful," he said, his words strained.

He lifted her hips, bringing her up to meet him, and took her with one quick, powerful thrust. And then he waited, unmoving, except for his labored breaths. Being inside her was heaven. Her body was home and comfort and incomparable pleasure.

He moved. Slowly. Back and forth. Teasing her with gentle strokes. Tormenting himself. Wolfe made love to Caroline with the utmost tenderness, savoring each moment their bodies were one, knowing that she would be a part of him forever. His sweet Caroline.

Her moist folds tightened around his shaft, squeezing and releasing until he thought he would die. When he sensed that she was on the verge of coming, he increased the tempo and deepened the lunges until she bucked and cried out, her climax hitting her hard. He pumped into her, not letting up until the moment of completion. In those seconds after he convulsed with shattering intensity, their bodies wrung every ounce of satisfaction from the culmination of their mating. It was a moment that Wolfe wanted to last forever.

Completely drained and totally sated, he eased himself up and off her, then settled at her side. Being extra careful, he pulled her close. They shared a kiss that held them bound together beyond the sexual experience.

"I love you, Wolfe." She snuggled against him. "Please, don't ever forget me and what we've shared."

Forget her? Impossible. She was a part of him. His mind, his heart, his very soul. "I won't forget you. I promise."

Long after she fell asleep in his arms, he held her and looked at her and savored each precious second. He stored up memories to last a lifetime. Finally, hours later, he slept.

The quiet tap at the bedroom door woke him the next morning. He slipped out of bed, adjusted the covers around Caroline's naked shoulders and reached for his pants lying in the nearby chair. He zipped up his slacks as he made his way to the door. When he opened the door, he found Jack Parker standing in the hall. He stepped outside and closed the door behind him.

"Sorry to disturb you." Jack glanced toward Caroline's bedroom. "But we just got a call from Sawyer. Seth Horton is dead."

"Goddammit! I was afraid of this. What the hell happened? I thought a couple of Sawyer's men were taking Horton directly from the hospital."

"A couple of Sawyer's agents were killed and whoever killed them took Seth. Dom was there when the feds showed up. He had no way of knowing these guys weren't who they said they were. They showed the sheriff's deputy the proper ID. Fake ID, we now realize. But Dom's blaming himself for not suspecting something.''

"Tell him not to. You're right—there's no way he could have known. But with Horton dead, we're no closer to discovering the identity of his superior in the Loyalists Coalition than we were from day one."

"Are you going to tell Miss Caroline?" Jack nodded to the bedroom.

"Later. Before someone else tells her." Wolfe looked directly at Jack. "Screen the calls for a few hours. She needs her rest."

"I can do that," Jack said, then hesitated before saying, "The boss called. She wanted to know how much longer you were going to need three of her top agents."

"What did you tell her?"

"I told Ms. Denby not to expect us back until you were a hundred percent sure Miss Caroline was safe."

"Thanks."

"After this mess is over and things are settled, are you going to hang around?" Jack asked. "If that woman looked at me the way she looks at you, dynamite couldn't blast me from her side for the rest of my life."

"It's none of your... Truth is that I want to stay with her, but it's not possible."

Jack nodded, then headed downstairs. David was grateful that the long, tall Texan hadn't pressed him for an explanation.

He grinned with triumph as he laid down the copy of the file he had *borrowed* from another Peacekeepers agent. Someone else had done a good job of finding out everything the Loyalists Coalition needed to know about David Wolfe. With the joy of discovery, he beat on his desk repeatedly, then shoved back his chair and bounded to his feet. At last, all the pieces had fallen into place. He'd known there was something not right about David Wolfe. Now he knew exactly what. He had Wolfe and Ellison Penn by the short hairs and they didn't even know it. A wide, self-satisfied smile spread across his face.

David Wolfe was Aidan Colbert! He had to be. Everything fit too neatly. With the help of a few reliable sources, he had unearthed the truth. And Ellison Penn had known all along, had probably even been the one to contact Wolfe and bring him in to guard Caroline McGuire. God, what irony—the man protecting Caroline was the same man who had executed her beloved stepfather.

Of course he couldn't prove David Wolfe's true identity, but he didn't have a single doubt. After all, two and a half years ago, Ellison Penn had taken a severely injured man to a clinic in Switzerland and admitted him under a John Doe alias. This had occurred only days after Aidan Colbert had supposedly died in a bomb explosion, giving his life to save a bunch of kids. This John Doe character had remained at the clinic for more than nine months, and when he left the clinic, he had walked out as David Wolfe, with all the credentials to prove he was a former CIA agent. The only thing was that there wasn't one CIA agent around who could remember David Wolfe. Hell, Ellison had even called in a favor from an old friend, Sam Dundee, to arrange a job for Wolfe.

He could understand Ellison taking care of a Peacekeepers agent, even falsifying records to show that Aidan Colbert had died and then resurrecting him as David Wolfe. But calling Wolfe in to protect Caroline had been a major mistake. And Ellison Penn didn't make mistakes. So, what was going on?

He snapped his fingers. Of course! That was it. Ellison wanted to make sure whatever evidence might be unlocked with Caroline's key would wind up in his hands. And the Peacekeepers' President didn't completely trust anyone the way he had trusted Aidan Colbert.

Ellison had taken a chance of exposing himself if anyone

discovered Wolfe's true identity, but then Ellison didn't think anyone would be smart enough to figure it out. He had a great deal to do if he was going to stop Ellison and protect the organization. The first step was to get Caroline McGuire away from David Wolfe. And he knew just how to accomplish that goal. One phone call was all it would take.

Once Caroline knew that Wolfe had killed Preston Shaw, she would turn against him and walk away, straight into the arms of the Loyalists Coalition. Then they would have Caroline—and more important, they would have the key to whatever hidden evidence might exist against them.

Caroline lounged cross-legged in the middle of the kitchen, all her mother's belongings spread out around her. Wolfe sat on the bar stool above, watching her as she fingered her mother's lingerie.

"My mother liked the finer things in life," Caroline said. "She bought only the best."

"The best thing in her life was you, but she never knew your true worth." Wolfe returned the smile Caroline gave him.

"People were never that important to Mother, not unless they could do something for her. Things were what mattered to her. The things money could buy."

Caroline neatly folded the lingerie and placed it in the suitcase to her left, then she picked up the jewelry chest. Wolfe watched her as she examined the twelve-inch-square brown alligator-skin case, trimmed and studded in brass. Caroline turned the small key, which was already in the lock, and opened the jewelry box. Inside were more than a dozen pieces of rather nice jewelry. Caroline inspected each piece. A couple of rings, one pearl and the other diamond. She held up the diamond.

"This was Mother's engagement ring…the one Preston gave her." She slipped the ring on her finger and found it a bit too loose. "Funny. I always thought my hands were larger than Mother's. She was so elegantly slender."

Caroline dropped the rings back into the case. She picked up several bracelets, then returned them, one by one. She lifted a necklace, rubies and diamonds, then dropped it back on its velvet bed. The final piece she retrieved was a large heart-shaped pendant on a gold chain.

"Preston gave this to Mother, too. For their anniversary, the year he died." Caroline held up what appeared to be an antique piece, perhaps from the 1920s, with tiny diamonds surrounding an onyx, diamond and gold filigree heart-shaped locket of some sort.

"That's an unusual pendant," Wolfe said. "May I see it?"

Caroline held it up and he reached down to grasp it in his hand, then sat back and cupped the necklace in his palm.

Wolfe's gut instincts kicked into play, alerting him that this piece of jewelry struck a chord in his memory. But why? What was it about this object that seemed familiar? The note! The note Shaw wrote to his wife Lenore. What had it said? Something about looking into her heart.

"Caroline?"

"Hmm-mmm?" She glanced up at him.

"I'd like to read the letter your stepfather left in the safe, one more time," Wolfe said.

"Why?"

"That locket triggered a memory," he told her. "Something in the note to your mother."

"I can tell you exactly what the note said. I've memorized it."

"Tell me the part about keeping the key safe and looking into your heart."

"All right," Caroline said, then quoted, *"Safeguard this key and the identical one in your possession. They unlock the means by which to keep our family safe, after I am gone. Look into your heart for the proof of my love for you and the children."*

"Look into your heart," Wolfe repeated. "For the proof."

Caroline stared at the pendant, then gazed at the jewelry box. "Oh, my God! Wolfe, do you think—"

"Lock the jewelry box, then remove the key and compare it to yours," he said. "Then use your key to see if it will unlock the box."

She followed his instructions. She locked the case, then removed the key. With shaky fingers she slipped the chain from around her neck, opened the catch and slipped the key off the chain. She held her key in one hand and the key to the box in the other, then brought them together.

"A perfect match," Wolfe said.

"Do you think...?"

She slid the key into the keyhole and turned, then smiled up at Wolfe when they heard a faint *click*. The box unlocked. She jumped up and threw her arms around Wolfe's neck.

"We found what the key unlocks," she said. "But there are no papers in there—" she pointed to the jewelry case "—so the evidence has to be here somewhere."

Wolfe held up the locket for her to see. "Look inside your heart."

"The heart-shaped locket!" Caroline gasped. "But what sort of evidence would fit into something so small?"

"There's one way to find out. Shall we open it?"

"Yes, please. Open it now."

Wolfe examined the pendant, trying to ascertain the exact location of the catch. Just as he found it and applied pressure to open it, Jack Parker stuck his head into the kitchen.

"Sorry to bother y'all," Jack said. "But I've got a rather insistent twosome out here demanding to see Miss Caroline."

"What twosome?" David asked.

"Lyle Jennings and Fletcher Shaw."

"What do they want?" David glared at Jack.

"I told you, they want to see Miss Caroline. Immediately."

"Jack, please show them into the living room," Caroline

said. "Wolfe and I will be right out." She turned to Wolfe, her face alight with happiness. "See if there's anything in the locket, then we'll be able to show whatever there is to Fletch and Lyle."

"Caroline!" Fletcher's voice called loudly.

"Oh, dear, something must be wrong," Caroline said. "I'd better go see what he's so upset about."

The moment Caroline's back was turned, Wolfe opened the locket. His pulse rate accelerated when he recognized the small dark coil of microfilm hidden away inside the golden heart. He turned the locket over and dumped the microfilm out into his hand. If this tiny photographic film contained the evidence Preston Shaw claimed it did, then Caroline would soon be safe from her stepfather's cohorts. Once the evidence came to light, with names and dates, Caroline would no longer be in danger.

Before Caroline reached the door, Fletcher and Lyle came barging into the kitchen. Right behind them Jack Parker reached out and grabbed both men by the backs of their necks. That's when Wolfe noticed that Fletcher Shaw had his hand in his pocket and the outline of a pistol showed plainly through the cloth. Wolfe slipped the microfilm into his pocket, along with the keys.

"Please, Jack, let them go," Caroline said.

Jack looked to Wolfe for permission. He nodded. Jack released his two captives.

"Wolfe, you're fired," Fletcher said as he straightened his crooked collar. "Or should I call you Aidan Colbert?"

Wolfe's gaze locked with his accuser's glare. At that precise moment, it really didn't matter now how Fletcher had found out who David Wolfe really was. What mattered was how much he knew and what he was going to tell Caroline.

"Fletcher, what are you talking about?" Caroline looked from her stepbrother to Wolfe. "Why does he think your name is Aidan Colbert?"

"Because that's what it is, isn't it?" Fletcher said, brandishing the 9 mm he'd whipped out of his pocket. "Don't get upset by this gun, Caroline. Its sole purpose is to make sure we don't have any trouble getting your bodyguard and his associates to leave."

Ignoring Fletcher and the weapon he held, she focused all her attention on Wolfe's face. "Is he right? Is Fletch right? Is your name not David Wolfe? Is it really Aidan Colbert?"

"Yes," Wolfe said.

"I'm afraid I don't understand why…" Caroline swayed slightly.

When Wolfe reached out for her, Lyle ran to her side. "Don't touch her."

"Please, someone tell me what's going on," Caroline said.

"Aidan Colbert was a trained assassin," Fletcher told her.

"What?" Caroline's violet-blue eyes rounded in disbelief. "Is that true? Is that what you did for the CIA?"

"He was never a CIA agent," Fletcher said. "He was a member of a secret society and his very first assignment was to kill a man who had been falsely accused of being a rogue agent."

"Caroline, please…" Wolfe went numb from the pain. He couldn't bear this helplessness, this inability to protect Caroline from the most devastating agony she would ever know.

"Aidan Colbert is the man who was sent to kill my father," Fletcher said, the hatred and contempt in his gaze practically searing the flesh from Wolfe's bones.

"No!" Caroline jerked out of Lyle's arms and confronted Fletcher. "Where did you get such ridiculous information?"

"I was told in confidence by someone with your best interests at heart," Fletcher said. "But I've been sworn to secrecy. It's a matter of national security. I brought Lyle with me to help persuade you to believe me, to realize that you've put your trust in the man who killed my father. We can't do anything to him because we have no proof that will stand up in court. But we can demand that he leave this house and stay away from you. From now on Lyle and I will make sure you're safe."

Caroline turned slowly and looked point-blank at Wolfe. "It isn't true, is it? None of it. It's all lies, isn't it?"

What could he possibly say or do that would reassure her? Absolutely nothing. He had betrayed her, lied to her, pretended to be someone he wasn't. But if he admitted the truth to her now, she would hate him and she would send him away. Without him, her life would be in danger. He didn't know who he could trust and who he couldn't. Was it possible that one of these men who had come running to her rescue might very well be the one intent on killing her? Or were Fletcher and Lyle simply pawns being manipulated by a brilliant strategist? Right now, his money was on Gavin Robbins, the sorry son of a bitch. Robbins had to have been the one who had somehow discovered David Wolfe's identity and gone to Fletcher. *And if it isn't Robbins?* his intuition asked. God help him. Don't let it be Ellison.

"Answer me, dammit!" Caroline screamed.

"Will you give me a chance to explain?" Wolfe pleaded. "I need to talk to you, just the two of us."

She shook her head. "Wolfe, please, answer my question."

"I can't," he said.

"Oh, God. Oh, God..." she gasped.

Caroline crumpled into Lyle's waiting arms. When Wolfe reached for her, Jack Parker clamped his hand down on Wolfe's shoulder and nodded toward Fletcher Shaw, warning Wolfe that Fletcher had his 9 mm aimed directly at the two of them. Fletch's hand trembled. Without much provocation, he might shoot, and as nervous as he was, he could easily fire the gun accidentally.

Chapter 20

Caroline refused to see him, refused to speak to him. Fletcher had ordered him out of her house, and without risking a confrontation that might end in bloodshed, he didn't have much choice. Caroline knew only half truths, as well as the ugliest, most painful truth. Right now she had to be confused and hurting, in more pain than she'd experienced since the night of Preston Shaw's death. And what made the situation unbearable for Wolfe was that then and now, he was responsible for her agony.

Jack stood in the doorway to the bedroom and watched Wolfe as he flung his clothes into his suitcase. "You know we can subdue Shaw and Jennings. Just say the word and Matt and I will—"

"And what happens if one of them accidentally gets hurt?" Wolfe asked as he whipped the suitcase zipper closed. "You have no idea what Fletcher might do with that damn gun. He could start shooting with the least provocation." Wolfe lifted his suitcase off the bed. "Besides, if Caroline doesn't want us here, then legally we can't stay. If we don't leave she can call the police and have us thrown out."

"The David Wolfe I know wouldn't be tucking tail and leaving without putting up a fight," Jack said.

Wolfe turned on Jack, his gaze narrowing as frustration and anger boiled inside him. "That's just it—you don't know me. Didn't you hear what Fletcher said? I'm not David Wolfe. I'm Aidan Colbert and you have no idea what Aidan Colbert is capable of doing."

"Colbert or Wolfe, I know one thing," Jack said. "You care about Caroline. My bet is that nothing and no one else matters to you, just her. So why leave her unprotected?"

Wolfe glowered at Jack, then headed toward him. Jack stepped back, allowing Wolfe to walk past him, then he followed Wolfe downstairs and out onto the porch where Matt O'Brien still stood guard.

"You two stay with her," Wolfe said. "Do whatever it takes to keep her safe. I have some business to take care of, then I'll contact y'all."

"What do we do if she orders us to leave, too?" Jack asked.

"Try to talk her into letting you stay. But if not, then you and Matt keep a watch on her, even if it has to be from a distance. And if she leaves this house, follow her. She won't be safe until I… Call Sawyer McNamara and ask him to meet me at the Peacekeepers International building in D.C. in two hours. I've got some rat killing to do and I just might need some federally authorized backup. But if anyone wants to know, he's to tell them he's a Dundee agent."

Wolfe got in the leased Mercedes and backed out of the driveway, not once looking back. He didn't have time for regrets or sentimentality. Not when Caroline's life was in more danger now than ever. The only way he could protect her was to find out what was on the strip of microfilm in his pocket and hope there was enough evidence to put the top men in the Loyalists Coalition behind bars. Later, when she was safe, he would face Caroline and accept his punishment. Unfortunately, he had a major problem at present. He didn't know who he could trust at Peacekeepers. His gut instincts told him that Ellison Penn was trustworthy. But on the off chance that he wasn't, David wanted the FBI present when they looked at the microfilm for the first time.

"You're coming with me," Fletcher told Caroline, all the while nervously scanning the room for any sign of a Dundee agent. He clasped the pistol with both shaky hands, as if preparing to shoot. "I don't want you here in this house alone. I've spoken to Oliver and he insists that I bring you to stay with them until we can sort through this mess. Their house is more secure than mine or Lyle's and Oliver has even offered to bring in bodyguards from the company he uses."

Caroline sat quietly in a chair at the kitchen table. A blessed numbness had thankfully taken control of her body and to some extent her mind. She could hear Fletcher speaking, could feel Lyle's hands holding hers, could sense the myriad emotions swirling around her. But only one thing truly registered at a deeper level—David Wolfe was a man named Aidan Colbert and that man had been the trained assassin who had executed Preston. No matter how many times she processed the information, her heart refused to believe it was true. Wolfe would never lie to her. Deceive her. Betray her. He loved her. He had risked his life to save her. Fletcher had to be wrong. But why hadn't Wolfe defended himself? Why had he acted like a guilty man?

Oh, Wolfe. My dear David... No, he wasn't *her David.* He never had been *her* David. And that had been her biggest mistake, allowing her heart to confuse the two men, to mix them together in her mind until they were one being. But if Fletcher was right, David Wolfe didn't exist. The man she had given herself to, her heart and her body, was Aidan Colbert—her stepfather's murderer.

Caroline trembled from head to toe. Uncontrollably. Then

quite suddenly she laughed, the sound alien to her ears. Shrill, hysterical laughter. And just as quickly as the laughter began, it died away and was replaced by gasping sobs. Oh, God, no! Please, help me. Don't let this happen to me again.

Somewhere outside herself, she sensed Fletcher and Lyle hovering over her, could hear them speaking, arguing, discussing. She felt them lifting her to her feet, gently shaking her, calling out her name. But she was too far away from them, buried too deep inside the panic-stricken laughter and tears of her own heartache, to respond to their concern.

"My God, she's gone berserk," Fletcher said. "Just like she did the night Father was killed."

Ellison Penn met Wolfe and Sawyer McNamara at the elevator and whisked them down the hall and to his office. Gavin Robbins and Barry Vanderpool watched with curiosity, but neither said a word.

Ellison closed the door, then turned and confronted Wolfe and McNamara. "What's going on? Do you know the risk you've taken coming here like this?" He eyed Sawyer. "And who is this with you?"

"McNamara. FBI," Sawyer said.

"McNamara is here to make sure what I'm about to turn over to you is kept safe," Wolfe explained.

Ellison's eyebrows lifted. "So, you don't trust me. Is that what this is all about? You've found the evidence Preston hid away and you're concerned that I might not be trustworthy."

"Someone told Fletcher Shaw that I'm Aidan Colbert and Fletcher told Caroline." Wolfe watched Ellison closely, gauging his reaction.

"I see. And you think I'm the one who revealed your identity."

"No, I don't think you would betray me," Wolfe said. "But at this point, I don't completely trust anyone."

"But you seem to have no problem trusting the FBI," Ellison said.

"I trust this particular federal agent. Sawyer's not interested in me or you or any classified Peacekeepers business. He wants what I want—to find out who's been trying to kill Caroline."

"As soon as we take a look at this microfilm Wolfe has in his possession, we should be able to tell who we can and can't trust," Sawyer McNamara said. "And once we have the evidence on these men, we can start making arrests."

"Microfilm, huh?" Ellison smiled. "Preston Shaw was a smart man. Unfortunately, he outsmarted himself."

Wolfe relaxed just a bit, feeling more reassured by the minute. Ellison didn't act like a man who had anything to hide.

"Let's take a look at the microfilm," Sawyer said. "If it contains what we hope it does, I can take things from here. For a very long time, we've been wanting to get our hands on proof that the Loyalists Coalition exists."

He dialed the private number and waited for the familiar voice to answer. His superior would be greatly interested in the news he had for him.

"Yes?" the voice said.

"Sir, I thought you would like to know that David Wolfe is at Peacekeepers International at this very minute and in conference with Ellison Penn and another gentleman."

"Who is this other gentleman?"

"I assume he's another Dundee agent. We suddenly seem overrun with them."

"Do you have any idea what's going on in Ellison's office?"

"No, but—"

"Call me back when you have more information."

"Yes, sir."

* * *

Wolfe answered his cell phone while Ellison and Sawyer prepared the microfilm for viewing on a projector.

"Wolfe, it's me, Jack Parker."

"Is something wrong?"

"Don't know," he said. "But I thought I'd better inform you that Jennings and Shaw didn't take Miss Caroline to Shaw's house in Baltimore."

Wolfe's heart lurched, apprehension tightening his gut. "Where did they take her?"

"To Alexandria, Virginia, straight to Oliver Harper's home," Jack said. "Matt and I are keeping watch. We're as close as we can get to the house without being spotted."

"Why would Fletcher take her to the Harpers'?"

The blood ran cold in Wolfe's veins. Jack was right. Somebody Caroline trusted was probably a member of the Loyalists Coalition. But who? Fletcher Shaw? Lyle Jennings? Or was it one or all of the Harpers?

"If the Loyalists Coalition have Miss Caroline, then it may take a squad of storm troopers to get her away from them," Jack said.

"I should never have let her send me away." Wolfe cursed himself for allowing this situation to happen. "I thought I could get things done here before the Coalition took action. I should have—"

"If you had stayed, at the very least Fletcher Shaw would have called the police and had you arrested. At worst, he could have lost his head and shot you. Or one of us could have been forced to kill him."

"Anything would be preferable to Caroline being held captive."

"We don't know for sure she's being held captive."

"Don't we?"

The doctor emerged from the bedroom in the Harper mansion where Caroline McGuire now slept peacefully. Oliver waited outside in the hallway. He hated the uncertainty, the sense of not having everything under control. But thanks to Fletcher's quick actions, they now had possession of Caroline. Unfortunately, she didn't seem to have the key. He had sent a couple of his men back to her house to search for it, but they had come up with nothing.

"Please, come with me, Dr. Johnson," Oliver said, and led the man across the hall into a private sitting room. "How is she?"

"I've sedated her. She should sleep for several hours."

"What were you able to learn from her?"

"She was rather incoherent, but with the proper medication, she was agreeable to answering all my questions."

Oliver smiled, a sense of relief relaxing the tension in his muscles. "What did she tell you about the key?"

"She and Mr. Wolfe discovered that the key opened a jewelry box that had belonged to Caroline's mother," the doctor said.

"A jewelry box? Then Preston was bluffing. There is no evidence. We've been fools to have worried."

"Perhaps. But it seems Mr. Wolfe thought that there might be something hidden inside a large heart-shaped locket they found among Caroline's mother's jewelry."

"A locket? Nonsense. What sort of evidence could be hidden in—" Damn! Microfilm! Of course. Preston had filmed classified documents for the Loyalists Coalition; why wouldn't he have used the same method to obtain evidence against his brethren? "A small piece of coiled microfilm might fit into a large locket. I can think of nothing else it could be." Oliver grabbed the doctor by the lapels of his expensive suit. "Did Wolfe get his hands on that microfilm?"

Dr. Johnson jerked out of Oliver's grip, then smoothed the lapels of his jacket. "Caroline is unaware of any microfilm. She did mention that Mr. Wolfe had been about to open the locket just as Fletcher arrived this morning. If there was anything in that locket, I swear to you that she knows nothing about it.''

"Wolfe wouldn't have left Caroline's house without checking that locket," Oliver said. "That means if there was anything inside, it's now in his possession.''

"Yes, that would be my guess.''

"We'll have to act quickly.'' Oliver paced the floor. "You keep Caroline sedated. I'll inform everyone that you've advised complete rest for her and she's not to be disturbed. In the meantime, I will contact David Wolfe and present him with a deal he can't refuse.''

"And that would be?''

"Caroline's life in exchange for whatever Wolfe removed from Lenore Shaw's locket.''

"Will this hold up in court?'' Wolfe asked, his hands damp with perspiration and his heartbeat racing wildly.

"Oh, yeah,'' Sawyer replied. "What we have here—'' he pointed to the viewing screen that enlarged the documents captured on the microfilm ''—is a journal that lists names, dates and events.'' Sawyer reached out and advanced the film. "And this is a signed confession by Preston Shaw that he assassinated Senator Harwell, following instructions from his superior, Oliver Harper.''

An overwhelming rush of emotion surged up inside Wolfe. Relief. Justification. Consolation. He had not executed an innocent man! Preston Shaw had not only been party to the plot to kill Senator Harwell, he had, as the evidence had shown and the Peacekeepers had acted upon, been the man who had pulled the trigger. But the relief was short-lived. Caroline was at this very moment in the home of Oliver Harper, the head honcho of the Loyalists Coalition!

"I knew Oliver had some extremist political views, but I never imagined him to be a true radical,'' Ellison said. "I've known the man since we were in college together and… When this comes out, it will kill Eileen and Brooke.''

"Harper's not the only bigwig on this list," Sawyer said. "We'll be rounding up ten other well-known citizens. A congressman, a senator and a federal judge among them."

"Are you sure Caroline didn't see the microfilm?" Ellison asked.

"I'm sure," Wolfe replied. "But she knew that I suspected there was something hidden in the locket. And if Harper had this Dr. Johnson use drugs on her, she would have told them whatever they wanted to know. And even without drugs, in her present mental state—" Emotion lodged in Wolfe's throat. He turned away from the other two men, clenched his hands into fists and shut his eyes as the pain and fear he could not control ran wild inside him.

"If Oliver learns about the locket, he will figure out what Preston hid inside it," Ellison said. "It wouldn't take a genius to come to the conclusion that the only evidence that would fit into something that size would be microfilm."

"And Harper's only bargaining chip is Caroline McGuire's life," Sawyer said. "It's his trump card, so he'll play it. And very soon."

The call came in on Ellison Penn's private line. He recognized the voice immediately. The devil himself—Oliver Harper. He would like nothing better than to get his hands around Oliver's neck and squeeze the life out of him. How could a man with every privilege life had to offer become the maniacal leader of a bunch of lunatics?

"I understand David Wolfe is there with you," Oliver said.

"That's right."

"Did he bring you a little present?"

Ellison held his breath. He knew…the damn bastard knew! Was there any point in playing games? "Yeah. All gift-wrapped and with a bow on top."

"I have a little gift-wrapped present of my own," Oliver

said. "I thought perhaps your Mr. Wolfe might like to trade."

Oliver's laughter sent chills up Ellison's spine. Oliver wanted a trade. Caroline for the microfilm.

"And if you're thinking of calling in the feds, I would advise you not to. As far as making copies of whatever evidence you have—don't," Oliver said. "After we've made the exchange, don't consider double-crossing me. If you do, you should know that I have no intention of going to jail. I'd kill myself first. And I wouldn't die alone. I find the Egyptian custom of burying the pharaoh's wife with him rather interesting, don't you? You see, David Wolfe isn't the only one with something valuable to lose. You do still love my wife, don't you, Ellison?"

"Why, you son of a bitch!"

"Tsk-tsk," Oliver said. "Now that we understand each other, put Mr. Wolfe on the phone. I do so love bringing a big man to his knees and hearing the fear in his voice. Tell me, Ellison, how long has it been since someone put the fear of God into you?"

Chapter 21

Caroline wanted David. Where was her David? She was alone and frightened. She'd been calling for him for what seemed like days, but someone kept telling her that she would have to wait. Whose voice was that? she wondered. She tried to open her eyes, but her eyelids felt heavy. She tried to move, but her limbs seemed to weigh a ton. What was wrong with her? Why couldn't she open her eyes and get up? She had to find David. He was lost and if she didn't find him soon, he would be lost forever. *Her David*, who had seen to all her needs. He had provided for her, protected her and loved her.

She could almost feel his strong arms around her, holding her, keeping the evil world at bay. He would never let anything bad happen to her. When everyone else failed her, disappointed her, hurt her, she could count on David to be her knight in shining armor.

Suddenly Caroline realized that someone was talking, issuing orders in a harsh voice. But who? And why? And what were they doing in her bedroom? Was she dreaming?

"Bring her around," the harsh voice said. "We're making the exchange in two hours. I want her up and walking by then."

Where am I? What's happening? Who are these people? Is this another nightmare or is this real? I need to know. Help me. Please help me. David...David...David!

Wolfe sat beside Ellison Penn in the back seat as the driver breezed the big black limousine toward the Mount Hope sanatorium and health spa in Montgomery County. Every nerve in Wolfe's body screamed, every muscle strained. Adrenaline pumped through him, preparing him for the most important battle of his life. Everyone else involved in this rescue had an agenda of their own, but for Wolfe the only thing that mattered was saving Caroline.

"We've done all we can," Ellison said. "Everything is set in place, and with a little luck, both your lady and mine will be saved from Oliver Harper."

Harper had to be a monster if he were willing to use his own wife as a bargaining tool. Wolfe had never seen Ellison as distraught and worried as he'd been since Harper's threatening phone call. But then Wolfe knew only too well how Ellison felt—they both had a great deal to lose if anything went wrong.

"We need more than luck," Wolfe said. "We need divine intervention. For our plan to work, everything has to come together perfectly. We have to take Caroline out of the sanatorium while the FBI take Brooke and Eileen Harper into protective custody. Since Harper isn't aware the FBI is involved, we'll have the element of surprise on our side. He's counting on our not bringing in outside help."

Ellison looked directly at Wolfe. "I understand how you must feel because I know what's at stake for you."

"Once Caroline is safe, I know you'll want to deal with Harper yourself. But if Robbins turns out to be the traitor within Peacekeepers, then I want to be allowed to deal with him personally.''

''With this exchange coming down, it's reasonable to assume the traitor will tip his hand and we will discover his identity,'' Ellison said. ''There are only a handful of men within the organization close enough to the top to be truly useful to the Loyalists Coalition.''

Yeah, Wolfe thought, only a handful. Robbins. His assistant, Latham. And Barry Vanderpool. They had ruled out Ellison's top agents, most of whom were out of the country on assignments at the moment. That left only the three suspects.

Wolfe's cellular phone rang. He responded. ''Yes?''

''Dom just reported in with some interesting information. Barry Vanderpool left the Peacekeepers building about an hour before you and Mr. Penn,'' Jack Parker said. ''Want to guess where he went?''

''To Mount Hope.''

''You got it.''

''Then he's—''

''Probably,'' Jack said. ''But guess who's on your tail? Robbins left the building shortly after y'all did, along with a couple of Peacekeepers agents, and he's been keeping a discreet distance behind Mr. Penn's limo.''

''Damn! If Robbins was in this with Harper, he wouldn't have to tail us. He'd know where we were going. That must mean he suspects Ellison and me of being up to something illegal and he's hoping to nail us and make himself look good. I sure as hell was hoping he was our traitor, but looks like he isn't.''

''I'll make sure Robbins doesn't interfere,'' Jack said. ''He might not be in with the bad guys, but if he gets in the way, he could foul things up for us. Sawyer's people are already in position and ready to strike the minute you get Caroline to safety.''

* * *

An attendant led Wolfe and Ellison into Dr. Johnson's private office and asked them to take a seat. They chose to stand. Wolfe checked his watch. The minute they walked out of here, the FBI would enter the Harper home to take Brooke and Eileen into protective custody, while a squad of FBI agents, led by Sawyer McNamara would swarm the sanatorium and arrest Oliver Harper. Within minutes of Harper's arrest, the other nine Loyalists Coalition leaders would also be arrested.

Oliver Harper entered the office, a charming smile on his face as he looked first at Wolfe and then at Ellison. "Right on time, I see. I appreciate your being prompt. Did you bring the microfilm?"

"We want to see Caroline," Wolfe said.

"She's being brought here as we speak." Oliver glanced into the outer office. "She's been kept drugged, so she'll still be a bit groggy."

It took every ounce of his self-control to keep from grabbing Harper and strangling the man. No matter who the other players were, Harper was the one truly responsible for the threats against Caroline. Wolfe would derive great pleasure out of seeing the mighty Mr. Harper spend the rest of his life behind bars.

"I'm sure you have a few Dundee men outside as backup, but I hope you haven't planned a double-cross," Oliver said. "You see, I have men posted in various positions throughout the sanatorium and even in the health spa that adjoins the sanatorium, so if you're thinking of creating problems, reconsider. Innocent people might die."

Dr. Johnson personally escorted Caroline into his office. Although her eyes were glazed, she walked under her own power, aided only by the doctor's hand on her elbow.

"Here's our little patient," the doctor said.

The sight of her, so fragile and weak, broke Wolfe's heart. She wore a hospital gown and was barefoot. Her hair was disheveled, her face pale. She stared at Wolfe and opened her mouth on a silent gasp.

"Come here, my dear." Oliver held out his hand to Caroline and she went to him willingly.

Ellison reached out and grabbed Wolfe's wrist, stopping him from doing what he knew instinct would tell Wolfe to do—rip Caroline away from danger and to hell with the consequences.

"The microfilm?" Oliver held out his hand. "Once I have it, then she's yours."

"Oliver, what's going on?" Caroline asked. "What microfilm are you talking about?"

"Nothing for you to worry about, Caroline," he said, his tone gentle and fatherly.

Ellison reached inside his coat pocket, removed the microfilm and held it out to the leader of the Loyalists Coalition. The look of triumph on Oliver's face was almost more than Wolfe could endure. Just as Oliver reached for the microfilm, they heard a commotion in the hallway and a voice calling out a warning.

"Don't turn her over to Wolfe! The whole thing is a trap."

Suddenly Ellison closed his fist around the microfilm. Oliver jerked Caroline to his side as he whipped a gun from his pocket just as Barry Vanderpool rushed into the office.

Breathing hard, his face slightly flushed, Barry said, "This place is swarming with agents. I recognized our Peacekeepers agents, including Gavin Robbins. They saw me and know that I saw them. They've already taken positions and my guess is we could already be surrounded."

Damn Gavin Robbins! Wolfe cringed at the thought of the gung-ho agent screwing this deal. Undoubtedly Robbins had somehow found a way to sidestep the Dundee agents.

"I should have known better than to trust you, Ellison," Oliver said. "You're not a gentleman. You never were. Too bad for Eileen. I have men ready to—"

"Eileen and Brooke are safe from you," Ellison said.

Oliver's eyes widened with surprise, as if it had never entered his mind that Ellison would have taken precautions so quickly. He held the gun to Caroline's head. "She isn't safe. Does she mean anything to you, Wolfe? If she does, you'll call off the Peacekeepers and Dundee agents. I can and will kill her in a split second."

"And I'll kill you if you hurt her," Wolfe said, his gaze locking with Caroline's. She stared at him, shock and puzzlement in her eyes.

Gunfire erupted outside, gaining the attention of everyone in the office. Damn! Vanderpool's spotting the agents had tipped their hand and set things into motion before the exchange had been completed. Now with Caroline still in his control, Oliver Harper was twice as dangerous.

Holding the gun to Caroline's temple, Oliver kept a tight hold on her as he pushed her toward the door. "We're leaving. Dr. Johnson has a helicopter pad on top of the building and I'll be taking Caroline with me as my own little insurance policy. Better tell your men not to fire at the helicopter because if I go down, Caroline goes down with me."

The minute Oliver and Caroline disappeared up the hallway, Ellison got on his cellular phone and contacted Sawyer McNamara. Wolfe grabbed Dr. Johnson and shoved him out the door.

"You're going to show me how to get to the roof." Wolfe pulled his Sig Sauer from his hip holster and pointed it straight at the doctor.

All hell had broken loose from the sound of it. The FBI agents were at war with the posted guards, members of the Loyalists Coalition trained in combat. Wolfe knew that the government agents would try their best to protect the innocent patients in the sanatorium and clients in the health spa. But right now, he didn't have time to worry about anyone except Caroline.

When he saw Jack Parker rounding a corner near the stairwell the doctor had indicated led to the roof, Wolfe flung Dr.

Johnson toward Jack and said, "Take this bastard to McNamara. I'm through with him."

"Wait and I'll—" Jack said.

"Can't wait."

Wolfe ran up the stairs, his heart racing, his thoughts wild with worry. When he reached the roof, he found Oliver dragging Caroline with him as he headed toward the parked helicopter. Wolfe aimed his pistol, but before he could fire, Oliver turned abruptly, placing Caroline in front of him as a shield. Wolfe realized that Oliver was about to open fire, so he dropped and rolled across the rooftop. Oliver began shooting. Wolfe came to a halt behind a row of empty barrels, took aim and waited for a clean shot, one that wouldn't endanger Caroline. Suddenly, Oliver pulled Caroline with him toward the edge of the roof.

"Throw your gun out where I can see it—right now. And come out with your hands behind your head," Oliver called. "If you don't, I'll kill her. I can shoot her in the head or toss her off the building. And I doubt she'd survive the bullet in her head or the five-story drop."

"No, Wolfe, don't!" Caroline screamed. "He'll kill you."

Everything happened at once. Wolfe tossed aside his gun, then stood and came out from behind the barrels. Caroline took advantage of Oliver concentrating on David's movements and aimed her elbow to his mid-section. He growled with pain and loosened his tenacious grip on her arm, but before she could run, he grabbed her wrist. A gunshot blast echoed in Wolfe's head and for a split second he thought Oliver had shot Caroline. *No! God, no!*

But Wolfe realized a moment later that someone had shot Oliver. The gun in Oliver's hand fired once, straight down. A reflex action that happened almost simultaneously with the other gunshot. As Oliver staggered backward, blood oozed from the wound where he had been hit in the head, but he kept a deadly hold on Caroline. She struggled to free herself, but to no avail. When Oliver toppled backward over the two-foot high metal railing and off the roof, he dragged Caroline over the edge. She screamed. The sound echoed inside Wolfe's head as he ran forward, adrenaline flooding his body. He wasn't able to reach her in time!

Wolfe cried out, his voice agonized. The roar of a wounded animal. Then he saw two hands clinging to the narrow decorative railing that circled the rooftop. Small, delicate hands. Caroline's hands. An instant prayer rose from his heart. Thank God she was a fighter. Thank God she hadn't fallen to her death. Thank God she was alive.

Wolfe knelt on his knees, reached down and grabbed her arms. "I've got you, sweetheart. Hang on. You're going to be all right."

She clasped his wrists. He dragged her up and onto her knees, then wrapped his arms around her and held her. She clung to him, her body trembling, as she sucked in deep breaths of air.

"You saved me," she murmured.

"You saved yourself," he told her.

He couldn't resist the urge to touch her, to reassure himself that she was alive and well. With shaky fingers, he caressed her face. She closed her eyes and sighed. He lifted her raw, bleeding hands and inspected them.

"Are you two all right?" Jack asked as he came running up to them.

Wolfe nodded. "Did you shoot Harper?"

"No, Ellison Penn shot him."

Jack inclined his head toward the open door that led to the stairwell. Ellison stood there, his pistol still in his hand.

"Miss Caroline, it's sure good to see that you're all right," Jack said. "We've got an FBI lady right over here. She's going to take care of you. She'll drive you to the hospital and stay with you." Jack motioned for the six-foot female agent, who then came forward and identified herself.

"Ms. McGuire, I'm Agent Lucie Evans."

Wolfe lifted Caroline to her feet, then released his comforting hold on her hands and gently shoved her toward Agent Evans. "Take good care of her."

He turned and walked away.

"Wolfe!" Caroline called out to him.

More than anything he wanted to go back to her. But that wasn't an option. As he passed Ellison, the two exchanged a knowing glance. This was the only way it could end. He had known from the beginning that his sojourn into Caroline's life would be brief and that once she was no longer in danger, he would have to leave her.

Wolfe took the steps two at a time on his way down the stairs, hurrying as fast as he could to escape. He had to leave now and put as much distance between Caroline and him as he possibly could. He'd been kidding himself to think he could ever explain to her, ever rationalize his past actions. The bottom line was that he had killed her stepfather and for that she would never be able to forgive him. Better to make a clean break now and not prolong the agony for either of them.

Caroline stayed at the church until the last minute. She threw handfuls of birdseed from the yellow net holders and waved goodbye to the bride and groom as they left for the D.C. airport in their white limousine. If ever two people deserved their happiness, Roz and Lyle did. Even the ladies of Lyle's church, who had so vehemently opposed the marriage in the beginning, had finally come around once they'd gotten to know Roz and saw beyond her flashy facade.

Today Roz had walked down the aisle on her uncle Henry's arm, wearing a pale yellow satin dress that hugged her slender curves. Her tulle veil, attached to a yellow rose headband, puffed out away from her face like a halo. Wearing a canary-yellow dress almost identical to the bride's, Caroline had been Roz's only attendant. Fletcher had been Lyle's best man.

Poor Fletch. He'd been duped by Oliver the way everyone

else had been. And feeling terribly guilty for being so gullible, he had taken more than his share of the blame for trusting Oliver. And he had lost the woman he loved. The day Oliver Harper died, Peacekeepers International had arranged for Eileen and Brooke to drop out of sight. They had left Alexandria without a trace five months ago.

As the limousine disappeared and the crowd dispersed, Fletch came up behind Caroline and slipped her coat around her shoulders. "It's good to see somebody happy, isn't it?"

Caroline sighed, then smiled at her stepbrother. "You miss Brooke, don't you? Do you still have no idea where she and Eileen are?"

"No idea whatsoever. It's as if they vanished off the face of the earth." Fletch walked Caroline to her car, then paused by the hood and took her hands into his.

"It's been five months," Caroline said. "I would have thought she might have contacted you by now." *Six months, two weeks and four days since Wolfe had walked out of her life.*

"Has David Wolfe contacted you?"

Caroline shook her head. "I didn't expect him to."

"Did you want to see him again?"

"I honestly don't know," she admitted. "I suppose a part of me hoped that... I should hate him, but I don't. I still care about him. What sort of person does that make me?"

"It makes you human, kiddo." Fletch squeezed her hands, then released her. "We don't get to choose who we fall in love with, do we?"

Caroline unlocked her car, opened the door and slid behind the wheel. Fletch leaned inside, kissed her on the cheek and smiled. "If Brooke gets in touch with you..."

"I promise that I'll call you if I hear from her."

When Caroline turned the bend in the road, she saw a black limousine stationed in front of her house. Her heart skipped a beat. Was it possible that Wolfe...? She parked her Lincoln in the driveway, then got out just as Ellison Penn emerged from the limo. He came toward her hesitantly, as if he thought she might ask him to leave. She hadn't seen him since the night he shot Oliver Harper and helped save her life.

Gavin Robbins, who never owned up to the fact that his overzealous behavior at the Mt. Hope sanatorium had wreaked havoc with Wolfe and Ellison Penn's plans, had visited Caroline when she'd spent several days in the hospital after her nearly fatal ordeal at the hands of the Loyalists Coalition. Although he had made himself available to answer any and all questions regarding Preston Shaw's death and the Loyalists Coalition, he had also taken the opportunity to remind her that he was one of the good guys, a Peacekeepers agent dedicated to the cause of freedom. And he didn't hesitate to also remind her that David Wolfe, aka Aidan Colbert, had been her stepfather's executioner.

After learning the truth about Preston Shaw, Caroline had spent the past five months, as had Fletch, trying to reconcile her memories of a kind, good man with reality, with the fact that Preston had been a traitor to his country, an assassin and a member of the Loyalists Coalition.

"Ms. McGuire, may I speak to you?" Ellison asked.

She nodded. "Please, come inside. I'll fix coffee."

He followed her onto the porch and into her home, then waited in the living room. After tossing her coat onto a kitchen chair and kicking off her canary-yellow heels, Caroline prepared the coffeemaker. As she removed two cups and saucers from the cupboard, she allowed herself to consider the reasons why Ellison Penn might be paying her a visit. An update on the trials of several prominent D.C. citizens that was sure to end in convictions? Word of another suicide attempt by Barry Vanderpool, who was awaiting his own trial? Perhaps news about Eileen and Brooke, something she could share with Fletch? Or would he actually share information about David Wolfe?

When she brought the cups out on a small serving tray, Ellison stood, took the tray from her and set it on the table in front of the sofa. She sat beside him, then lifted her coffee from the tray.

"Did Lyle and Roz have a nice wedding?" he asked.

"Lovely. A perfect November afternoon, with bright sunshine and clear skies. A church filled with friends, relatives and well-wishers. And a bride and groom deeply in love. Who could ask for more?"

"Indeed." Ellison inhaled deeply, then exhaled and looked directly at Caroline. "I suppose you wonder why I've come to see you."

"Yes, I am wondering what brought you to my doorstep."

"I'm retiring from Peacekeepers," he said. "Gavin will be taking my place, at least temporarily. I don't see him keeping the top job for long. He's not suited to it." Ellison cleared his throat. "I'm flying out tomorrow for London to join Eileen and Brooke. They've been living in my London town house for the past five months. Both Brooke and her mother have needed time to adjust and to recover from the shock they suffered when they found out what kind of man Oliver truly was. At first Brooke didn't want to see anyone, not even Fletcher. And of course, she had her hands full taking care of Eileen. But they're both recovering now. Slowly but surely."

"May I tell Fletch where he can find Brooke?" Caroline sipped her coffee, then set the cup and saucer down on the tray. "Do you think she's ready to see him, now?"

"In my telephone conversation with Brooke only this morning I asked her that very question." Ellison smiled. "I intend to speak to Fletcher tonight and see if he'd like to fly to London with me tomorrow."

Caroline smiled. "Two happy endings. I like that."

"Would you like to know where you can find David Wolfe?"

Caroline's heart skipped a beat. "Don't you mean Aidan Colbert?"

"He followed orders. He did his duty like any good soldier. Preston Shaw was an enemy, a rogue agent who had to be eliminated." Ellison reached out and laid his hand on Caroline's shoulder. "You weren't supposed to be there that night. We would never have sent in an agent to kill a man in front of his child."

Caroline pulled away from Ellison's grasp. "When I found the key and my life was threatened, why did you call in David Wolfe to guard me, knowing as you did who he really was?"

"There's something you have a right to know, need to know. Something more about David. You see, after that night when Preston was executed, Aidan Colbert had a difficult time dealing with the fact that you had found Preston's body and had seen his killer. He was a man with a soft spot in his heart for children. He cared very much what happened to you. I think in the beginning, you reminded him of his little brother."

"Brendan."

Ellison nodded. "I sent Aidan to London, to keep him out of the way until we were sure you couldn't identify him. And during the years he spent there, I sent him reports on you. Pictures, too. And it was while he was in London that he arranged, through a lawyer, to begin taking care of you financially. He was appalled that your mother had abandoned you. I believe he spoke to your aunt Dixie only once and all other transactions were taken care of by the lawyer I arranged for him. Money was provided to take care of your psychiatrist's bills, to pay for your medical and dental bills, as well as clothes and items for school. And of course, there were the birthday and Christmas presents.

"And later on college tuition and a bank loan so that you could open your own studio. Whatever you needed, he made sure you had. He took care of you, became your keeper, but always from afar. So, who else would care more about protecting you from the Loyalists Coalition, who else had a bigger stake in your life than Aidan Colbert, the man you only knew as David.''

Caroline rose from the sofa, her heartbeat thundering inside her head, drowning out all other sounds. ''Are you trying to tell me that Aidan Colbert was my benefactor? That David Wolfe and *my David* are one and the same?''

''Yes, that's exactly what I'm telling you.''

Caroline paced the floor as she tried to assimilate the information. A part of her wanted to deny the possibility, but in her heart she knew it was true. Hadn't she, on a subconscious level, always known? The moment she saw David Wolfe for the first time, her soul had recognized his. She had responded to him as she'd never responded to another man, been swept off her feet by her own unbridled passion for a man who was little more than a stranger. But he hadn't been a stranger. He had been her David. The man who had been her guardian angel for fifteen years.

But her beloved David was also Preston Shaw's killer!

''David lives in Tennessee, in a log cabin in the Smoky Mountains.'' Ellison reached inside his coat pocket and withdrew an envelope. ''Here's the directions, along with his address and phone number. But I would suggest you surprise him, otherwise he might bolt and run.''

''You seem awfully sure that I'll go to him,'' Caroline said.

''Not sure, just hopeful.'' Ellison rose to his feet. ''If ever a man needed to be forgiven, your David does.''

For hours after Ellison Penn departed, Caroline sat alone in her living room looking at the pictures she had taken of David Wolfe the night he'd made love to her for the first time. She had been so desperately in love with this man. And from studying the look on his face in the photographs, she saw the truth—he had been in love with her, too. The sun set and the moon came up and still she sat, as her heart and mind fought a battle. And in the end her soul triumphed.

Wolfe brought in a load of wood and dumped it into the bin by the fireplace. The weatherman was predicting a light snowfall tonight. He had always loved the snow up here in the mountains, but even now, after fifteen years, a light snowfall brought back memories of a December night in Baltimore. Don't think, he told himself. Put the past out of your mind. And forget about Caroline McGuire. She is no longer a part of your life. Not in any way. If Ellison had done as he requested, then Caroline would receive a letter from David's lawyer this week, informing her of her benefactor's death. Once that deed was done, then the last connection between them would be severed.

He had quit the Dundee agency, sublet his Atlanta apartment and moved to the mountains five months ago, hoping to escape from the memories of Caroline. But unfortunately those memories followed him, tormented him, plagued him. More than once he had been tempted to call Ellison to ask about her. But somehow he'd found the strength to resist.

Wolfe sniffed, savoring the smell of the homemade vegetable soup he'd put on to cook earlier in the day. After his long hike, he'd read for a while and then gone out to bring in more firewood, and during all this activity, he'd forgotten lunch. He pulled a big bowl off the open rack, then lifted the lid from the soup pot and ladled up the vegetable concoction. He carried the bowl, along with a handful of crackers, over to the kitchen table and sat down to eat. When he had finished three-quarters of the soup, he heard a car pull into the gravel driveway. Who the hell? he wondered. Somebody lost, no doubt. He wasn't expecting anyone and his was the only cabin on this road. He heard a car door slam. Damn. Now he'd have to go out into the cold evening to give some lost tourist directions on how to get to Pigeon Forge or Gatlinburg.

The moment he opened the front door, he recognized his guest, but he couldn't believe his eyes. He must have fallen asleep after dinner and was now dozing in front of the fire. Dreaming.

"Caroline?"

She lifted her hand and waved, then walked toward him. She was even lovelier in this dream than he remembered. She wore a red wool coat, a black-and-red plaid scarf and a matching cap.

"May I come in?" she asked.

"Yes, please," he replied.

Please, come into my dreams, sweet Caroline, and stay here with me forever.

When she entered the cabin, he followed her. She removed her coat, gloves, scarf and hat to reveal a pair of black slacks and a red sweater. She handed him the discarded items and when she did, their hands brushed lightly against each other.

If this was a dream, then it was a damn realistic dream, Wolfe thought. He laid the coat and other items on a nearby chair, then turned back to Caroline. Her hair shimmered a lustrous blue-black in the firelight. She stared at him, tears in her blue-violet eyes.

"I'm not dreaming, am I?" he asked. "You're really here, aren't you?"

"Yes, Wolfe, I'm really here."

"How? Why?"

"Ellison Penn told me where you were and gave me directions to find this place." She glanced around inside the cabin. "Nice home. But it's terribly isolated. I lost my way several times before getting here. I thought I'd never find you."

I have been lost without you, he wanted to tell her. *Lost and alone and afraid that my life was over.* "Why did you come here?"

"I know everything," she said. "Ellison told me."

"Everything?"

"I know that Aidan Colbert was my benefactor, David," she said. "I think my heart and soul recognized you the moment we met."

He couldn't bear for her to be kind to him, to be grateful, when what he wanted—all that he wanted—was for her to love him. "Aidan Colbert killed your—"

She rushed to him and placed her fingers over his lips. "I know who Aidan Colbert was and what he did." The touch of her flesh against his, the nearness of her body, the smell of her delicate perfume aroused him. If only he could take her into his arms. If only...

"Despite how kind and good Preston Shaw was to me, he was a man capable of doing some very bad things. And he was a member of an evil organization. I understand that you acted under orders to eliminate an enemy of Peacekeepers and a traitor to your country. It's taken me five months, but I have finally come to accept the truth about my stepfather. And about you. Even before Ellison told me that you were my David, I had already forgiven you."

"You've forgiven me?" Was it possible? Dare he believe what he was hearing?

"I've come here because I want to help you learn how to forgive yourself." She reached out and took both of his hands into hers. "Not just for executing Preston, but for killing your father."

Caroline had not come to him because she loved him and wanted to be with him. She had come to help him find redemption. But didn't she realize that without her love, there could be no atonement, no salvation?

"Thank you for coming to see me to tell me that you've forgiven me," he said. "But I think you should go now. Leave before the snow sets in."

"I'm afraid you don't understand." She lifted his hands and pulled his arms around her waist. "I've come here to stay with you."

"For how long?" Did she think he needed daily therapy, with her as his nursemaid?

"For the rest of my life," she said.

"What?"

She wrapped her arms around his neck. "Of course, I'll expect you to marry me, eventually. Before we have children."

"Caroline?"

"Hmm-mmm?" She stood on tiptoe and kissed him.

"If you're doing this because you're grateful—"

"But I am grateful," she said.

"I don't want your gratitude."

"What do you want?"

"What the hell do you think I want?" He jerked free, turned his back on her and walked away.

She came up behind him, close enough to touch him, but she allowed a hairbreadth to remain between her chest and his back. "I think you want exactly what I do. To put the past behind us and accept what can never be changed. And to love each other with all our hearts, to get married and have babies and grow old together."

He closed his eyes as tears clouded his vision. Was it possible? Was she really offering him his heart's desire? "Are you telling me that my dream and your fantasy can become a reality, despite the past?"

"That's exactly what I'm telling you. Oh, Wolfe—my darling David—don't you know how much I love you?"

He spun around to face her and without shame allowed her to see the tears trickling down his cheeks. "And I love you, my sweet Caroline. I always have. With all my heart and soul."

Epilogue

"They're here." Caroline rose slowly from the overstuffed chair by the fireplace and waddled toward the front door. David hurried up from the basement where he'd spent the past two hours puttering in his carpentry shop while Caroline napped.

They spent their weekends and holidays here in David's mountain cabin and weekdays at their house in Maryville, where Caroline had opened her photography studio. David had taken up a new hobby that quickly turned into a new profession—carpentry. He had only a month ago opened his own handcrafted furniture shop.

David rushed to Caroline's side just as she opened the front door. "You stay in here," he ordered. "It's too cold outside for you and—" he patted her protruding tummy "—little Brendan. I'll go help Lyle and Roz with the babies and their suitcases."

Caroline sighed. She loved the way David had become even more protective of her during her pregnancy, but sometimes she wanted to scream at the way he kept her from doing anything these days, to tell him that she wasn't an invalid. But she never said anything, realizing how happy it made him to take care of her.

Roz, decked out in a fake leopard-skin coat and matching hat, came scurrying up the steps, one of the twins in her arms. Lyle followed closely behind with the other twin. Since they were bundled up so securely, Caroline couldn't tell the babies apart.

David brought the two suitcases inside and their guests placed the infant carriers on the sofa while they shucked off their winter coats. Caroline removed the blankets from the babies and cooed to them. Instantly she recognized Dixie as the placid infant on the right and Betsy as the squalling babe on the left. The two redheaded darlings had been named in honor of their deceased grandmothers.

"So, how are you doing?" Roz asked. "You look great, but my God, you're twice as big as you were Thanksgiving when you two came to Maryland."

"I feel wonderful and the doctor says I'm fine," Caroline replied. "And I'll have you know that even though I'm in my seventh month, I've gained only twenty pounds. Not like someone else I know who had gained fifty-five pounds by her third trimester."

"Yes, but I had an excuse. I was expecting twins."

"Both of whom are now awake and hungry," Lyle said. "Three months old and all these girls do is eat, sleep, cry and then eat some more."

"Don't forget diaper changes," Roz said. "Daddy doesn't like changing the dirty ones, but I make him do them, anyway. While we're here, we'll let Uncle David change a few. It'll be good practice for him."

David wrapped his arm around Caroline's shoulders and she snuggled against him. "I'll change every diaper, wet ones and dirty ones. And if Caroline didn't plan to breast-feed, I'd be more than happy to take care of all the feedings, too."

"Boy, do you have him trained right." Roz laughed. "Hey, Lyle, get those bottles warmed up and we'll let Uncle

David and Aunt Caroline feed the girls while we change into our bathing suits and hit the hot tub out on the deck.''

Thirty minutes later, Caroline and David sat side by side on the sofa, Dixie in David's arms and Betsy in Caroline's. Both girls slept peacefully. In unison David and Caroline rose from the sofa, took the babies into the guest bedroom and placed them in matching bassinets. When they returned to the living room, they heard Lyle's and Roz's laughter coming from the deck outside. David flipped the wall switch and turned off the rustic overhead chandelier, leaving the room bathed only in a sparkling glow from the twinkling white lights on the Christmas tree.

He wrapped his arms around her and nuzzled her neck. ''Merry Christmas Eve, Mrs. Wolfe.''

Caroline sighed. ''Life is good, isn't it? Fletch and Brooke called from London to tell us that they've planning a double wedding with Ellison and Eileen for next spring and want us all to fly over there for the big event. Roz and Lyle are happily married and the parents of two perfect little girls.'' Caroline laid her arms over David's, where they crisscrossed her big belly. ''And you and I have everything. Each other and now a baby on the way. Oh, David, I'm so happy.''

''And that's exactly how I plan to keep you for the rest of your life, my sweet Caroline.''

She turned in his arms and they shared a kiss. Baby Brendan drew back a foot and kicked his father. Caroline and David laughed, then kissed again, the love growing stronger every day, their lives complete.

* * * * * *

*Look for Jack Parker's story
when Beverly Barton's exciting series,
THE PROTECTORS, continues.
Available in November!*

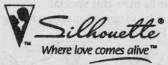

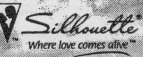

Babies are en route in a trio of
brand-new stories of love found on the
way to the delivery date!

Labor of Love

Featuring

USA Today bestselling author
Sharon Sala

Award-winning author
Marie Ferrarella

And reader favorite
Leanne Banks

On sale this July at your favorite retail outlet!

Only from
Silhouette Books

THE COLTONS

When California's most talked about dynasty is threatened, only family, privilege and the power of love can protect them!

On sale...

June 2001	**December**
Beloved Wolf	*The Housekeeper's Daughter*
Kasey Michaels	Laurie Paige
July	**January 2002**
The Virgin Mistress	*Taking on Twins*
Linda Turner	Carolyn Zane
August	**February**
I Married a Sheik	*Wed to the Witness*
Sharon De Vita	Karen Hughes
September	**March**
The Doctor Delivers	*The Trophy Wife*
Judy Christenberry	Sandra Steffen
October	**April**
From Boss to Bridegroom	*Pregnant in Prosperino*
Victoria Pade	Carla Cassidy
November	**May**
Passion's Law	*The Hopechest Bride*
Ruth Langan	Kasey Michaels

Only from

Silhouette®
Where love comes alive™

Available wherever Silhouette books are sold.